The proceeds from the sale of this book will be
used to support the mission of Library of America,
a nonprofit organization that champions the
nation's cultural heritage by publishing America's
greatest writing in authoritative new editions
and providing resources for readers to
explore this rich, living legacy.

BREECE D'J PANCAKE

THE COLLECTED
BREECE D'J PANCAKE

Stories, Fragments, Letters

··

INTRODUCTION BY
Jayne Anne Phillips

LIBRARY OF AMERICA

Interior design and composition by Gopa & Ted2, Inc.

Distributed to the trade in the United States by Penguin Random House Inc.
and in Canada by Penguin Random House Canada Ltd.

Library of Congress Control Number: 2020930767
ISBN 978-1-59853-672-0

1 3 5 7 9 10 8 6 4 2

CONTENTS

....

INTRODUCTION

······················

BY JAYNE ANNE PHILLIPS

BREECE D'J PANCAKE'S dozen stories, completed in the last four or five years of his life, include some of the best short stories written anywhere, at any time. Readers who first encounter his work here, collected with letters that imply his profound commitment so clearly, enjoy a special privilege. Those who read them again, who've passed them hand-to-hand in the way of writers, and word-of-mouth in the way of dedicated booklovers, will celebrate their lines anew. Forty years of the author's absence cast no shadow. The shadings, the broad arcs of interior, antediluvian time, are inside the sentences. The ancient hills and valleys of southern West Virginia remain Breece Pancake's home place; the specificity and nuance of his words embody the vanished farms, the dams and filled valleys, the strip-mined or exploded mountains. His stories are startling and immediate: these lives informed by loss and wrenching cruelty retain the luminous dignity that marks the endurance of all that is most human.

Breece Pancake's stories are the only stories written in just this way, from inside the minds of protagonists coming of age in the mountains of an Appalachian world closed to others. I've said, in a quote for an earlier edition of his work, "Breece Pancake's stories comprise no less than an American *Dubliners*." I meant, not that the author's style is similar to Joyce's, but that the stories are a map of their physical locality, above and below ground, just as Joyce's stories are a map of Dublin's streets in Joyce's youth. And that the links between the stories are as finely calibrated, and as naturally present in the material itself, as those in Joyce's *Dubliners.* Colly's mourned father in "Trilobites" is a literary relation to Bo's dead father in "Fox Hunters" and foster son Ottie's never-known father of "In the Dry"; the stories share a generational, nearly biblical sense of time. There is the long-ago time in which men and women brought forth their issue in the isolated, virginal hills they owned and farmed and hunted; there is the loss of the land, of livings from it; there is industrialization, exploitation, ruin.

"Trilobites," the first story in this volume, is a portal to other stories as tone-perfect and wholly accomplished: "Fox Hunters," "Hollow," "In the Dry," "A Room Forever," "The Scrapper," "The Honored Dead"—readers will have their favorites—but "Trilobites" comes first, as though clearing the way and claiming haunted ground with exhilarating precision. Colly, the story's protagonist, *was born in this country and . . . never very much wanted to leave,* but his father, who paid his dues in combat on the Elbe, died alone in a West Virginia field, *a khaki cloud in the canebrakes.* Colly is no good at farming the beautiful hilly land, with its dust devils and wind-furled rows of cedars, its brief rainstorms and willow-wisps, the patchy fog *that curls little ghosts into the branches and gullies.* All of time is a grave. *I look again at the spot of ground where Pop fell. He had lain spread-eagled in the thick grass after a sliver of metal from his old wound passed to his brain. I remember thinking how beaten his face looked with prints in it from the grass.* The loansman stands by with a contract to buy the farm, build a housing project, fill the bottoms with dirt and raise the flood line. The Permian certainty of geologic time, eons of graves, striations of rock and shifting landmass, flows through the stories, and the prehistoric Teays River, gargantuan and mighty, vanished underground, seems to pulse with absence in the prose. Colly gaffs for a turkle in a drying creek, as though wrestling a fellow survivor from its shrinking dominion; equipped with the author's vision, he looks at the land and sees the past. *I look down the valley to where bison used to graze before the first rails were put down. Now those rails are covered with a highway, and cars rush back and forth in the wind.*

Breece's suicide on June 8, 1979, twenty-one days before his twenty-seventh birthday, left others to champion the survival of his work. His widowed mother, Helen Pancake, dedicated herself to seeing his book published. James Alan McPherson's foreword, and John Casey's afterword, were written for the stories' first publication as a collection in 1983. Both writers were his teachers; they tell us what they can of who he was, how they learned of his death, and the ways in which he approached them later in dreams and memory. They weren't his mother or his sisters, or Emily Miller, the girl who begged John Casey to "go see" because she couldn't. But they were his mentors and continued to support his work after his death. Like everyone intimate with a suicide, "they will take his death to their graves": the phrase creates a burden so gravid that it defies cliché. His death, for those who knew him and are still alive, is a long time ago now, but it never goes away. That's why suicide is a moral crime. As surely as homicide, matricide, or fratricide, it ends a lived life and opens a wound. We attend to the story of his death, a limited, fractured story, to move beyond it, past limitations and personal history. His fiction is the world he lived in, the world he made. *A long time before me or these tools, the Teays flowed here. I can almost feel the cold waters and the tickling the trilobites make when they crawl.*

I never knew Breece D'J Pancake except through his work, but his life brushed past mine three times. Born the same year, twenty-one days apart, we were raised in different versions of West Virginia. He was from the small town of Milton (population 2,500) in the southwest part of the state, and attended, in his freshman year, West Virginia Wesleyan, a Methodist college in Buckhannon, my hometown. Buckhannon (population 6,000) is in north-central West Virginia, part of the Tri-state Ohio, Pennsylvania, West Virginia region then linked by straight-ticket Democratic sympathies and strong unions. I was a senior in high school in 1969-70; Buckhannon-Upshur High School won their third Triple AAA football championship and I was in passionate "first love" with the tight end, a brilliant boy whose musician brother died in Vietnam that November. It's odd to think of Breece living in Buckhannon. He joined the Drama Club but left Wesleyan ("Still nothing to do in Buckhannon?" he wrote to a former classmate) to attend Marshall University in Huntington, near his parents. After graduation, he went south, to teach at military academies in Fork Union and Staunton, Virginia. I went west, to San Francisco, then Boulder, waitressing. I'd published a few poems and wrote my first story, "El Paso," for application to MFA programs. He taught cadets, sent his work to John Casey at the University of Virginia, and began driving the forty minutes from Staunton to Charlottesville to sit in on Casey's weekly workshops. Casey "tried to send him off to Iowa for a year to get him some more time to write," and Vance Bourjaily accepted him into the Iowa Writers' Workshop, class of '76-'78 (my class), but apparently didn't offer him financial aid—or perhaps financial aid decisions were already made by the time Bourjaily read Breece's work.

Iowa's MFA program was famous, but I went there because they offered the best financial support—in-state tuition and a small stipend. Workshop students at Iowa, pitted against each other for second-year funding, were viciously competitive, but there were no southern codes of honor as at UVA, and class-conscious noblesse oblige did not enter into things. It would not have mattered that Breece wore jeans, flannel shirts, and boots—most of us did. And Breece's work, in any case, would have distinguished him at Iowa, where the work itself finally defined one's status. He would have encountered a larger, more broadly ranging group in a midwestern landscape that promised a remove from the past.

But Breece was accepted full-time at UVA, and saw himself as John Casey's apprentice. He went south to the antebellum-by-nature UVA campus for grad school, was eventually awarded a Hoynes Fellowship, and moved to One Blue Ridge Lane, near the university. His 12 x 12 apartment, in the east wing of a building that had been servants' quarters for the manor house on the property, shared a circular drive with a few other cottages. His landlady, Mrs. Virginia Meade, gave occasional English Department parties and "had the gall," Breece wrote his mother, to ask Breece to tend bar: "Said if I didn't, she'd have to hire a colored, and they don't mix a good drink." Georgia expat James Alan McPherson, who won the Pulitzer for *Elbow Room* while Breece was his student, called UVA "a finishing school for the sons of the southern upper class," and the English Department, "the interior of a goldfish bowl . . . an environment reeking of condescension."

Breece felt excluded, looked down upon, even as he achieved success. He wrote to his sister Donetta, "Made it! *Atlantic* bought "Trilobites" for $750 . . . This has really set fire to Wilson Hall and the (Cross yourself) English Department. Poor second rate citizen Pancake who can't speak the King's English . . . that turkey made it." According to his teachers and fellow students, he played up his "otherness," exaggerated his accent, spread tales of eating roadkill and fighting in bars. The surname Pancake is an Anglicized version of the German name, *Pfannkuchen*; he was Scottish (Frazier) on his mother's side and took his middle initials from a printer's error in *The Atlantic* galley of "Trilobites": D. J. for Dexter John translated to the aristocratic D'J with the grace of an apostrophe. He was courtly toward women, if defensive concerning "Women's Lib"; James Alan McPherson remembered that Breece "spoke contemptuously of upper-class women with whom he had slept on a first date, but was full of praise for a woman who had allowed him to kiss her on the cheek only after several dates." His sympathies were for the dispossessed, the underdog, the working poor. "I am sick to my stomach of people who drive fine cars, live alone in big apts., never worked a day in their lives," he wrote to his mother of Albemarle County, Virginia, soon after moving to Charlottesville. "This county is second in the country for millionaires—LA county being first. It do get hard to swallow."

Milton, in southern West Virginia, did not breed millionaires. Novelist Mary Lee Settle, a West Virginia native who taught at UVA, addressed West Virginia/Virginia cultural dissonance in her novel *Clamshell*: "Physically, [VA] is only a barrier of mountains away, across the Allegheny Divide, but to us Virginia is our Europe, hated and loved, before which we are shy, as Americans are shy in Europe." Northern West Virginia towns were more like small towns in Pennsylvania or Ohio; Virginians didn't matter at all to us. My family's Ohio relatives hosted my brothers when they worked summer jobs in Youngstown's steel mills; we would have seen antebellum pretensions as laughable. But southern West Virginians, even those descended from aristocratic Lost Cause Virginians, can still find themselves particularly disparaged by Virginians.

This was news to me until a somewhat famous Virginia writer delighted in informing me that he and his wife had grown up deriding West Virginians across the Tug Fork River: "We could actually see them on the opposite bank at high school parties, and we'd throw beer cans and cat-call them." He seemed to think that real or imagined disparities of wealth and "prestige" on two sides of a river had to do with the inbred superiority of Virginians, rather than the economic advantage of slave-state evil that plantation Virginia practiced so enthusiastically. Most Americans, even now, are unaware that West Virginia seceded from Virginia in 1863 to stand with the Union, that West Virginia's state motto, "Mountaineers are always free," is a reference to Virginia's slavery economy and unjust taxation of its "western frontier." West Virginia, the only Appalachian state entirely located within the Allegheny, Blue Ridge, and Appalachian mountain ranges, was and remains geographically and culturally isolated. Virginia considered the land—so towering, pristine, majestic, navigable only by river—worthless, until Big Timber and Big Coal colonized the state anew.

Breece was insulted by what he considered superficial

representation of his home place, as in Harry Caudill's influential *Night Comes to the Cumberlands*, and the "selling short" of his frugal, morally upright people. He connected, through his idolized father's experience, to Depression-era, World War II standards of masculinity. *The wrinkly old boundary post* in "Trilobites" is a monument: *Pop set it when the hobo and soldier days were over. It is a locust-tree post and will be there a long time.* Like many writers, Breece didn't belong in the place where he was born, but knew its history in myriad detail, swearing eternal allegiance in his writing and being. He didn't play sports, which so define boys in rural small towns; he wasn't meant for mine or factory work (his father once warned him, "Son, you'd better get an education because those hands will never fit a shovel"), but loved the land down to the strata and composition of the mountains themselves. A good student, he wrote about working-class characters whose families did not possess the measure of security his own had managed to attain. A farmer in "The Honored Dead" angrily refuses his son an education: *Everybody's going to school to be something better. . . . I don't care if they end up shitting gold nuggets. Somebody's got to dig in the damn ground.* The farmer isn't wrong. Every word and phrase and punctuation mark in a Pancake story are perfectly chosen; each story engages our complex empathy and presents unresolvable dilemmas. Breece did meticulous research on doghole mining, long-distance trucking, Holiness congregations, serpent handling, and more; typically, he wrote fifteen drafts of each story, but his unerring sense of the culture and sound of his characters was bred-in-the-bone.

His father, C. R. "Bud" Pancake, returned from World War II a decorated Army veteran for service in the Rhineland, the

Ardennes, and Central Europe; he went back to work at Union Carbide Chemical Company in nearby South Charleston but struggled with alcoholism. Thomas E. Douglass, in his masterful book about Breece's life and work, *A Room Forever,* notes that C. R. joined AA in Huntington, a half-hour drive from Milton, in 1953. "Helen would drive him and wait outside in the car during the meetings, holding 18-month-old Breece in her lap." There's not much mention in Pancake lore of how successfully C. R. battled the disease, but he kept his job for thirty-two years, rising to the status of shipping clerk, to sustain his family: wife Helen, two daughters, Donetta and Charlotte, and his only son, Breece. He warned Breece, "Never enter the gates of a plant. Once you do, they've got you." He taught his son reverence for the mountains, for animals, taught him to hunt and dress game, took him fishing and camping, and to numerous amateur "Golden Gloves" competitions around the state that inform stories like "The Scrapper": *As he threw a right cross to Gibson's chest, Skeevy felt the fine bones of his jaw shatter and tasted blood. . . . As he went down he could hear Trudy screaming his name above the cheers.* After Breece went off to college, C. R. wrote to his son of an aborted camping trip: "You know what. After I left you I went back to the tent and went to sleep untell about 10 pm. got up, packed the tent and took off. Camping is nothing alone . . . Listen Pal . . . It was so good having you here this summer and thank you for all the good things you did for us . . . Looking forward to your next trip home. You see I consider you my very best friend as well as my son."

C. R. and Helen Pancake sent their three children to college. They didn't need to lecture about sacrifice and honor; they embodied both. Breece grew up well aware of his father's hard work, and shadowed by his father's fate: *I picture my father—a young hobo with the Michigan sunset making him squint, the lake behind him. His face is hard from all the days and places he fought to live in, and of a sudden, I know his mistake was coming back here to set that locust-tree post on the knob.* C. R. had earned a decent pension and planned to retire early, at fifty-five, but contracted virulent MS. Progressively crippled, he died within a few years of diagnosis. Helen nursed him at home. She began taking extension courses at Marshall University and became the children's storytelling librarian at the Milton Public Library after her husband's death. She grew even closer to Breece, often researching facts for his stories, sending him clippings. "The story is coming along . . . many thanks for telling me that weird story this summer. Without you, I might be writing like John-Boy Walton—soft soap." She felt her son's grief at his father's death on September 8, 1975. Twenty-one days later, his close friend, Matt Heard, with whom he'd taught at Fork Union Military Academy, died, horribly mutilated, in a car accident. Breece had just begun teaching in Staunton, and wrote to Helen: "I mailed them Matt's watch. I don't think I told you why I had his watch—we got pretty polluted after the first week here, and I woke up with his watch. Never saw him again." He once told his mother of restricting himself to "six beers after nine o'clock," but there's no record of any voiced concern by Helen that his father's alcoholism made Breece vulnerable. She concentrated on encouraging her son's work, and his hopes, and tried to send him checks that he often refused. She curated his letters and papers after he died, destroying whatever she deemed too private, and hosted several writers who were researching essays or articles about him.

"Breece drank, like all the boys," she told an interviewer, "but I think when he drank he got remorseful and sad."

The Main Street of Milton, known as Route 60, passes just in front of the modest two-story house in which Breece grew up. Route 60 was first a Shawnee "Buffalo Trail," then a stagecoach route and colonial road known as the Teays River Turnpike. It was named for the ancient preglacial Teays River, formed more than two million years ago. Once the size of the Ohio, it carved a series of buried prehistoric valleys through several states. Massive ice sheets buried the Teays, and numberless Pleistocene-era fossils. Breece saw the mythic past in the present (*I like to hold little stones that lived so long ago*). The elusive trilobite was, in his imagination and his work, a miniature Holy Grail (*I pull this globby rock from my pocket and slap it on the counter in front of Jim. He turns it with his drawn hand. . . . "Gastropod," he says. "Probably Permian. You buy again." I can't win with him. He knows them all. "I still can't find a trilobite," I say*).

Breece was proud, and honor-bound by defined codes. James Alan McPherson observed that UVA had only recently opened its campus "to the sons and daughters of the southern lower and middle classes" and saw Breece as a "particular kind of mountain-bred southerner, or part-southerner." The qualification is important. West Virginians are not southerners or northerners. They belong nowhere, and when they leave home, they've left forever. Breece wrote to his mother, "I'm going to come back to West Virginia when this is all over. There's something ancient and deeply rooted in my soul. I like to think that I've left my ghost up one of those hollows and I'll never be able to leave for good until I find it."

I'll never be able to leave. Which means he knew he had to. UVA did not comprise a departure but a dropping down, into a culture that did not respect him or see him. He was interested in genealogy, in meeting up with the "Virginia" Pancakes, who were accepted in the "upper echelons" of Staunton society and disappointed him with their snobbery: "It makes you afraid to have a beer because your name's Pancake," he wrote Helen, "What a trip these Southerners are." His mother recalled with some bitterness after his death that Breece was attracted to girls from "monied" families, daughters of "doctors, brokers, lawyers" who "did him dirty." They didn't put him above all others, or love him unconditionally. She raised a son who was respectful to his elders and partial to "good girls"—obedient daughters who didn't defy their families or backgrounds. He spoke disparagingly in letters to Helen of a fellow student who "was talking about her abortion, and she shit a brick when I said I hunted—'You kill the little animals?'" and of "swearing off the Tube for life" after watching an episode of *The Awakening Land,* a 1978 miniseries in which "that guy grabbed Elizabeth Montgomery's tit on national T.V." The standard seems to belong to a previous era, but Breece was not a Hendrix or Janis Joplin fan; he loved Phil Ochs, Tom Waits, Gordon Lightfoot, white guy troubadours who sung of class prejudice and the loner's honor. Though raised a Methodist, Breece was confirmed in the Catholic Church in June 1977, within ten months of moving to Charlottesville. Drawn like a penitent to a religion in which suicide, then as now, was a mortal sin, he embraced Rome's dictates long before waves of revelation about clergy child abuse rocked the Church. Sex outside of marriage was a sin; any other expression of sexual love was perversion. Maybe he hoped Catholicism would protect him, provide boundaries even stricter than those he set for himself.

He fell in love that fall with Emily Miller, a UVA graduate student raised in Richmond society, and proposed marriage in June '78. She seems to have returned his feelings but turned him down due to her family's strong objections. They continued dating; Breece likely hoped he could change her mind. "Her parents have decided I'm not good enough for her," he wrote his mother, "and they've been after her to give me the boot and look for more promising material among her own kind . . . a good Southern Virginia family . . . if I got angry it wouldn't hurt anyone but Emily." The marriage proposal was not his first. At twenty, an undergraduate at Marshall University, he proposed marriage to his girlfriend, a doctor's daughter from Huntington who rented a post office box to receive his letters; she apparently lived with her family and kept the relationship secret. They were to marry in March 1972. Breece had already rented their apartment but she phoned to break everything off on New Year's Eve. Breece left school, visited his sister in Phoenix, camped in the Rockies, and traveled to Mexico. He wanted a marriage like his parents' steadfast relationship, but didn't live long enough, or go far enough from home in his sensibilities, to question the sexual preconceptions he'd internalized. Though he joked with friends about casual sexuality, Breece was drawn to the Catholic doctrine of sex as a spiritual bond between married—or at least betrothed—partners.

In the stories, Breece's female characters mirror the waste and harm his men inflict, focusing male futility like kindling set afire in relentless sunlight. Women are prey, like the squirming lump of unborn faun Buddy kicks aside in "Hollow," and Bo's high school classmates in "Fox Hunters," Dawn Reed and Anne Davis, who drown when their (likely pursued) car *went off the road up by French Creek Church*. Women are whores, like Buddy's live-in girlfriend Sally, in "Hollow," who taunts men seemingly as hungry as the circling dogs scenting Lindy, Buddy's bluetick bitch. The nameless protagonist in "A Room Forever" is second mate on a tug docked in a river town on New Year's Eve. He initially sympathizes with the fourteen-year-old runaway he hires, but her *little girl's body that won't move . . . a kid playing whore, and I feel ugly with her, because of her. I force myself on her like the rest.* Women are abused possessions. Reva, in "The Mark," haunted by the compulsive copulating of monkeys in a cage, lives out her brother Clinton's warning that marriage will see her *slapped down like an 'ol catfish*. Rarely, as in "Trilobites," he writes about women who insist on a measure of independence and sexual choice, women who leave home and their captive men behind. Ginny, the high school lover who *talk[s] through her beak*, drives her own car to collect Colly, then leaves him stranded outside an abandoned, glass-strewn depot. *"What is it Colly? Why can't we have any fun?" . . . I know she doesn't understand. I slide her to the floor. Her scent rises to me and I shove crates aside to make room. I don't wait. She isn't making love, she's getting laid . . . I think, all right. Get laid.* He "ruts" her because she's left this town and this life, while Colly time-travels in place, borne down by grief and loss. *"Let me go with you," I say. I want to be sorry, but I can't.* Pancake is an accomplished enough artist to allow his young male protagonists to go wrong, destroy, self-destruct, attempt escape, and to represent his female characters as acted upon, acted against: their emotional and physical survival seems almost accidental.

Breece wrote women as seen by trapped men coming of age in mountain towns, not women as themselves, not yet. His application letter to the Mary Roberts Rinehart Foundation, laced with the self-deprecating humor so evident in his letters, describes a proposed story titled "Of Time and Virgins": a "stream of consciousness narrative as a young man tried to make a decision whether he should propose to a virgin . . . he reviews the four great loves of his life, sees how each falls prey to sexual promiscuity . . . decides he is tainted but not beyond help. Since he has been with this girl more than a year without bedding her, he decides she is more to him than the others and decides to 'propose' tomorrow."

In a lyrical unmailed letter left for John Casey, Breece asks, "Remember Emily Miller? 'Then Kerrigan said there weren't any virgins left in this day and time—but—I'm afraid he—well, he was wrong.' So I decided she was right. I wanted to marry her but later, when it became clear I would have no work. . . . Still, I love this girl, and time flew its course. . . . " Breece and Emily Miller never lived together. We have one letter to her, found in his notebook after his death, in which he writes, "My God, Emmer, I love you. . . . Am I such a ghoul at heart? Is your papa right to ask you to re-consider?" In the letter, he doesn't seem to intend to die so young. He sees futures for his characters, real to him as his own life, in a novel to be titled *Generations* or *Water in a Sieve*. He continues in the same letter: "I want Ottie to wander the country . . . I want Colly in Vietnam's last days, a leg torn off by our own fire . . . I want Ottie tired, alone . . . to return and finding Sheila gone—meet with the strong, good woman (a kind of you) and begin his small settling."

Breece was leaving UVA and Emily was not going with him.

Publishing in *The Atlantic* was no comfort when it seemed he could not find a teaching job or the refuge of a residency. Why had he spent nearly three years as an outsider at Mr. Jefferson's university, living in one room on the fringes of Mrs. Meade's impressive property, scrimping by, writing feverishly, to find no work? "I could stay, I know, John, were I to beg," he wrote John Casey, ". . . would you love me if I did? I love you . . . because when my father and my friend were dead you helped me hang on . . . I'm not good enough to work or marry, but I'm good enough to write."

In just a few days, less than a week after his suicide, Breece would have received letters from the Millay Colony granting him a residency, and, even more important, from the Province-town Fine Arts Work Center, accepting him for an eight-month residency. Such news came in letters then, not instantly, by email. The letter he would have received from FAWC listed my name among the Fellows for that fall, just as the letter I received in Iowa City listed his. I'd read "Trilobites" in *The Atlantic* and noted his name: the place he evoked, the ache he described.

His death should not have happened, not that night at One Blue Ridge Lane, in a lawn chair under an apple tree, with the one gun he hadn't given away to friends in the preceding weeks. He'd kept that gun, a .30-.30 over a .20-gauge shotgun, a weapon lethal enough to kill a deer at seventy-five yards, and knew it was there for him. Saturday evening, June 7, he'd seen the film *Deer Hunter* with Emily Miller; later that night, alone, he phoned his mother to tell her, three times, that he loved her. Palm Sunday, June 8, he skipped church with Emily but stopped to see her before attending 3 P.M. Mass. Then he went home. *He drank, like all the boys.* Late that Sunday, Breece walked a few yards from his room to a cottage on the grounds. He knew the man who rented the cottage, but the man's girlfriend seems not to have known Breece at all. She came into the shadowy cottage with groceries in her arms and saw him slumped in a chair in the dark. It's said that he left immediately, saying he meant no harm, but the frightened girl called the police and ran to tell the landlady, Mrs. Meade. Why was he there? Helen's early assertion that he was sleepwalking seems a mother's hope. "I think he was startled," she said later, "he was frightened, he was confused, he was pushed, he was . . . sick." The Albemarle County sheriff's report includes a statement: "The complainant stated that Mr. Pancake cornered her and explained that he had a drinking problem and had a tendency to wander around." Breece fled back to his own rented room. Mrs. Meade, his irritated landlady, knocked on his door. "The police are coming, looking for a Breece Pancake," she said. "Yes, I know," he answered, "I'm sorry." *I know I will always be to blame, but it can't just be my fault.* As soon as she was gone, quickly, he grabbed the shotgun and went outside, to the chair under the apple tree.

He was alone, except for the words he'd written, the stories he'd worked to perfection. *I see myself scattered, every cell miles from the others. I pull them back and kneel in the dark grass.* He pulls us with him, into the work, narratives so immersed in sense memory, so tensile, so hard and true and redolent with the smell and time and feel of one place, as to render them actually timeless. He had to be gone when the police arrived. *I get up. I'll spend tonight at home. I've got eyes to shut in Michigan—maybe even Germany or China. I don't know yet. I walk, but I'm not scared. I feel my fear moving away in rings through time for a million years.*

Any little detail might have changed the outcome, but each

was firmly set. Mrs. Meade, a week or so after, hired a laborer to dig up the earth stained with Breece's blood and replace it.

In that unmailed letter to Emily Miller, he professed faith in the novel he envisioned: "I believe that would be a book—and a good one to read for any man of any class . . . The woman will be written up when I return—she must have four stories to her like the two men—and they must never be too innocent or loving or 'decadent.'" Breece's quotation marks, end of letter.

A book for *any man of any class*, a woman's stories *never be too "decadent."* He needed to leave Charlottesville for Provincetown: eight supported months in a quiet seaside town in the republic of Massachusetts, so far from UVA and West Virginia. Let's imagine him after that, in Paris or Berlin (*eyes to shut*).

Breece was never, truly, anyone's apprentice. His tone-perfect dialogue, infallible, instructive, teaches the reader to hear. His prose has the clarity of a struck bell, an authority that strengthens as one reads the lines; his stories build their own rhythm and throb, shift past to far past to present in ghostly dissolves, sculpt their lonely, ineffable power. Desire and yearning ricochet from one story to another. Very much by the author's design, these young men sabotage their desperate need for the women they penetrate; they want the temporary warmth and stopped time and melding of identity that sex can offer, but they close down their vulnerability in rage, hurt, anger. Those who love most, love secretly, like Ottie, the protagonist of "In the Dry," who longs for green trees but *stares at the knotted purple glow along the curve of his jaw, the wreck-scar. . . . No breaks are his; no breaks for foster kids, for scab truckers.* He's held Sheila, the daughter of his foster parents, *his fingers laced under her breasts . . . felt her blood pumping,* but the truth about a long-ago accident drives Ottie from this place where he never belonged. Eagle, in "The Honored Dead," tricks the draft and grows his hair long, while his best friend Eddie goes to war. Eagle marries the girl they both dated, *my own darling Ellen,* but scares his daughter Lundy with tales of bloody Shawnee raids and the Mound Builders' centuries-old burial mound in the back pasture. *Tomorrow I'll set her straight. The only surefire thing I know about Mound Builders is they must have believed in a God and hereafter or they never would have made such big graves.*

A large rectangular slab marks Breece's grave in Milton Cemetery. Its border, the letters of his name, his dates, a small, centered cross, are raised in brass. His parents' graves are just beside. His stone, flat to the ground, seems to deepen into the earth like a pillar. Two weeks before he died, Breece wrote to his mother about a dream he'd had: "I came to a place where the days were the best of every season, the sweetest air and water in spring, then the dry heat where deer make dust in the road, the fog of fall with good leaves. And you could shoot without a gun, never kill, but the rabbits would do a little dance, as if it were all a game, and they were playing it too. Then winter came with heavy powder-snow, and big deer, horses, goats and buffaloes— all white—snorted, tossed their heads, and I lay down with my Army blanket, made my bed in the snow, then dreamed within the dream."

The miraculous, exhilarating truth is that Breece D'J Pancake fought his way out of any dream, no matter how pervasive or foretold, with the sheer power of his dedication and intent, his genius and his passion, in language that is his alone. Truly great work delivers worlds that are *known* rather than merely understood or apprehended. His stories will be read as long as American stories survive, passed on, head to heart.

BREECE D'J PANCAKE

PART ONE
The Stories of Breece D'J Pancake

FOREWORD

· · · · · · · · · · · · · · · · · · · ·

I think you should come over (drive or train, I'll pay your
expenses and "put you up") because if you do the preface
I feel you should be more familiar with this valley and
[my son] Breece's surroundings as well as what you knew
of him in Charlottesville.

—Letter from Mrs. Helen Pancake,
February 10, 1981

He never seemed to find a place
With the flatlands and the farmers
So he had to leave one day
He said, To be an Actor.

He played a boy without a home
Torn, with no tomorrow
Reaching out to touch someone
A stranger in the shadows.

Then Marcus heard on the radio
That a movie star was dying.
He turned the treble way down low
So Hortense could go on sleeping.

—"Jim Dean of Indiana,"
Phil Ochs

IN LATE September of 1976, in the autumn of the Bicentennial year, I began my career as a teacher at the University of Virginia. I had been invited to join the writing program there by John Casey, who was then on leave. I had been lent the book-lined office of David Levin, a historian of Colonial American literature, who was also on leave that year. I had been assigned the status of associate professor of English, untenured, at my own request. I had come to Virginia from a Negro college in Baltimore. I had accepted Virginia's offer for professional and personal reasons: I wanted to teach better-motivated students and, on a spiritual level, I wanted to go home.

If I recall correctly, 1976 was a year of extraordinary hope in American politics. James Earl Carter, a southerner, was running for the presidency, and people in all parts of the country, black and white, were looking to that region with a certain optimism. Carter had inspired in a great many people the belief that *this* New South was the long-promised one. And there were many of us who had followed the ancestral imperative, seeking a better life in the North and in the West, who silently hoped that the promises made during the Reconstruction were finally going to be kept. While in the "white" American community Jimmy Carter's candidacy provoked an interest in the nuances of southern speech and in the ingredients of southern cooking, in the "black" American community the visibility of Carter—his speaking in a black Baptist church, his walking the streets of Harlem and Detroit—seemed to symbolize the emergence of a southern *culture*, of which they had long been a part, into the broader American imagination. The emergence of Carter suggested a kind of reconciliation between two peoples shaped by this common culture. His appearance was a signal to refugees from the South—settled somewhat comfortably in other regions—that we were now being encouraged to reoccupy native ground. There were many of us who turned our imaginations toward the ancestral home.

I had left the South at twenty-one, a product of its segregated schools and humanly degrading institutions, and had managed to make a career for myself in the North. Growing up in the South, during those twenty-one years, I had never had a white friend. And although, in later years, I had known many white southerners in the North and in the West, these relationships had been compromised by the subtle fact that a southerner, outside the South, is often viewed as outside his proper context, and is sometimes as much of an outsider as a black American.

Friendships grounded in mutual alienation and self-consciously geared to the perceptions of others are seldom truly tested. They lack an organic relationship to a common landscape, a common or "normal" basis for the evolution of trust and mutual interest. Mutual self-interest—the need of the white southerner to appear "right" in the eyes of sometimes condescending northerners (the South being the traditional scapegoat on all matters racial) and the need of the black southerner for access to somewhat commonly held memories of the South and of southern culture—is the basis for political alliances rather than friendships. To achieve this true friendship, it is necessary for the two southerners to meet on southern soil. And if growing up in the South never presented this opportunity, and if one is still interested in "understanding" that part of oneself that the "other" possesses, it becomes necessary to return to the South. Ironically, while the candidacy of Jimmy Carter represented a political alliance between white and black southerners, the real meaning of the alliance, in 1976 at least, resided in the quality of the personal relationships between these two separate but same peoples on their home ground, in the homeplace. Perhaps this is what I was looking for in the fall of 1976, at Thomas Jefferson's University of Virginia.

I remember two incidents from those first days at Virginia, while I sat in David Levin's book-lined office. An overrefined and affected young man from Texas came in to inquire about my courses, and as I rose from my chair to greet him, he raised his hand in a gesture that affirmed the Old South tradition of noblesse oblige. He said, "Oh, no, no, no, no! You don't have to get up."

The second incident was the sound of a voice, and came several days later. It was in the hall outside my office door and it was saying, "I'm Jimmy Carter and I'm running for President, I'm Jimmy Carter and I'm running for President." The pitch and rhythms of the voice conveyed the necessary messages: the rhythm and intonation were southern, lower-middle-class or lower-class southern, the kind that instantly calls to mind the word *cracker*. Its loudness, in the genteel buzz and hum of Wilson Hall, suggested either extreme arrogance or a certain insecurity. Why the voice repeated Carter's campaign slogan was obvious to anyone: the expectations of the South, especially of the lower-class and middle-class South, were with Carter. He was one of them. His campaign promised to redefine the image of those people whom William Faulkner had found distasteful, those who were replacing a decadent and impotent aristocracy. These were the people whose moral code, beyond a periodically expressed contempt for black Americans, had remained largely undefined in the years since Faulkner.

The bearer of this voice, when he appeared in my doorway,

conformed to the herald that had preceded him. He was wiry and tall, just a little over six feet, with very direct, deep-seeing brown eyes. His straw-blond hair lacked softness. In his face was that kind of half-smile/half-grimace that says, "I've seen it all and I still say, 'So what?'" He wore a checkered flannel shirt, faded blue-jeans, and a round brass U.S. Army-issue belt buckle over a slight beer belly. I think he also wore boots. He stood in the doorway, looking into the handsomely appointed office, and said, "Buddy, I want to work with you."

His name, after I had asked it again, was still Breece Pancake.

There was something stiff and military in his bearing. I immediately stereotyped him as of German ancestry (in the South, during its many periods of intolerance, German names have been known to metamorphose into metaphorical Anglo-Saxon ones, Gaspennys and perhaps Pancakes included). He had read some of my work, he said, and wanted to show me some of his. His directness made me wary of him. While I sat at a desk (in academia, a symbol of power), he seemed determined to know me, the person, apart from the desk. In an environment reeking with condescension, he was inviting me to abandon my very small area of protection.

He asked if I drank beer, if I played pinball, if I owned a gun, if I hunted or fished. When these important *cultural* points had been settled, he asked, almost as an afterthought, if he could sign up to do independent study with me. When we had reached agreement, he strolled back out into the hall and resumed shouting, "I'm Jimmy Carter and I'm running for President! I'm Jimmy Carter and I'm running for President!" I recall now that there was also in his voice a certain boastful tone. It matched and complemented that half-smile of his that said, "So what?" Breece

Pancake was a West Virginian, that peculiar kind of mountain-bred southerner, or part-southerner, who was just as alienated as I was in the hushed gentility of Wilson Hall.

The University of Virginia, during that time at least, was as fragmented as the nation. There were subtle currents that moved people in certain directions, toward certain constituency groups, and I soon learned that it was predictable that Breece Pancake should come to my office seeking something more than academic instruction. The university, always a state-supported school, had until very recently functioned as a kind of finishing school for the sons of the southern upper class. About a generation before, it had opened its doors to the sons of the middle class. And during the 1960s it had opened them farther to admit women and black students. In an attempt to make the institution a nationally recognized university, an effort was made to attract more students from the affluent suburbs of Washington and from the Northeast. More than this, an extraordinarily ambitious effort was made to upgrade all the departments within the university. Scholars had been recruited from Harvard and Princeton and Stanford and Berkeley and Yale. The institution claimed intellectuals from all parts of the world. The faculty was and remains among the best in the nation.

But these rapid changes, far from modifying the basic identity of the institution, caused a kind of cultural dislocation, a period of stasis in the attempted redefinition of the basic institutional identity. In many respects, it was like a redecoration of the interior of a goldfish bowl. Many of the sons of the southern gentry, seeking the more traditional identity, began attending Vanderbilt, Tulane, Chapel Hill, and Washington and Lee. And while the basic identity of the school remained southern, very few southerners were visible. One result was the erosion of the values that had once given the institution an identity. Another was stratification by class and color considerations. Preppies banded together. So did women. So did the few black students. So did, in their fraternities and clubs, the remnants of the old gentry.

Ironically, the people who seemed most isolated and insecure were the sons and daughters of the southern lower and middle classes. They had come to the place their ancestors must have dreamed about—Charlottesville is to the South what Cambridge is to the rest of the nation—and for various reasons found themselves spiritually far from home. Some of them expressed their frustrations by attacking the traditional scapegoats—black teachers and students. Others began to parody themselves, accentuating and then assuming the stereotyped persona of the hillbilly, in an attempt to achieve a comfortable identity. Still others, the constitutional nonconformists like Breece Pancake, became extremely isolated and sought out the company of other outsiders.

A writer, no matter what the context, is made an outsider by the demands of his vocation, and there was never any doubt in my mind that Breece Pancake was a writer. His style derived in large part from Hemingway, his themes from people and places he had known in West Virginia. His craftsmanship was exact, direct, unsentimental. His favorite comment was "Bull*shit*!" He wasted no words and rewrote ceaselessly for the precise effect he intended to convey. But constitutionally, Breece Pancake was a lonely and melancholy man. And his position at the university— as a Hoyns Fellow, as a teaching assistant, and as a man from a small town in the hills of West Virginia—contributed some to the cynicism and bitterness that was already in him. While his vocation as a writer made him part of a very small group, his middle-class West Virginia origins tended to isolate him from the much more sophisticated and worldly middle-class students from the suburbs of Washington and the Northeast, as well as from the upper-class students of southern background. From him I learned something of the contempt that many upper-class southerners have for the lower- and middle-class southerners, and from him I learned something about the abiding need these people have to be held in the high esteem of their upper-class co-regionalists. While I was offered the opportunity to be invited into certain homes as an affirmation of a certain tradition of noblesse oblige, this option was rarely available to Breece (an upper-class southerner once told me: "I like the blacks. They're a lot like European peasants, and they're *cleaner* than the poor whites"). Yet he was always trying to make friends, on any level available to him. He was in the habit of giving gifts, and once he complained to me that he had been reprimanded by a family for not bringing to them as many fish as he had promised to catch. To make up this deficiency, he purchased with his own money additional fish, but not enough to meet the quota he had promised. When he was teased about this, he commented to me, "They acted as if they wanted me to tug at my forelock."

You may keep the books or anything Breece gave you—he loved to give but never learned to receive. He never felt worthy of a gift—being tough on himself. His code of living was taught to him by his parents—be it Greek, Roman or whatever, it's just plain old honesty. God called him

home because he saw too much dishonesty and evil in
this world and he couldn't cope.

> —Letter from Mrs. Helen Pancake,
> February 5, 1981

And I won't be running from the rain, when I'm gone
And I can't even suffer from the pain, when I'm gone
There's nothing I can lose or I can gain, when I'm gone
So I guess I'll have to do it while I'm here.

And I won't be laughing at the lies, when I'm gone
And I can't question how or when or why, when I'm gone
Can't live proud enough to die, when I'm gone
So I guess I'll have to do it while I'm here.

> —"When I'm Gone,"
> Phil Ochs

Breece Pancake seemed driven to improve himself. His ambition was not primarily literary: he was struggling to define for
himself an entire way of life, an all-embracing code of values
that would allow him to live outside his home valley in Milton,
West Virginia. The kind of books he gave me may suggest the
scope of his search: a biography of Jack London, Eugene O'Neill's
plays about the sea—works that concern the perceptions of men
who looked at nature in the raw. In his mid-twenties Breece
joined the Catholic church and became active in church affairs.
But I did not understand the focus of his life until I had driven

through his home state, along those winding mountain roads, where at every turn one looks down at houses nestled in hollows. In those hollows, near those houses, there are abandoned cars and stoves and refrigerators. Nothing is thrown away by people in that region; some use is found for even the smallest evidence of affluence. And eyes, in that region, are trained to look either up or down: from the hollows up toward the sky or from the encircling hills down into the hollows. Horizontal vision, in that area, is rare. The sky there is circumscribed by insistent hillsides thrusting upward. It is an environment crafted by nature for the dreamer and for the resigned.

Breece once told me about his relationship with radio when he was growing up, about the range of stations available to him. Driving through those mountains, I could imagine the many directions in which his imagination was pulled. Like many West Virginians, he had been lured to Detroit by the nighttime radio stations. But he was also conscious of the many other parts of the country, especially those states that touched the borders of his own region. Once, I asked him how many people there were in the entire state of West Virginia. He estimated about two or three million, with about a hundred thousand people in Huntington, then the state's largest city. It was a casual question, one with no real purpose behind it. But several days later I received in my mailbox a note from him: "Jim, I was wrong, but proportionally correct (Huntington, WV has 46,000 people). To the West, Ohio has approximately 9 million. To the East, Virginia has approx. 4 million. To the South, Kentucky has approximately 3 million. To the North, Pa. has approx. 11 million. West Virginia—1,800,000—a million more than Rhode Island. P.S. See you at lunch tomorrow?" It need not be emphasized that he was very self-conscious about the poverty of his state, and about its image in certain books. He told me he did not think much of Harry Caudill's *Night Comes to the Cumberlands*. He thought it presented an inaccurate image of his native ground, and his ambition, as a writer, was to improve on it.

This determination to improve himself dictated that Breece should be a wanderer and an adventurer. He had attended several small colleges in West Virginia, had traveled around the country. He had lived for a while on an Indian reservation in the West. He had taught himself German. He taught for a while at a military academy in Staunton, Virginia, the same one attended by his hero, Phil Ochs. He had great admiration for this song-writer, and encouraged me to listen closely to the lyrics of what he considered Ochs's best song, "Jim Dean of Indiana." Breece took his own writing just as seriously, placing all his hopes on its success. He seemed to be under self-imposed pressures to "make it" as a writer. He told me once: "All I have to sell is my experience. If things get really bad, they'll put you and me in the same ditch. They'll pay *me* a little more, but I'll still be in the ditch." He liked to impress people with tall tales he had made up, and he liked to impress them in self-destructive ways. He would get into fights in lower-class bars on the outskirts of Charlottesville, then return to the city to show off his scars. "These are stories," he would say.

He liked people who exhibited class. He spoke contemptuously of upper-class women with whom he had slept on a first date, but was full of praise for a woman who had allowed him to kiss her on the cheek only after several dates. "She's a lady," he bragged to me. I think that redefining himself in terms of his *idea* of Charlottesville society was very important to Breece, even if that idea had no basis in the reality of the place. Yet there was also an antagonistic strain in him, a contempt for the conformity imposed on people there. We once attended a movie together, and during the intermission, when people crowded together in the small lobby, he felt closed in and shouted, "Move away! Make room! Let people through!" The crowd, mostly students, immediately scattered. Then Breece turned to me and laughed. "They're clones!" he said. "They're *clones!*"

He loved the outdoors—hunting and fishing and hiking in the Blue Ridge Mountains. Several times he took me hiking with him. During these outings he gave me good advice: if ever I felt closed in by the insularity of Charlottesville, I should drive up to the Blue Ridge and walk around, and that would clear my head. He viewed this communion with nature as an absolute necessity, and during those trips into the mountains he seemed to be at peace.

He also loved to play pinball and pool and to drink beer. He was very competitive in these recreations. He almost always out-drank me, and when he was drunk he would be strangely silent. He sat stiff and erect during these times, his eyes focused on my face, his mind and imagination elsewhere. Sometimes he talked about old girlfriends in Milton who had hurt him. He related once his sorrow over the obligation imposed upon him—by a librarian in Milton—to burn and bury hundreds of old books. He liked old things. He talked about hunting in a relative's attic for certain items that once belonged to his father. He recollected letters his father had written, to his mother and to him, in the years before his death.

Breece Pancake drank a great deal, and when he drank his imagination always returned to this same place. Within that private room, I think now, were stored all his old hurts and all his fantasies. When his imagination entered there, he became a melancholy man in great need of contact with other people. But because he was usually silent during these periods, his presence tended often to make other people nervous. "Breece always hangs around," a mutual friend once said to me. He almost never asked for anything, and at the slightest show of someone else's discomfort, Breece would excuse himself and compensate— within a few hours or the next day—with a gift. I don't think there was anyone, in Charlottesville at least, who knew just what, if anything, Breece expected in return. This had the effect of making people feel inadequate and guilty.

> Jim, "Bullshit" was one of B's choice sayings—in fact he used to say he wanted his short stories entitled "Bullshit Artist." Love his heart!
>
> —Letter from Mrs. Helen Pancake,
> February 5, 1981

> The mad director knows that freedom will not make
>   you free,
> And what's this got to do with me?
> I declare the war is over. It's over. It's over.
>
> —"The War Is Over,"
> Phil Ochs

In the winter of 1977 I went to Boston and mentioned the work of several of my students, Breece included, to Phoebe-Lou Adams of *The Atlantic*. She asked to be sent some of his stories. I encouraged Breece to correspond with her, and very soon afterward

several of his stories were purchased by the magazine. The day
the letter of acceptance and check arrived, Breece came to my
office and invited me to dinner. We went to Tiffany's, our favorite seafood restaurant. Far from being pleased by his success, he
seemed morose and nervous. He said he had wired flowers to
his mother that day but had not yet heard from her. He drank a
great deal. After dinner he said that he had a gift for me and that
I would have to go home with him in order to claim it.

He lived in a small room on an estate just on the outskirts
of Charlottesville. It was more a workroom than a house, and
his work in progress was neatly laid out along a square of plywood that served as his desk. He went immediately to a closet
and opened it. Inside were guns—rifles, shotguns, handguns—of
every possible kind. He selected a twelve-gauge shotgun from
one of the racks and gave it to me. He also gave me the bill of
sale for it—purchased in West Virginia—and two shells. He then
invited me to go squirrel hunting with him. I promised that I
would. But since I had never owned a gun or wanted one, I asked
a friend who lived on a farm to hold on to it for me.

Several months later, I found another gift from Breece in my
campus mailbox. It was a trilobite, a fossil once highly valued by
the Indians of Breece's region. One of the stories he had sold *The
Atlantic* had "Trilobites" as its title.

There was a mystery about Breece Pancake that I will not
claim to have penetrated. This mystery is not racial; it had to
do with that small room into which his imagination retreated
from time to time. I always thought that the gifts he gave were
a way of keeping people away from this very personal area, of
focusing their attention on the persona he had created out of

the raw materials of his best traits. I have very little evidence, beyond one small incident, to support this conclusion, but that one incident has caused me to believe it all the more.

The incident occurred one night during the summer of 1977. We had been seeing the films of Lina Wertmuller, and that evening *Seven Beauties* was being shown at a local theater. I telephoned Breece to see if he wanted to go. There was no answer. When I called later I let the telephone ring a number of times. Finally, a man answered and asked what I wanted. I asked for Breece. He said I had the wrong number, that Breece did not live there anymore. There was in the tone of his voice the abrupt authority of a policeman. He then held the line for a moment, and in the background I could hear quick and muffled conversation between Breece and several other people. Then the man came on the line again and asked my name and number. He said that Breece would call me back. But then Breece himself took the telephone and asked what it was I wanted. I mentioned the movie. He said he could not see it because he was going to West Virginia that same evening, but that he would get in touch with me when he returned. I left town myself soon after that, and did not see Breece again until early September. That was when he gave me the trilobite, and shortly afterward he made me promise that I would never tell anyone about the night I called him the summer before.

In the early summer of 1978 I left Charlottesville for New Haven, Connecticut. Carter was still President, but my ideas about the South had changed dramatically. I hoped that, with luck, I would never have to return to Charlottesville. I began making plans to resume my old life-style as a refugee from the

South. But if life has any definition at all, it is the things that happen to us while we are making plans. In the early fall of that year I found out that I would be a father before spring arrived. Around that same time, a package from Breece, mailed from Charlottesville, arrived at my apartment in New Haven. I did not open it. I knew there would be a gift inside, but I also knew that renewing my connection with Breece would take my memories back to Charlottesville, and I wanted to be completely free of the place. The package from Breece remained unopened until the late evening of April 9, 1979.

On the evening of April 8 I had a dream that included Breece. I was trapped in a room by some menacing and sinister people and they were forcing me to eat things I did not want to eat. Breece was there, but I cannot remember the part he played in the drama. I woke up before dawn to find that my wife's contractions had begun. The rest of the day was spent in the delivery room of the Yale-New Haven Hospital. In the late afternoon I went to the Yale campus and taught a class, which earned me one hundred dollars. Then I walked home, happy with the new direction my life had taken as the hardworking father of Rachel Alice McPherson. At my apartment, however, there was a telegram from John Casey, sent from Charlottesville. It informed me that on the previous night Breece Pancake had killed himself.

I called Charlottesville immediately and was told certain facts by Jane Casey, John's wife: Breece had been drinking. He had, for some reason, gone into the home of a family near his little house and had sat there, in the dark, until they returned. When he made a noise, either by getting up or by saying something, they became frightened and thought he was a burglar. Breece ran from the house to his own place. There, for some reason, he took one of his shotguns, put the barrel in his mouth, and blew his head off.

I have never believed this story.

I speculate that Breece had his own reasons for hiding in a neighbor's house. They may have had to do with personal problems, or they may have had to do with emotional needs. Whatever their source, I am sure his reasons were extraordinary ones. As a writer, if I am to believe anything about Breece's "suicide," extract any lesson from it, that lesson has to do with the kind of life he led. I believe that Breece had had a few drinks and found himself locked inside that secret room he carried around with him. I believe that he had scattered so many gifts around Charlottesville, had given signals to so many people, that he felt it would be all right to ask someone to help him during what must have been a very hard night. I believe that he was so inarticulate about his own feelings, so frightened that he would be rejected, that he panicked when the couple came home. Whatever the cause of his desperation, he could not express it from within the persona he had created. How does one say he expects things from people after having cultivated the persona of the Provider? How does one explain the contents of a secret room to people who, though physically close, still remain strangers? How does one reconcile a lifetime of indiscriminate giving with the need for a gesture as simple as a kind word, an instant of basic human understanding? And what if this need is so bathed in bitterness and disappointment that the attempt itself, at a very critical time, seems hopeless except through the written word? In such a situation, a man might look at his typewriter, and then at the rest of the world, and just give up the struggle. Phil Ochs hanged himself. Breece Pancake shot himself. The rest of us, if we are lucky enough to be incapable of imagining such extreme acts of defiance, manage to endure.

Very late in the evening of the day I got the news, I opened the package that Breece had sent me the previous fall. It contained some old photographs of railroad workers, some poetry, and a letter. The first line of the letter told the entire story: "You are under no obligation to answer this." But he had hoped anyway that I would. The pictures were from his family collection, given to him in trust by his Aunt Julia, who was soon to die. He wanted to give them away rather than sell them. The poetry represented an extension of this same impulse. "Also enclosed are some poems you might find interesting—again, I'm not asking for response, just sharing news. I went to Staunton Correctional Institution (the pen) and stumbled onto this guy [an inmate]. Not knowing anything about poetry, I gave [his poems] to [the poet] Greg Orr. . . . He liked them and is doing what he can to help find the proper market thru CODA. Anyway, what was that Latin phrase about the Obligation of Nobility? If it's what I think it means—helping folks—it isn't bad as a duty or a calling. We'd both better get back to work."

Looked at in purely sociological terms, Breece Pancake's work was helping people, giving to people. I think that part of him, the part of West Virginia that borders on Virginia, wanted to affirm those old, aristocratic, eighteenth-century values that no longer had a context, especially in Charlottesville. He was working toward becoming an aristocrat in blue jeans. But he was from the southern lower-middle class, his accent had certain associations, he could find no conventional way to express his own needs, and while he was alive there were many of us who could not understand who or what he was.

Several weeks later, I sent the fossil he had given me, the trilobite, to the girl who had allowed him to kiss her cheek after several dates. She had left Charlottesville, and was then working in New York.

JAMES ALAN MCPHERSON

TRILOBITES

••••••••••••••••••••

I OPEN the truck's door, step onto the brick side street. I look at Company Hill again, all sort of worn down and round. A long time ago it was real craggy and stood like an island in the Teays River. It took over a million years to make that smooth little hill, and I've looked all over it for trilobites. I think how it has always been there and always will be, at least for as long as it matters. The air is smoky with summertime. A bunch of starlings swim over me. I was born in this country and I have never very much wanted to leave. I remember Pop's dead eyes looking at me. They were real dry, and that took something out of me. I shut the door, head for the café.

I see a concrete patch in the street. It's shaped like Florida, and I recollect what I wrote in Ginny's yearbook: "We will live on mangoes and love." And she up and left without me—two years she's been down there without me. She sends me postcards with alligator wrestlers and flamingos on the front. She never asks me any questions. I feel like a real fool for what I wrote, and go into the café.

The place is empty, and I rest in the cooled air. Tinker Reilly's little sister pours my coffee. She has good hips. They are kind of like Ginny's and they slope in nice curves to her legs. Hips and legs like that climb steps into airplanes. She goes to the counter end and scoffs down the rest of her sundae. I smile at her, but she's jailbait. Jailbait and black snakes are two things I won't touch with a window pole. One time I used an old black snake for a bullwhip, snapped the sucker's head off, and Pop beat hell out of me with it. I think how Pop could make me pretty mad sometimes. I grin.

I think about last night when Ginny called. Her old man drove her down from the airport in Charleston. She was already bored. Can we get together? Sure. Maybe do some brew? Sure. Same old Colly. Same old Ginny. She talked through her beak. I wanted to tell her Pop had died and Mom was on the warpath to sell the farm, but Ginny was talking through her beak. It gave me the creeps.

Just like the cups give me the creeps. I look at the cups hanging on pegs by the storefront. They're decal-named and covered with grease and dust. There's four of them, and one is Pop's, but that isn't what gives me the creeps. The cleanest one is Jim's. It's clean because he still uses it, but it hangs there with the rest. Through the window, I can see him crossing the street. His joints are cemented with arthritis. I think of how long it'll be before I croak, but Jim is old, and it gives me the creeps to see his cup hanging up there. I go to the door to help him in.

He says, "Tell the truth, now," and his old paw pinches my arm. I say, "Can't do her." I help him to his stool.

I pull this globby rock from my pocket and slap it on the counter in front of Jim. He turns it with his drawn hand, examines it. "Gastropod," he says. "Probably Permian. You buy again." I can't win with him. He knows them all.

"I still can't find a trilobite," I say.

"There are a few," he says. "Not many. Most of the outcrops around here are too late for them."

The girl brings Jim's coffee in his cup, and we watch her pump back to the kitchen. Good hips.

"You see that?" He jerks his head toward her.

I say, "Moundsville Molasses." I can spot jailbait by a mile.

"Hell, girl's age never stopped your dad and me in Michigan."

"Tell the truth."

"Sure. You got to time it so you nail the first freight out when your pants are up."

I look at the windowsill. It is speckled with the crisp skeletons of flies. "Why'd you and Pop leave Michigan?"

The crinkles around Jim's eyes go slack. He says, "The war," and sips his coffee.

I say, "He never made it back there."

"Me either—always wanted to—there or Germany—just to look around."

"Yeah, he promised to show me where you all buried that silverware and stuff during the war."

He says, "On the Elbe. Probably plowed up by now."

My eye socket reflects in my coffee, steam curls around my face, and I feel a headache coming on. I look up to ask Tinker's sister for an aspirin, but she is giggling in the kitchen.

"That's where he got that wound," Jim says. "Got it on the Elbe. He was out a long time. Cold, Jesus, it was cold. I had him for dead, but he came to. Says, 'I been all over the world'; says, 'China's so pretty, Jim.'"

"Dreaming?"

"I don't know. I quit worrying about that stuff years ago."

Tinker's sister comes up with her coffeepot to make us for a tip. I ask her for an aspirin and see she's got a pimple on her collarbone. I don't remember seeing pictures of China. I watch little sister's hips.

"Trent still wanting your place for that housing project?"

"Sure," I say. "Mom'll probably sell it, too. I can't run the place like Pop did. Cane looks bad as hell." I drain off my cup. I'm tired of talking about the farm. "Going out with Ginny tonight," I say.

"Give her that for me," he says. He takes a poke at my whang. I don't like it when he talks about her like that. He sees I don't like it, and his grin slips. "Found a lot of gas for her old man. One hell of a guy before his wife pulled out."

I wheel on my stool, clap his weak old shoulder. I think of Pop, and try to joke. "You stink so bad the undertaker's following you."

He laughs. "You were the ugliest baby ever born, you know that?"

I grin, and start out the door. I can hear him shout to little sister: "Come on over here, honey, I got a joke for you."

The sky has a film. Its heat burns through the salt on my skin, draws it tight. I start the truck, drive west along the highway built on the dry bed of the Teays. There's wide bottoms, and the hills on either side have yellowy billows the sun can't burn off. I pass an iron sign put up by the WPA: "Surveyed by George Washington, the Teays River Pike." I see fields and cattle where buildings stand, picture them from some long-off time.

I turn off the main road to our house. Clouds make the sunshine blink light and dark in the yard. I look again at the spot of ground where Pop fell. He had lain spread-eagled in the thick grass after a sliver of metal from his old wound passed to his brain. I remember thinking how beaten his face looked with prints in it from the grass.

I reach the high barn and start my tractor, then drive to the knob at the end of our land and stop. I sit there, smoke, look again at the cane. The rows curve tight, but around them is a sort of scar of clay, and the leaves have a purplish blight. I don't wonder about the blight. I know the cane is too far gone to worry about the blight. Far off, somebody chops wood, and the ax-bites echo back to me. The hillsides are baked here and have heat ghosts. Our cattle move to the wind gap, and birds hide in caps of trees where we never cut the timber for pasture. I look at the wrinkly old boundary post. Pop set it when the hobo and soldier days were over. It is a locust-tree post and will be there a long time. A few dead morning glories cling to it.

"I'm just not no good at it," I say. "It just don't do to work your ass off at something you're not no good at."

The chopping stops. I listen to the beat of grasshopper wings, and strain to spot blight on the far side of the bottoms.

I say, "Yessir, Colly, you couldn't grow pole beans in a pile of horseshit."

I squash my cigarette against the floor plate. I don't want a fire. I press the starter, and bump around the fields, then down to the ford of the drying creek, and up the other side. Turkles fall from logs into stagnant pools. I stop my machine. The cane here is just as bad. I rub a sunburn into the back of my neck.

I say, "Shot to hell, Gin. Can't do nothing right."

I lean back, try to forget these fields and flanking hills. A long time before me or these tools, the Teays flowed here. I can almost feel the cold waters and the tickling the trilobites make when they crawl. All the water from the old mountains flowed west. But the land lifted. I have only the bottoms and stone animals I collect. I blink and breathe. My father is a khaki cloud in the canebrakes, and Ginny is no more to me than the bitter smell in the blackberry briers up on the ridge.

I take up my sack and gaff for a turkle. Some quick chubs flash under the bank. In the moss-dapples, I see rings spread where a turkle ducked under. This sucker is mine. The pool smells like rot, and the sun is a hardish brown.

I wade in. He goes for the roots of a log. I shove around, and feel my gaff twitch. This is a smart turkle, but still a sucker. I bet he could pull liver off a hook for the rest of his days, but he is a sucker for the roots that hold him while I work my gaff. I pull him up, and see he is a snapper. He's got his stubby neck curved around, biting at the gaff. I lay him on the sand, and take out Pop's knife. I step on the shell, and press hard. That fat neck gets skinny quick, and sticks way out. A little blood oozes from the gaff wound into the grit, but when I slice, a puddle forms.

A voice says, "Get a dragon, Colly?"

I shiver a little, and look up. It's only the loansman standing on the creekbank in his tan suit. His face is splotched pink, and the sun is turning his glasses black.

"I crave them now and again," I say. I go on slitting gristle, skinning back the shell.

"Aw, your daddy loved turtle meat," the guy says.

I listen to scratching cane leaves in the late sun. I dump the tripes into the pool, bag the rest, and head up the ford. I say, "What can I do for you?"

This guy starts up: "I saw you from the road—just came down to see about my offer."

"I told you yesterday, Mr. Trent. It ain't mine to sell." I tone it down. I don't want hard feelings. "You got to talk to Mom."

Blood drips from the poke to the dust. It makes dark paste. Trent pockets his hands, looks over the cane. A cloud blocks the sun, and my crop glows greenish in the shade.

"This is about the last real farm left around here," Trent says.

"Blight'll get what the dry left," I say. I shift the sack to my free hand. I see I'm giving in. I'm letting this guy go and push me around.

"How's your mother getting along?" he says. I see no eyes behind his smoky glasses.

"Pretty good," I say. "She's wanting to move to Akron." I swing the sack a little toward Ohio, and spray some blood on Trent's pants. "Sorry," I say.

"It'll come out," he says, but I hope not. I grin and watch the turkle's mouth gape on the sand. "Well, why Akron?" he says. "Family there?"

I nod. "Hers," I say. "She'll take you up on the offer." This hot shadow saps me, and my voice is a whisper. I throw the sack to the floor plate, climb up to grind the starter. I feel better in a way I've never known. The hot metal seat burns through my jeans.

"Saw Ginny at the post office," this guy shouts. "She sure is a pretty."

I wave, almost smile, as I gear to lumber up the dirt road. I pass Trent's dusty Lincoln, move away from my bitten cane. It can go now; the stale seed, the drought, the blight—it can go when she signs the papers. I know I will always be to blame, but it can't just be my fault. "What about you?" I say. "Your side hurt all that morning, but you wouldn't see no doctor. Nosir, you had to see that your dumb boy got the crop put proper in the ground." I shut my trap to keep from talking like a fool.

I stop my tractor on the terraced road to the barn and look back across the cane to the creekbed. Yesterday Trent said the bottoms would be filled with dirt. That will put the houses above flood, but it'll raise the flood line. Under all those houses, my turkles will turn to stone. Our Herefords make rusty patches on the hill. I see Pop's grave, and wonder if the new high waters will get over it.

I watch the cattle play. A rain must be coming. A rain is always coming when cattle play. Sometimes they play for snow, but mostly it is rain. After Pop whipped the daylights out of me with that black snake, he hung it on a fence. But it didn't rain. The cattle weren't playing, and it didn't rain, but I kept my mouth shut. The snake was bad enough, I didn't want the belt too.

I look a long time at that hill. My first time with Ginny was in the tree-cap of that hill. I think of how close we could be then, and maybe even now, I don't know. I'd like to go with Ginny, fluff her hair in any other field. But I can see her in the post office. I bet she was sending postcards to some guy in Florida.

I drive on to the barn, stop under the shed. I wipe sweat from my face with my sleeve, and see how the seams have slipped from my shoulders. If I sit rigid, I can fill them again. The turkle is moving in the sack, and it gives me the creeps to hear his shell clinking against the gaff. I take the poke to the spigot to clean the game. Pop always liked turkle in a mulligan. He talked a lot about mulligan and the jungles just an hour before I found him.

I wonder what it will be like when Ginny comes by. I hope

she's not talking through her beak. Maybe she'll take me to her house this time. If her momma had been anybody but Pop's cousin, her old man would let me go to her house. Screw him. But I can talk to Ginny. I wonder if she remembers the plans we made for the farm. And we wanted kids. She always nagged about a peacock. I will get her one.

I smile as I dump the sack into the rusty sink, but the barn smell—the hay, the cattle, the gasoline—it reminds me. Me and Pop built this barn. I look at every nail with the same dull pain.

I clean the meat and lay it out on a piece of cloth torn from an old bed sheet. I fold the corners, walk to the house.

The air is hot, but it sort of churns, and the set screens in the kitchen window rattle. From inside, I can hear Mom and Trent talking on the front porch, and I leave the window up. It is the same come-on he gave me yesterday, and I bet Mom is eating it up. She probably thinks about tea parties with her cousins in Akron. She never listens to what anybody says. She just says all right to anything anybody but me or Pop ever said. She even voted for Hoover before they got married. I throw the turkle meat into a skillet, get a beer. Trent softens her up with me; I prick my ears.

"I would wager on Colly's agreement," he says. I can still hear a hill twang in his voice.

"I told him Sam'd put him on at Goodrich," she says. "They'd teach him a trade."

"And there are a good many young people in Akron. You know he'd be happier." I think how his voice sounds like a damn TV.

"Well, he's awful good to keep me company. Don't go out none since Ginny took off to that college."

"There's a college in Akron," he says, but I shut the window.

I lean against the sink, rub my hands across my face. The smell of turkle has soaked between my fingers. It's the same smell as the pools.

Through the door to the living room, I see the rock case Pop built for me. The white labels show up behind the dark gloss of glass. Ginny helped me find over half of those. If I did study in a college, I could come back and take Jim's place at the gas wells. I like to hold little stones that lived so long ago. But geology doesn't mean lick to me. I can't even find a trilobite.

I stir the meat, listen for noise or talk on the porch, but there is none. I look out. A lightning flash peels shadows from the yard and leaves a dark strip under the cave of the barn. I feel a scum on my skin in the still air. I take my supper to the porch.

I look down the valley to where bison used to graze before the first rails were put down. Now those rails are covered with a highway, and cars rush back and forth in the wind. I watch Trent's car back out, heading east into town. I'm afraid to ask right off if he got what he wanted.

I stick my plate under Mom's nose, but she waves it off. I sit in Pop's old rocker, watch the storm come. Dust devils puff around on the berm, and maple sprigs land in the yard with their white bellies up. Across the road, our windbreak bends, rows of cedars furling every which way at once.

"Coming a big one?" I say.

Mom says nothing and fans herself with the funeral-home fan. The wind layers her hair, but she keeps that cardboard picture of Jesus bobbing like crazy. Her face changes. I know what she thinks. She thinks how she isn't the girl in the picture on the mantel. She isn't standing with Pop's garrison cap cocked on her head.

"I wish you'd of come out while he's here," she says. She stares across the road to the windbreak.

"I heard him yesterday," I say.

"It ain't that at all," she says, and I watch her brow come down a little. "It's like when Jim called us askin' if we wanted some beans an' I had to tell him to leave 'em in the truck at church. I swan how folks talk when men come 'round a widow."

I know Jim talks like a dumb old fart, but it isn't like he'd rape her or anything. I don't want to argue with her. "Well," I say, "who owns this place?"

"We still do. Don't have to sign nothin' till tomorrow."

She quits bobbing Jesus to look at me. She starts up: "You'll like Akron. Law, I bet Marcy's youngest girl'd love to meet you. She's a regular rock hound too. 'Sides, your father always said we'd move there when you got big enough to run the farm."

I know she has to say it. I just keep my mouth shut. The rain comes, ringing the roof tin. I watch the high wind snap branches from the trees. Pale splinters of light shoot down behind the far hills. We are just brushed by this storm.

Ginny's sports car hisses east on the road, honking as it passes, but I know she will be back.

"Just like her momma," Mom says, "racin' the devil for the beer joints."

"She never knew her momma," I say. I set my plate on the floor. I'm glad Ginny thought to honk.

"What if I's to run off with some foreman from the wells?"

"You wouldn't do that, Mom."

"That's right," she says, and watches the cars roll by. "Shot her in Chicago. Shot hisself too."

I look beyond the hills and time. There is red hair clouding the pillow, blood-splattered by the slug. Another body lies rumpled and warm at the bed foot.

"Folks said he done it cause she wouldn't marry him. Found two weddin' bands in his pocket. Feisty little I-taliun."

I see police and reporters in the tiny room. Mumbles spill into the hallway, but nobody really looks at the dead woman's face.

"Well," Mom says, "at least they was still wearin' their clothes."

The rain slows, and for a long time I sit watching the blue chicory swaying beside the road. I think of all the people I know who left these hills. Only Jim and Pop came back to the land, worked it.

"Lookee at the willow-wisps." Mom points to the hills.

The rain trickles, and as it seeps in to cool the ground, a fog rises. The fog curls little ghosts into the branches and gullies. The sun tries to sift through this mist, but is only a tarnished brown splotch in the pinkish sky. Wherever the fog is, the light is a burnished orange.

"Can't recall the name Pop gave it," I say.

The colors shift, trade tones.

"He had some funny names all right. Called a tomcat a 'pussy scat.'"

I think back. "Cornflakes were 'pone-rakes,' and a chicken was a 'sick-un.'"

We laugh.

"Well," she says, "he'll always be a part of us."

The glommy paint on the chair arm packs under my finger-nails. I think how she could foul up a free lunch.

Ginny honks again from the main road. I stand up to go in, but I hold the screen, look for something to say.

"I ain't going to live in Akron," I say.

"An' just where you gonna live, Mister?"

"I don't know."

She starts up with her fan again.

"Me and Ginny's going low-riding," I say.

She won't look at me. "Get in early. Mr. Trent don't keep no late hours for no beer drinkers."

The house is quiet, and I can hear her out there sniffling. But what to hell can I do about it? I hurry to wash the smell of turkle from my hands. I shake all over while the water flows down. I talked back. I've never talked back. I'm scared, but I stop shaking. Ginny can't see me shaking. I just walk out to the road without ever looking back to the porch.

I climb in the car, let Ginny kiss my cheek. She looks different. I've never seen these clothes, and she wears too much jewelry.

"You look great," she says. "Haven't changed a bit."

We drive west along the Pike.

"Where we going?"

She says, "Let's park for old times' sake. How's the depot?"

I say, "Sure." I reach back for a can of Falls City. "You let your hair grow."

"You like?"

"Um, yeah."

We drive. I look at the tinged fog, the colors changing hue.

She says, "Sort of an eerie evening, huh?" It all comes from her beak.

"Pop always called it a fool's fire or something."

We pull in beside the old depot. It's mostly boarded up. We drink, watch the colors slip to gray dusk in the sky.

"You ever look in your yearbook?" I gulp down the rest of my City.

She goes crazy laughing. "You know," she says, "I don't even know where I put that thing."

I feel way too mean to say anything. I look across the railroad to a field sown in timothy. There are wells there, pumps to suck the ancient gases. The gas burns blue, and I wonder if the ancient sun was blue. The tracks run on till they're a dot in the brown haze. They give off clicks from their switches. Some tankers wait on the spur. Their wheels are rusting to the tracks. I wonder what to hell I ever wanted with trilobites.

"Big night in Rock Camp," I say. I watch Ginny drink. Her skin is so white it glows yellowish, and the last light makes sparks in her red hair.

She says, "Daddy would raise hell. *Me* this close to the wells."

"You're a big girl now. C'mon, let's walk."

We get out, and she up and grabs my arm. Her fingers feel like ribbons on the veins of my hand.

"How long you in for?" I say.

"Just a week here, then a week with Daddy in New York. I can't wait to get back. It's great."

"You got a guy?"

She looks at me with this funny smile of hers. "Yeah, I got a guy. He's doing plankton research."

Ever since I talked back, I've been afraid, but now I hurt again. We come to the tankers, and she takes hold on a ladder, steps up.

"This right?" She looks funny, all crouched in like she's just nailed a drag on the fly. I laugh.

"Nail the end nearest the engine. If you slip, you get throwed clear. Way you are a drag on the fly'd suck you under. 'Sides, nobody'd ride a tanker."

She steps down but doesn't take my hand. "He taught you everything. What killed him?"

"Little shell fragment. Been in him since the war. Got in his blood . . ." I snap my fingers. I want to talk, but the picture won't become words. I see myself scattered, every cell miles from the others. I pull them back and kneel in the dark grass. I roll the body face-up, and look in the eyes a long time before I shut them. "You never talk about your momma," I say.

She says, "I don't want to," and goes running to an open window in the depot. She peeks in, turns to me. "Can we go in?"

"Why? Nothing in there but old freight scales."

"Because it's spooky and neat and I want to." She runs back, kisses me on the cheek. "I'm bored with this glum look. Smile!"

I give up and walk to the depot. I drag a rotten bench under the broken window and climb in. I take Ginny's hand to help her. A blade of glass slices her forearm. The cut path is shallow, but I take off my T-shirt to wrap it. The blood blots purple on the cloth.

"Hurt?"

"Not really."

I watch a mud dauber land on the glass blade. Its metal-blue wings flick as it walks the edge. It sucks what the glass has scraped from her skin. I hear them working in the walls.

Ginny is at the other window, and she peers through a knot-hole in the plywood.

I say, "See that light green spot on the second hill?"

"Yeah."

"That's the copper on your-all's roof."

She turns, stares at me.

"I come here lots," I say. I breathe the musty air. I turn away from her and look out the window to Company Hill, but I can feel her stare. Company Hill looks bigger in the dusk, and I think of all the hills around town I've never set foot on. Ginny comes up behind me, and there's a glass-crunch with her steps. The hurt arm goes around me, the tiny spot of blood cold against my back.

"What is it, Colly? Why can't we have any fun?"

"When I was a young punk, I tried to run away from home. I was walking through this meadow on the other side of the Hill, and this shadow passed over me. I honest to god thought it was a pterodactyl. It was a damned airplane. I was so damn mad, I came home." I peel chips of paint from the window frame, wait for her to talk. She leans against me, and I kiss her real deep. Her waist bunches in my hands. The skin of her neck is almost too white in the faded evening. I know she doesn't understand.

I slide her to the floor. Her scent rises to me, and I shove crates aside to make room. I don't wait. She isn't making love, she's getting laid. All right, I think, all right. Get laid. I pull her pants around her ankles, rut her. I think of Tinker's sister. Ginny isn't here. Tinker's sister is under me. A wash of blue light passes over me. I open my eyes to the floor, smell that tang of rain-wet wood. Black snakes. It was the only time he had to whip me.

"Let me go with you," I say. I want to be sorry, but I can't.

"Colly, please . . ." She shoves me back. Her head is rolling in splinters of paint and glass.

I look a long time at the hollow shadows hiding her eyes. She is somebody I met a long time ago. I can't remember her name for a minute, then it comes back to me. I sit against the wall and my spine aches. I listen to the mud daubers building nests, and trace a finger along her throat.

She says, "I want to go. My arm hurts." Her voice comes from someplace deep in her chest.

We climb out. A yellow light burns on the crossties, and the switches click. Far away, I hear a train. She gives me my shirt, and gets in her car. I stand there looking at the blood spots on the cloth. I feel old as hell. When I look up, her taillights are reddish blurs in the fog.

I walk around to the platform, slump on the bench. The evening cools my eyelids. I think of how that one time was the only airplane that ever passed over me.

I picture my father—a young hobo with the Michigan sunset making him squint, the lake behind him. His face is hard from all the days and places he fought to live in, and of a sudden, I know his mistake was coming back here to set that locust-tree post on the knob.

"Ever notice how only blue lightning bugs come out after a rain? Green ones almost never do."

I hear the train coming. She is highballing all right. No stiffs in that blind baggage.

"Well, you know the Teays must of been a big river. Just stand on Company Hill, and look across the bottoms. You'll see."

My skin is heavy with her noise. Her light cuts a wide slice in the fog. No stiff in his right mind could try this one on the fly. She's hell-bent for election.

"Jim said it flowed west by northwest—all the way up to the old Saint Lawrence Drain. Had garfish—ten, maybe twenty foot long. Said they're still in there."

Good old Jim'll probably croak on a lie like that. I watch her beat by. A worn-out tie belches mud with her weight. She's just too fast to jump. Plain and simple.

I get up. I'll spend tonight at home. I've got eyes to shut in Michigan—maybe even Germany or China, I don't know yet. I walk, but I'm not scared. I feel my fear moving away in rings through time for a million years.

HOLLOW

....

HUNCHED ON his knees in the three-foot seam, Buddy was lost in the rhythm of the truck mine's relay; the glitter of coal and sandstone in his cap light, the setting and lifting and pouring. This was nothing like the real mine, no deep tunnels or man-trips, only the setting, lifting, pouring, only the light-flash from caps in the relay. In the pace he daydreamed his father lowering him into the cistern: many summers ago he touched the cool tile walls, felt the moist air from the water below, heard the pulley squeak in the circle of blue above. The bucket tin buckled under his tiny feet, and he began to cry. His father hauled him up. "That's the way we do it," he laughed, carrying Buddy to the house.

But that came before everything: before they moved from the ridge, before the big mine closed, before welfare. Down the relay the men were quiet, and Buddy wondered if they thought of stupid things. From where he squatted he could see the gray grin of light at the mouth, the March wind spraying dust into little clouds. The half-ton cart was full, and the last man in the relay shoved it toward the chute on two-by-four tracks.

"Take a break" came from the opening, and as Buddy set his shovel aside, he saw his cousin Curtis start through the mouth. He was dragging a poplar post behind him as he crawled past the relay toward the face. Buddy watched while Curtis worked the post upright: it was too short, and Curtis hammered wedges in to tighten the fit.

"Got it?" Buddy asked.

"Hell no, but she looks real pretty."

Estep, Buddy's front man, grunted a laugh. "Damn seam's gettin' too deep. Ain't nothin' but coal in this here hole. When we gonna hit gold?"

Buddy felt Estep's cap-light on his face and turned toward it. Estep was grinning, a purple fight cut oozing through the dust and sweat on his cheek.

"Chew?" Estep held out his pouch, and Buddy took three fingers before they leaned against each other, back to back, stretching their legs, working their chews.

"Face is a-gettin' pretty tall," Estep said. Buddy could feel the voice in his back.

"Same thin's happenin' up Storm Creek," he said, pulling the sagging padding up to his knees.

"An' Johnson's scratch done the same."

"Curt," Buddy shouted, "when'd they make a core sample on this ridge?"

"Hell's bells, I don't know," he said, trying to work in another wedge.

"Musta been sixty years ago," Estep said. "Recollect yer grandaddy shootin' at 'em. Thought they's Philadelfy law'ers."

"Yeah," Buddy laughed, remembering the tales.

From near the opening, where the rest of the relay gathered for air, came a high-pitched laugh, and Buddy's muscles went tight.

"One a-these days I'm gonna wring that Fuller's neck," he said, spitting out the sweet tobacco juice.

"What he said still eatin' at ya?"

"He ain't been worth a shit since he got that car."

"It's Sally, ain't it?"

"Naw, let'er go. Worthless . . ."

The group laughed again, and a voice said, "Ask Buddy."

"Ask 'im what?" Buddy shined his light along the row of dirty faces; only Fuller's was wide with a grin.

"Is Sal goin' back to whorin'?" Fuller smiled.

"Goddamn you," Buddy said, but before he could get up, Estep hooked both his elbows in Buddy's, and Fuller laughed at his struggle. Curtis scrambled back, grabbing Buddy's collar.

"I reckon you all rested 'nough," Curtis shouted, and when they heard coal rattling from the bin to the truck, they picked up their shovels, got into line.

Buddy loosened up, giving in to Curtis and Estep. "Tonight at Tiny's," he shouted at Fuller.

Fuller laughed.

"Shut up," Curtis said. "You and Estep work the face."

Estep let go, and they crawled to the coal face and took up their short-handled spades. The face was already four feet high, and both men could stretch out from their knees, knocking sparkling chunks into the pile, pushing it back for the relay.

"Bet this whole damn ridge is a high seam."

"Make it worth more than ten swats a day."

"By God," Buddy said, and as he dug, wondered if the money would make Sally stay. Remembering Fuller, he hit the face harder, spraying coal splinters into the air.

Estep stopped digging and ran a dirty sleeve across one eye. Buddy was coughing a raspy wheeze, flogging coal to his feet. "Stop killin' snakes—throwin' stuff in my eyes."

Buddy stopped digging. Estep's voice washed over his anger, leaving him small and cold in the glint of the coal face, yet bold and better than Estep or Fuller.

"Sorry, it's just I'm mad," he coughed.

"Get yer chance tonight. Cmon, pace off—one, two . . ."

Together they threw the relay back into rhythm, added speed. The chink of spades and scrape of shovels slipped into their muscles until only the rumble of the returning truck could slow them. The seam grew where it should have faulted, and they hunkered to their feet, digging toward the thin gray line of ceiling.

"Get some picks," Buddy grinned.

"Naw, needs shorin' yet."

Curtis slipped through the relay to the face, his light showing through the dust in up-down streams. When he got down to them, they leaned against the sidewalls to give him room, and he stuck a pocket level to the ceiling, watching as the bubble rose toward the face.

"Knock off till Monday," he said. "We ain't got the timbers fer this here."

As the men crawled out toward the bloom pile, a whisper of laughter seeped back through the mine to the face, and Buddy dropped to his belly to slink outside, unhurried. Even a clam crawl had winded him, and he waited by the chute for Estep and Curtis as the cold air dried his sweat, sealing the dirt to his skin. He could hear, beneath the whining low gears of the coal truck, the barking of a dog down in the hollow. He sat down hard and leaned against the chute.

From the entrance to the hilltop was a wold of twenty yards, the dead stalks of broom sedge rippling in the wind. Buddy figured the overburden of dirt could be moved in a month, the coal harvested in less than a year. He knew Sally would not wait, was not sure he wanted her.

He remembered a time when the price of her makeup and fancy habits would have fed his mother and sisters something besides the mauve bags of commodities the state handed out.

Estep came out, and Buddy offered him a smoke as they watched the truck shimmy under the bin, leveling its load.

"Goddamned cherry picker," Estep grunted toward the driver far down the hill.

"Gonna be lots more cherry—all that goddamned coal." Buddy looked to the western ridges where the sun set a cold strip of fire.

Curtis came up behind them, smiling. "I'm goin' home an' get all drunked up."

"Last time I done that," Estep said, "got me a new baby. Gonna watch ol' Mad Man here so's he don't tear up Tiny's."

"That's where I'll be, by God," Buddy said, as if there might still be something to hold to.

"Just leave 'nough of Fuller to crawl in that doghole on Monday," Curtis said, taking off his cap. Buddy stared at the lines of gray in his hair where the coal dust had not settled.

"I ain't makin' no promises," Buddy said as he started down the path toward the road.

"Pick ya up about eight tonight," Estep yelled, watching Buddy wave his lunch bucket from the trail.

Night rose up from the hollow, and as he came to the dusty access road, Buddy could feel the cold air washing up around him, making him cough. Patches of clouds gathered over the hollow, glowing pink. He turned onto the blacktop road, banging his lunch box against his leg as he walked, and remembered hating Fuller as a boy because Fuller had called him a ridge runner. After twenty years of living in the hollow, he knew why Fuller hated him.

He laughed again at the thought of the coal. He would have a car by fall, and a new trailer—maybe even a double-wide. He tried to think of ways to get Curtis to give up dogholing, and for a moment thought of asking Sally to go into Chelyan with him to look at trailers, but remembered all her talk of leaving.

Through the half-light, he could make out the rotting tipple where his father was crushed only ten days before they shut it down, leaving the miners to scab-work and DPA. The tipple crackled in the cold as the sun's heat left it, and on a pole beside it an unused transformer still hummed. No more coal, the engineers had said, but Buddy had always laughed at engineers— even when he was in an engineer company in the Army. At the foot of the smoldering bone pile where the shale waste had been dumped, Estep's little boy stopped, searching.

"What ya doin' there, Andy?"

"Rocks," the boy said. "They's pitchers on 'em." He handed Buddy a piece of shale.

"Fossils. Ol' dead stuff."

"I'm collectin' 'em."

"What ya wanna save ol' dead stuff for?" he said, handing the shale back.

The boy looked down and shrugged.

"You get on home, hear?" Buddy said, watching as Andy disappeared down the secondary, leaving him to the hum of the transformer. He wondered why the boy looked so old.

As he started back up the road, he could hear the dogs packing up, their howls echoing from the slopes, funneling through the empty tipple. The clouds had thickened, and Buddy felt the first fine drops of a misty rain soak through the dirt on his face. When the trees thinned, he saw his trailer, rust from the bolts already streaking the white paint of last summer. The dogs were just up the road, and he wondered if they could smell Lindy, his bluetick bitch, in the trailer. Sally sat by the window, looking, waiting, but he knew it was not for him.

Lindy smiled at Sally, wagged at the sound of Buddy's footsteps from the bedroom and down the hall. Sally walked away from the door window and set the plates by the stove.

"Estep's stoppin' 'round eight," Buddy said, frowning at the turnips and beans beneath the potlids of supper. "No meat?"

Sally said nothing, but took up her plate and dolloped out her food, leaving the side meat for Buddy. She watched him serve himself, and found herself staring at the freckles of black dust embedded in his face. A dog bark broke her stare, and she went to the table. She could hear them sniffing under the floor.

"They bother hell outa me," she said when Buddy sat.

"Well, she stays in. I don't need no litter of mutts." Buddy mashed fat between his fork prongs, fishing the lean from the mess, and watched Sally eat. "They's gonna be money, Sal."

"Don't start up. They's al's *gonna*, but they ain't never any."

"This time's for sure. Estep an' me, we worked that stuff today. A D-nine dozer an' steam-shovel'd a-fixed us real quick. Curt's got the deed an' all."

"Thought yer folks settled these here ridges."

He remembered standing in the sun at a funeral—he could not say whose, but the scent of Vitalis from his father's hands had turned his stomach, and his new shoes pinched his feet.

"Never had a pot to piss in, neither. Stick 'round, Sal."

With her fork, Sally drew lazy curves in her beansoup, and shook her head. "Naw, I'm tired of livin' on talk."

"This ain't talk. What made ya stay with me this long?"

"Talk."

"Love? Love ain't talk."

"Whore's talk."

His hand flashed across the table, knocking her head askance, and she flushed. She got up slowly, put her plate in the sink, and walked down the hall to the bedroom. Buddy heard her turn on the TV, but the sound died down, leaving only the whimper of the dogs. He watched his plate turn cold, grease crusting the edges.

Getting bourbon for his coffee, he sat his plate on the floor for the bitch, and went to the window. With lamplight shining green in their eyes, the pack circled the trailer, talking, waiting. He turned off the lamp and looked for the thing Sally stared after, but only the light gray sky and near-black ghost of the road touched the hollow.

In the darkness he found his .30-.30 rifle and flashlight, opened the slatted window, and poked them through. Passing over two strong-boned hounds, his beam landed on a ragged spitz, and he fired into the marble-lights, the shot singing through the washes and gullies.

The dogs scattered into the brush beyond the road, leaving the thrashing spitz to die in the yard. Lindy paced the trailer's length to the sound of the whines, but when they stopped, she settled on the couch, her tail flapping each time Buddy moved.

The shot jerked Sally from her half-sleep, but she settled back again, watching the blue TV light play against the rusty flowers of ceiling leaks as the last grains of cocaine soaked into her head. She stretched, felt afloat in an ocean of blue light rippling around her body, and relaxed. She knew she was prettier than the girls in the Thunderball Club, or the girl on the TV, and lots more fun.

"Lotsss," she whispered, over and over.

Buddy's silhouette stood in the doorway. "They won't be back," he said.

"Who?" Sally sat up, letting the sheets slide away from her breasts.

"The dogs."

"Oh, yeah."

"Ya can't make any money at it, Sal. Too much free stuff floatin' 'round."

"Yeah? An' all this money yer makin's gonna keep me here?"

He turned back down the hall.

"Buddy," she said, and heard him stop. "C'mon."

As he shed his shoes, she noticed the slope in his back more than usual, but in turning to her, his chest swelled when he unbuttoned his shirt. From where he stood, the hall light mixed with the TV, flashing her eyes white and pink as she moved in the blanket-wave to make room for him.

He climbed in, his cold hands stroking her waist, and she felt the little tremors in his muscles. She dragged a single finger down his spine to make him shiver.

"When ya leavin'?"

"Pretty soon," she said, pulling him closer.

Estep honked his horn again, and Lindy danced by the door, howling.

"I'm comin', dammit," Buddy muttered, buttoning his shirt. The clock on the nightstand glowed ten after eight.

Sally propped her pillow against the headboard and lit another cigarette. As she watched Buddy dress, her jaw tightened, and she rolled ashes from the tip of her cigarette until the fire came to a point. "See ya," she said as he started down the hall.

"Yeah. See ya," he answered, keeping the dog inside as he closed the door.

Outside, the mist mingled with snow, and the spitz lay cold as the water beaded on its fur. Buddy left it to warn the pack, and walked toward the clicking of Estep's engine and the soft clupping of wipers. Before he could open the door, a pain jabbed his lungs, but he held his breath against it, then tried to forget it in the blare of the car's radio.

"Whadya know, Mad Man?" Estep said as Buddy climbed in, coughing.

"Answer me this—Why'd ya reckon Curt wants props for?"

"To shore the damn face, dumbshit."

"An' doghole that goddamn seam, too. He's a ol'-time miner. He loves doin' all that ol'-time shit."

"Whadya drivin' at?"

"How many ya reckon'd walk out if I's to dump the water Monday?"

"Buddy, don't go callin' strike. I got family."

"C'mon—how many ya reckon?"

"Most," Estep said. "Maybe not Fuller."

Buddy nodded. "I'd say so, too."

"Yer talkin' weird. Curt's kin—ya can't go callin' strike on yer kin."

"I like Curt fine," Buddy coughed. "But I'm tellin' ya they's a easy way to run that coal."

"Won't work, Buddy. Operation like that'd put ever'body outa work. 'Sides, land ain't good fer nothin' after ya strip."

"That land," he gagged, "that land ain't no good noway, and we could so use work. We'd use ever'body in our hole. An' Storm Creek. An' that piddlin' of Johnson's. Fair an' equal. Know how much that'd be?"

"Can't be much with all the fellars in the line."

"Try on fifty thou. Does it fit?" He slapped Estep's arm. "Well, does it?"

"Where'd we get the machines?"

"Borrow on the coal. Curt's got the deed—just needs some new thinkin' put in his head's all. You with me?"

"I reckon."

They rode, watching the snow curve in toward the lights, melting on the windshield before the wiper struck it. Through the trees, Buddy could see the string of yellow light bulbs above the door and windows of Tiny's.

"Johnson found out who's stealin' his coal," Estep said, letting the car slow up. "Old Man Cox."

"How's he know fer sure?"

"Drikked a chunk an' put in a four-ten shell. Sealed 'er over with dust an' glue."

"Jesus H. Christ."

"Aw, didn't hurt 'im none. Just scared 'im," Estep said, guiding the car between chugholes in the parking lot.

Buddy opened his door. "Man alive, that's bad," he mumbled.

Inside Tiny's, Buddy nodded and waved to friends through the smoke and laughter, but he did not see Fuller. He asked Tiny, but the one-eared man only shrugged, setting up two beers as Buddy paid. He walked to the pool table, placed his quarter beside four others, and returned to lean against the bar with Estep.

"Slop," Buddy yelled to one of Johnson's shots.

"Slop you too," Johnson smiled. "Them quarters go fast."

Fuller came in, walked to the bar, and shook his head when Tiny came up.

"'Bout time ya got here," Buddy said.

"Sal's out yonder. Wants to talk to ya."

"Whadya got? Carload of goons?"

"See fer yerself." Fuller waved toward the window. Sally sat with Lindy in the front seat of Fuller's car. Buddy followed Fuller outside motioning for Sally to roll down the window, but she opened the door, letting Lindy out.

"You baby-set for a while," she said.

Fuller laughed as he started the car.

Buddy bent to collar Lindy, but she stayed by him. Straightening himself, Buddy looked after the car and saw his TV bobbing in the back seat.

"C'mon," Estep said from behind him. "Let's get drunked up an' shoot pool."

"Yer on," Buddy said, leading the dog into the bar.

Buddy lay on the trailer's carpet, a little ball of rayon batting against his nostril as he breathed, and tried to remember how he got there, but Sally's smile in his mind jumbled him. He remembered being driven back by Estep, falling down in the parking lot, and hitting Fred Johnson, but he did not know why.

He stood up, shook himself, and leaned down the hall to the bathroom. The blood flow from his head and the shock of the light turned the room purple for a moment, and he ran water from the shower on his head to clear the veil. Looking into the mirror, he saw the imprints of the carpet pattern on his cheek, the poison hanging beneath his eyes. He wanted to throw up but could not.

"Ol' dead stuff," he muttered, and heaved dryly.

Atop the commode sat a half-finished bourbon Coke, and he tossed it down, waiting for it to settle or come up again. Leaning against the wall, he remembered the dog, called to her, but she did not come. He looked at his watch: it was five-thirty.

He went into the living room and opened the door—the wet snow was collecting in patches. He called Lindy, and she came to him from behind the trailer, a hound close behind her. He shut the door between the dogs and sat on the couch. Lindy hopped up beside him. "Poor old girl," he said, patting her wet side. "Yer in fer the works now." His knuckles were split, and blood flaked from his fingers, but he could not feel any burning.

"Sal's gone, yes, she is. Yes, she is. Couple of months, an' we'll show her, yes we will." He saw himself in Charleston, in the Club, then taking Sally home in his new car . . .

"Hungry, ol' girl? C'mon, I'll fix ya up."

In the kitchen, he looked for fresh meat to treat her, and finding none, opened a can of sardines. Watching her lap them up, he poured himself a bourbon, and feeling better, leaned against the counter. Sally's plate lay skinned with beansoup in the sink, and for a moment he missed her. He laughed to himself: he would show her.

Lindy walked under the table and coughed up her sardines.

"Don't blame ya a damn bit," he said, but in the roil of sardines and saliva, he saw himself cleaning it up, knew the smell would always be there. There was no reason he should have to clean up, no reason he could not have meat, or anything he wanted. He took up his rifle, leaning where he had left it, and Lindy barked around his heels. "No," he shouted, hanging her by the collar from his forefinger until he could shut the door.

Outside the snow fell harder and in thick, wet lumps, making patterns in the darkness. The climb up the hill to the ridge behind the trailer stirred his lungs to bleeding, and he stopped to spit and breathe. Rested, he walked again in a quiet rhythm with the rustle of snow on the dead leaves.

In the brush by the trail, a bobcat crouched, waiting for the man to clump by, its muscles tight in the snow and mist. Claws unsheathed, it moved only slightly with the sounds of his steps until he was far up the trail, out of sight and hearing. The cat moved down the trail, stopping only to sniff the blood-spit the man had left behind.

By the time Buddy crested the ridge, he could feel the pain of trailer heat leave his head, and he stopped short of the salt blocks he had laid out last fall. He held in a breath to slow the wheezing, and when it stopped, sat on his old stump, watching the first mild light of the sky glow brown. He loaded his gun and watched a low trail in the brush, a trail he saw through outlines of snow in the ghost light. From the hollow, dog yelps carried to the ridge. The trail was empty.

Behind him, something rattled in the leaves, and he turned his head slowly, hearing the bones in his neck click. In the brown light he made out the rotted ribs of an old log barn he had played in before they sold the land, moved to the hollow. Something scurried past it, ran away from him, and up the ridge. From the baying of the dogs below, he was sure it was a fox.

Between the clouds and the hills hung the sun, moving fast enough to track, making the snow glisten on the branches. When he looked away from the sun, his eyes were drawn to the cool shadow of a deer standing against the yellow ribbon of sunlight.

He moved slowly, lifting the gun to his face, aiming into the shadow, and before the noise splintered into the hollow, he saw a flash of movement. He ran to the place where the deer had stood, but there was no blood. He tracked the animal only ten yards to where it had fallen. It was a doe with a pink lip of wound near her shoulder, but no blood.

Working quickly, he split her hind tendons, threaded them with a stringer, and hoisted her from a low limb. He cut across the throat, and blood dripped into the snow, but as he ran the knife up the belly, something inside the carcass jolted, moved against the knife point. He kept cutting, and when the guts sagged out, a squirming lump fell at his feet.

He kicked the unborn fawn aside, disconnected the doe's guts, sliced off the hindquarters, and let the rest of the carcass fall for the scavengers to find. He laid three small slices of liver aside in the snow to cool.

Warm doe blood burned his split knuckles, and he washed

them with snow, remembering why he had hit Fred Johnson—for spiking Old Man Cox's coal. He began to laugh. He could see Old Man Cox screaming his head off. "Shit," he laughed, shaking his head.

He bit off a piece of the cool raw liver, and as it juiced between his teeth, watched the final throes of the fawn in the steamy snow. He could not wait to dump the water at the mine tomorrow, and laughed as he imagined the look on Curtis's face. "Strike," he muttered over and over.

On a knoll in the ridge, run there by the dogs, the bobcat watched, waiting for the man to leave.

A ROOM FOREVER

•••••••••••••••••••

BECAUSE of New Year's I get the big room, eight-dollar room. But it seems smaller than before; and sitting by the window, looking out on the rain and town, I know the waiting eats at me again. I should never show up in these little river towns until my tug puts in—but I always come early, wait, watch people on the street. Out there vapor lamps flicker violet, bounce their light up from the pavement, twist everything's color. A few people walk along in the drizzle, but they don't stop to look into cheap-shop windows.

Aways past the streets I see the river in patches between buildings, and the black joints of river are frosted by this foggy rain. But on the river it's always the same. Tomorrow starts another month on the river, then a month on land—only the tales we tell will change, wrap around other times and other names. But there will be the same crew on the *Delmar*, the same duty for eighteen hours a day, and pretty soon there won't be tales. For now, I wait, watch the wind whip rain onto the panes and blur the glass.

I plug in the hot plate for coffee, look through the paper for something to do, but there is no wrestling or boxing for tonight, and even the bowling alley is closed for New Year's. I could maybe go down to a bar on First Avenue, sort of tie one on, but not if I have to watch barge rats and walk the wet steel edges tomorrow. Better to buy a pint and whiskey myself into an early sack, better not to think about going out.

I down my coffee too soon, burn my mouth. Nothing ever goes just the way it should. I figure that is my bitch with New Year's—it's a start all right—only I think back on parties we had in the Navy, and how we pulled out the stops the year we got to be short-timers, and it leaves me feeling lousy to sit here thinking about parties and work and the baby year and the old worn-out year. I want to haul my ass out of here—I have been inside too long.

I get my jacket and watch cap, then stand outside my door and light a cigarette. The hall and stairwell are all lit up to keep away the whores and stumblebums. The door across the hall opens and the drag queen peeks out, winks at me: "Happy New Year." He closes his door quietly, and I cut loose, kick the door, smudge the paint with my gum soles. I hear him in there laughing at me, laughing because I am alone. All the way down the stairs I can hear his laugh. He is right: I need a woman—not just a lousy chip—I need the laying quiet after that a chip never heard of. When I come to the lobby full of fat women and old men, I think how this is all the home I have. Maybe I have bought this room forever—I just might not need another flop after tonight.

I stand under the marquee, smoke, look back into the lobby at the old cruds. I think how all my fosters were old and most of them dead by now. Maybe it's better they are dead or I might go back and visit them and cramp their style. There wouldn't be any welfare check tied to me now, and I am too big to be whipped.

I toss my cigarette, watch it bob down the gutter-wash and through the grate. It will probably be in the Mississippi before the *Delmar*. Moping around these towns for nine months has made me screwy; walking barges and securing catheads in high water has finally got me down here with the rest of the cruds. Now my mouth hurts from the coffee burn, and I don't even feel like getting soused. I walk down the street, watch people as they pass, and think how even the chippies in their long vinyl coats walk like they have someplace to be. I think I am getting pretty low if these old sows are starting to look good.

I walk until I see a stumblebum cut into a passage between two buildings. He has got his heat in him and he is squared away. I stop to watch this jake-legger try to spread out his papers for a bed, but the breeze through the passage keeps stirring his papers around. It's funny to watch this scum chase papers, his old pins about ready to fold under him. The missions won't let him in because he is full of heat, so this jake-legger has to chase his papers tonight. Pretty soon all that exercise will make him puke up his heat, and I stand and grin and wait for this to happen, but my grin slips when I see her standing in that doorway.

She is just a girl—fourteen, fifteen—but she stares at me like she knows what I'm thinking, what I'm waiting to see with this old bum, and she keeps looking at me like she is the Wrath of God or something. My eyes hurt to watch her from the side while I keep my face on the stumblebum, but I watch just the same. I can tell right off she is not a chippy. Her front is more like a kid who had a home once—jeans, a real raincoat, a plastic scarf on her head. And she is way too young for this town—the law won't put up with fresh chicken in this place. I think she has probably run off, and that type is hard to figure out. I walk past her, pay no attention, then duck into a doughnut shop.

Prince Albert sits at the counter talking to himself, running rusty fingers through his hair and beard. His skin is yellowish because he cauterized his brain with a forty-volt system aboard the *Cramer*. I hear he was a good wireman, but now he is just a gov't suck, and he is dirty and smells like any wino on the street.

I eat my sinker, sip coffee and look out the window. Traffic thickens, the parties are building up. That girl walks by, looks in the storefront at me like she knows exactly when I'm going to fall between two barges in a lurch. It gives me the creeps and I leave my coffee, go for some whiskey and a nap, but when I get outside, she is far down the street, going toward the shanty bars on First Avenue. The rain blows up a howl, whipping sheets of water along the sidewalks. I follow her until she gets into another doorway. My watch cap is soaked, and water starts running down my face and neck, but I go to her doorway, stand in the rain looking at her.

She says, "You want to buy me?"

I stand there for a long time trying to figure if it's a coneroo. "You got a room?" I say.

She shakes her head, looks across the street, then up and down it.

"We'll use mine, but I want some booze."

"All right, I know a place that sells it," she says.

"I know a better place." I am wise to that trick. I am not about to let her pimp roll me. But it bugs me—I can't figure what kind of pimp wouldn't keep a room. If she is working alone she won't last two days between the cops and the pimps.

We go on down the street to a state store. It is good to have somebody to go along with, but she looks too serious, like all she thinks about is the business end of this. I buy a pint of Jack Daniel's, try to joke. "Jack and me go way back," I say, but she acts like she can't hear me.

When we walk into the lobby of the hotel, two old men stop talking to look at us. I think how they must have the hots for her, envy me, and I am glad these cruds are paying attention. At my door, I take my time unlocking, and hope the queen peeks out, but he is off getting buggered. We go in, and I get us a towel to dry off, make coffee for the whiskey.

"It's nice here," she says.

"Yeah. They spray regular."

For the first time she smiles, and I think how she ought to be off playing jacks or something.

"I'm not much good at this," she says. "The first guys hurt me pretty bad, so I'm always sort of scared."

"That's because you ain't cut out for it."

"No, it's just I need a place. I got to stop moving around, you know?"

"Yeah." In the window I see our ghosts against the black gloss of glass. She puts her arm around me, and I think how we maybe never left the business end.

"Why'd you come to me?" she says.

"You looked at me funny—like you seen something awful was going to happen to me."

She laughs. "Well, I didn't. I was sizing you."

"Yeah. I'm just jittery tonight. I'm second mate on a tug. It's kind of dangerous."

"What's a second mate do?"

"Everything the captain or first mate won't do. It ain't much of a life."

"Then why don't you just quit?"

"Some things are worse. Quits ain't the answer."

"Maybe not."

Her hand on my neck teases me into smiling about her, liking her. "Why don't you quit trying to be a chippy? You ain't got the stuff. You're better than that."

"It's nice you think so," she says.

I look at her, think what she could be if she had a break or two. But she won't get them here. Nobody here gets a break. I could tell her about my fosters or the ladies in the welfare offices, and the way they looked at me when they put me on a bus for another town, but it wouldn't make any sense to her. I turn off the light and we undress, get into bed.

The darkness is the best thing. There is no face, no talk, just warm skin, something close and kind, something to be lost in. But when I take her, I know what I've got—a little girl's body that won't move from wear or pleasure, a kid playing whore, and I feel ugly with her, because of her. I force myself on her like the rest. I know I am hurting her, but she will never get any breaks. She whimpers and my body arches in spasms, then after, she curls in a ball away from me, and I touch her. She is numb.

I say, "You could stay here this month. I mean if you wanted to, I could pay up the rent and you could get a real job and pay me back."

She just lays there.

"Maybe you could get work uptown at Sears or Penney's."

"Why don't you just shut-the-fuck-up." She climbs out of bed. "Just pay me off, okay?"

I get up, find my pants, peel off twenty and give it to her. She doesn't look at the bill, but grabs her coat, runs out the door.

I sit on the bed, light a cigarette, and my skin crawls to think what could happen to that girl; then I tell myself it was just a waste of time and money. I think back to high school when I was courting Jane. Her parents left us alone in the living room, but her poodle kept screwing at my leg. There we were trying to talk and her dog just kept humping my leg. I think I'd like to get a car and go back looking for that dog, but it is always like that—a waste of time and money.

I snipe my cigarette, lay back on the bed with the light on, and think about Prince Albert with sinker crumbs in his beard, coffee stains on his shirt. I think how there must be ten of his kind in every town down to the delta, and how the odds on ending up that way must be pretty low. Something goes screwy and they grab the wrong wire, make a stupid move on the locks. But if nothing goes wrong, then they are on for a month, off for a month, and if they are lucky they can live that way the rest of their days.

I dress and go out again. It is still raining and the cold pavement shines with new ice. Between the buildings the bums are sleeping in the trash they have piled up, and I think about some nut in California who cut winos' throats, but I can't see the percentage. The stumblebums are like Prince Albert, they ran out of luck, hit the skids.

I turn onto First Avenue, walk slowly by the row of crowded taverns, look in the windows at all the lucky people getting partied up for New Year's. Then I see her sitting at a table near the back door. I go in, take a stool at the bar, order a whiskey, neat. The smoke cloud is heavy, but I see her reflection in the mirror behind the bar. From the way her mouth is hanging limp I see she is pretty drunk. I don't guess she knows she can't drink her way out of this.

I look around. All these people have come down from their flops because there are no parties for them to go to. They are strangers who play a little pool or pinball, drink a little booze. All year they grit their teeth—they pump gas and wait tables and screw chippies and bait queers, and they don't like any of it, but they know they are lucky to get it.

I look for her in the mirror but she is gone. I would have seen her going out the front, so I head for the back door to look for her. She is sitting against a building in the rain, passed out cold. When I shake her, I see that she has cut both wrists down to the leaders, but the cold rain has clotted the blood so that only a little oozes out when I move her. I go back inside.

"There's some girl out back tried to kill herself."

Four guys at the bar run out to her, carry her inside. The bartender grabs the phone. He says to me, "Do you know her?"

I say, "No. I just went for some air." I go on out the door.

The bartender yells, "Hey, buddy, the cops'll want to see you; hey, buddy..."

I walk along the avenue thinking how shit always sinks, and how all these towns dump their shit for the river to push it down to the delta. Then I think about that girl sitting in the alley, sitting in her own slough, and I shake my head. I have not gotten that low.

I stop in front of the bus station, look in on the waiting people, and think about all the places they are going. But I know they can't run away from it or drink their way out of it or die to get rid of it. It's always there, you just look at somebody and they give you a look like the Wrath of God. I turn toward the docks, walk down to see if the *Delmar* maybe put in early.

FOX HUNTERS

••••••••••••••••••••

THE PASSING of an autumn night left no mark on the patchwork blacktop of the secondary road that led to Parkins. A gray ooze of light began to crest the eastern hills above the hollow and sift a blue haze through the black bowels of linking oak branches. A small wind shivered, and sycamore leaves chattered across the pavement but were stopped by the fighting-green orchard grass on the berm.

The opossum lay quietly by the roadside. She had found no dead farm animals in which to build her winter den; not even a fine empty hole. She packed her young across the road and into the leaves where the leathery carcass of another opossum lay. She did not pause for sniffing or sentiment.

Metalclick. She stopped. Fire. She hunkered in tight fear against the ground, her young clutching closer to her fur. Soft, rhythmless clumpings excited her blood, and she sank lower. With day and danger advancing, fear was blushing in her as she backed cautiously into higher brush. From her hiding, she watched a giant enemy scuffling on the blacktop, and a red glow bouncing brightly in the remnant of her night.

Bo felt this to be the royal time of his day—these sparse, solitary moments when the rest of the world was either going to bed or not up yet. He was alone, knew the power in singularity, yet was afraid of it. Insecurity crawfished through his blood, leaving him powerless again. Soon he began a conversation to make the light seem closer to the road.

"Coffee, Bo," he said to himself.

"Yeah, and Lucy, toosie," he answered.

"And putin*tane.*"

"Yeah," and he quickened his pace, imitating a train.

"*Put*intane, *putin*tane, put*n*tane, p'*tane*, woooo."

The opossum crouched lower. Her unready, yet born, offspring clung to her belly, nudging to nurse.

His pace lagged back. Maybe Lucy was a whore, but how in the hell would he know? He liked the way she leaned over the grill, showing slip and garters, and knowing it, still, acting vaguely embarrassed. He liked the way she would cock her head to the right, nod solemnly, brows pursed in wrinkled thought, while he talked about cities he had seen on TV. Or about his dad, who sucked so much mine gas, they had to bury him closed-coffin because he was blue as jeans. Bo would live out a reckless verbal future with Lucy. She listened. Occasionally she advised. Once he was going to run off to New York and get educated. Just chuck it all, leave his mother, and get educated in New York. He had felt silly and ashamed when Lucy said to finish high school first. Times like that, he left the dinette convinced Lucy was a whore.

From up the road, he could hear the rumble of Enoch's truck. Instinctively, he jumped over the embankment, slipped into the brush, and squatted. A hiss came from within the brush. Bo turned to see a gray-white form in the fog beside him. It looked like a giant rat with eyebrows. They stared, neither wanting any part of the other—the opossum frozen between acting dead or running, Bo crouching lower as the headlights neared. It was only two more miles to Parkins, but if Enoch saw him he would stop; then Bo would be "crazy boy" at the garage for another week because he would rather walk than ride with his boss.

The truck clattered by, its pink wrecker rig swinging, erratic pendulum of pulley, hook, and cable.

Bo unzipped his pants and pissed with frozen opossum eyes looking on. Steam rose from the puddle, and he shuddered as it drifted to intermingle with the blue mist. He began wading leaves up the embankment.

As he trampled the orchard grass at the berm, another truck could be heard up the road, and he fought the urge to slide back down the slope. He could not explain why he wanted to walk, nor was he certain he wanted to walk anymore. He stepped onto the pavement feeling tired and moved a few paces until headlights flooded his path, showing up the highway steam and making the road give birth to little ghosts beneath his feet.

The truck thundered up behind, then let three high-pitched whines pierce the road spirits of the morning. Bo waited for the truck to stop. When it did, a voice called: "Git in er git ober."

Bo whirled to look at the driver but found his eyes drawn to the white oblivion of the headlights. "Bill?" was all he was able to say as his eyes made red and purple dots appear in the lights.

"Hell yes. You blind?"

Bo looked to the gray hills to drag his attention from the lights, and slowly remembered every detail of Lucy's body as it disintegrated into his brain. Breast hair. Jesus Christ, how long had he stood in that light like a fool? Bill would tell everybody that Bo Holly was out of his goddamned mind. He groped to the truck, rubbing the red dots into his eyes with his hands.

"Git in," said Bill, while his eyes explored Bo with the same scrutiny he had once used to search a two-headed calf for stitches around either head. Bo gave a little sigh as he climbed into the truck's cab, and Bill pounced with the question: "You sick?"

"Just not awake yet," Bo lied. He felt professional about lying, and once started, would not stop. "Momma overslept. Got me up and out without coffee and half dressed. Said I was late to work. What time is it, Bill?" Questions and complex sentences, Bo had learned, were the great shield of liars. Bill studied his wrist-watch, then sneered at the sky as if *The Black Draught Almanac* had been two days off on its sunrise schedule.

"Ten abter seben," he growled, pounding his hand against the wheel.

"Shit," Bo yelled, watching Bill jump a little. "But Enoch probably ain't there yet. He's always late. Didn't come in last Saturday till eleven."

"Ain't none of *my* biz-whacks," Bill snapped. "By god, I mind my own biz-whacks." But Bo knew Bill would remember this as a gossip gift to a bored wife.

"I's talkin' to Larry up to the Union Hall," said Bill, experimenting shamefully, "an' he says yer faberite song's that damn 'Rockin' Riber.'"

"'Rollin' on the River'?" Questions don't give offense, he thought, besides, the song's "Proud Mary."

"Stupid song, Bo. You oughta know better."

Bo said nothing.

"Son' like that's ber a riber town. We ain't got no riber in Parkins."

"Got the Elk in Upshur. Watch this pothole." The truck jolted twice. "Guess it's eat up the whole road." Bill had to think to remember where he had left off. Elk?

"The Elk ain't nothin' to sing about," he cackled. "Now, Merle Haggard, he can tell ya . . ."

"S'matter, Bill, ain't you proud to be a West Virginian?"

"Sure, goddammit, but a song like that's ber eberbody eberwhere. You just don't listen to no good stuff, do ya?"

Bo settled back in his seat, stuck his feet under the heater, and once they were warm enough to feel cold, decided why he liked Lucy: she was a genuine person.

In the silence, the opossum thawed, and was carefully slipping up the bank, sniffing after the danger once so close. It paused in the sycamore leaves and wet orchard grass, then scuttered across the blacktop and back into the woods the way it had come. It was almost morning.

When Bill's truck topped the final grade into Parkins, the sun had already begun to ricochet from the western slopes, and the eastern hills cast a gray shadow over the town. From that grade, Bo could see who was up and who wasn't by the positions of yellow squares of light on the houses. Lucy was in the kitchen of her boardinghouse, her tenants in the bathrooms. The two Duncan sisters, who did nothing, rose early to get on with it. They gossiped about their neighbors, mostly about Lucy. She ignored them. Bo thought she liked to be talked about.

Brownie Ross was opening his general store near the railroad; turning on lights, raising blinds, shoveling coal into the stove. Bo wondered why Brownie opened so early—Enoch, too. Brownie never sold anything bigger than a quarter-sack of nails before noon, and if your car broke down, you'd have to walk to Parkins for a phone.

Bill worked for the railroad—station manager—and Lucy boarded the few men the reopened mine demanded, so both had to be up and going by six. Enoch opened early because Brownie did, and Brownie was just old. Mornings changed very little in Parkins.

"Just let me off at the boardin'house, Bill. I want a cuppa coffee."

"Ain't none of *my* biz-whacks," Bill snapped as the truck stopped beside the laughing yellow bear Brakes-and-Alignment sign. Out of the truck, Bo turned to thank the driver, but "Ain't none of *yours*, neither" was fired back at him. The truck jumped forward, and Bo let the lurch shut the door. He walked to the garage-door window and peeked in: the yellow night-light was still burning, the workshop bench still scattered with tools and parts from the night before. The green Dodge was gone.

Musta done somethin' right, he thought, they drove her away.

Neither Enoch nor wrecker were in sight. The portent of Bill's attack hit home: Enoch was up to tricks again, but only the men were supposed to know. "Not even the angels in heaven shall know the hour of his coming." Bo laughed as he entered the oppressive smell of red clay, grease, and gasoline. He straightened the tool bench, washed, locked up, and headed for Lucy's.

The boardinghouse was ugly. It loomed three stories straight up from the flat hollow-basin, as plain and ponderous as the great boulders Bo had seen on TV westerns. Noise echoed through its walls; sounds of plumbing malfunctions and boarder disagreements. On the back, a lean-to had been converted into a dinette.

Inside, Bo rediscovered the aromas of breakfast. Ten miners were eating; Lucy was packing their lunches in arch-topped tin boxes. Bo swaggered to the jukebox, punched F-6 in defiant remembrance of Bill, and sauntered to the counter. But nobody had watched as he thought they would have. Ike Turner's bass voice chanted the rhythm; Tina whispered in.

Lucy coldly asked if he wanted coffee. He did not answer, but got his coffee anyway. The miners left and the straw bosses came down. Unlike their men, who whispered labor and safety secrets, the straw bosses ate alone and silently.

Bo, withdrawn, watched them. He wondered why he could not claim kin to men by tolerating their music, their cards, their fox hunting, but he knew a scab of indifference to keep away sociability.

When the foremen left, Lucy refilled Bo's cup. Too many color treatments had left her hair the same red as a rusty Brillo pad. She wore only a hint of green eye-makeup, and her skin was the texture and color of toadstools. On each hand she wore a diamond engagement ring. Bet ya can still throw 'em, Bo thought.

"How's goin', Bo?" She meant it, and that was appealing.

"Ain't too clear on it, Lucy. Bored, I guess."

"Try a different song tomorrow."

"Tomorrow's Sunday. 'Sides, I ain't bored with my song."

"How old are you again?"

"Sixteen, last count."

"Took sixteen years to bore ya?"

"Took that long to take effect."

Lucy laughed. Bo watched her face contort, wondered if she was laughing with him or at him, decided that was why the other men called her a whore, and smiled.

"You look hell-bottom low. Somethin' eatin' at ya? Yer momma sick er somethin'?"

"Nobody wants to talk to me, Lucy."

"Quit cryin' in yer coffee. You ain't old enough to be a blub-berin' drunk."

"Well, it's the truth."

"Got a girl?"

"Had one this summer. Her daddy moved off to Logan. We wrote, only I don't hear much since school started up again."

Lucy remembered growing up. "Yer okay. Just growin' pains."

"I guess it's just I don't say nothin' worth listenin' to."

"Bo, listenin's worth more to the listener."

He would remember to look for meaning later; he sought another avenue of talk, but Lucy was too quick.

"Case of the lonesomes, huh?"

"Yeah."

"Must be pretty bad if your best talker's a whore."

Bo hung his head and waited for the roof to fall. When it didn't, he slowly added support.

"You ain't that," he said, looking as serious as he could without looking stupid.

Lucy searched for hand business, and found ten seconds in turning off the grill and wiping up a drop of coffee. "I like it . . . you sayin' that. Yer the only one to believe it. Could be right good for ya. Could be dangerous. Don't go talkin' it around, hear?"

Bo shrugged. "Sure, Lucy," he said, withdrawing to his scab and his coffee. He watched her clear the straw-bosses' tables, showing bits of garter each time she bent. He rubbed his finger around the rim of the empty cup.

"How about another, Lucy?" he asked, as she bent long over a table to get at the corner. She smiled in a vague, sleepy way as she tugged her skirt down from her hips.

"Sure, Bo," she said, moving behind the counter for the pot, and added, "Past time for work," as she poured. "When the cat's away . . ."

"Cat's been doin' some playin' on his own."

"Huh?"

Bo gave Lucy the dime, then placed a quarter under the saucer. Nobody tipped Lucy, which compelled Bo to do it. The tip was a game between them, a secret. All the coffee Bo could drink for thirty-five cents.

As he slid from the stool, Lucy asked, "What's the rush? Tired of talkin'?"

"Need to look through the junk pile. Parts for my car. Gonna break out like gangbusters."

"Take me with ya."

"Sure," he said for the sake of play, and stepped out into the creeping shade of morning. Somehow he thought of how fine he felt in a new way, a knowing way.

It was nearly nine when Enoch came in. Bo lay on a crawler under Beck Fuller's Pontiac, draining excretions from the crankcase and twisting a filthy rag around the grease tits to remove warts of clay.

"Be a damn sight easier on the lift," Enoch grumbled. Bo avoided the hole. He was forbidden to use the lift.

He scooted the crawler into the light, shoved his welder's beanie back, and studied Enoch. Everything in the man's posture had slipped to the lowest support. His jaws drooped, dragging the scalp tight on his close-cropped head. His belly pulled the same way against whatever power was left in his shoulders. All of this converged on his khaki pants, making the cuffs gather in little bundles at his feet.

"Don't mind the work. Only thing doin' all mornin'. Where ya been at?"

Enoch lit a cigarette. "Checkin' out a wreck. Dawn Reed and Anne Davis went off the road up by French Creek Church. Car rolled int' the creek. Found 'em dead 'smornin'." He smiled at Bo, but Bo did not smile back. "Wasn't they 'bout your age?" he sputtered.

Bo stood up and brushed his jeans. "Jesus, yes. I go to school with 'em. Drunk?"

"Don't know yet. They was full of water. All scrunged up like raisins.

"Hey, her car was an Impala. I dropped it up to my house till the state cops are done with it. I'll sell ya parts real cheap. It ain't the same year as yours, but you could—"

"No thanks." Bo's stomach contracted, his nose, ears, and hands felt cold. Enoch cocked his head in wonder, took another draw from his cigarette, and turned away.

"Yer crazy," he said, turning back. "Just nuts. *They—are—dead*. Got that? Don't need no car no more." He turned again to ward off fury. Bo traced a stick figure in the Pontiac's dust with his finger, then wiped it out again. Another preachin', he thought.

"I come in here 'smornin' to get that miner's Dodge out," Enoch said. "Them tools was ever'where. You wasn't nowhere. Sleepin'? Sleep more'n ya work. Snuck in t' put 'em away while I's down to the station. Figger Bill wouldn't tell me you's at that whore's house?"

"She ain't that," Bo whispered, looking for something to throw at Enoch.

"She ain't, huh? Well, how do you think she got that boardin'house? Bartram didn't give it to her—she blackmailed 'im for it the way she done them other guys in Charleston. You stay clear of her, Bo, she'll ruin ya."

"Don't tell me what to do," Bo shouted.

"I gotta watch out for my interests. You work for me, you stay outa that house."

"I quit!" he shouted so loudly his throat hurt. He threw his rag in the barrel for effect, adding, "I got enough on you to earn my keep without workin'." Half out the door the lie frightened him; he wanted to turn back, blame Lucy, and keep his chance to leave forever. You blew it, something whispered, but pride pointed his way outside.

Inside, Enoch worried. Bo was probably lying. But what if he knew about him and the boys and Dawn? He looked up the road, but Bo was walking too fast to catch on foot. Enoch ground the wrecker to a start and whirled off up the road.

As the wrecker pulled up beside him, Bo set his jaw in silence. He looked at Enoch, and the flabby jaws said, "Git in, Bo, we gotta talk." Once he had Bo inside, Enoch let the subject of blackmail sleep, and went on with his sermon:

"I know'd your daddy. That's why I give ya this job. You're a good mechanic, but you proved you ain't no man by walkin' out on me.

"I tried to be good to ya. Let you use my tools on yer car, even teached you how to be a mechanic . . . but I can't teach ya how to be a man."

"Try treatin' me like one," Bo hissed.

"All right. You want to work? Your daddy wouldn't want me to let ya after the way you acted. I'm sorry to his memory, but I'll let you come back."

Bo looked out on the broom-sedge slopes. He could swear his daddy's ghost answered, "Yech."

"All right," said Enoch. "Tonight we're goin' fox huntin'. I figger yer daddy woulda took ya by now."

Bo hated fox hunting, but nodded and smiled. He wanted his job; he'd need a stake.

When he had finished servicing Beck's car, Bo washed his hands, lit a cigarette, and waited to become hungry. Enoch had said he would be back, but Bo was glad to be alone.

Dawn and Anne were dead. He boiled memories of them in his mind. Dawn was chesty and popular. She was dumb, but smart enough to act smart. Bo respected and spoke to her. Anne was built so slightly she always wore white blouses so onlookers could tell she had a bra, and therefore something to hold up. Her only friend was Dawn, her only beauty was in her eyes. She'd never stare down a husband, Bo thought, so maybe it's best. Dawn brushed against him a lot, not always so he would notice, but enough to make him wonder what she had meant.

Bo leaned his head against the red battery-charger and closed his eyes on Dawn's memory, while a vision of Lucy rocked smiling in his brain.

He saw a clapboard house, worn silver by weather, now glistening in the sun. He felt the intruder-sun on his head and the power he loved coax him toward the cool shade of the house. He saw movement up the moss-green sandstone steps, across the grooved porch-floor, and through the screen door. In the cool dampness of the linoleum living room, his cousin Sally stood; her hair pressed in ragged bangs on her forehead, the rest pinned loosely behind. Little chains of grime made sweaty chokers around her throat, but she looked cool and remote as she moved toward him and took his hand. "I don't love you," he said, viciously. Images soon ran together in flesh tones, and he awakened.

The dream had excited him as the cold August rain blowing through a porch might break the monotony of heat and pleasure-chill his blood. He searched for a reason for the dream. Maybe, he thought, I made it up. Maybe it happened.

Hunger drove him beyond Enoch's Law, and he ran quickly to the dinette. The door was locked, so he dragged himself to Brownie's, where he bought cheese, crackers, pork-rind snacks, and two Big Orange drinks.

"Dolla-fourtee." Bo handed the old man the money, tore into the cheese and Big Orange. "Don't eat it here," Brownie added, bagging the lunch.

Bo sat outside the garage in the cold sun and ate. He watched the Duncan sisters as they sat by their window and watched him with peeping sparrow-eyes. When he had drained the last Big Orange, he felt a wickedness rise in him as he chucked the empty bottle at the Duncan house, and he smiled to see them retreat behind their curtains.

Enoch returned at two-twenty, found Bo asleep against the battery charger. Cuffy had suggested cutting Bo's throat, and now was the time, but Cuffy was not around, and Enoch was not a cutter of throats.

"Wake up, Bo, goddammit, wake yourself up."

"Wha?"

"Look, I'm goin' to get the dogs. You lock up at three, an' be on the road afront of your house by six. I'll get ya there."

"Who alls comin'?" Bo yawned.

"Cuffy an' Bill an' Virg Cooper."

"Cuffy an' Bill don't like me," he warned.

"Don't be a smart-ass an' they will. Dress warm, hear?"

Bo nodded, thinking, son of a bitch.

He waited until Enoch's wrecker silhouetted the grade and passed over, then he locked up and headed for Lucy's. She sat alone reading a magazine and looking day-worn. Maybe she caught a man, Bo thought, but he threw her back. Over coffee he poured out his roil of sickness, hate, and confusion. Soon they were wrestling with the go or don't-go of the hunt.

"Bo, ya drive people off an' dump 'em. Go ahuntin'—they're just tryin' to be good to ya."

He looked up sternly. "You don't kick a dog in the ass then give 'im a bone."

Then with a sudden fervor: "Maybe I could take Daddy's forty-five automatic."

"Can't shoot foxie, Bo," she warned. "Be nothin' left to chase."

"I know," he said, as if a veteran of hunts. "I just want to show 'em I can shoot. You know, plug some cans."

"Make damn sure them cans ain't got legs," she grinned.

He gulped his coffee and left so quickly he forgot to leave his tip.

The clay trail from the secondary to Bo's hillside house was worn a smooth red in the center, bordered with a yellow crust. He followed the path into the perpetual dusk and sweet-chill of a pine grove. There the path forked, one toward the garbage pile, the other into a clearing where the house stood, rudely shingled in imitation-brick tar paper.

The clearing was scattered with pin-oak and sugar-maple

leaves lodged in fallow weeds. The sugar maples blended their colors to camouflage the undying plastic daffodils his mother had planted around the porch.

Bo panicked when he saw the shedded skin of a copperhead on the porch steps, then laughed at the dusty suggestion, bounced on it daringly, and up to the porch. He opened the whining screen door, burst the jammed wooden door open, and heard his mother: "'Sat you, Bo?" He remembered how she used to call him her "only Bo." As a boy he had liked it; now it made him shudder. But it didn't matter; she no longer called him in that fashion.

"Yeah, Momma."

As he washed his hands at the sink, he looked out the kitchen window at the heap in the backyard. It was slowly becoming a '66 Impala again. "Like gangbusters," he had said to Lucy, then asked himself, "When?" Turning his attention to his soap-lathered hands dissolved the question, but another sprang in its place: Why not use Dawn's car as a parts department?

He tried to find peace in cooking, but while he chopped potatoes and onions into the skillet, he heard his mother stirring in the bedroom. The aroma of pork grease had reached her, and she shouted, "Smells good." Instead of answering, Bo turned to sawing chops from a whole loin. These he fried also, not turning them until the blood oozed out and turned gray in the skillet.

His mother slipped into the kitchen with short, uneasy steps and dropped into the cushioned chair by the table. She had been resting. The doctor told her to rest eight years ago, when her husband died. Miner's insurance paid her to rest until the rest sapped her strength.

She leaned a tired, graying, but still-brown head of hair

against the wall, and let her eyelids sag complacently. She wore two print cotton dresses—one over the other. Two-dress fall, Bo thought, means a three-dress-and-coat winter.

Bo put the food on the table and was about to shovel pork into his mouth when his mother asked for her medicine. "It's in the winder above the sink."

"Has been for eight years," said Bo, scooting his chair out. As he gathered the bottles of colored pills, his glance went once again to the car. The tires were flat.

"I need my medicine," said his mother, while mashing her food into a mush between the fork prongs. She spoke over a mouthful: "When you gonna junk that thing like your Momma ast?"

"Never," he said, setting the bottles and himself at the table. "Probably die workin' on it. Enoch's got . . ." He did not want to mention the wreck at supper.

"Enoch's got what?"

"Got some parts, but I need more."

"It'll get snakes next spring."

"It al's gets snakes, and I al's run 'em off. Now will you leave my car be?"

"TV movie looks like a good 'un tonight," she said in penance.

"Gotta date at the dance in Helvetia."

When the supper dishes were finished, Bo dressed quickly while his mother rested from the walk back to the bedroom. Once wrapped, he slipped to the hall closet and took the .45 from its hatbox. He checked the clip: it was loaded with brightly oiled brass shells. The gun even smelled good. Shoving the weapon into his pocket, he shouted, "Night, Momma," and heard her whimper instructions as he closed and locked the door.

The sun was not setting, nor was it seen. It hid behind the

western slopes so only a hint of sun rose upward, firing the ridges with a green fire, and leaving everything in the hollow a clean, cold shadow. Bo knew a freeze was coming. It was too cold to snow. He would have to go now.

Bo watched the trees and houses go by as he only half-listened to Enoch's chatter about his two blueticks, Mattingly and Moore.

"Now Matt, he knows how to run, but Moore can figger if a fox is throwed the pack and he knows just where to look for him."

Bo thought: "I shoulda stayed and watched that movie. Wish Spanker hadn'ta run off. Couldn't stand to be tied up, though."

Houses and tales drifted by. Bo looked back at Matt and Moore, wobbly legged and motion sick.

"I was younger'n you the first time my daddy taked me ahuntin'." Enoch shifted down, and the transmission rattled like a bucket of chains. "Got drunk on two spoons of shine an' half a chew. Man. That was a time. Sittin' back . . . listen to them ol' honkers, and sittin' back. I growed up quick. Had to to stay alive. You ever know my daddy?"

"Nope," said Bo, thinking, wonder what that movie was.

"Your daddy knowed 'im. Meaner'n a teased snake. Got me laid when I's eight. Took me t' a house in Clarksburg—ol' gal said I couldn't come in—so he left me in the car an' went back with a tire tool—then he come an' got me an' showed me that ol' gal an' her man conked out on the floor."

"Musta been some excitement," Bo said, looking at the patterns trees threw against the sky as the truck passed.

"Yeah, an' that ain't all. He taked me t' this room an' busted in on this gal an' made her lay real still till I's finished. Then she called Daddy a SOB cause all he give her was fifty cents, an' he knocked her teeth out."

Enoch laughed wildly, but Bo only smiled. Old Man Enoch was dead, but the rumors of strangers' graves found in pigpens still grew.

"When'd ya git yer first?"

Bo told the afternoon dream as a fact, adding color and characters as he went until he was only inches out of shotgun range when "the sweet thing's old man cut down on me with his sixteen-gauge."

"Damn, who was she?"

"Think I'd tell you so's you could go an' tell on me an' get me killed?"

"Just never figgered you for the type. Guess I been takin' you all wrong." Enoch added in consideration: "Yer pretty slick."

Once they topped the hill, small slashes of light broke through the trees; enough to see rabbits and the road without headlights. Bo was about to mention his gun, but they pulled so quickly off the timber trail, he forgot it. The truck rumbled into a small room in the forest: it was walled with trees, hearthed by a pit of cold ashes, and furnished with broken car-seats. Now, Bo thought, climbing from the truck. Now loose. Alone. Smell power in the air—smells like good metal in temper. Dawn never brush against me again. Alone.

"Git some firewood," Enoch ordered.

Bo swung around. "Look, I work for you from the time I git there till when I leave. You want somethin' t'night, better ask like a friend."

"Cocky, ain't ya?"

"I gotta right."

"You ain't actin' like a man."

"You ain't treatin' me like one."

Bo and Enoch combed the littered hill for shed-wood and abandoned timber.

Two miles beyond, an owl watched a meadow from the branches of a dead hickory tree. Hidden in the underbrush, the fox watched the owl and the meadow. Both saw the rabbit meandering through the dying ironweed and goldenrod, and both waited for the best condition of attack. When the moment came, the owl was on wing before the fox had lifted a pad.

The wind changed, and the fox changed cover while keeping close watch on the feasting owl. The fox crept carefully, judged the distance to the nearest cover, then rushed the owl with a bark. The bird flew straight up in alarm, aimed at the thief, and dropped, only to bury its talons in ironweed and earth. Fox and prey were under cover, leaving the bird robbed and hungry in the silver dusk.

Bo built a fire while Enoch tended the dogs. Mattingly and Moore sniffed the air as they overcame their sickness. They pranced and bit the chains as Enoch checked their feet for stones or cuts. As the fire came to life, Bo felt a baseness growing within himself, felt he knew the forest better than the man with the dogs, and, for a moment, wanted to run into the darkness.

Bill began to honk his horn at the foot of the hill and continued to honk his way up the hill trail. The dogs barked from the pain in their ears. "Drunk already," Enoch shouted, laughing. Under a persimmon bush, the fox gnawed rabbit bones and rested, pausing between chews to listen.

The truck lunged into camp; Cuffy fell out, the other men

stumbling behind, leaving the frothing dogs tied to the bed of the truck.

"What the hell's he doin' here?" said Cuffy, pointing at Bo.

"I invited him," Enoch said.

"Hey, Enoch," shouted Virg, looking from man to dog and back again. "You an' Matt are beginnin' to look alike."

Cuffy sauntered to the fire, took the seat opposite Bo, and they eyed each other with disgust.

"Wha's Nutsy doin' here?" he taunted.

"I like it here," Bo fired back.

"Don't git too used to it."

Bo left Cuffy to join the group.

"B'god, don' tell me that dog can run," Enoch yelled at Bill.

"Bender's the best runner. Bet he sings first *and* leads 'em," Bill answered.

"I'll bet on Moore to sing out first," said Bo. "And Bender to lead."

"Least you got *half* a brain," said Bill.

"How much?" asked Bo.

"Dollar."

"Done," said Bo. Enoch bet Bill on his own, and they shook hands all around before releasing the dogs.

The men brought out their bourbon, and Enoch gave Bo a special present—moonshine in a mason jar. Then they retired to the fire to swap tales until trail broke.

From his post in the brush the fox could hear sniffing searches being carried out. Dabbing his paws in rabbit gore for a head start, he darted over the bank toward the hollow. Queen, Bill's roan hound, was first to find the trail. Instead of calling, she cut back across the ridge to where cold trail told her he was prone to cross. Moore sang out lowly as he sniffed to distinguish fox from rabbit.

"Moore," Enoch shouted, "I'd know 'im anyplace."

"Dog's keen-mouthed all right," said Virg.

Bill paid each man the dollar he owed.

"Made a mistake about that boy," Enoch bragged, embarrassing Bo. "Tell 'em 'bout yer first woman, Bo." The men leaned forward, looking at Bo.

"You tell 'em, Enoch, I ain't drunk enough."

Bo corrected Enoch's rehash from time to time as the listeners hooted their approving laughter.

"Fred said he couldn't go ahuntin'," said Cuffy, watching Bo for some reaction. "Seems somebody's been messin' whit his wife whilst he's gone." Bo stared Cuffy down, then took a full drink from his jar.

"Maybe 'twas that hippie back of Fred," Virg offered.

"Hippie just screws animals," said Cuffy.

"Or other hippies," Enoch added.

"That's what he means," Bo explained, and they all broke into a wild wind of laughter.

The last of the firewood was burning when Bill was finishing his tale. The dogs had been forgotten.

"Like I said, we's all drunk an' Cuffy an' Tom got to argyin' 'bout the weight of them two hogs . . . had 'em all clean and butchered an' packed. Them two bastards loaded 'em on the truck—guts an' all—an' took 'em to Sutton to weigh 'em. Got the guts all mixed up, an' fit ober what head went to what hog."

"Weren't much kick to that hog when I gutted 'im," Cuffy reminisced.

"'Bout like you kicked when they brained you," Virg spouted. And the men belched laughter again.

The fox was climbing the trail to camp, the pack trailing behind. Queen waited in the brush near the men, cold-trail sure the fox would cross here. The fox circled trees, his last trick to lose the pack.

Bo was woven into the gauze-light, torn between passing out and taking another drink. He caught bits of conversation, then his mind drifted into hollow sleep, and the voices jerked him awake again.

"He's sittin' in the Holy Seat," said Bill's voice in Bo's darkness. Bo kept his eyes closed.

"That was one helluva wreck," said Enoch. "Way I figger it, she drowned."

"Whycome?" asked Virg.

"She was all wrinkly—sorta scrunged up."

"The Holy Pole is in your hold, so work yer ass to save your soul," Cuffy proclaimed.

"She was damn good, all right." Enoch's voice drifted away.

"Hell," said Virg, "I al's went last."

"First come, first served," said Bill.

"Shut up," said Cuffy. "I'm horny again."

"Hell, we all are," said Virg. "Let's dig her up."

"Maybe she's still warm," added Cuffy. The men giggled until they were coughing.

"Told her old man she had a job," Enoch laughed.

"I miss her," sighed Virg.

"I don't," shouted Cuffy. "She coulda hung us all if'n somebody didn' marry her. Nosir, I'm glad she's dead."

Bo fingered the .45 in his pocket.

But the men had whittled the time away telling lies mingled with truth until Bo could no longer distinguish between the two. He had told things, too; no truth or lie could go untold. It was fixed now; the truth and lies were all told.

The fox broke through the clearing, pausing at the sight of fire and man. Queen burst to attack just as the confused fox retreated toward her. There was a yelp, and the fox dashed for the hollow with Queen running a sight chase.

"That damn cutter," Bill shouted. Bo drunkenly swung the .45 from his coat pocket, shot at Queen, and missed. Cuffy screamed as the shot echoed from the dark western ridges. Queen paused to look at Bo, then went back to trail. Virg jumped up and kicked the gun from Bo's hand.

"Try'n save foxie," Bo slurred.

"You stupid son of a bitch," said Cuffy, and Bo looked for the pistol to kill him, but it was lost in the leaves and darkness. His head throbbed, and he looked stupidly at the men.

"Leave 'im alone," said Enoch. "Nobody never teached 'im no better."

Bo stood wavering, and said to Virg, "I's sorry, but I's tryin' to save foxie."

Cuffy spat on Bo's shoe, but he ignored it, walked to the bushes, and threw up.

"You guys piss on the fire," said Enoch. "I'll call the dogs."

Bo nearly missed the clearing in the strange, misty-gray light of Sunday afternoon. Dried oak leaves whispered in the sapless branches above him, and an autumn-blooming flower hung limply on its stem, frostbitten for its rebellion.

The remnants of the night lay strewn about the leaf-floor like a torpid ghost. The mason jar was empty, but his head felt fine—only an ache of change, like a cold coming on. He could smell cold ashes and vomit in the air, but the molten smell was gone from the wind, or perhaps the wind had carried it on.

He found his father's pistol, laced with rusty lines from the wet leaves, and shoved it into his coat pocket. As he lurched down the clay timber-trail toward the secondary, he wondered if the Impala would be ready to roll by spring.

TIME AND AGAIN

....

MR. WEEKS called me out again tonight, and I look back down the hall of my house. I left the kitchen light burning. This is an empty old house since the old lady died. When Mr. Weeks doesn't call, I write everybody I know about my boy. Some of my letters always come back, and the folks who write back say nobody knows where he got off to. I can't help but think he might come home at night when I am gone, so I let the kitchen light burn and go on out the door.

The cold air is the same, and the snow pellets my cap, sifts under my collar. I hear my hogs come grunting from their shed, thinking I have come to feed them. I ought to feed them better than that awful slop, but I can't until I know my boy is safe. I told him not to go and look, that the hogs just squeal because I never kill them. They always squeal when they are happy, but he went and looked. Then he ran off someplace.

I brush the snow from my road plow's windshield and climb in. The vinyl seats are cold, but I like them. They are smooth and easy cleaned. The lug wrench is where it has always been beside my seat. I heft it, put it back. I start the salt spreader, lower my shear, and head out to clean the mountain road.

The snow piles in a wall against the berm. No cars move. They are stranded at the side, and as I plow past them, a line falls in behind me, but they always drop back. They don't know how long it takes the salt to work. They are common fools. They rush around in such weather and end up dead. They never sit still and wait for the salt to work.

I think I am getting too old to do this anymore. I wish I could rest and watch my hogs get old and die. When the last one is close to dying, I will feed him his best meal and leave the gate open. But that will most likely not happen, because I know this stretch of Route 60 from Ansted to Gauley, and I do a good job. Mr. Weeks always brags on what a good job I do, and when I meet the other truck plowing the uphill side of this road, I will honk. That will be Mr. Weeks coming up from Gauley. I think how I never met Mr. Weeks in my life but in a snowplow. Sometimes I look out to Sewel Mountain and see snow coming, then I call Mr. Weeks. But we are not friends. We don't come around each other at all. I don't even know if he's got family.

I pass the rest stop at Hawks Nest, and a new batch of fools line up behind me, but pretty soon I am alone again. As I plow down the grade toward Chimney Corners, my lights are the only ones on the road, and the snow takes up the yellow spinning of my dome light and the white curves of my headlights. I smile at the pretties they make, but I am tired and wish I was home. I worry about the hogs. I should have given them more slop, but when the first one dies, the others will eat him quick enough.

I make the big turn at Chimney Corners and see a hitchhiker standing there. His front is clean, and he looks half frozen, so I stop to let him in.

He says, "Hey, thank you, Mister."

"How far you going?"

"Charleston."

"You got family there?" I say.

"Yessir."

"I only go to Gauley Bridge, then I turn around."

"That's fine," he says. He is a polite boy.

The fools pack up behind me, and my low gears whine away from them. Let them fall off the mountain for all I care.

"This is not good weather to be on the road," I say.

"Sure ain't, but a fellow's got to get home."

"Why didn't you take a bus?"

"Aw, buses stink," he says. My boy always talked like that.

"Where you been?"

"Roanoke. Worked all year for a man. He give me Christmastime and a piece of change."

"He sounds like a good man."

"You bet. He's got this farm outside of town—horses—you ain't seen such horses. He's gonna let me work the horses next year."

"I have a farm, but I only have some hogs left."

"Hogs is good business," he says.

I look at him. "You ever see a hog die?" I look back at the road snow.

"Sure."

"Hogs die hard. I seen people die in the war easier than a hog at a butchering."

"Never noticed. We shot and stuck them pretty quick. They do right smart jerking around, but they're dead by then."

"Maybe."

"What can you do with a hog if you don't butcher him? Sell him?"

"My hogs are old hogs. Not good for anything. I just been

letting them die. I make my money on this piece of road every winter. Don't need much."

He says, "Ain't got any kids?"

"My boy run off when my wife died. But that was considerable time ago."

He is quiet a long time. Where the road is patched, I work my shear up, and go slower to let more salt hit behind. In my mirror, I see the lights of cars sneaking up behind me.

Then of a sudden the hitchhiker says, "What's your boy do now?"

"He was learning a mason's trade when he run off."

"Makes good money."

"I don't know. He was only a hod carrier then."

He whistles. "I done that two weeks this summer. I never been so sore."

"It's hard work," I say. I think, this boy has good muscles if he can carry hod.

I see the lights of Mr. Weeks's snowplow coming toward us. I gear into first. I am not in a hurry. "Scrunch down," I say. "I'd get in trouble for picking you up."

The boy hunkers in the seat, and the lights from Mr. Weeks's snowplow shine into my cab. I wave into the lights, not seeing Mr. Weeks, and we honk when we pass. Now I move closer to center. I want to do a good job and get all the snow, but when the line of cars behind Mr. Weeks comes toward me, I get fidgety. I don't want to cause any accidents. The boy sits up and starts talking again, and it makes me jittery.

"I was kinda scared about coming through Fayette County," he says.

"Uh-huh," I say. I try not to brush any cars.

"Damn, but a lot of hitchhikers gets killed up here."

A man lays on his horn as he goes past, but I have to get what Mr. Weeks left, and I am always too close to center.

The boy says, "That soldier's bones—Jesus, but that was creepy."

The last car edges by, but my back and shoulders are shaking and I sweat.

"That soldier," he says. "You know about that?"

"I don't know."

"They found his duffel bag at the bottom of Lovers' Leap. All his grip was in there, and his bones, too."

"I remember. That was too bad." The snow makes such nice pictures in my headlights, and it rests me to watch them.

"There was a big retard got killed up here, too. He was the only one they ever found with all his meat on. Rest of them, they just find their bones."

"They haven't found any in years," I say. This snow makes me think of France. It was snowing like this when they dropped us over France. I yawn.

"I don't know," he says. "Maybe the guy who done them all in is dead."

"I figure so," I say.

The hill bottoms out slowly, and we drive on to Gauley, clearing the stretch beside New River. The boy is smoking and taking in the snow.

"It snowed like this in France the winter of 'forty-four," I say. "I was in the paratroops, and they dropped us where the Germans were thick. My platoon took a farmhouse without a shot."

"Damn," he says. "Did you knife them?"

"Snapped their necks," I say, and I see my man tumble into the sty. People die so easy.

We come to Gauley, where the road has already been cleared by the other trucks. I pull off, and the line of cars catches up, sloshing by. I grip the wrench.

"Look under the seat for my flashlight, boy."

He bends forward, grabbing under the seat, and his head is turned from me. But I am way too tired now, and I don't want to clean the seat.

"She ain't there, Mister."

"Well," I say. I look at the lights of the cars. They are fools.

"Thanks again," he says. He hops to the ground, and I watch him walking backward, thumbing. I am almost too tired to drive home. I sit and watch this boy walking backward until a car stops for him. I think, he is a polite boy, and lucky to get rides at night.

All the way up the mountain, I count the men in France, and I have to stop and count again. I never get any farther than that night it snowed. Mr. Weeks passes me and honks, but I don't honk. Time and again, I try to count and can't.

I pull up beside my house. My hogs run from their shelter in the backyard and grunt at me. I stand by my plow and look at the first rims of light around Sewel Mountain through the snowy limbs of the trees. Cars hiss by on the clean road. The kitchen light still burns, and I know the house is empty. My hogs stare at me, snort beside their trough. They are waiting for me to feed them, and I walk to their pen.

THE MARK
••••••••••••••••••••

ON THE morning of the fair the smell came to Reva in the kitchen, slicing through the thick odors of coffee and fish roe. She left the dishes and carried her coffee through the tunneling light of the hallway, past her brother's neatly framed arrowheads, past the charcoal portrait of her grandfather, beyond the cool darkness, onto the porch. The land and river were hidden under a thick brown fog that the sun was peeling away. The fog smelled of ore and earth, and Reva sat to breathe it in, rubbing weariness from the bones in her hands. She felt thick with worry for her brother; working the same river that had killed their parents only eight years ago. The worry was making one of her spells come, and she promised herself to forget.

In the yard, chuckleheaded Jackie, the tenant, curried Tyler's prize bull, singing some idiot's tune quietly. The bull shifted his huge weight from side to side, shuddering against the unnatural ripples Jackie's brush had put into his black fur. As "the Pride and Promise of Cutter's Landing" whipped his ropish tail against early flies, Reva mocked, "Peeepeee," before sipping her coffee. The bull shifted again.

"Holt still, damn ya," Jackie grunted, losing his song.

Peepee, Reva grinned to herself. Pea-brained Peepee pees on his heifers. Peeepeee.

Tyler, her husband, came to the porch wearing his green plaid shirt and blue trousers.

"This okay?" he asked, modeling in a pivot.

"For a sideshow, yeah," she laughed.

"I can't help it," he said, embarrassed for his color blindness.

"Find the light-colored slacks, Big T.," she said, knowing they were tan, and watched him shuffle down the hall like a little boy, and not her husband of two winters.

She felt the spot where the baby should be, closed her eyes, and tried to imagine her blood in the rabbit's veins. It would pump into the ovaries, making them swell, the doctor had said, if she was pregnant. They were going to kill the rabbit and look for her secret in its organs, but the sinkings in her belly came on too hard and frightening, too much like her worst month. She told herself they would find no confessions in the rabbit ovaries.

She remembered her brother Clinton holding a litter of baby rabbits close to his naked chest while the mowing machine droned behind him in a dead hum. Was that the summer she began to want him?

She looked to where the fog had lifted away from the road and was crossing the acres of tobacco in the river bottom, leaving a glistening coat of dew. Clinton had helped them top and worm the crop before shipping out, and she squinted to think of a whore holding her brother's strong body, smelling the smoky scent of their grandfather. By next week there would be only dry stubble for snakes to shed in, and a dusty smell from the crackling curing-barn.

Tyler came back in light-blue jeans, a pair Reva had forgotten. She took a deep breath of the August heat.

"What the hell's Jackie up to?" he asked, watching the tenant.

Reva did not answer. A grasshopper landed on the banister, and Reva watched its armored jaws bubble juice. On the same spot, once, her grandfather had told his boatman's tales and sung the chanteys, and she had traded dark secrets with her brother.

"Go on an' put him in the truck, Jackie," Tyler shouted, then murmured, "Goddamn ignoramus'll just have to do it all over at the fair. But he does look down right champeen, don't he? Even had Jackie polish his ring."

"Don't that beat all," she said, going to fetch the pants herself.

"Yessir," Tyler said to the bull, "you look downright elegant."

Coming back through the hallway, Reva locked eyes with the stare of her grandfather but, not knowing his young face, kept her pace to the porch.

"Go put these on 'fore Bill an' Carlene gets here," she said, handing Tyler the trousers.

"Don't ya wanta help?" he said, hooking his arm around her waist and grinning as he kissed her neck. He smelled of Aqua Velva, but his chin was rough.

"You missed a spot," she said, brushing her hand across his face and pushing away. He went into the house.

Jackie goaded "Pride and Promise" into the straight-bed truck, tied him, and latched the gate. Reva watched him hang his chuckled head as he jogged to the barn, knock-kneed. She wondered if he had a bottle hidden there.

The fog was gone, and she could see the hills beyond the river—hills that soon gave way to the plains of Ohio. On the eastern shore, nearly hidden in the vines and weeds, stood the ship-lapped wooden lockhouse where her grandfather once worked. Even as it stood empty in their youth, it had been her playhouse or Clinton's fort. By its concrete foundation, they dug for the bones of a body their grandfather said he had fished from the river as a boy, but never found them. Up and down the shore, paths were worn slick in the black river-clay. On the smooth gray bark of a water maple, its roots breaking the abutment of a lock gate, Clinton had carved their parents' initials on the cold December Friday the bridge collapsed.

A small dusty breeze moved across the porch, and Reva shivered in its heat, closing her eyes to tears from staring too long. A tiny pain screwed into her back, and she tried to hate against being left here, alone. She tried to blame Clinton, her parents, even the river, but opened her eyes to the white knuckles of her tiny fist.

The bull stomped indifferently in the truck bed, and the early sun warmed the locust into buzzing, but the good air had gone with the fog. When she saw Bill's new Buick turn off the highway, she got up heavily and went inside.

"She stares 'bout all the time," Tyler said, watching the bull, waiting for his brother's answer.

The brother sat slightly higher on the banister, smoking. The locust buzz only thickened the air, and the dusty leaves of the water-maple hills hung limp green, showing no flags of wind. Bill yawned.

Tyler looked up at his brother. "I figgered I'd give her a baby to keep her mind offa Clint. Boy, she was ripe the day he left. Now she just misses that sassy talk of his."

Bill still said nothing, and Tyler got up to stand beside his brother. Bill scratched at Tyler's worry.

"Aw shit, T., quit worryin' like some ol' woman. You got a farm to work. Worry 'bout that."

"Sure 'nough there. Weren't for that tobacca yonder, I'd be up shit creek."

Reva stood in the hallway, her index finger tracing the serrated edge of a rose-colored arrowhead. Clinton had called it a Shawnee war-point, and gave it center honor because it was her favorite. Upstairs the toilet flushed, and she heard her sister-in-law humming as she primped. She went out.

"Ready?" Tyler said, springing off the steps.

"Where's Carlene?" Bill asked.

"In the john, I have an idee," she said, snapping her purse closed.

"Wife's got a straight pipe," Bill said to his brother.

"Lookee there," Reva said, pointing to where a mole was tunneling in the yard. Tyler walked out and poised his heel over the moving earth.

"Tyler, that mole ain't botherin' us," she said, bored with her husband's grin.

"I know it," he said, dropping down at the head of the tunnel. "Dug his own grave."

"I heard tell ever'thin's poison on dog days," said Bill.

Reva shot him a cross look.

"What's poison?" said Carlene, coming to the porch.

"Nothin'." Reva brushed her hair back, then walked down the steps toward the Buick.

Jackie leaned against the truck, his big head lolling back on the sideboards. "Purty day," he said as Reva passed, and she nodded, smiling, knowing any sort of day was good for Jackie. Waiting in the car's building heat made the throb in her forehead bloom back between her ears. She stared at the sycamores and water maples along the riverbank. Secret totems hung there as gifts to the ghost-trees of her parents: a necklace from Reva, a charmed dog-bone from Clinton, bits of glass on fishing line to make the trees glitter in the winter sun. Her head cleared, and she heard the others coming to the car, whispering. Only Tyler's voice came up low from within him, ". . . but they been dead a long time."

In the silence of the car, Carlene felt bad about her sister-in-law's spells. She remembered Grandfather Cutter standing for weeks in the cold wind on the riverbank, watching the cars come up, water spewing from the lips of their torn metal. Only when rumor of a Ford truck met him would he move closer, watching. When his son's finally came up empty, he only walked to the truck where his grandchildren sat, staring at the masses of twisted steel.

The smooth blacktop was interrupted suddenly by a four-mile section of concrete slabs. The car jolted over each one as it passed, and Tyler slowed down, motioning Jackie to back off his tail.

"Damn idiot," he said, then, glancing into the mirror to where Bill sat behind him, "You seen Layman's bull, 'Rangoon'?"

"Sounds more like a disease," Bill chuckled.

"Probably got it in 'Nam."

"The name or the disease?" Reva grinned wickedly. No one laughed.

"I'll lay odds he made the papers on it," Tyler continued. "Good-looker without a line."

"Naw," Bill drawled, "Layman ain't that smart."

Carlene leaned forward to Reva. "I can't wait till ya hear from the doc. Scared?"

"Just mad," she said for Tyler's ears.

"Want a boy or a girl?" Carlene's blue eyes widened with her question.

"Don't matter. Just let it be till I know for sure."

Tyler took her hand, and she could feel the worry in his cold fingers. The ride was making her carsick, and she closed her eyes thinking Clinton might never come back after the baby was born.

"New Angus in the county," she heard Bill say, and felt Tyler's fingers flex.

"Whose?"

"Feller name of Jordan or Jergan—I forget, but the bull's called 'Imperial Sun'—*S-u-n*. All the way from Virginia."

"Good stock?"

"You couldn't afford the fee."

Carlene leaned up again. "What you gonna call the baby?"

"'Imperial Sun,'" Reva's voice was hollow.

"Ain't neither," Tyler tried to joke. "Gonna call him a'ter ol' Jeff D. Cutter. Ain't that so, Reva?"

"Sure, Big T."

"Who won last year?" Tyler looked at Bill's image, and waved Jackie back again.

"You know," Bill said, "I don't rightly recall."

The FFA boy shifted his tobacco chew as he handed Reva her ham sandwich, smiling tightly against the juice in his mouth. With the afternoon sun in his eyes, his squint reminded her of her brother's, and she smiled back as she paid.

"I don't for the life of me know how ya eat that trash," Carlene sneered.

Remembering the boy's smile, Reva took a big bite and pulled a slice of meat from the sandwich. She wagged it at Carlene like a tongue, and her eyes brightened a little. "Good," Reva said, stuffing the meat into her mouth.

The sawdust midway was full of the scent of dirt and people and fun, not like the stock pens or stinking the same. As they strolled, they looked at blank faces gazing on their own. The children chased each other with shrieks and laughter. A redheaded boy was pulling mats of cotton candy from his hair while his sister slapped on more, laughing. On the bench, their mother stared into the forest of faces.

Reva remembered Clinton's teasings after her wedding. "Gonna get slapped down like a ol' catfish," he had said, laughing. Afterward, he had called her Catfish, and always warned her about beef bait and hooks before she went to Tyler's bed.

Again they passed the gut-jolting rides, and Carlene was edging toward the Dodg'em cars. "C'mon," she said.

"Naw, I been whipped up 'nough for today."

"Well, we done it all," Carlene said, disappointed.

"Ain't seen the sideshows nor the animals neither."

"Those?" Carlene snarled and squinted, but followed Reva down the midway to the shows.

Even with the barkers, the sideshow lane seemed quiet, and whispering adults made a drone below the barkers' calls. They passed the Monster of Calcutta and the Living Torch, listening as the whispers grew into voices when the shows cleared out. The stripper had no barker, needed none.

"Bill said she smokes a cigar with her you-know-what," Carlene whispered.

"Now that there's a trick," Reva answered. Her face lightened thinking about it. Her brother would come upriver, not in his boatman's clothes, but as a naked Indian hiding in the pawpaw tunnels. In the lockhouse she would show him that trick. Her mood shifted back when she thought some whore might already have shown him.

"Lookee, snakes," Reva shouted under her breath.

"Don't want to pay to see nothin' I got too much of."

"Aw c'mon, Carlene," Reva said, handing the barker her quarters. Carlene dragged behind, pushing through the crowd to where Reva had squeezed a place by the canvas-lined pit. In the pit among the harmless snakes sat a shoeless old man, his voice running on professionally, but laced with boredom.

"Now you can all see this is a living thing," he said, holding up a small snake. Then he dropped it down his throat. Carlene gagged, and the crowd whispered.

"You sir," he continued, pointing to a man in bib overalls, "do you see the snake hidden?" and he gaped his toothless jaws. The man in overalls did not look up, but shyly shook his head. The snake eater belched the snake into his hands and freed it to crawl with the others. Whispers rolled through the tent, but Reva followed Carlene outside. She felt sorry for Tyler and his mole-killing foot, but knew it would always be that way with him.

"I'm goin' back to the yards," Carlene said. "This here's makin' me sick."

"Well, lookee there." Reva pointed to a chicken-wire cage where two spider monkeys bucked in their breeding. Another lay on a shelf near the roof, stroking himself, awaiting his turn.

"I knowed a woman to mark her baby thataway."

Reva drew her stare away from the monkeys and leveled off scornfully at Carlene's blue eyes.

"Well," Carlene continued bitterly, "my momma told me all about it. Said the gal was nigh onto seven months, an' her husband couldn't drag her away from them monkeys."

Reva looked at the female monkey awaiting her new mount. The other male climbed down for his share as the female's empty face looked back at Reva, blinking.

"That baby was born lookin' just like a monkey," Carlene said, bending herself to talk between Reva and the cage. "Momma swears it's the mark of the beast, but she's real partial to that kinda talk."

"Where is it now?" Reva asked, as if to seek it out.

"Died, I think."

Both males rested, stretched full-length on the floor of the cage, while the female huddled in the corner, glaring. The wind carried their stench away. Now Reva wanted to go to the lockhouse, wanted to feel the chilly floor against her buttocks and shoulders.

The pains in her belly were sharp and familiar. The soreness left her tired and empty. "My stomach hurts," she said to Carlene.

"That sandwich. I tol' ya."

Tyler took her arm, startling her. "We been all to hell an' back tryin' to find ya'll. You look sick," he said, watching a cold paleness rise in her cheeks.

"How'd ol' Peepee do?" she asked above the grasp of cramps.

Tyler shook his head.

"Sorry, T.," she said, stroking his cheek. It was already rough.

"You all right?" he asked.

She leaned her face against his chest, letting him hug her. He smelled sweaty and good, but the scent of roe and livestock clung to his skin.

"Yeah, T.," she said, feeling a menstrual slip. She was sorry the rabbit had died for nothing.

As she went down the steps, Reva did not look for the crushed tunnel of the mole. Instead, she made her way through clouds of gnats toward the river as the moon drove the darkness from the bottom. From deep in the grasses where the snakes were waking up, she saw fireflies speckling the sky and thought she caught scent of something moist in the dry air.

Tyler watched from the porch as his wife passed under the shadows of maples along the riverbank, their foliage making lace of the rising moon across the river. He had lost the prize and the child in the same day, and grew bitter about her spells. "Hey, Jackie," he called, waiting for the tenant to shuffle out to the yard.

"Whut?" The tenant almost screamed from in front of his shack.

"C'mon an' have a drink."

By the moss-softened locks, Reva stared at two moons, one hanging quietly above Ohio, the other broken by the slow current of the river. Mosquitoes buzzed about her ears, taking blood from beneath her tender scalp, but she did not move. Upstream, a deer's hoof sucked in the soft mud, but Reva kept watching the swimming moon—the same moon she knew Clinton watched with his Cincinnati whore. She felt her belly for the child that had never been, and almost wanted the deed undone, even forgotten.

Across the river, a tiny fisherman's-fire danced, and sometimes she thought she could smell its smoke. She stood up, her joints popping from sitting in the dew too long, and traced the carvings in the tree with her cold fingers; felt all that was left of her family: *L.C.N.C. '67.*

Jackie was smiling at the second drink. Tyler made them stronger, laughing at Jackie's stupid grin.

"Whut ya gonna call yer kid?" the tenant asked.

"Ain't gonna be no *kid*," Tyler answered.

"But I's of a mind—"

"You ain't got no mind. Ain't gonna be no *kid*."

Jackie looked stupidly at Tyler. The farmer rubbed his forehead, looking for words.

"She lost her heat," he finally said, hoping Jackie would understand.

They heard a low, simpering whine coming from the porch and went out. Reva sat on the steps, rocking back and forth, hugging herself, whining.

"Goddammit to hell," Tyler said, seeing the orange blades of fire wave out from the lockhouse.

"I done it," Reva said to Jackie, who stood on the step in front of her. She looked up on the porch to her husband. "I done a awful thing, T."

"C'mon, git up'ar," Jackie said, grabbing her arm to help her up. His huge head hid the moon, and, when she cried against him, the fire. He smelled like coal and whiskey.

THE SCRAPPER

IN THE silence between darkness and light, Skeevy awakened, sick from the dream. He rolled over, feeling his head for bumps. There were only a few, but his bones ached from being hit with chairs and his bloody knuckles stuck to the sheets. The shack was dark and hollow as a cistern, and he heard his voice say, "Bund."

The dream had been too real, too much like the real fight with Bund, and he wondered if he had really tried to kill his best friend. His mother begged him to quit boxing when they brought punchy Bund home from the hospital. "Scrap if'n you gotta," she had said, touching the bandage over Skeevy's eye, "but don't you never wear no bandages again. Don't never hurt nobody again."

Trudy mumbled softly in her own dreams, and he slipped from under the covers slowly, trying not to make the springs squeak. He felt empty talking to her, and did not want to be there when she woke up. He dressed and crept to the refrigerator. There was only some rabbit left; still, it was wild meat, and he had to have it.

Outside, a glow from the east was filtering through the fog and turning the ridge pink. Skeevy knew Purserville was across that hill, but he knew the glow could not be from their lights. He started up the western hill toward Clayton wishing he was farther away from Hurricane, from Bund.

As he crested the first knoll, he looked back to the hollow, where he knew Trudy was still sleeping, and far beyond the horizon, where he knew Bund would be sitting on a Coke case in front of the Gulf station begging change, his tongue hanging limp. Skeevy felt his gut skin, and he figured it was just a case of the flux.

At the strip mine, Skeevy sat on a boulder and ate cold rabbit as he looked down on the roofs of Clayton: the company store, company church, company houses, all shiny with fog-wet tin. He saw a miner steal a length of chain from the machine shop where Skeevy worked during the week, promised himself to report it, and forgot it as quickly. Around the houses, he could see where the wives had planted flowers, but the plants were all dead or dying from the constant shower of coal dust.

Just outside of town, across the macadam from the Free Will Church, was The Car, a wheelless dining car left behind after the timber played out. The hulk gleamed like a mussel shell in the Sunday sun.

Skeevy threw his rabbit bones in the brush for the dogs to find, wiped his hands on his jeans, and went down the mountain toward The Car. As he crossed the bottle-cap-strewn pavement of the diner's lot he looked back to where he had sat. The mountain looked like an apple core in the high sun.

Inside, the diner still smelled of sweat and blood from the fight the night before. He shoved the slotted windows open and wondered how ten strong men could find room to fight in The Car. He rubbed his knuckles and smiled. He yawned in the doorway while he waited for the coffee-maker, and through the fog saw Trudy's yellow pantsuit coming down the road.

"Where you been?" he asked.

"You're a'kiddin' me, Skeevy Kelly." She came through the lot smiling, and hooked her arm around him. "You don't show me no respect. Just up an' leave without a good-mornin' kiss."

"I bet you respect real good. I'd respect you till you couldn't walk."

"You're a'kiddin' again. What you want to do today?"

"Bootleg."

"Stop a'kiddin'."

"I ain't, Trudy. I gotta work for Corey," he said, watching her pout.

"Them ol' chicken-fights . . ."

"Well, stick around and talk to Ellen."

"Last time that happened, I ended up smellin' like a hamburger." Skeevy laughed, and she hugged him. "I'll go visit the preacher or somethin'."

"You watch out that 'somethin' ain't about like that," he said, measuring off a length with his arm. She knocked his hand down and started toward the road, until he could only see her yellow slacks pumping through the fog. He liked her, but she made him feel fat and lazy.

"Hey, Trudy," he shouted.

"What?" came from the foggy road.

"Get respected," he said, and heard "I swan to goodness . . ." sigh out of the mist.

A clatter came from the church across the road as two drunken miners dusted themselves down the wooden steps and drifted up the road toward the houses.

Skeevy took two cups from the shelf, filled them, and crossed the road to the church. There was only a shadow of light seeping through the painted window. The old deacon was sweeping bottles from between the pews, talking softly to himself as the glass clanked in empty toasts.

"Here, Cephus." He offered the heavy mug. "Ain't good to start without it."

The skinny old man kept to his chore until the mug grew too heavy for Skeevy and he set it on the pew.

"They had a real brawl," Skeevy offered again.

"Ain't right, drinkin' in a church." The old man looked up from his work, his brown eyes catching the hazy light. He took up his coffee and leaned on his broom. "How many?" he asked, blowing steam from his brew.

"Even 'nough. 'Bout twenty-five to a side."

"Oooowee," the old man crooned. "Let's get outa here. Lord's abotherin' me for marvelin' at the devil's work."

Once outside, Skeevy noticed how the old man stood straighter, making an effort, grimacing with pain in his back.

"Who won?" Cephus asked.

"Clayton, I reckon. C'mon, I gotta show you a sight."

They crossed the blacktop to the abandoned mill basement beside the diner. There, with its wheels in the air, lay Jim Gibson's pickup truck.

"Five Clayton boys just flipped her in there."

"Damn" was all Cephus could say.

"Nobody in her, but she made one hell of a racket."

"I reckon so." He looked at Skeevy's knuckles.

Skeevy rubbed his hands against his jeans. "Aw, I just tapped a couple when they got bothersome. Those boys fight too serious."

"I usta could," Cephus said, looking back to the murdered truck.

Skeevy looked to the yellow pines on the western hills: the way the light hit them reminded him of grouse-hunting with Bund, of pairing off in the half-day under the woven branches, of the funny human noises the birds made before they flew, and how their necks were always broken when you picked them up.

"You chorin' the juice today?" Cephus kept looking at the truck.

"Sure. Where's the cockfight?"

"I figger they'll meet-up someplace or another," he said, handing Skeevy the cup with "'Preciate it" as he started for the church. Skeevy side-glanced at the old man to see if his posture drooped, but it did not.

He returned to the diner, plugged in the overplayed jukebox, and threw a few punches at his shadow. He felt tired, and only fried one cheeseburger for breakfast.

Because the woman's back was toward him, Skeevy kept looking at the soft brown scoops of hair. It was clean. Occasionally the man with her would glance at Skeevy to see if he was listening. Being outsiders, they shouted in whispers over their coffee.

Tom and Ellen Corey pulled up in their truck. Ellen's head was thrown back with laughter. Before coming in, they reviewed the upended truck in the neighboring basement. Ellen kept laughing at her short husband as they entered, keeping to the upper side of the counter and away from the customers.

As he leaned over the counter to catch Corey's whispers, Skeevy noticed how Corey's blue eyes were surrounded by white. He had seen the same look in threatened horses.

"Jeb Simpkin's barn," he whispered. "One o'clock."

"Okay."

"Was he all right when he left?" Corey asked.

"Who?"

Skeevy kept his face straight while Ellen sputtered beside him, her hand over her mouth. The outsiders were listening.

"Gibson, dammit. How hard did I lay him?"

"Too hard. You used the club, remember?"

"Oh, shit."

"Yeah," said Skeevy as Ellen broke out laughing.

Skeevy took the keys and went to the Coreys' truck. Across the road, children, women, and old people were shuffling to church. Rev. Jackson and the deacon greeted them at the door, shaking hands. Cephus shot Skeevy a crude salute, and Skeevy made the okay sign as he climbed into the cab. He wondered if Cephus could see it.

As the truck rumbled down the blacktop, Skeevy leaned back behind the wheel, letting his eyes sag, and he could feel his belly bouncing with the jolts of the truck. He took the revolver from beneath the seat, and watched the roadside for groundhogs to shoot. Between the diner and Corey's coal-dust driveway he saw nothing.

From the cellar of Corey's house he loaded the truck with pint cases of Jack Daniel's and Old Crow: four-dollar bottles that would sell for eight at the cockfight. When he first came to Clayton, he had hated bourbon. He noticed the flies were out, and in Hurricane they would be crawling quietly on Bund's tongue. He opened a case, took a bottle, and drank off half of it. Before the burning stopped, he was at Simpkin's barn, and could hear the chickens screaming.

Warts Hall, a cockfighter from Clayton, came from the barn with a stranger, catching Skeevy as he finished the pint.

"Got any left?" Warts asked. His face was speckled with small cancers.

"More than you can handle," said Skeevy, throwing back the blanket covering the cases. Warts took out two Crows, handing Skeevy a twenty.

"Kindy high, ain't it?" the stranger asked, seeing the change.

"This here's Benny the Punk from Purserville."

"Just a Pursie?" Skeevy asked.

Benny looked as if to lunge.

"Well," Skeevy continued, "I don't put no price on it."

The Punk pretended to read the label on his bottle.

Gibson came out of the barn and Skeevy sidestepped to the cab where the revolver was hidden.

"Got one for me, Skeev?" Gibson asked.

"Sure," Skeevy answered, moving to the truck bed. "I reckon I forgot my cigarettes."

Gibson offered one from his pack and Skeevy took it, handing the man the bottle and pocketing the cash. He noticed the yellow circle around Gibson's eye and temple where the club had met him. Gibson stood drinking as Skeevy counted cases and pretended to be confused.

"Where's the mick?" Gibson asked.

Skeevy turned back smiling. "Ain't got no idy."

"You see him, you tell him I'm alookin'."

"Sure."

The Punk followed Gibson back into the barn, where the gamecocks were crowing.

A wind was rising, pushing the clouds out of the hollow and high over head. Cally, Jeb's daughter, stood on the high front porch of the farmhouse. Skeevy watched her watching him. He had heard Jeb talk of her at work and knew she had been to college in Huntington; he believed Trudy when she said college girls were all looking for rich boys. He watched her clomp down the steps in chunky wooden shoes, and as she crossed the yard between them, he saw how everything from the curve of her hair to the fit of her jeans was too perfect. She looked like the girls he had seen in *Playboy,* and he knew even if she stood beside him, he couldn't have her.

"Your name's Kelly, isn't it?" Her voice was just like the rest of her.

"Yeah," he said, not wanting to say his first name. He knew she would laugh.

"Mom said you were related to Machine Gun Kelly . . ."

He pulled a case out onto the tailgate as if to unload it, wishing somebody had shot the bastard the day he was born.

"He was a cousin of mine—second or third—ever'body's sort of ashamed of him. I don't know nothin' 'bout him."

"I thought you might know something. I'm doing a paper on him for Psych."

"Say what?"

"A paper for Psychology."

Skeevy wondered if she collected maniacs the way men collect gamecocks. He hoisted the case. "Comin' to the main?" he asked.

"Gross."

"They don't have to fight if they don't want to," he smiled, carrying the case inside. Seeing Cally standing at the door, he went back for another. She followed him slowly on her chunky shoes.

"Where do you live?" Cally asked.

"In the holler 'twixt Purserville an' Clayton."

She looked puzzled. "But there's nothing there."

"Sure," he said, and wondered if she would add him alongside his cousin in her collection.

They watched as Cephus's truck bounced through the creek and climbed, dripping, up to the barn. Cephus rushed in without speaking, and Skeevy left Cally standing as he followed with another case. When he came out, Corey had her cornered.

"Gibson's lookin' for you," he said to Corey.

"Been talkin' 'bout that very thing to Cally, here—"

"All Mr. Gibson wants is to restore his dignity," she interrupted.

"So I thought we'd arrange a little match. Since you got boxin' in your blood, I'd be willin' to let you stand in. Loser pays for the truck—'course I'd be willin' to do that, but I know you won't lose."

"I quit boxin' five years ago," Skeevy said, playing with the chain on the tailgate.

"You're quick, boy. I seen you. Don't even have to box. Just dance Gibson to death," Corey laughed. "'Sides," he said to Cally, "Skeevy loves to scrap."

She giggled.

"Hell, scrappin's different. This here's business."

Cally giggled again.

He looked to the pasture field where wind-pushed clouds were blinking the sun on and off. He spotted a holly tree half-way up the slope. His mother had always liked holly trees. He had never told anybody about his promise to her; he knew they would laugh.

"Two-huntert bucks," he heard himself say.

Corey's eyes grew white rims, but they receded quickly. "Half profit on the booze," he bartered.

"Take it or leave it," Skeevy said, watching Cally smile.

"All right," Corey said. "Cally, you talk good to Jim. Get him to agree on Saturday."

Watching her walk into the barn, Skeevy knew Cally could probably make Jim forget the whole thing. But he was glad for the fight, and began starving for wild meat.

"Where's lunch?" he asked Corey.

In the pit, two light clarets rose in flapping pirouettes. Skeevy neither watched nor bet: newly trained cocks had no form and spent most of their time staying clear of one another.

"Lay off," Cephus yelled. "Ain't no need to make no bird fight. Break for a drink."

For ten minutes, Skeevy and Corey were run ragged handing out bottles and making change. Suddenly there were no more takers, and they still had half a truckload.

"The Pursies ain't buyin' from me after last night," Corey whispered. They loaded all but a half-case into the truck, and Corey took it back to his house.

Leaving the half-case unguarded, Skeevy walked to the pit to examine Warts's bird, a black leghorn with his comb trimmed back to a strawberry. Warts had entered him in the main against a black-breasted red gamer. Skeevy watched as the men fixed two-inch gaffs to the birds' spurs. The Punk stood by him, cleaning his nails with a barlow knife.

"What you want laid up, Benny?"

"Give you eight-to-ten on the red," he said, his knife searching to the quick for a piece of dust.

"Make it," said Skeevy. They placed their money on the ground between them, watching as the two owners touched the birds together, then drew them back eight feet from center.

"Pit!" Cephus yelled, and the cocks strutted toward each other, suddenly meeting in a cloud of feathers.

Warts's rooster backed off, blood gleaming from a gaff mark beneath his right wing.

"Give me—" But before the bettor could finish, the two birds were spurring in midair, then the gamecock lay pinned by the leghorn's gaff.

"Handle!" said the judge, but neither owner moved; they were waiting to hear new odds.

"Dammit, I said 'handle,'" Cephus groaned. The birds were wrung together until they pecked, then set free.

"Even odds," someone shouted. Benny leaned forward for the money, and Skeevy stepped on his hand.

"Get off!"

"Leave it there."

"You heard. It's even."

"You made a bet, Punk. Stick it out or get out."

The Punk left the money.

The birds spun wildly, and again the leghorn came down on the red, his gaff buried in the gamer's back.

"Handle." Cephus was getting bored.

The red's owner, a C&O man from Purserville, poured water on his bird's beak, and blew down its mouth to force air past the clotting blood.

"He's just a Pursie chicken," Skeevy grinned. Benny threw him a cross look.

Warts rubbed his bird to the gamer but got no response.

"Ain't got no fight left," Cephus grumbled.

"Don't quit my bird," the C&O man shouted, his hands and shirt speckled with blood.

"If I's as give out as that rooster, I'd need a headstone. Break for a drink."

"Pleasure," Skeevy said to Benny as he picked up his money and returned to the half-case. After selling all but the two bottles in his hip pockets, Skeevy started out the door to look for Cally. Gibson stopped him, smiling.

"I'll make you fight like hell," he warned.

"Well," said Skeevy, "anytime you get to feelin' froggy, just hop on over to your Uncle Skeevy."

"See you Saturday," Gibson laughed.

Outside, he looked for Cally, but she was not around. He went down the farm road, across the blacktop, and up the hills toward his shack. When he topped the first hill, he could see rain coming in from Ohio; and looking back on the tiny people he had left behind, he could see Benny standing with Cally. He wondered if Benny would have to clean his nails again.

Trudy's silence was building as he poured another bourbon and wondered why he gave a good goddamn. When he switched on the light, he disturbed the rest of a hairy winter-fly. He watched it beat against the screen, trying to get to another fly somewhere to breed and die.

"It ain't like I'm boxin' Joe Frazier . . ." He watched her cook and could not recall when she had cared so much about her cooking. "You done tastin' them beans, or you just run outa plates?"

She granted a halted laugh, turned and saw him grinning, and broke into a laughing fit.

"I swan, you made me so mad . . ." she snorted, sitting.

"Ain't nothin' to get mad over."

"Ain't your fight, neither."

"Two-huntert bucks makes it pretty close." He had meant to keep quiet and send the money to Bund. For a moment he saw her eyes open then sag again, and he knew she was worried about the hospital bills. He went back to watching the fly.

Outside the rain fell harder, making petals in the mud. He saw his ghost in the window against the outside's grayness and felt his gut rumble with the flux. Lightly, he touched the scar above his eye, watching as his reflection did the same.

He got up, opened the screen, and let the black fly buzz out into the rain. When he saw the deep holes the drops were making, he wondered if the fly would make it.

"Why don't winter-flies eat?" he asked Trudy.

"I figger they do," she said from the stove.

"Never do," he said, going to the sink to wash.

Taped to the wall was a snapshot of a younger self looking mean over eight-ounce gloves. That was good shape, he thought, fingering the picture. Because it was stained with fat-grease, he left it up.

Trudy put supper down, and they sat.

"You reckon that money would do for a weddin'?" she asked.

"Maybe," he said. "We'll think on it."

They ate.

"Did I ever tell you 'bout the time me an' Bund wrecked the Sunflower Inn?"

"Yeah."

"Oh."

In the stainless steel of the soup machine, Skeevy could see his distorted reflection—real enough to show his features, but not the scar above his eye. His mouth and nose were stuffed with bits of torn rags for padding, and breathing through his mouth made his throat dry.

"Too tight?" Corey asked as he held the bandages wrapped around Skeevy's knuckles. Skeevy shook his head and splayed his fingers to receive the gray muleskin work gloves. He twisted his face to show disgust, and sighed.

"Well, you're the damn boxer," Corey said. "Where's your gloves?"

Skeevy made a zipping motion across his lips and stuck out his right hand to be gloved. He knew it would hurt to get hit with those gloves, but he knew Gibson would hurt more.

A crowd had formed around Corey's truck, and he had Ellen out there to guard it. She was leaning against the rear fender, talking to a longhair with a camera around his neck. Cally came out of the crowd, put her arm around the longhair, and said something that made Ellen laugh. Skeevy squeezed the gloves tighter around his knuckles.

When Skeevy and Corey came outside the crowd howled with praise and curses; the longhair took a picture of Skeevy, and Skeevy wanted to kill him. They cornered the diner and skidded down the embankment to the newly mown creek-basin. The sun was only a light brown spot in the dusty sky.

Jim Gibson stood naked to the waist, his belly pooching around his belt, his skin so white Skeevy wondered if the man had ever gone shirtless. He grinned at Skeevy, and Skeevy slapped his right fist into his palm and smiled back.

It was nothing like the real fight: Cephus rang a cowbell, Gibson threw one haymaker after another, the entire crowd cursed Skeevy's footwork.

"Quit runnin', chickenshit," someone in the crowd yelled.

In his mind the three minutes were up, but nobody told Cephus to ring the bell. Six minutes, and he knew there would be no bell. Gibson connected to the head. And again. Cheers.

Skeevy tried to go low for the sagging belly, made heavy contact twice, but was disappointed to see the results. He danced some more, dodging haymakers, knowing Gibson could only strike thin air a number of times before weakening. When he saw the time come, he sighted on the man's bruised temple, caught it with a left hook, and dropped him. Then came the bell.

Skeevy felt a stinging in his eye and knew it was blood, but this was nothing like the real fight. This was crazy—Gibson wanted to kill him. Gotta slow him, he thought. Gotta stop him before he kills me.

Cephus rang the bell. Can't believe that goddamned bell, he thought. What the hell is this? Can't see shit. Chest. Wind him. He sighted on the soft concave of Gibson's chest and moved in.

As he threw a right cross to Gibson's chest, Skeevy felt the fine bones of his jaw shatter and tasted blood. Gibson did not fall, and Skeevy danced with the flagging pain. He went again with a combination to the temple. He wanted to tear the eye out and step on it, to feel its pressure building under his foot . . . pop.

As he went down he could hear Trudy screaming his name above the cheers. He lay for a time on the cold floor of the Sunflower Inn: the jukebox played, and he heard Bund coughing.

He rolled to his side.

Cephus threw water on Skeevy, and he spat out the bitten-off tip of his tongue. Gibson waited as Skeevy raised himself to a squat. His head cleared, and he knew he could get up.

THE HONORED DEAD

....

WATCHING LITTLE Lundy go back to sleep, I wish I hadn't told her about the Mound Builders to stop her crying, but I didn't know she would see their eyes watching her in the dark. She was crying about a cat run down by a car—her cat, run down a year ago, only today poor Lundy figured it out. Lundy is turned too much like her momma. Ellen never worries because it takes her too long to catch the point of a thing, and Ellen doesn't have any problem sleeping. I think my folks were a little too keen, but Lundy is her momma's girl, not jumpy like my folks.

My grandfather always laid keenness on his Shawnee blood, his half-breed mother, but then he was hep on blood. He even had an oath to stop bleeding, but I don't remember the words. He was a fair to sharp woodsman, and we all tried to slip up on him at one time or another. It was Ray at the sugar mill finally caught him, but he was an old man by then, and his mind wasn't exactly right. Ray just came creeping up behind and laid a hand on his shoulder, and the old bird didn't even turn around; he just wagged his head and said, "That's Ray's hand. He's the first fellow ever slipped up on me." Ray could've done without that, because the old man never played with a full deck again, and we couldn't keep clothes on him before he died.

I turn out the lamp, see no eyes in Lundy's room, then it comes to me why she was so scared. Yesterday I told her patches of stories about scalpings and murders, mixed up the Mound Builders with the Shawnee raids, and Lundy chained that with the burial mound in the back pasture. Tomorrow I'll set her straight. The only surefire thing I know about Mound Builders is they must have believed in a God and hereafter or they never would have made such big graves.

I put on my jacket, go into the foggy night, walk toward town. Another hour till dawn, and both lanes of the Pike are empty, so I walk the yellow line running through the valley to Rock Camp. I keep thinking back to the summer me and my buddy Eddie tore that burial mound apart for arrowheads and copper beads gone green with rot. We were getting down to the good stuff, coming up with skulls galore, when of a sudden Grandad showed out of thin air and yelled, "*Wah-pah-nah-te-he.*" He was waving his arms around, and I could see Eddie was about to shit the nest. I knew it was all part of the old man's Injun act, so I stayed put, but Eddie sat down like he was ready to surrender.

Grandad kept on: "*Wah-pah-nah-te-he.* You evil. Make bad medicine here. Now put the goddamned bones back or I'll take a switch to your young asses." He watched us bury the bones, then scratched a picture of a man in the dust, a bow drawn, aimed at a crude sun. "Now go home." He walked across the pasture.

Eddie said, "You Red Eagle. Me Black Hawk." I knew he had bought the game for keeps. By then I couldn't tell Eddie that if Grandad had a shot at the sixty-four-dollar question, he would have sold them on those Injun words: *Wah-pah-nah-te-he*—the fat of my ass.

So I walk and try to be like Ellen and count the pass-at-your-own-risk marks on the road. Eastbound tramples Westbound: 26–17. At home is my own darling Ellen, fast asleep, never knowing who won. Sometimes I wonder if Ellen saw Eddie on his last leave. There are lightning bugs in the fog, and I count them until I figure I'm counting the same ones over. For sure, Lundy would call them Mound Builder eyes, and see them as signals without a message, make up her own message, get scared.

I turn off the Pike onto the oxbow of Front Street, walk past some dark store windows, watch myself moving by their gloss, rippling through one pane and another. I sit on the Old Bank steps, wait for the sun to come over the hills; wait like I waited for the bus to the draft physical, only I'm not holding a bar of soap. I sat and held a bar of soap, wondering if I should shove it under my arm to hike my blood pressure into the 4-F range. My blood pressure was already high, but the bar of soap would give me an edge. I look around at Front Street and picture people and places I haven't thought of in years; I wonder if it was that way for Eddie.

I put out my hand like the bar of soap was in it and see its whiteness reflect blue from the streetlights long ago. And I remember Eddie's hand flattened on green felt, arched knuckles cradling the cue for a tough eight-ball shot, or I remember the way his hand curled around his pencil to hide answers on math tests. I remember his hand holding an arrowhead or unscrewing a lug nut, but I can't remember his face.

It was years ago, on Decoration Day, and my father and several other men wore their Ike jackets, and I was in the band. We marched through town to the cemetery in the rain; then I watched the men move sure and stiff with each command, and the timing between volleys was on the nose; the echoes rang four times above the clatter of their bolt weapons. The rain smelled from the tang of their fire, the wet wool of our uniforms. There was a pause and the band director coughed. I stepped up to play, a little off tempo, and another kid across the hills answered my taps. I finished first, snapped my bugle back. When the last tone seeped through to mist, it beat at me, and I could swear I heard the stumps of Eddie's arms beating the coffin lid for us to stop.

I look down at my hand holding the bugle, the bar of soap. I look at my hand, empty, older, tell myself there is no bar of soap in that hand. I count all five fingers with the other hand, tell myself they are going to stay there a hell of a long time. I get out a cigarette and smoke. Out on the Pike, the first car races by in the darkness, knowing no cops are out yet. I think of Eddie pouring on the gas, heading with me down the Pike toward Tin Bridge.

That day was bright, but the blink of all the dome lights showed up far ahead of us. We couldn't keep still for the excitement, couldn't wait to see what happened.

I said, "Did you hear it, man? I thought they'd dropped the Bomb."

"Hear? I felt it. The damn ground shook."

"They won't forget that much noise for a long time."

"For sure."

Cars were stopped dead-center of the road, and a crowd had built up. Eddie pulled off to the side behind a patrol car, then made his way through the crowd, holding his wallet high to show his volunteer fireman's badge. I kept back, but in the break the cops made, I saw the fire was already out, and all that was left of

Beck Fuller's Chevy was the grille, the rest of the metal peeled around it from behind. I knew it was Beck's from the '51 grille, and I knew what had happened. Beck fished with dynamite and primer cord, and he was a real sport to the end. Beck could never get into his head he had to keep the cord away from the TNT.

Then a trooper yelled: "All right, make way for the wrecker."

Eddie and the other firemen put pieces of Beck the Sport into bags, and I turned away to keep from barfing, but the smell of burning hair drifted out to me. I knew it was the stuffing in old car-seats, and not Beck, but I leaned against the patrol car, tossed my cookies just the same. I wanted to stop being sick because it was silly to be sick about something like that. Under the noise of my coughings I could hear the fire chief cussing Eddie into just getting the big pieces, just letting the rest go.

Eddie didn't sit here with any bar of soap in his hand. He never had much gray matter, but he made up for it with style, so he would never sit here with any bar of soap in his hand. Eddie would never think about blowing toes away or cutting off his trigger finger. It just was not his way to think. Eddie was the kind who bought into a game early, and when the deal soured, he'd rather hold the hand a hundred years than fold. It was just his way of doing.

At Eight Ball, I chalked up while Eddie broke. The pool balls cracked, but nothing went in, and I moved around the table to pick the choice shot. "It's crazy to join," I said.

"What the hell—I know how to weld. They'll put me in welding school and I'll sit it out in Norfolk."

"With your luck the ship'll fall on you."

"Come on, Eagle, go in buddies with me."

"Me and Ellen's got plans. I'll take a chance with the lottery."
I shot, and three went in.

"That's slop," Eddie said.

I ran the other four down, banked the eight ball to a side pocket, and stood back, made myself grin at him. The eight went where I called it, but I never believed I made the shot right, and I didn't look at Eddie, I just grinned.

I toss my cigarette into the gutter, and it glows back orange under the blue streetlight. I think how that glow would be just another eye for Lundy, and think that after a while she will see so many eyes in the night they won't matter anymore. The eyes will go away and never come back, and even if I tell her when she is grown, she won't remember. By then real eyes will scare her enough. She's Ellen's girl, and sometimes I want to ask Ellen if she saw Eddie on his last leave.

Time ago I stood with my father in the cool evening shadow of the barn to smoke; he stooped, picked up a handful of gravel, and flipped them away with his thumb. He studied on what I said about Canada, and each gravel falling was a little click in his thoughts; then he stood, dusted his palms. "I didn't mind it too much," he said. "Me and Howard kept pretty thick in foxhole religion—never thought of running off."

"But, Dad, when I seen Eddie in that plastic bag . . ."

He yelled: "Why the hell'd you look? If you can't take it, you oughtn't to look. You think I ain't seen that? That and worse, by god."

I rub my hand across my face, hang my arm tight against the back of my neck, think I ought to be home asleep with Ellen.

I think, if I was asleep with Ellen, I wouldn't care who won. I wouldn't count or want to know what the signals mean, and I wouldn't be like some dog looking for something dead to drag in.

When Eddie was in boot camp, me and Ellen sat naked in the loft at midnight, scratching fleas and the itch of hay. She went snooping through a box of old books and papers, and pulled out a bundle of letters tied with sea-grass string. Her flashlight beamed over my eyes as she stepped back to me, and watching her walk in the color tracings the light left in my eyes, I knew she would be my wife. She tossed the package in my lap, and I saw the old V-mail envelopes of my father's war letters. Ellen lay flat on her back, rested her head on my thigh, and I took up the flashlight to read.

"*Dear folks. We are in*—the name's been cut out."

"Why?" She rolled to her stomach, looked up at me.

I shrugged. "I guess he didn't know he couldn't say that. *The way they do thes people is awful bad. I found a rusky prisoner starven in the street and took him to a german house for a feed.*" I felt Ellen's tongue on the inside of my thigh and shivered, tried to keep reading. "*They didn't do nothin for him till I leveled off with my gun and Howard he raised hell with me only I seen that rusky eat one damn fine meal.*" I turned off the flashlight, moved down beside Ellen. He had never told that story.

But it's not so simple now as then, not easy to be a part of Ellen without knowing or wanting to know the web our kisses make. It was easy to leave the house with a bar of soap in my pocket; only the hardest part was sitting here, looking at it, and remembering.

I went through the hall with the rest of the kids between classes, and there stood Eddie at the top of the stairs. He grinned at me, but it was not his face anymore. His face had changed; a face gone red because the other kids snickered at his uniform. He stood at parade rest, his seaman's cap hanging from his belt, his head tilting back to look down on me, then he dragged his hands around like Jackie Gleason taking an away-we-go pool shot. We moved on down the hall to ditch my books.

"You on leave?" I said.

"Heap bad medicine. Means I'm getting shipped."

"How long?" I fumbled with the combination of my locker.

"Ten days," he said, then squinted at the little upside-down flag on my open locker door. "You sucker."

I watched him until he went out of sight down the steps, then got my books, went on to class.

The butt of my palm is speckled with black spots deep under the skin: cinders from a relay-race fall. The skin has sealed them over, and it would cost plenty to get them out. Sometimes Ellen wants to play nurse with a needle, wants to pry them out, but I won't let her. Sometimes I want to ask Ellen if she saw Eddie on his last leave.

Coach said I couldn't run track because anyone not behind his country was not fit for a team, so I sat under the covered bridge waiting for the time I could go home. Every car passing over sprinkled a little dust between the boards, sifted it into my hair.

I watched the narrow river roll by, its waters slow but muddy like pictures I had seen of rivers on the TV news. In history class, Coach said the Confederate troops attacked this bridge, took it, but were held by a handful of Sherman's troops on Company

Hill. Johnny Reb drank from this river. The handful had a spring on Company Hill. Johnny croaked with the typhoid and the Yankees moved south. So I stood and brushed the dust off me. My hair grew long after Eddie went over, and I washed it every night.

I put my fist under my arm like the bar of soap and watch the veins on the back of my hand rise with pressure. There are scars where I've barked the hide hooking the disk or the drag to my tractor; they are like my father's scars.

We walked the fields, checked the young cane for blight or bugs, and the late sun gave my father's slick hair a sparkle. He chewed the stem of his pipe, then stood with one leg across a knee and banged tobacco out against his shoe.

I worked up the guts: "You reckon I could go to college, Dad?"

"What's wrong with farming?"

"Well, sir, nothing, if that's all you ever want."

He crossed the cane rows to get me, and my left went up to guard like Eddie taught me, right kept low and to the body.

"Cute," he said. "Real cute. When's your number up?"

I dropped my guard. "When I graduate—it's the only chance I got to stay out."

He loaded his pipe, turned around in his tracks like he was looking for something, then stopped, facing the hills. "It's your damn name is what it is. Dad said when you was born, 'Call him William Haywood, and if he ever goes in a mine, I hope he chokes to death.'"

I thought that was a shitty thing for Grandad to do, but I watched Dad, hoped he'd let me go.

He started up: "Everybody's going to school to be something better. Well, when everybody's going this way, it's time to turn around and go that way, you know?" He motioned with his hands in two directions. "I don't care if they end up shitting gold nuggets. Somebody's got to dig in the damn ground. Somebody's got to."

And I said, "Yessir."

The sky is dark blue and the fog is cold smoke staying low to the ground. In this first hint of light my hand seems blue, but not cold; such gets cold sooner or later, but for now my hand is warm.

Many's the time my grandfather told of the last strike before he quit the mines, moved to the valley for some peace. He would quit his Injun act when he told it, like it was real again, all before him, and pretty soon I started thinking it was *me* the Baldwin bulls were after. *I* ran through the woods till my lungs bled. *I* could hear the Baldwins and their dogs in the dark woods, and *I* could remember machine guns cutting down pickets, and all *I* could think was how the One Big Union was down the rathole. Then I could taste it in my mouth, taste the blood coming up from my lungs, feel the bark of a tree root where I fell, where I slept. When I opened my eyes, I felt funny in the gut, felt watched. There were no twig snaps, just the feeling that something was too close. Knowing it was a man, one man, hunting me, I took up my revolver. I could hear him breathing, aimed into the sound, knowing the only sight would come with the flash. I knew all my life I had lived to kill this man, this goddamned Baldwin man, and I couldn't do it. I heard him move away down the ridge, hunting his lost game.

I fold my arms tight like I did the morning the bus pulled up. I was thinking of my grandfather, and there was a bar of soap under my arm. At the draft physical, my blood pressure was clear out of sight, and they kept me four days. The pressure never went down, and on the fourth day a letter came by forward. I read it on the bus home.

Eddie said he was with a bunch of Jarheads in the Crotch, and he repaired radio gear in the field. He said the USMC's hated him because he was regular Navy. He said the chow was rotten, the quarters lousy, and the left side of his chest was turning yellow from holding smokes inside his shirt at night. And he said he knew how the guy felt when David sent him into the battle to get dibs on the guy's wife. Eddie said he wanted dibs on Ellen, ha, ha. He said he would get married and give me his wife if I would get him out of there. He said the beer came in Schlitz cans, but he was sure it was something else. Eddie was sure the CO was a fag. He said he would like to get Ellen naked, but if he stayed with this outfit he would want to get me naked when he came back. He asked if I remembered him teaching me to burn off leeches with a cigarette. Eddie swore he learned that in a movie where the hero dies because he ran out of cigarettes. He said he had plenty of cigarettes. He said he could never go Oriental because they don't have any hair on their twats, and he bet me he knew what color Ellen's bush was. He said her hair might be brown, but her bush was red. He said to think about it and say Hi to Ellen for him until he came back. Sometimes I want to ask Ellen if she saw Eddie on his last leave.

When I came back, Ellen met me at the trailer door, hugged me, and started to cry. She showed pretty well with Lundy, and

I told her Eddie's letter said to say Hi. She cried some more, and I knew Eddie was not coming back.

Daylight fires the ridges green, shifts the colors of the fog, touches the brick streets of Rock Camp with a reddish tone. The streetlights flicker out, and the traffic signal at the far end of Front Street's yoke snaps on; stopping nothing, warning nothing, rushing nothing on.

I stand and my joints crack from sitting too long, but the flesh of my face is warming in the early sun. I climb the steps of the Old Bank, draw a spook in the window soap. I tell myself that spook is Eddie's, and I wipe it off with my sleeve, then I see the bus coming down the Pike, tearing the morning, and I start down the street so he won't stop for me. I cannot go away, and I cannot make Eddie go away, so I go home. And walking down the street as the bus goes by, I bet myself a million that my Lundy is up and already watching cartoons, and I bet I know who won.

THE WAY IT HAS TO BE
•••••••••••••••••••

ALENA STEPPED under the awning of the Tastee Freeze and looked out at the rain draining into the dust, splattering craters with little clouds. When it stopped, cars hissed along the highway in whorls of mist. She stood by the slotted window, peering through the dirty glass to empty freezers and sills speckled with the crisp skeletons of flies. Far down the parking lot stood a phone booth, but as she stirred circles in the bottle caps and gravel, she knew she could not call home.

She sat on a lip of step by the porcelain drinking fountain and watched Harvey's head lolling against the car window, his holster straps arching slack above his shoulders. She felt her stomach twitch, and tried to rub her eyes without smearing. She didn't want it this way, but knew Harvey would never change. She laughed a little; she had only come from West Virginia to see the cowboys, but all this range was farmed and fenced. The openness freed and frightened her.

Harvey jostled, rolled down the window. There was a white dust of drool on his chin. "Wanna drive?" he said.

She started toward the car. "All last night I worried. Momma's cannin' stuff today."

"Lay off," he said. "You gotta right to get out." He tightened his holster and pulled on his jacket.

"You love that thing?"

"He's got it comin'."

"Parole catches you, you got lots more."

"Lay off, it's too early," he said, reaching for a cigarette.

While she drove, Alena saw the haze lift, but not like a dew. Instead, it left a dust film and far ahead there was always more haze. As they skirted Oklahoma City, it thickened, and the heat stuck to their skin. She pulled off at a hamburger stand and Harvey got out while she looked at the map. In a side panel, a picture of the Cowboy Hall of Fame called her away from the route. Harvey came back with a bag of sandwiches and coffee.

"Harv, let's go here," she said, offering the picture.

He looked, then grabbed her thigh just below the crotch and kissed her. "There'll be plenty of time after this."

As they ate, Harvey took a slip of paper from his shirt pocket and checked the map. He stared at the dashboard for a long time, thinking. Alena watched his brow draw tight, but she could not ask him to give it up. She hoped Harvey was not dumb enough to kill him.

Harvey took the wheel and they drove down a small secondary toward a farm. Alena watched the land slip by, growing flatter, longer in the new heat. Always the steady haze hid the horizon, and she wished she would see a cowboy.

The stairwell was empty, quiet, yet Alena's nerves twisted again as she looked at Harvey. He walked uneasily and his eyes were crossed from the whiskey. Two flights up and they opened their door. The room was small and old-fashioned, and opened to the street, where the dust storm turned the streetlights yellow. Harvey took off his jacket, opened his satchel and got out the whiskey. He was shaking, and his gun flapped loosely in its holster.

"Jesus, Harvey," she said, sitting on the bed.

"Will you shut up?"

She could still see it: the man reached out to shake and Harvey handed him three in the chest. "I'm afraid," she said, and could not forget the old woman sitting on the porch, stringing beans. Alena wondered if she still sat there, her mouth open, her son dead in the yard.

"Have a drink," Harvey said. He had stopped shaking.

"I'm gonna barf."

"Barf then, dammit." He rubbed his neck hard.

She stood by the sink and looked into the drain, but nothing would come up. "What're we gonna do?"

"Stay here," he said, finishing the pint, looking for another.

"I'm sorry I'm scared," she said, and turned on the water to wash her face.

"Lay down," Harvey said, standing by the window.

Alena sat in the chair by the sink, watching Harvey. His pint half gone, he leaned against the window casement. Not the man she knew in the hills, he looked skinny and meaner to her, and now she knew he was a murderer, that the gun he always carried had worked. She was not part of him now; it was over so easily she wondered if they had ever loved.

"We'll go to Mexico and get married," he said.

"I can't, I'm too scared."

Harvey turned toward her, the yellow light of the street glowing against his face and chest.

"The whole time I was in," he said, "I waited for two things: to kill him, and to marry you."

"I can't, Harvey. I didn't know."

"What? That I love you?"

"No, the other. I thought it was talk."

"I don't talk," he said, and took a drink.

"God, I wish you hadn't."

"Whadaya want? To be back in the hills?"

"Yes, I don't want this anymore. I hate this."

He pulled his gun and pointed it at her. She sat, looking at him, his eyes wide with fear, and she leaned over the chair and threw up a stream of yellow bile. When she stopped coughing and wiped her chin, Harvey sat slumped in the corner, the pistol dangling in his hand.

"You goddamned bitch," he muttered. "Now I need you and you're a goddamned bitch." He lifted the pistol to his temple, but Alena saw him smile. A puff of air came from his lips, and he put the gun in its holster.

"I'm gonna get drunk," he said, standing up. "You suit yourself. I'm not comin' back." Down the hall, she could hear him bumping against the walls.

Alena washed herself, then turned on the light. Her eyes were circled and red, her lips chapped. She put on makeup and went out.

As she walked down the street, the dust blew papers against her ankles, and she went into a café with a Help Wanted sign. The girl behind the counter looked bored when Alena ordered a beer.

"You need help?"

"Not now, only in the morning. Come in the morning and ask for Pete. He'll probably put you on."

"Thanks," she said, and sipped.

In the back was a phone booth, and Alena carried her beer to it. She made the call, and the phone rang twice.

"Hello, Momma."

"Alena," her voice trembled.

"I'm in Texas, Momma. I come with Harvey."

"Stringin' round with trash. We spoiled you rotten, that's what we done."

"I just didn't want you all to worry."

There was a long quiet. "Come on back, Alena."

"I can't, Momma. I got a job. Ain't that great?"

"Top shelf in the cupboard fell down and made a awful mess. I been worried it's a token."

"No, Momma, it's all right, you hear? I got a job."

"All that jelly we put up is busted."

"It's all right, Momma, you got a bunch left."

"I reckon."

"I gotta go, Momma. I love you."

The phone clicked.

The night calmed, and most of the dust settled in eddies by the curb. As she walked along to the hotel, Alena felt better. Harvey was gone, but it didn't matter. She had a job, and she was in Texas.

As she passed through the lobby of the hotel, the clerk smiled at her, and she liked it. But on the landing to the room, Harvey waited. Cigarette butts were all around his feet, and he was rumpled, cripple-looking.

"I come back to apologize," he said, standing to hold her. She fell against him.

"Nothin's changed," she said. "I'm stayin' here."

"That's it?"

She nodded. "I got a job, so I called home. Everything's okay."

"Can we talk upstairs?"

"Sure," she said.

"Then let's talk," and his hand brushed against the revolver as he reached for another cigarette.

THE SALVATION OF ME

••••••••••••••••••••

CHESTER WAS smarter than any shithouse mouse because Chester got out before the shit began to fall. But Chester had two problems: number one, he became a success, and number two, he came back. These are not your average American problems like drinking, doping, fucking, or being fucked, because Rock Camp, West Virginia, is not your average American problem maker, nor is it your average hillbilly town.

You have never broken a mirror or walked under ladders or celebrated Saint Paddy's day if you have never heard of Rock Camp, but you might have lost a wheel, fallen off a biplane wing, or crossed yourself left-handedly if you have. The three latter methods are the best ways to get into Rock Camp, and any viable escape is unknown to anybody but Chester, and he is unavailable for comment.

It was while Archie Moore—the governor, not the fighter—was in his heyday that the sweet tit of the yellow rose of Texas ran dry, forcing millions of Americans down to the survival speed of 55 mph. I have heard it said that Georgians are unable to drive in snow, and that Arizonans go bonkers behind the wheel in the rain, but no true-blooded West Virginia boy would ever do less than 120 mph on a straight stretch, because those runs are hard won in a land where road maps resemble a barrel of worms with Saint Vitus' dance. It was during this time that Chester discovered people beating it through West Virginia via Interstate 64 on their way to more interesting places like Ohio and Iowa, and for the first time in his life Chester found fourth gear in his Chevy with the Pontiac engine. Don't ask me what the transmission was, because I was sick the day they put it in, and don't ask me where Chester went, because I didn't see him again for four years, and then he wasn't talking.

All I know for sure is that Chester made it big, and came back to show it off, and that I never hated him more in the years he was gone than I did the two hours he was home. The fact that without Chester I had twice as many cars to fix, half as much gas to pump, and nobody to road-race or play chicken with on weekends made up for itself in giving me all my own cigarettes, since Chester was the only bum in the station. And his leaving warmed over an old dream.

Back in '61 when I was a school kid, everybody from one end of Rock Camp to the other switched over from radio to TV, and although I still believe that was a vote purchase on Kennedy's part, everyone swears it was a benefit of working in the pre-Great Society days. So the old Hallicrafters radio found its place next to my desk and bed, looking at me, as it later did through hours of biology homework, like any minute the Day of Infamy would come out of its speakers again.

What did come out, and only between the dusk and dawn, was WLS from Chicago. Chicago became a dream, then more of a habit than pubescent self-abuse, replaced beating off, then finally did what the health teacher said pounding the pud would do—made me crazy as a damn loon.

Chicago, Chicago, that toddlin' town . . .

Don't ask me to sing the rest, because I have forgotten it, and don't ask me what became of the dream, either, because I have a sneaking suspicion Chester did it in for me when he came back. But the dream was more beautiful than the one about Mrs. Dent, my sex-goddess math teacher, raping hell out of me during a tutoring session, and the dream was more fun because I believed it could happen. When I asked Mr. Dent, the gym teacher, if the angle of his dangle was equal to the heat of her meat, he rammed my head into a locker, and I swore forever to keep my hand out of my Fruit of the Looms. Besides, Chicago had it over Mrs. Dent by a mile, and Chicago had more Mrs. Dents than could rape me in a million years.

Dex Card, the then-night jock for 'LS, had a Batman fan club that even *I* could belong to, and the kids in Chicago all had cars, wore h.i.s. slacks—baked by the friendly h.i.s. baker in his own little oven so the crease would never wash out. They all chewed Wrigley gum, and all went to the Wrigley Building, which for some reason seems, even today, like a giant pack of Juicy Fruit on end. The kids in Chicago were so close to Motown they could drive up and *see* Gladys Knight or the Supremes walking on the goddamned street. And the kids in Chicago had three different temperatures: if it was cold at O'Hare Airport, it was colder in the Loop, and it was always below zero on the El. It took me ten years to get the joke. It took us two days to get the weather—if it rained in Chicago on Monday, I wore a raincoat on Wednesday, and thought of it as Chicago rain.

After the dream came the habit. I decided to run off to Chicago, but hadn't figured what I could do to stay alive, and I didn't know Soul One in the town. But the guys on 'LS radio sounded like decent sorts, and they had a real warmth you could just hear when they did those Save the Children ads. You knew those guys would be the kind to give a poor kid a break. And that is where the habit and the dream got all mixed up.

I would maybe take the train—since that was the only way I knew to get out, from my father's Depression stories—and I might even meet A-Number-One on some hard-luck flatcar, and him tracing old dreams on the car floor with a burned-out cigarette. Then me and old A-Number-One would take the Rock Island out of Kentucky, riding nonstop coal into the Chicago yards, and A-Number-One would tell about whole trains getting swallowed up, lost, bums and all, in the vastness of everything, never found. But I would make it off the car before she beat into the yards, skirt the stink on that side, and there I was at the Loop.

I would find WLS Studios and ask for a job application, and the receptionist, sexier than Mrs. Dent and a single to boot, would ask me what I could do. I would be dirty from the train, and my clothes would not be h.i.s., so what could I say but that I would like to sweep up. Bingo, and they hire me because nobody in Chicago ever wants to sweep up, and when I get down to scrape the Wrigley's off the floor, they think I'm the best worker in the world. I figure I'd better mop, and Dex Card says I'm too smart to mop and for me to take this sawbuck, go buy me some h.i.s. clothes and show up here tomorrow. He says he wants me to be the day jock, and he will teach me to run the board, make echoes, spin the hits, double-up the sound effects, and switch to the news-weather-and-sports. Hot damn.

So I sat at the desk every night, learning less biology, dreaming the dream over and over, until one night I looked at my respectable—nevertheless Woolworth—slacks, and realized that the freight trains no longer slowed down at Rock Camp. There was always the bus, but in all three times I collected enough pop bottles for a ticket to where the train slowed down, the pool balls would break in my ears, and quarters would slip away into slots of time and chance.

"You can't see the angles," Chester said to me one day after he ran the table in less than a minute.

I was in the tenth grade and didn't give two shits for his advice. All I knew was all my quarters were gone, there were no more pop bottles along the Pike, and Chicago was still a thousand miles away. I just leaned on my stick: I was sheared and I knew it.

"You know anything about cars?" I shook my head no. "Can you work a gas pump?" Again no. "You *can* wash a car." I sneered a who-the-hell-couldn't.

And from that day I went to work for E. B. "Pop" Sullivan in his American Oil station at seventy-five cents an hour, one-third of which went to Chester for getting me the job. I told myself it didn't matter, I wasn't going to make a career of it, I was hitting it for Chicago as soon as I got the money—I'd ride the buses all the way, I'd drive. What the hell, I'd save up and buy a car to take me to Chicago in style.

When I told Chester I wanted to buy a car, he let me off the hook for his fee, even took me to look at the traps on the car lot. Then I told Chester I didn't want a trap, I wanted a real car.

"That's the way you get a real one," he said. "You make it to suit yourself—Motown just makes them to break down."

We looked at a Pontiac with only 38,000 and a 327. Somebody had lamed in the rear and pushed the trunk into the back seat. There was a clump of hair hanging from the chrome piece around the window. Chester crawled under this car and was gone for almost five minutes, while I was more attracted to a

Chevy Impala with a new paint job and a backyard, install-it-yourself convertible top that came down of its own when you pressed a button. Chester came out from under the Pontiac like he had found a snake, then walked over to me grinning.

"She's totaled to hell and back, but the engine's perfect."

I told Chester I liked the Impala, but he just sucked his teeth like he knew what happened to tops that come down of their own. He walked all around the car, bent over to look under it, rubbed his fingers along the tread of the tires, and all the time I kept staring at the $325 soaped on the windshield. Sure, the Pontiac was cheaper, but who wanted to pay $130 to walk around with an engine under his arm? Not me, I wanted to drive it away, make the top go up and down.

"Tell you what," he said. "I got me a nice Chevy for that Pontiac's motor. You buy the motor—I'll rent the body to you."

I wasn't about to bite, so I shook my head.

"We'll be partners, then. We'll each only sell out to the other, and we'll stick together on weekends. You know, double dates."

That made a little more sense, and the rest of that month the Chicago dream went humming away to hide someplace in my brain. I had nightmares about adapters being stretched out to fit an engine that shouldn't be in a Chevy. I worried about tapping too far from the solid part of the block, could just see cast steel splintering the first time we forced her up to 80. I went to drag races, asked anybody I saw if you could put a Pony engine in a Chevy, and most people laughed, but one smart-ass leaned back in his chair: "Son," says the smart-ass, "go play with yourself."

But the month went by, and the engine, for some reason I never understood, went in, but all the fire wall and all the fender wells came out. When Chester came down to the transmission problem, I came down with the flu, and for three days I neither dreamed of Chicago nor my car because I was too busy being sick. On returning to school, I saw her in the parking lot, the rear end jacked up with shackles, and when I looked in on the gearshift, Chester had a four-speed pattern knob screwed on it. I thought it was a joke, because I never saw the last gear used. She did 50 wound tight in third, and that was enough for the straight piece in the Pike.

That summer was just one big time. Chester and I spent every cent we earned on gas and every free minute on the back roads. We discovered a bridge with enough hump that hitting it at 45 would send us airborne every time and make the buggy rock like a chair until we could get new shocks on it. Unbeknownst to him, Pop Sullivan supplied shocks all summer. We found a curved section of one-lane that was almost always good for a near head-on with a Pepsi truck. A couple of times, Pop supplied red-lead to disguise the fact that we had gotten too close to the Pepsi truck. Pepsi, I take it, got the message and rerouted the driver. Chester told me, "They sent a boy to do a man's job."

But the best fun came when a Cabell County deputy was on his way to summons some ridge runner to court for not sharing his liquor revenues with the state. Deputy met us coming downhill and around a curve at top speed, and there was little else for Deputy to do but give us the right-of-way or kiss all our sweet asses good-bye. Deputy was a very wise man. Figuring that anybody coming from nowhere that fast had something to hide, Deputy then radioed ahead the liquor was in our car. They nabbed us at the foot of the hill, stone-cold sober, and found us holding no booze at all. What they did find were Deputy's two daughters—both out with their momma's permission. Chester got three days for driving away from a deputy, and neither of us was allowed to call the girls again. Don't ask me what their momma got, as I am not sure if Deputy was the wife-beating kind or not.

Chester served his three days in Sundays reading the paper at the county jail, and the first Sunday changed him considerably for the worse. At work the next day he wouldn't talk about who he wanted to go out with or where we were going to find money for the next tankful, but by the weekend he loosened up. "It's all a matter of chance," he said. I thought he was trying to explain his jail sentence. It took four years before I figured it out. After his second Sunday, he came back with a sneak in his eyes like he was just waiting for something to drop on his back out of thin air. "It's out there for sure, but it's just a matter of being in the right place when the shit falls." I agreed all the way. It was all in Chicago, and school was starting and I was still in Rock Camp.

The next morning, Chester went on the lam in a most interesting manner. It was his turn to cruise around town in the car during lunch, smooching his woman, and I would get snatch for my grab on the high-school steps. We had both been caught getting too fresh with our girls, and now there was not a decent girl in Rock Camp that wouldn't claim one of us raped her after her football boyfriend knocked her up. So it was that Chester's main squeeze was a girl from Little Tokyo Hollow, where twice-is-nice-but-incest-is-best and all the kids look like gooks. So it was I had no woman that day. And Chester was making the main circuit with regular rounds so that from where I sat, I could see every move this slant-eye made.

The first three go-arounds were pretty standard, and I could almost measure the distance her hand had moved on the way to

Chester's crotch, but on the fourth trip she had him wide and was working the mojo. I knew Chester had done some slick bargaining to get that much action that soon, and I figured it was over from there, since I saw him turn around and head west back to the school. He was still only cruising, taking his time like he knew the bell would never ring unless he had gone to his locker. Then on the way by, I saw the slant-eye going down on him, her head bobbing like mad, Chester smiling, goosing the gas in short spurts. It wasn't until he stopped at the town limits and put the girl out that I figured Chester didn't care about coming back to class, but I went on anyway, sure as I could be that he'd be back tomorrow.

That afternoon the guidance counselor called me in and asked me what I was doing with the rest of my life. It seemed Chester's slant-eye had spilled the beans, and they were thinking there was something in me they could save. I told the guidance counselor I wanted to work for a radio station in Chicago—just as a joke.

"Well, you'll have to go to college for that, you know."

It was news to me, because Dex Card didn't sound like a teacher or a doctor, and I said no.

That evening, when Chester didn't show for work, I asked Pop Sullivan to sponsor me through college. I promised to stay at the station until I got my journalism degree, then send him the difference.

"I got all the difference I need" was all Pop would say. He kept looking out the window for Chester to come fix his share of cars. Chester never came, so I stayed until the next morning and figured out how to fix both our shares of cars with a book, and I thought maybe that was the way Chester had done it all along.

A week later, Pop hired another kid to pump gas and raised me to minimum wage, which by Archie's heyday was about a buck fifty. That was when I got a telegram from Cleveland saying: "Sorry Pard, I got it into fourth and couldn't get it out. I'll make it up sometime, C."—and I wondered why Chester bothered to waste four cents on the "Pard."

I left the radio off and my grades went up a little, but I didn't think I'd learned much worth knowing. The guidance counselor kept this shit-eating grin for when she passed me in the hall. Then weird stuff started happening—like my old man would come to bed sober at night and go to church twice on Sunday and drink orange juice at breakfast without pitching a bitch at me. And I got invited to parties the football players' parents threw for them and their girls, but I never went. Then a teacher told me if I made a B in World History before Christmas I would be a cinch for the Honor Society, but I told that teacher in no uncertain terms what the Honor Society could go do with themselves, and the teacher said I was a smart-ass. I agreed. I still got the B. I started dating Deputy's youngest daughter again, and he acted like I was a quarterback.

Then the real shit came down. It was snowing tons before Christmas, so I cut school to help Pop clear the passage around the pumps, and he called the principal to tell him what was up. I was salting the sidewalks when Pop yelled at me to come inside, then he loaded his pipe and sat down behind the desk.

"What'd I tell you about stealing?" he says, but I set him straight that I wasn't holding anything of his. "I don't mean you are, only I want to know if you remember." I told him that he had said once-a-thief-always-a-thief about a million times. "Do you think that's so?" I asked him if he'd stolen before. "Just once, but

I put it back." I told him once-a-thief-always-a-thief, but he just laughed. "You need a college sponsor. I need another Catholic in this town." I assured Pop that my old man had suddenly seen the light, but I was in no way, shape, or form walking his path with him, and he was Methodist to boot. "You think about it." I said I would think about it and went in to grease a car. All I could think was, Dex Card doesn't sound like a Catholic name.

I walked home in the snow that night, and it did not seem like Chicago snow—it seemed like I was a kid before the radio moved into my room, and like when I got home from sledding and my old lady was still alive, still pumping coffee into me to cut the chill, and I missed her just a little.

I went inside hoping my old man would have a beer in his hand just so I could put things back to normal again, but he was sitting in the kitchen reading a newspaper, and he was stoned sober out of his mind.

I fixed us some supper, and while we ate he asked me if Pop had said anything to me about college. I said he would sponsor me if I turned mackerel-snapper. "Not a bad deal. You going to take it?" I assured him I was thinking on it. "There's mail for you," and he handed me an envelope postmarked Des Moines, Iowa. Inside was seventy-five bucks and a scrap of paper that said: "Less depreciation. *Adios*, C." I put the money in my wallet and balled up the note. "You can buy some clothes with that wad," he said. I assured my old man that I would need a car more if I was to drive to college every day, but he just laughed, gave me a dutch rub from across the table. He told me I was a good kid for a punk. Even the women in the school cafeteria sent me a card saying I was bound to become a man of letters—on the inside was a cartoon mailman. It took me a while to get the joke.

And about that time the price of gas went up. I bought a '58 VW without a floor, drove it that way until it rained, then bought a floor for more than I paid for the whole car. Deputy's daughter missed a couple of months and decided it was me, and it probably was, so she joined me in catechism and classes at the community college in Huntington, and we lived in a three-room above Pop's station. The minute Deputy's daughter lost the kid, Deputy had the whole thing annulled, and Pop made me move back in with my old man. My old man started drinking again. I quit school, but stayed on at Pop Sullivan's garage to pay him back, and it was about then that I saw the time had gone by too soon. I had not turned the old radio on in all these years and I couldn't stand to now. I decided working for Pop wasn't too bad, and pretty soon my old man was going to have to be put away, and I'd need the money for that.

I drove home in the VW singing, "*Chicago, Chicago, that toddlin' town . . .*" and that was when I knew I had forgotten the rest of the words.

Then I saw it coming down the Pike, just a glimpse of metallic blue, a blur with yellow fog-lights that passed in the dusk, and the driver's face was Chester's. I wheeled the bug around, headed back into town, wound the gears tight to gain some speed, but he was too far gone to catch up with. I cruised town for an hour before I saw him barreling down the Pike again, and this time I saw the blond in his car. When they pulled in on Front Street to get a bite at the café, I wheeled up beside the new Camaro. I had seen that girl of his lick her teeth in toothpaste ads on TV.

I asked Chester how it was going, but he forgot to know me: "Beg pardon?" I saw all his teeth were capped, but I told him who I was. "Oh, yes," he said. I asked him where he got the mean machine, and his girl looked at me funny, smiled to herself. "It's a rental." His girl broke out laughing, but I didn't get the joke. I told Chester he ought to go by and say hello to Pop on the way out. "Yes, yes, well, I will." I invited them out to eat with me and my old man, but Chester got a case of rabbit. "Perhaps another time. Nice to see you again." He slammed the car door, went into the café ahead of his girl.

I sat there in the VW, stared at the grease on my jeans, thought I ought to go in there and shove a couple of perhaps-another-times down Chester's shit-sucking face. Don't ask me why I didn't do it, because it was what I wanted most to do all my life, and don't ask me where the dream went, because it never hummed to me again.

When Chester left town, he left a germ. Not the kind of germ you think makes a plant grow, but a disease, a virus, a contagion. Chester sowed them in the café when Deputy recognized him, asked what he'd been doing with himself. Chester told Deputy he was on Broadway, and gave away free tickets to the show he was in, and a whole slough of people went up to New York. They all came back humming show songs. And the germ spread all over Rock Camp, made any kid on the high-school stage think he could be Chester. A couple of the first ones killed themselves, then the real hell was watching the ones who came back, when Pop told them there was no work at the station for faggots.

But one thing was for sure good to know, and that was when Chester was chewed up and spit out by New York because he thought his shit didn't stink, or at least that was what the folks said. I don't know what happened in New York, but I think I've got a hitch on what Chester did here. He was out to kill every-body's magic and make his own magic the only kind, and it worked on those who believed in Archie's heyday, or those who thought the sweet tit would never go dry, and it worked on Chester when he came back, started to believe it himself.

Standing in the station on a slow day, I sometimes think up things that might have happened to Chester, make up little plays for him to act out, wherever he is. When I do that, I very often lose track of when and where I am, and sometimes Pop has to yell at me to put gas in a car because I haven't heard the bell ring. Every time that sort of thing happens, I cross myself with my left hand and go out whistling a chorus of "Chicago."

Check the oil? Yessir.

IN THE DRY

....

HE SEES the bridge coming, sees the hurt in it, and says aloud his name, says, "Ottie." It is what he has been called, and he says again, "Ottie." Passing the abutment, he glances up, and in the side mirror sees his face, battered, dirty; hears Bus's voice from a far-off time, *I'm going to show you something.* He breathes long and tired, seems to puff out the years since Bus's Chevy slammed that bridge, rolled, and Ottie crawled out. But somebody told it that way—he only recalls the hard heat of asphalt where he lay down. And sometimes, Ottie knows. Now and again, his nerves bang one another until he sees a fist, a fist gripping and twisting at once; then hot water runs down the back of his throat, he heaves. After comes the long wait—not a day or night, but both folding on each other until it is all just a time, a wait. Then there is no more memory, only years on the hustle with a semi truck— years roaring with pistons, rattling with roads, waiting to sift out one day. For this one day, he comes back.

This hill-country valley is not his place: it belongs to Sheila, to her parents, to her cousin Buster. Ottie first came from out- side the valley, from the welfare house at Pruntytown; and the Gerlocks raised him here a foster child, sent him out when the money crop of welfare was spent. He sees their droughty valley, but cannot understand—the hills to either side can call down rain. Jolting along the Pike, he looks at withered fields, corn tassling out at three feet, the high places worse with yellowish leaves. August seems early for the hills to rust with dying trees, early for embankments to show patches of pale clay between milkweed and thistle. All is ripe for fire.

At a wide berm near the farmhouse, he edges his tractor truck over, and the ignition bell rings out until the engine sputters, dies. He picks up his grip, swings out on the ladder, and steps down. Heat burns through his T-shirt under a sky of white sun; a flattened green snake turns light blue against the blacktop.

The front yard's shade is crowded with cars, and yells and giggles drift out to him from the back. A sociable, he knows, the Gerlock whoop-de-doo, but a strangeness stops him. Something is different. In the field beside the yard, a sin crop grows—half an acre of tobacco standing head-high, ready to strip. So George Gerlock's notions have changed and have turned to the bright yellow leaves that bring top dollar. Ottie grins, takes out a Pall Mall, lets the warm smoke settle him, and minces a string of loose burley between his teeth. A clang of horseshoes comes from out back. He weaves his way through all the cars, big eight-grand jobs, and walks up mossy sandstone steps to the door.

Inside smells of ages and of chicken fried in deep fat, and he smiles to think of all his truckstop pie and coffee. In the kitchen, Sheila and her mother work at the stove, but they stop of a sudden. They look at him, and he stands still.

The old woman says, "Law, it's you." Sunken, dim, she totters to him. "Where on earth, where on earth?"

He takes the weak hand she offers and speaks over her shoulder to Sheila. "Milwaukee. Got to get a tank trailer of molasses from the mill. Just stopped by—didn't mean to barge your sociable."

"Aw, stay," Sheila says. She comes to him and kisses his cheek. "I got all your letters and I saved ever one."

He stares at her. She is too skinny, and her face is peeling from sunburn with flecks of brown still sticking to her cheek, and along her stomach and beneath her breasts, lines of sweat stain her blouse. He laughs. "You might of answered a few of them letters."

The old woman jumps between them. "Otto, Buster's awful bad off. He's in a wheelchair with two of them bags in him to catch his business."

Sheila goes to the stove. "Ottie don't need none of that, Mom. He just got here. Let him rest."

Ottie thinks of the abutment, the wear on his face. "It's them steel plates. They don't never get any better with them plates in their heads."

Old Woman Gerlock's eyes rim red. "But hush. Take your old room—go on now—you can table with us."

Sheila smiles up at him, a sideways smile.

Upstairs, he washes and shaves. Combing out his hair, he sees how thin it has gone, how his jaw caves in where teeth are missing. He stares at the knotted purple glow along the curve of his jaw—the wreck-scar—and knows what the Gerlocks will think, wonders why it matters. No breaks are his; no breaks for foster kids, for scab truckers.

He sits on the edge of the bed, the door half open, and hears talk of the *ugly accident* creep from the kitchen up the stairs. Ottie knows Old Gerlock's voice, and thinks back to how the old man screamed for Bus, how his raspy yells were muffled by saws cutting into twisted metal.

As he tries to find the first thing to turn them all this way, the pieces of broken life fall into his mind, and they fall without the days or nights to mend them. He opens a window, walks back to his low table. Those things are still there: dried insects, Sheila's mussel shells from Two-Mile Creek's shoals, arrowheads, a plaster angel. All things he saved.

He picks up the angel, likes its quiet sadness. A time ago, it peeked through flowers when he came to himself in the hospital, and the old woman prayed by his bed while he scratched the bandage-itch. He hears children shouting. When he was a child, he held a beagle puppy, looked into the trunk of a hollow tree: on the soft inner loam was the perfect skeleton of a mouse, but grabbing for it, his hand brought up a mangle of bones and wet wood. He puts the angel on the table, and looking into the yard, he sees no such tree. *Show you something*

In the hot yard, Gerlocks unfold their tables, and their laughter hurts him. They are double-knit flatlanders long spread to cities: a people of name, not past. He has been in their cities, and has jockeyed his semi through their quiet streets seeing their fine houses. But always from the phone book to the street he went, and never to a doorstep. Fancy outside is fancy inside, and he never needs to look. He knows why they come back—a little more fancy.

The sun makes long light-bars on the floor; walking through them, he thinks of the wire grille bolted to his window at Pruntytown, so far from this valley, and he wonders what became of all the boys waiting for homes. From the closet he takes an old white shirt, its shoulders tan with coat-hanger rust, with years. He puts it on, strains to button it across his chest. He wore this same shirt to church back then, sat alone, saw the fancy way Bus and Sheila dressed. This time he knows himself better, stronger, and it is good to wear the shirt.

On the closet shelf is a box of old photographs of distant Gerlock kin, people from a time so far that names have been forgotten. Years ago, wet winters kept him in, and he laid out pictures, made up lives for these people, and made them his kin and history. He felt himself part of each face, each person, and reached into their days for all he could imagine. Now they seem only pictures, and he carries the box downstairs to the porch.

The back porch catches a breeze, and he lets it slip between the buttons of his shirt, sits in the swing, and listens to the first dead water-maple leaves chattering across the hard-packed path. His hand shuffles through old photographs, some cardboard, some tin. They show the brown and gray faces of Gerlock boys; men he almost knew, old men, all dead. The women are dressed in long skirts; only half-pretty women, too soon gone old. He wonders about the colors of their world: flour-sack print dresses, dark wool suits; a bluer sky by day, a blacker night. Now days and nights blur, and the old clothes are barn rags, brown with tractor grease. He puts the box on the floor, watches the Gerlock families.

The families walk the fields to see how neatly generations laid out this farm. Ottie knows the good way it all fits: hill pasture, an orchard with a fenced cemetery, bottoms for money crops. He can see what bad seasons have done to warp barn siding, to sag fences he drew tight, to hide posts with weeds.

Wasps swarm under the porch's eave. Warming in the late sun, they hover, dip, rise again, and their wings fight to cool the air around their nest. Beyond the hills, where the landline ends, he sees the woods creeping back, taking over with burdock, ironweed, and sassafras. A day forgotten comes to him.

On the spring day he spent with Sheila, they caught a green-gold bass, and watched it dangle as the light sprinkled on it.

Sheila said, "I think the belly's the prettiest part."

Ottie grabbed her, laughed. "All that color and you pick the white?"

Sheila giggled and they held each other, fighting for breath, and leaned against the spotted bark of a sycamore. Then the fish flopped from the hook, and slipped into black water. They sat on roots, rested, listened to their breathing. With his fingers laced under her breasts, Ottie felt her blood pumping.

One wasp reels, circles, butts beaded ceiling, and Ottie watches the brown wings flash over bright yellow bands, and knows he can pack his grip, be in Columbus by midnight. He lights another cigarette, wonders if being with Sheila that day has turned them.

The old woman's voice tunnels through the hall to the porch, a soft cry: "It's for disgrace you want Bus here."

"Done nothing like it," the old man yells. "He's a part of us. He's got a right if the murderous devil yonder has got a right."

Hearing Sheila calm them, he breathes out smoke, rubs fingers along the fine stubble near his scar.

Old Gerlock comes out, Sheila and her yellow dog behind him; Ottie stands to shake hands, looks again at the old man's stiff face. He sees eyes straining from hard years, and there are lines and wrinkles set long ago by the generations trying to build a place.

Old Gerlock says, "Otto."

"Good to see you, sir." He feels heavy, stupid, and bends to pet Sheila's dog.

"That's a sugar-dog," Old Gerlock says. "Worthless mutt."

Ottie hears Sheila laugh, but deeper than he remembers. Her laugh was high then, and the old woman worried them around the porch, saying, "Please don't, honey. A thing alive can feel." But Sheila held her paper-cone torch to another nest, careful to keep flames and falling wasps from her hand. She balanced on the banister, held the brace, and he saw the curve of a beginning breast crease her shirt. Then he looked to Bus, knew Bus had seen it too. He stops petting Sheila's dog, and straightens.

The old man paws his shoulder. "Otto, you always got a place here, but when Buster comes, you help make him feel at home."

"Yessir." Bus's face comes back to Ottie: a rage gone beyond fear—the thought almost makes him know. "I hadn't figured he'd be here."

"Soon enough. You don't recollect nothing of what happened?"

"Nosir. Just me and Sheila fishing and Bus coming to say he wants me to ride with him and listen for a noise."

"Not even after all these years?"

Sheila hugs the old man with one arm. "Dad, time just makes it go inside. Ottie won't ever know."

Old Gerlock shuffles and pshaws: "I just figured . . ."

The old woman comes out, a dish towel in her hand, and Ottie watches her gasp to keep down sobs. "Otto, don't you take no disgrace at Bus coming here. Wickedness brung him. Pure-T devilment."

The old man looks hard at her, then to Sheila and Ottie, and his face goes gray-blue with blood. "Sheila, take him yonder to see my new dog—only don't be sugaring over her, now, you can't do such to a hunting dog."

Sheila and Ottie go down the steps, take the clay path to the barn. Ottie squints in the coarse sun. Along low slopes of parched hills, fingers of green twist into gullies where water still hides. Looking back, he sees the old man go inside, but the old woman stands alone, with hands over her eyes.

"This is a hell of a game," Sheila says. "They wasn't going to bring Bus. Then Dad hears you're here—up and calls them, says, 'Bring Buster hell or high water.'"

"Don't matter. Just makes me feel tired, sort of."

She takes his hand. "Why'd you never come in before?"

"Never been back this way. Had to get out sooner or later. I don't see what made you stay."

"No place *to* go but here. You changed, Ottie. You used to be rough as a damn cob, but you're quiet. Moody quiet the way Bus was."

He squints harder. "What about you?"

"Nothing much happens here. Lots happens to you with all your shifting around. Don't that ever bother you?"

He laughs short and low. "You-all pity me my ways, don't you? Only I'm better off—ain't a thing here to change a one of you."

"Ain't nothing to make us any worse off, if that's what you're after."

She looks away from him, and her frizzy hair, faded with the long years, hides her face. At sixteen she was nothing to look at, and he has always dreamed her as looking better. Now he sees her an old maid in a little town, and knows her bitterness.

"This is my last haul anyplace," he says, waits until she looks at him. "I'm getting me a regular job with regular guys. I'm black-listed, so I can't drive union, but I know a place in Chicago that rebuilds rigs . . ."

"You won't stick, Ottie. You don't know what it is to stay in a place, and there ain't any place you'll stick."

He has half hoped, kept the hope just a picture of thought, a thought of sending Sheila the fare and working regular hours. Now he puts it away, seeing too soon how dim it gets.

He looks into the pen. Old Gerlock's dog is a square-headed hound, and Ottie knows to pet her means nothing. She stares at them blankly, beats her tail in the dusty shadow of her house. Blue-green flies hum her, but she does not snap them the way Beagle had. *Got something, something to show*

When they were boys, he and Bus chopped brush along the fence all that day. Toward dusk, with chimney swifts clouding the sky, they cut into the scattered bones of a white-tailed buck—the yellowed ribs still patchy with leathered meat. Bleached antlers clung to the skull.

Bus up and grabbed the skull as Ottie leaned for it. "Lookee, I bet it was killed by Injuns."

Ottie pulled at an antler until Bus let loose, then chucked the skull into thick green woods. "Hell, them's common as sin." He hooked brush again, stood straight only to watch when Beagle scared up a rabbit, set a sight-chase. He saw Bus far behind him, staring into meshed underbrush. The woods were already dark.

Bus was half crying. "I would of made me a collection like yours."

"Beagle jumped another one," Ottie said. He went back to work, heard Bus whipping with his sickle to catch the pace.

Bus said, "I don't like Beagle."

A bottle fly buzzes Ottie's eyes, and he fans it away, watches Sheila's dog sniff the wire-edged pen. The dog tries to jump over, and Sheila catches his collar.

Ottie says, "Boy and a girl."

"Not this one. He's been fixed."

"Yeah, but they still know what to do." He looks at ridges made brown fire by sun, and thinks back to a boy with mouse bones, a hollow tree, a beagle puppy.

A triangle rings up from the backyard, and Ottie goes with Sheila around the barn; but looking up, he sees them wheel Bus into the shade of a catalpa. Sheila gives Ottie a hasty, worrisome glance, and Ottie walks slowly to Bus, tries to see each day of the hidden time, but only sees the way Bus is now. Bus sits crooked to one side, his hands bone-bunches in his lap, head bending. He is pale, limp, and his face is plaster-quiet. Ottie smells a stink, and knows it is from the bags hanging on the chair.

"Here's Ottie," says Bus's mother. She leans over the chair. "You know Ottie."

Bus looks up at her, and his face wrenches tight. He rocks side to side in his chair. "Cig'ret'." In the shadow of the tree, blue veins show through his skin. A tube runs yellow from his crotch, and he lifts it, drains it into its bag.

"Oh, honey, you smoke so much." She looks at Ottie. "His Uncle George wants him to stop, but it's the only thing he gets any pleasure from."

Ottie shrugs.

"Here's Ottie."

Ottie squats, sticks out his hand. "Hey, Bus."

Bus takes the hand, then growls up at his mother. "Cig'ret." He shows his teeth.

Ottie gives him a Pall Mall, lights it. A curl of smoke wisps Bus's eyes, and he blinks once, slowly. Pieces of tobacco cling to his gray lips, and he spits weakly at them. The woman's bare hand wipes her boy's chin. Ottie glances from the grass to Bus's face, but all the days of waiting are not there, only a calm boy-smile. Ottie scratches at his scar, and his hand smells of Bus's— the smell of baby powder and bedsore salve.

"Buster, it's Ottie," she says again.

"Otto." On the porch, the old man holds his Bible against his chest, one finger parting the leaves.

Ottie stands. "Yessir?"

"Get the plow from the toolshed yonder."

On the path to the shed, a strangeness creeps through him: he remembers walking this way—nights, years ago—and Bus yelling, "I'm going to show you something, Ottie." Bus grinned, made Beagle dance on his hind legs by holding back the collar. Then Bus shoved hard with his sickle blade, and Beagle stumbled, coughing, into a corner. First his bandy legs folded, then he fell to his side, did not breathe, and his flanks filled, swelled. Ottie found no blood, only the pink-lipped wound in one dimple of Beagle's chest. Then he carried the dog toward dark hills.

In the hot shed, he gathers himself and finds the plow. With its handles and traces rotted away, the blade seems something from an unreal time, and his fingers track warm metal now pitted with rust. The Gerlocks always tell that this plow was first to break the bottoms of their valley, and Ottie wonders what it means or if they just made it up.

Sawdust falls into his eyes and he steps back, looks to the

ceiling; a bumblebee drills the rafters. The joists are spotted where Old Gerlock has daubed other holes with axle grease. Still, the bee drills. Ottie dwells on Sheila's laugh, a laugh high and happy at burning wasps. He remembers the nest in her hand, the fresh smile on her face, and the wasp worms popping from their paper cells under her fingertips.

He carries the single-blade to the porch, puts it on the banister, and brushes at the rusty streaks on his good shirt, smears brownish dust into the threads. He goes to the yard's edge, away. Sheila comes to stand with him, and he feels her eyes on him from the side, feels her fingers pressing inside his forearm.

On the porch, the old man preaches from his Bible, and his voice is a wind and whisper; the words of his god have the forgotten colors of another time. As the gathered families listen, Ottie watches them, their clothes fitting so well, and he knows the old man is the only Bible-beater among them. He hears false power in the preacher's voice, sees outsiders pretending. Old fool, he thinks, new fools are here to take your place.

Old Gerlock shouts to the hills: "For if they do these things in a green tree, what shall be done in the dry?"

Heads bow to the prayer, the unfixed wish, the hope offered up, and every head turns to Bus.

"Godspeed the plow," they say.

A line forms for supper, and Ottie sees the folding table set for Bus, a special table alone, and he knows Bus has no right—nobody has any right. They should all eat alone, all with no past, no life here.

On another table sit foods long forgotten: pinto beans, fried tomatoes, chowchow relish. He is hungry and keeps close behind Sheila, fills his plate, sits with her where he can see Bus.

Old Gerlock wanders to their table, rests skinny arms by his plate as he prays to himself. Sheila elbows Ottie, jerks her head toward her father, and her mouth stretches out to a grin. Ottie shrugs, eats, watches Bus's mother strip chicken and spoon it to her boy.

The old man looks up, blends his food. "Is it a good life, the way you live?"

Ottie puts down his fork the way the old woman taught him. "It keeps me busy enough."

"Must help you forget, I figure."

"Yessir. There's mistreatment galore from you I don't recollect."

Sheila takes Ottie's hand. "Stop it, you two."

The old man's lips go pale with a smile. "Just what happened to wreck that car, Otto?"

A dull flash passes over him; a sickness and a pain streaming from his neck down his back. Beyond the old man sits Bus—Bus with eyes of hard sadness. Ottie knows. "We been through that before."

Sheila squeezes his hand. "Goddamn, let it alone."

The old man draws to hit her, and her head turns.

Ottie yells, "Hit *me*."

Old Gerlock drops his hand. "No, you have got your suffering—just like her." He eats, does not look up.

Bus's eyes fix Ottie with a helpless gaze, but his lips skin back in rage. He sits straight in his chair, one hand waving away the spoon of chicken. He moans, "Ot'ie."

Sheila takes Ottie's arm. "C'mon, that's enough."

He shakes her off, walks under the waning shade of the

catalpa, and bends over Bus. He draws his face close, and smells the smoked oil of Bus's skin.

Bus cries, shakes his head, "Ot'ie."

He whispers, tries to hiss, "Bus."

"Ot'ie."

With the lumped knuckles of Bus's hand, he saw the far-hidden minutes of racing along the Pike. He saw Bus's face go stiff to fight, saw the sneer before that hand twisted the wheel a full turn and metal scraped and warped against bridge sides. *Show you, you got some* Ottie looks to the hills: in their hollows were outcrops, shallow caves where he hid with leaf-bedding and fire pit, where he waited out the night beside Beagle's cool carcass.

He squats, puts his hand on Bus's shoulder. "Bus?"

Bus blinks, bows his head.

Standing, Ottie sees the families staring, and he goes from the yard into open, brown bottoms. Sheila follows, catches his hand to slow him. He curves uphill to the orchard, stops at its crest. Far below are black splotches of Two-Mile Creek showing between patches of trees, the only green spreading slowly out from the marshy banks.

He remembers standing in that creek with Old Gerlock. He almost knew again the cool sweep against his knees, felt the hand cover his face, then the dipping into a sudden rush. Only that once he prayed; asked to stay, always live here. Sheila's arms go around his waist.

The ground is thick with fruit: some ripe, some rotten, some blown by yellow jackets. Ottie pulls a knotted apple, bites into dry meal. Even the pulp has no taste, and he sees the trees need pruning. He tosses the fruit away. "We used to cut props for the branches."

"Mom worked me all week making apple butter, but it's been a while." She snorts a small laugh, holds the back of her hand to her forehead, mocks: "Oh, dear. What *shall* we do in the dry?"

"Blow away, I guess."

"Yes," she says, pulls on him. "Asses to asses and bust to bust."

Ottie feels too close, lets go, and watches as she picks up something, holds it out to him. It is the pale blue half of a robin's egg left from the spring.

He says, "They throw it out if it don't hatch."

"You told me that before. I thought you saved such stuff."

He thinks of the low table in his room, the arrowheads, the plaster angel. Again he sees the buck-skull sailing, turning through the branches, shattering. His smile falls away. "No, I quit saving stuff."

She crushes the shell in her palm, makes it blue-white paste. "I ain't never been loved."

"Bullshit, Sheila. Buster loved you."

"Bus?" Her hand shades her eyes against the last sun.

"He thought we was making it down at the creek."

She clasps her hands around his neck, smiles again. "I ain't never even had a man, but I wanted both of you. Didn't you ever want to?"

He shakes his head.

She squints, and her hands slip from around his neck; she backs away, turns, hurries toward the house. Watching her go through timothy and trees, he hopes she will not look back, and hopes she will be lost to him in the crowded yard.

He sits against the cemetery's fence, scratches up dead moss with a stick, and feels the back of his shirt ripping on ribbed bars. The sun makes an ivory scar in the sky behind the hills; from the creek, a killdeer cries flying from marshes into the line of sun. A blue-brown light creeps up from the ground, and the leaves make patterns against a shadowy sky.

One by one, he picks up the fallen leaves nearest him, gathers them to himself with the years of hurried life. Feeling the crinkled edges of a scorched leaf, he sees, in the last of light, colors still splotching its skin. Everything is so far away, so buried, and he knows more than any buck-skull turned them all.

He walks the darkening fields alone. Heat lightning flashes, and he hears the slow drone of locusts cooling in the trees. He wonders how many deer have died in all the winter snows, how many mice have become the dirt. Walking the fencerow, Ottie knows Bus owns this farm, and has sealed it off in time where he can live it every day. And Ottie sees them together a last time: a dying dog and two useless children, forever ghosts, they can neither scream nor play; even dead, they fight over bones.

The cars leave the dusky yard, bound for cities and years far into the night. He stands until the farmhouse lights go out, then walks back through the yard, up to the porch.

"You'll be heading out tomorrow?" Old Gerlock sits hidden away in the shadows.

"Yessir."

"Stick around and help to strip tobacco."

Ottie grins. "Cutting knife don't fit my hand."

"Can't you tell the truth about Buster?"

He shrugs, rubs his hand across his face, but smells no salve or powder; only the dust of leaves. "I reckon Bus was trying to . . . I guess it was accidental."

The old man goes to the door, holds it open, then spits over the banister. "God forgive my wore-out soul, but I hope you burn in hell." Old Gerlock goes inside.

Ottie sits in the swing, thinks of the bars on his window at Pruntytown, and laughs. They never needed bars. They had always been safe from him. *Do what in the dry*

His voice is smoky: "Blow away."

Rustling metal leaves of tintypes, he takes a cardboard picture from the shoe box, lights it, sees the photograph crinkle into orange, blue, and purple against the night. He lights another, makes flames eat the long-forgotten faces. *Blow away* The third he wants to hold to the wasp nest, wants to make singed insects fall through colored flames, wants to see worms bubble and the rough edges of their paper nest smolder. It is not his way of doing. He shakes his head, waves out the fire. He stands until the last spark glows, rises, burns out.

"Blow away."

Inside is close, and it sucks the air from him. The scent of chicken seeps into the walls and already it is becoming the smell of old times. He takes the stairs quietly, sees no light under Old Gerlock's door, but a film clings to his skin the closer he comes to the landing.

Going down the hall to his old room, he passes Sheila's door, looks up. He sees her standing naked in the doorway; gray, waiting. He stops, waiting; he listens to her breathing. Slowly, he moves up his hand, touches her face, and he feels the sweat of her cheek mingle with the dust of his palm. He knows her better, and he knows her way of doing.

He steps into his room, strips off the white rag, and leaves it lying on the bed. He packs his grip with a razor, soap, and comb, all things he brought. Pulling on a clean T-shirt, he zips shut the grip and carries it into the hall. Sheila's door is closed, and Ottie knows what turned them all will spin them forever.

Outside, the yard is empty, dark. He climbs the ladder into his semi's cab and tries to remember a wide spot by the mill, a place to pull over. The ignition bell rings out, and gears—ten through forward—strain to whine into another night, an awful noise.

FIRST DAY OF WINTER

••••••••••••••••••••

HOLLIS SAT by his window all night, staring at his ghost in glass, looking for some way out of the tomb Jake had built for him. Now he could see the first blue blur of morning growing behind bare tree branches, and beyond them the shadows of the farm. The work was done: silos stood full of corn, hay bales rose to the barn's roof, and the slaughter stock had gone to market; it was work done for figures in a bank, for debts, and now corn stubble leaned in the fields among stacks of fodder laced with frost. He could hear his parents shuffling about downstairs for their breakfast; his old mother giggling, her mind half gone from blood too thick in her veins; his father, now blind and coughing. He had told Jake on the phone, they'll live a long time. Jake would not have his parents put away like furniture. Hollis asked Jake to take them into his parsonage at Harpers Ferry; the farm was failing. Jake would not have room: the parsonage was too modest, his family too large.

He went downstairs for coffee. His mother would not bathe, and the warm kitchen smelled of her as she sat eating oatmeal with his father. The lids of the blind man's eyes hung half closed and he had not combed his hair; it stuck out in tufts where he had slept on it.

"Cer'al's hot." His mother giggled, and the crescent of her mouth made a weak grin. "Your daddy's burnt his mouth."

"I ain't hungry." Hollis poured his coffee, leaned against the sink.

The old man turned his head a little toward Hollis, bits of meal stuck to his lips. "You going hunting like I asked?"

Hollis sat his cup in the sink. "Thought I'd work on the car. We can't be with no way to town all winter because you like squirrel meat."

The old man ate his cereal, staring ahead. "Won't be Thanksgiving without wild game."

"Won't be Thanksgiving till Jake and Milly gets here," she said.

"They said last night they ain't coming down," his father said, and the old woman looked at Hollis dumbly.

"I got to work on the car," Hollis said, and went toward the door.

"Car's been setting too long," the old woman yelled. "You be careful of snakes."

Outside, the air was sharp, and when the wind whipped against his face, he gasped. The sky was low, gray, and the few Angus he had kept from market huddled near the feeder beside the barn. He threw them some hay, brought his tool chest from the barn, began to work on the car. He got in to see if it would start, ground it. As he sat behind the wheel, door open, he watched his father come down from the porch with his cane. The engine's grinding echoed through the hollows, across the hills.

Hollis's knuckles were bloody, scraped under the raised hood, and they stung as he turned the key harder, gripped the wheel. His father's cane tapped through the frosty yard, the still of December, and came closer to Hollis. The blind man's mouth was shut against the cold, the dark air so close to his face, and Hollis stopped trying the engine, got out.

"You can tell she's locking up." The blind man faced him.

"This ain't a tractor." Hollis walked around, looked under the hood, saw the hairline crack along one side of the engine block.

His father's cane struck the fender, and he stood still and straight beside his son. Hollis saw his father's fingers creeping along the grille, holding him steady. "She sounded locked up," he said again.

"Yeah." Hollis edged the man aside, shut the hood. He didn't have the tools to pull the engine, and had no engine to replace it. "Maybe Jake'll loan you the money for a new car."

"No," the old man said. "We'll get by without bothering Jake."

"Put it on the cuff? Do you think the bank would give us another nickel?"

"Jake has too much to worry with as it is."

"I asked him to take you-all last night."

"Why?"

"I asked him and Molly to take you in and he said no. I'm stuck here. I can't make my own way for fighting a losing battle with this damn farm."

"Farming's making your way."

"Hell."

"Everybody's trying for something better anymore. When everybody's going one way, it's time to turn back." He rationalized in five directions.

In the faded morning the land looked scarred. The first snows had already come, melted, and sealed the hills with a heavy frost the sun could not soften. Cold winds had peeled away the last clinging oak leaves, left the hills a quiet gray-brown that sloped into the valley on either side.

He saw the old man's hair bending in the wind.

"Come on inside, you'll catch cold."

"You going hunting like I asked?"

"I'll go hunting."

As he crossed the last pasture heading up toward the ridges, Hollis felt a sinking in his gut, a cold hunger. In the dry grass he shuffled toward the fence line to the rising ridges and high stand of oaks. He stopped at the fence, looked down on the valley and the farm. A little at a time Jake had sloughed everything to him, and now that his brother was away, just for this small moment, Hollis was happier.

He laid down his rifle, crossed the fence, and took it up again. He headed deeper into the oaks, until they began to mingle with the yellow pine along the ridge. He saw no squirrels, but sat on a stump with oaks on all sides, their roots and bottom trunk brushed clean by squirrel tails. He grew numb with waiting, with cold; taking a nickel from his pocket, he raked it against the notched stock, made the sound of a squirrel cutting nuts. Soon enough he saw a flick of tail, the squirrel's body hidden by the tree trunk. He tossed a small rock beyond the tree, sent it stirring and rattling the leaves, watched as the squirrel darted to the broadside trunk. Slowly, he raised his rifle, and when the echoes cleared from the far hills across the valley, the squirrel fell. He field-dressed it, and the blood dried cold on his hands; then he moved up the ridge toward the pine thicket, stopping every five minutes to kill until the killing drained him and his game bag weighed heavily at his side.

He rested against a tree near the thicket, stared into its dark wavings of needles and branches; there, almost blended with the red needles, lay a fox. He watched it without moving, and thought of Jake, hidden, waiting for him to break, to move. In a fit of meanness, he snapped his rifle to his shoulder and fired. When he looked again the fox was gone, and he caught a glimpse of its white-tipped tail drifting through the piny darkness.

Hollis dropped the gun, sat against the tree, and, when the wind snatched at his throat, fumbled to button his collar. He felt old and tired, worn and beaten, and he thought of what Jake had said about the state home he wanted the folks in. They starve them, he said, and they mistreat them, and in the end they smother them. For a moment, Hollis wondered what it would be like to smother them, and in the same moment caught himself, laughing; but a darkness had covered him, and he pulled his gloves on to hide the blood on his hands. He stumbled up, and, grabbing his gun, ran between trees to the clearing nearest the fence, and when he crossed into the pasture felt again a light mist of sweat on his face, a calming.

He crossed the fields and fences, slogged across the bottoms and up to the house. Inside, his mother sat in the tiny back room, listening, with the husband, to quiet music on the radio. She came to Hollis, and he saw in her wide-set eyes a fear and knowledge—and he knew she could see what insanity had driven him to.

He handed her the squirrels, dressed and skinned, from his game bag, and went to wash his hands. From the corner of his eye, he saw her, saw as she dropped the squirrels into soaking brine, saw her hand go up to her mouth, saw her lick a trace of blood and smile.

Sitting at the table, he looked down at his empty plate, waited for the grace, and when it was said, passed the plate of squirrel.

He had taken for himself only the forequarters and liver, leaving the meaty hinds and saddles.

"Letter come from Jake." The ol man held a hindquarter, gnawed at it.

"And pitchers of them." His mother got up, came back with a handful of snapshots.

"He done fine for himself. Lookee at the pretty church and the children," she said.

The church was yellow brick and low, stained windows. In the picture Jake stood holding a baby, his baby girl, named after their mother. His face was squinted with a smile. The old woman poked a withered finger into the picture. "That's my Mae Ellen," she said. "That's my favorite."

"Shouldn't have favorites." His father laid down the bones.

"Well, you got to face that he done fine for himself."

Hollis looked out the window; the taste of liver, a taste like acorns, coated his mouth with cold grease. "Coming snow," he said.

His father laughed. "Can't feel it."

"Jake says they're putting a little away now. Says the church is right nice people."

"They ain't putting away enough to hear him tell it."

"Now," she said, "he's done fine, just let it be."

When the meal was finished, Hollis pushed back his chair. "I asked Jake to help by taking you-all in; he said no."

The old man turned away; Hollis saw tears in his blind eyes, and that his body shook from crying. He wagged his head again and again. The old woman scowled, and she took up the plates, carried them to the sink. When she came back, she bent over Hollis.

"What'd you figure he'd say? He's worked like an ox and done good, but he can't put us all up."

The old man was still crying, and she went to him, helped him from the chair. He was bent with age, with crying, and he raised himself slowly, strung his flabby arm around the woman's waist. He turned to Hollis. "How could you do such a goddamned thing as that?"

"We'll take our nap," she said. "We need our rest."

Hollis went to the yard, to where his car stood, looked again at the cracked block. He ran his hand along the grille where the old man's hands had cleared away dust. The wind took his breath, beat on him, and the first light flecks of ice bounced from the fenders. The land lay brittle, open, and dead.

He went back to the house, and in the living room stretched out on the couch. Pulling the folded quilt to his chest, he held it there like a pillow against himself. He heard the cattle lowing to be fed, heard the soft rasp of his father's crying breath, heard his mother's broken humming of a hymn. He lay that way in the graying light and slept.

The sun was blackened with snow, and the valley closed in quietly with humming, quietly as an hour of prayer.

AFTERWORD

....

I FIRST met Breece Pancake in the spring of 1975, a little more than four years before he killed himself. He was big, raw-boned, slightly slope-shouldered. He looked like one who'd done some hard work outdoors. At that time he had a job teaching English at the Fork Union Military Academy. He put the student-cadets to bed at ten and then wrote from taps till past midnight. He got up with the boys at the six-o'clock reveille. Breece showed up in my office at the University of Virginia one day and asked me to look at some things he'd written. The first story I read was pretty good; it turned out to be the best of his old stuff. Possibly he was testing me with something old before showing the pieces he'd just done. He asked me to look at some more, and luckily I said yes. The next batch were wonderful.

At that time the University of Virginia didn't have much money for writing-students, so I tried to send Breece off to Iowa for a year to get him some more time to write. Iowa wanted him, but they were running low on funds. Breece got a job at the Staunton Military Academy for the next year and started coming to my story-writing class at the university. I thought he should start sending his stories out, but he held back for a while.

Breece had gone to college at Marshall University in Hunting-ton, West Virginia, but what was striking about his knowledge and his craft was how much he'd taken in on his own. He must have had an enormous concentration at an early age. He had a very powerful *sense* of things. Almost all his stories are set in the part of West Virginia that he came from, and he knew that from top to bottom. He knew people's jobs, from the tools they used to how they felt about them. He knew the geology, the prehistory, and the history of his territory, not as a pastime but as such a deep part of himself that he couldn't help dreaming of it. One of the virtues of his writing is the powerful, careful gearing of the physical to the felt.

He worked as hard at his writing as anyone I've known, or known about. I've seen the pages of notes, the sketches, the numbers of drafts, the fierce marginal notes to himself to expand this, to contract that. And of course the final versions, as hard and brilliantly worn as train rails.

When he sold his first story to *The Atlantic* he scarcely took a breath. (He did do one thing by way of celebration. The galley proofs came back with the middle initials of his name set up oddly: Breece *D'J* Pancake. He said fine, let it stay that way. It made him laugh, and, I think, it eased his sense of strain—the strain of trying to get things perfect—to adopt an oddity committed by a fancy magazine.) He was glad, but the rhythm of his work didn't let him glory or even bask. He had expected a great deal from his work, and I think he began to feel its power, but he also felt he was still far from what he wanted.

Not long before Breece and I got to be friends, his father and his best friend both died. Sometime after that Breece decided to become a Roman Catholic and began taking instruction. I'm as uncertain finally about his conversion as I am about his suicide. I've thought about both a lot, and I can imagine a lot, but there is nothing certain I would dare say. Except that it was (and still is) startling to have had that much fierce passion so near, sometimes so close.

Breece asked me to be his godfather. I told him I was a weak reed, but that I would be honored. This godfather arrangement soon turned upside down. Breece started getting after me about going to mass, going to confession, instructing my daughters. It wasn't so much out of righteousness as out of gratitude and affection, but he could be blistering. And then penitent.

As with his other knowledge and art, he took in his faith with intensity, almost as if he had a different, deeper measure of time. He was soon an older Catholic than I was. I began to feel that not only did he learn things fast, absorb them fast, but he aged them fast. His sense of things fed not only on his own life but on others' lives too. He had an authentic sense, even memory, of ways of being he couldn't have known firsthand. It seemed he'd taken in an older generation's experience along with (not in place of) his own.

He was about to turn twenty-seven when he died; I was forty. But half the time he treated me (and I treated him) as if I were his kid brother. The other half of the time he treated me like a senior officer in some ancient army of his imagination. I knew a few things, had some rank, but he felt surely that I needed some looking after. There was more to it than that of course. More than these cartoon panels can show, he was a powerful, restless friend.

After his year commuting from Staunton, we got some money for him. The creative-writing program at the university was coincidentally, and luckily, endowed, and Breece was among the first to get one of the new fellowships. He had time now to get to know some of the other writers on the faculty (Peter Taylor, James Alan McPherson, Richard Jones) and some of the new band of graduate students in writing. This was, on the whole, good. The University of Virginia English department is a sophisticated place, both in a good, wide sense and a bad, narrow sense. The program in writing is just one of the many subdivisions—which is also, on the whole, good. On the good side, there were (and are) people on the regular faculty and among the regular Ph.D. candidates who understood and cared for Breece and his work. On the bad side of life in the department, there is a neurotic cancellation of direct, open expression, perhaps out of self-consciousness about how one's opinion will be regarded, since opinion is the chief commodity. Sometimes it's hard to get a straight answer. And sometimes it's clear that some people hold that criticism is the highest bloom of the literary garden, and that actual stories or novels or poems are the compost.

There was just enough of this attitude to give a young writer, however good, a sense of what social theorists call "status-degradation." Breece didn't know how good he was; he didn't know how much he knew; he didn't know that he was a swan instead of an ugly duckling. This difficulty subsided for Breece, but there was always some outsider bleakness to his daily life, a feeling that he was at the university on sufferance.

Of course, Breece could be pretty thorny himself, and he spent some time getting mad uselessly—that is, over things that I thought were better ignored, or at the wrong people. One effect of Breece's irritated energy was that he began campaigning for an M.F.A. degree for the apprentice writers, a so-called "terminal degree" to replace the uneasy M.A. The university now offers an M.F.A. in English, and it's on the whole an improvement in that it's a license for some of the subsistence-level jobs a writer might need along the way. Breece was a good union man.

He was also a wonderful reader. He screened prose fiction submissions for *Virginia Quarterly Review* and, in the spring of 1979, for the Hoyns Fellowships. He and I and another friend of ours went through a bale (that's a file-cabinet drawer, stuffed). In some ways we were engaged in the most functional form of criticism—picking twelve potential writers out of the bale.

From his clearheadedness and good humor then, and from the way his work was going, I guessed Breece was in good shape. He'd sold another two stories. He gave a reading of yet another to a full house. He had some job prospects, and he was getting ready to leave Charlottesville. He began giving away his possessions to his friends. He'd always been a generous gift-giver—when he came for a meal he'd bring trout he caught, or something for my daughters (for example, bathtub boats he'd whittled, with rubber-band-powered paddle wheels). When he began to give away his things, it looked as if he was just preparing to travel light.

A month later a friend of his showed me a letter from Breece in which he'd written, "If I weren't a good Catholic, I'd consider getting a divorce from life."

No one close to him guessed. Even that sentence about getting a divorce from life is only clear in retrospect. And from other signs and letters it's hard to say how intentional, how accidental his state of mind was when he killed himself.

Breece had a dream about hunting that he logged in his note-books, I think not long before he died. In the dream there were wooded mountains and grassy bottomland. Clear streams. Game was abundant. But best of all, when you shot a quail, a rabbit, or a deer, it fell dead and then popped back to life and darted off again.

There are a number of things that strike me about this dream. One is that it's about immortality and paradise. It is the happy hunting ground. And so it's still another case of a lore that Breece acquired sympathetically and folded into his own psyche. But the most powerful element is this: a theme of Breece's life and stories is the bending of violence into gentleness. He struggled hotly to be a gentle person.

One of Breece's favorite quotations was from the Bible—Revelation 3:15-16.

> I know thy works, that thou art neither cold nor hot: I would thou wert cold or hot.
>
> So then because thou art lukewarm, and neither cold nor hot, I will spew thee out of my mouth.

This is a dangerous pair of verses. Untempered by other messages, by the gentler tones of voice of the Spirit, they can be a scourge. It may have been simply a bad accident that Breece didn't allow himself the balms that were available to him after his self-scourgings.

I have three kinds of reminders of Breece. The first is the surprising number of people who have come by to talk about their friendships with him, or who have sent me copies of their correspondence with him. They all know how bristly Breece could be, how hard on himself. (On one postcard to a friend, in the spot for the return address, which was 1 Blue Ridge Lane, Breece wrote: "One Blow Out Your Brain." The friend hadn't noticed it. But the *message* on the card was to encourage the friend—keep on, keep on writing, have a good time, damn it.) But these people speak more of what Breece gave them by his heat.

I also have what Breece wrote.

And then there is a third way—perhaps memory, perhaps a ghost. I'm not sure what ghosts are. The reflective, skeptical answer I give myself is that the vivid sense of dead people that you sometimes have may be like the phantom-limb syndrome— you still feel the arm that's been cut off, still touch with the missing fingers. In like manner, you feel the missing person.

Two weeks after Breece's death, and after a lot of people who knew Breece peripherally had asked the inevitable unanswerable question, I was walking home, dog-tired. It was about two A.M. I was on the Lawn, going toward the Rotunda, the dome bright under the moon. I was walking automatically and only slowly realized I'd stopped. I smelled something. I tasted metal in my mouth. I didn't recognize the smell for an instant. It was a smell I'd known well years before. Gun bluing. But inside this sense of taste and smell was a compelling sympathy, beyond the sympathy of *that's* what it smelled like to have the muzzle in his mouth. There was a deep, terrifying thrill that I would never have dreamed of, a thrill and a temptation that sucked at the whole body. I wouldn't have thought of that. I wouldn't have *dared* to think of that.

In that dizzy urgency of sense, even while I was opening to it, there was something reassuring about it. As much as the letter he left, it was alarming, but loving: Don't go on thinking about why. Feel what I felt for an instant.

Breece and I used to argue a lot. The rhythm of it would often be that he would get up and go just before he lost his temper.

He'd come back into my office after a bit and either tell me calmly I was still wrong, or say something funny, allowing he might be not *entirely* right. Now that my own temper's worse, I appreciate his efforts. A month after the experience on the lawn, I was lying in the bathtub trying to think of nothing. I heard a short laugh. Then Breece's voice, an unmistakable clear twang: "That's one way to get the last word."

You don't have to believe anything but this—that's just the way he said things.

There were several more of these sentences over the next year. One a rebuke, the next two gently agreeable. Then recently, again late at night in a lukewarm bath, only a distant murmuring. What? I thought. What?

"—It's all right. You've got your own conscience."

Now there's the less excited working of my mind alone: Breece would have liked this or that, this stream, this book, this person. This would have made him angry, this made him laugh. A lot of people miss him, and miss what he would have gone on to write.

I think about the many things I learned from Breece. I think, with somewhat more certainty than a wish, that Breece's troubles don't trouble him or the people who struggled with him and loved him, that a good part of what he earned from struggling with his troubles remains.

JOHN CASEY

PART TWO

Fragments

———

SHOUTING VICTORY[1]

....

WE HADN'T had a real Glory meeting since we turned the snakes loose back in September, so Reverend Sam mixed up a cup of strychnine and passed it around. My faith isn't holding up so good, and I never bother with drinking any, but Darlene is full of the ghost, and she takes some. It never hurts her neither, but her father, Reverend Sam, is growing a sight pale and he falls down just like he'd been stomped on.

Everybody drops down beside him and lays hands on him and there is an awful commotion of tongues. I get me a chair and sit down and commence to pray, but I can't. I keep thinking about all the good things Reverend Sam does for folks in Cave Creek. I think about how he prays for dying folks and gives them the comfort of Jesus on their way out and how he always shows up at the mines to pray at every shift. I look up and see his eyes have gone glassy.

Darlene, her sister, and mother are standing up, bobbing their heads sort of pigeon-like—getting socked around by the Ghost. I knew I'd done that because they said I done it the first time Glory came on me. I used to get Glory at every meeting, and be so wore out on Monday that I couldn't work and my throat would be sore from shouting in tongues. But I look at Reverend Sam, and I can't get the Ghost.

"Shat. Hala ma shat ma te!" Darlene says.

Even in the crowd of bodies I can feel the cold soaking into the little room. Sam has stopped twitching and shouting, and lies really still while the others pray and speak in the tongues of men and angels.

I try again to pray, but my mind keeps drifting back to Sam that first day in the mine. I keep seeing the greasy blackened face, the thin line of smile.

"The snakes is God's creatures," he had said in the dinner hole. "You ain't got fear with faith in the Lord."

That night I took a serpent from Sam's hand and strung it around my neck in Glory, talking the whole time in tongues. It feels bad to remember all that and see Sam dying.

Darlene has both hands on Sam's belly, and her forehead is pressed down to them, and she is shaking from her prayers. I take her shoulders in my hands, ease her up. Her eyes are still closed, and she stands, swaying until her mother comes to hold her.

I get on my knees, put my ear against Sam's chest, hear the flutterings.

"I reckon we better get him a doctor," I say.

"He needs Jesus!" Darlene's mother says. "Don't need nothing but faith!" She looks at me like I've fallen from grace. Darlene's eyes are open but I'm not sure she can see me.

I walk back through the crowd to the door, step into the cold night. The air is sweet and dry. I walk up the road to Sam's house, sit on the porch swing and watch the clapboard building with them inside.

I try to think of what ugly sin Sam might be guilty of to be stricken. Sam is a godly man, a wise one to take the way of the

Lord, to lead his family and their friends. Sam had smiled at me just before the blue flash knocked us to the floor and the kettles of rock fell leaving craters in the ceiling. Sam had walked me out to the main shaft, and up top Sam fell to his knees and for the first time I knew why. I, too, had dropped to my knees.

I see Fred come out of the church and run down the road toward town. A few others step outside, then go back in, but I can not move from the swing. I watch the doctor's Ford pull up and the doctor get out. Two men drag Sam out and put him in the back seat. Darlene's mother gets in with the doctor and the car drives up the road toward Williamson.

In the yellow squares of the building's windows I can see the people milling around, putting on coats. The ones who pass Sam's porch on their way home see me and stop talking until they walk out of earshot.

Darlene walks by herself, and when she comes to the porch to go in, she doesn't see me.

"Who asked for the doctor?" I say.

Darlene looks up, then softly lets the screen door shut. "I did," she says. She comes to the swing, sits beside me. "I just of a sudden lost my faith and started yelling for a doctor."

"Well, nothing's wrong with having a doctor."

"But if I'd of kept my faith he'd of lived. I won't be able to stand it if he dies. It'll be my fault."

"It'll be the poison's fault. I don't trust strychnine."

"You got to have faith."

"I got faith with the snakes, but I ain't had none with the strychnine."

"But it's in the same scripture."

"I know but snakes is God's creatures. It's like he moves in them." I look at her and she is falling asleep. "C'mon, you better go to bed."

"No, I don't want to." She sits straight up. "Take me for a walk Henry, please?"

We walk along the railroad track, past the tipple and out of town. There is a new moon and we watch the ties, adjusting our steps. When we come to a low trail, we veer off up the hillside to an open world. We sit against a tree to rest and look down on the hollow-town.

She takes my hand.

"Pray with me so Daddy won't die," she says.

"All right, but we'll pray our own prayers."

She leans against me, lowering her head to her knees. I look out on the hollow and hills where the other miners have been buried—fifty-seven burned to a crisp, but Sam had walked me out and now I can't pray for the man who taught me how.

We sit there for a long time holding onto one another. Her head resting on her knees, her grip slackening in my hand. Somehow we are both warm and we fall asleep.

I awaken first at the sound of the car horn. Darlene stirs, nestled against me. I think whoever is coming down to the hollow is laying pretty heavy on the horn, just one long note getting closer. Then I think of Sam.

Sam must have lived and his wife is coming back with him, shouting victory and blowing the horn. But instead of stopping in town, the noise comes up the railroad tracks, through the brush, and blasts in my brain. I rub my face, pray it will stop. "Ke su comj klair su ke," I say. It does.

I shake Darlene. "Sam's home. I done been told."

As we walk down the path, the gray morning crosses the sky, seeps into the hollow.

I walk Darlene to her house, and as we stop to kiss, her mother and father come to the porch.

"Where you all been?"

"Just sitting out and praying for you," I say to Sam, smiling at him. "Angel of the Lord came upon me to tell me you was home."

Sam looks at us. I know what Sam thinks we've been doing. "If you had neither one of you lost your faith, I'd not have gone away."

"Nothing happened, Sam," I say. "We sat up on the ridge and prayed."

"Her mother said you's first to take temptation into Darlene's heart and turn your back on God."

"Daddy!" she says.

"Go away Satan," Sam says to me. "Go to the harlots, but leave my daughter pure."

I turn to the street, already the dawn is half-over the ridges.

CONQUEROR[2]

....

Now he lay awake on the shack's floor, huddled in his jacket, and listened to the field mice scratching at the walls. The rain drizzled, turned into mist, and tree frogs clicked, groaned: it was almost morning, and he knew Boss Pruitt would fire him if he didn't set up the ferris wheel in Kitty Hawk today. He watched a blue glow of early light outside the door until he saw Carolina pines against a foggy sky. He stood, squeezing water from his shoes, and brushed dirt from his clothes. He switched on his flashlight, found a last slosh of wine in the bottle, finished it; then he threw the bottle on the floor littered with rags, all dry, but no wood among them for fire. He wanted coffee. He thought of his home in West Virginia, then smiled; years with the carnies, years with the ferris wheel, years gave him no word like home.

He walked through the doorway into the yard. At his feet, packed in mud and ringed by the rain, lay a shiny yellow cat's-eye marble. He picked it up, rolled it between his fingers, and it showed yellow lights high in the air, turning. He switched off his flashlight, dropped the marble in his pocket, and looked back at the tar-paper shack. Walking through the white-clay fields with broken rows of long-dead cotton, he came to the highway's berm where his convertible was parked. Patches of tape had peeled away in the rain, soaking the seats and leaving puddles in the floor. He raised the hood, looked again at the hairline crack along one side of the engine block, then slammed it shut. From the trunk he took a suitcase and a large wooden tool box, left the keys dangling from the lock. Behind the road's eastern rise, the sunlit pines and a breeze shook drops from them in yellow sparks. He leaned against the fender and watched light glinting from chrome as the first few cars whistled past his thumb.

He had seen Boss fire slackers and no-shows: Boss called them crotch-licking punks and first-of-Mays, and his eyes bugged as he yelled. He tried to think of a sharp answer, but Boss never left room for sharp answers.

He smoked a cigarette and watched a higher sun seep through the fog. Along the edge of the field a quail piped and led her chicks into the woods; when he looked westward again, a new station wagon was pulling up. An old man rolled down the window, his face straining as he leaned, and he spoke through the half-opened window, a voice without breath: "Can you drive?"

He nodded, but when the old man slid across the seat, he saw the pinchers of an artificial hand unclamp the wheel. He put his suitcase and tools in the back, and climbed in to drive.

The old man laughed, held up his plastic arm. "Long drive wears me out. Leg's the same way." He tapped his left leg with the pinchers, then jerked his head toward the convertible as they pulled away. "Your car?"

"Nobody's now." He watched the car disappear in the wing mirror; when they topped the eastern hill, the sun started overhead, out of his eyes. He stared at the road, tried not to look at the old man's arm. "How far you going?"

"To the last stop sign before you hit the ocean. Going for a reunion at the airbase at the outer banks."

"I'll drive as far as Kitty Hawk." He took a ticket book from his shirt pocket, handed it to the old man. "I work for Pruitt's Amusements. You and your buddies have fun on me. Say Max sent you."

"Appreciate it. Got any show girls?" The old man leafed through the tickets and his claw clicked as he turned each one.

"None worth seeing."

He handed Max the book. "Thanks, but I ain't been to a carnival since my boy was little. He didn't take to it much either."

"Kids are funny that way."

The old man reached under the seat, dragged out a fifth of whiskey, poured a cup full and offered Max the bottle. "Kids are a pain in the ass."

He waved the bottle away, pointed to a thermos, and the old man poured Max a cup of coffee then sloshed down his liquor.

"Kids done this to me." He held up his arm, shuffled his leg. "One of them dedicated German youths. Yessir, kids and wives both. You married, Max?"

He shook his head, watched the pines blur by and the bright yellow lines slip past his window.

"Good for you. I been married thirty-five years and this is the first time I been away from her since the war."

Max looked at the bottle and grinned: a half-pint was already gone. "Careful you don't founder yourself on that stuff."

"Goddamn it, can't a man take a drink without a tee-totaling wise crack?"

"Didn't mean nothing by it." Max watched the pines fade away to open fields of beans and young cotton. Far back in every field were shacks; some standing, some caved in, some still with families. The field steamed in the sun, and down one side road to a shack he saw ruined toys.

The old man capped the bottle, stuck it under the seat, and leaned his head against the window. He closed his eyes and his jaws went slack, then he opened his eyes, turned to face Max. "Why'd you join a carnival?"

Max shrugged. "Got tired of using a mule's ass for a compass. I wanted to look around."

RIDGE-RUNNER[3]

●●●●●●●●●●●●●●●●●●

BUDDY UNCOVERED himself to get out of bed, but lay still—half-thinking, half-asleep. He tried to retrace the dream, to hook and snag the sneering way he felt; but he found only what he had seen. His family had been together again. It seemed like they had been at the old house on the ridge; just sitting, not doing anything. He had seemed a boy again, a boy who played with a toy truck at his Grandad Thacker's feet. Now that he was awake, the dream slipped and feeling fell away into times before they sold their grant-lands, moved to the hollow.

Through the trailer's slat-windows, he saw the first dark-blue sky before day, and knew the ridges would already be bright. He heard Sally's breathing. She would not make his breakfast, not even this last time. She was going, and he knew she would do nothing special about good-bye. Now she was far from him in a dream of white-powder and music, a dream busy with strange poems she wrote, a dream of things she would never tell him. He saw how slim she was; even under lumpy comforts and a wedding-ring quilt, the lines of her body lay smooth and lean. He rolled, fitted the curve of her back to his chest and belly, felt her skin and smelled of the spray on her hair. He slipped one arm around her waist, brought his hand up to the curve of her breasts, felt the slow and simple flow of her blood. She did not move to him, but drew closer into herself.

He remembered red bar-lights, the sparks they made in her hair, and he remembered the way she sat so straight on a stool in the Thunderball Club. At first she smiled, eyes heavy with metal-flakes that caught the red lights, then her smile softened, and she mocked his hicky accent: "'Scuse me, Miss, but could I have a dance?" In all the nights of dancing, she had never left the Club with him, never drank the drinks he bought. And when he was laid off his job in the railyards, she left with him, and they moved back to the hollow beneath the ridges where he was born. It rained so hard that night that leaves were knocked from the trees, and traffic on the streets crept to a drone. He had picked a sticky leaf from the sidewalk, placed it underside the plastic umbrella, and had seen her smile, wet with the oil of lipstick.

He shook her a little. "Sal, I got a dream to tell you."

She stirred, moaned, moved his hand away.

"It was just like when I's little. None of the folks was dead, and they's all up to the old house on the ridge . . ."

She rolled to face him. "Goddamn. Go on to work or something—the coke's still on. Just leave me *alone*." She turned away again, pulled the covers tight.

He got up, went down the hall to the bathroom. On a rack above the tub, his dried-out workclothes hung, stiff with shale, mud, coal grit. He dressed in two layers, spreading fine dust through the air, and pulled on his steel-toed boots, laced them to the knee.

He stared at the bathroom floor, told himself Sally had to go because it wasn't her way to stay. He had been alone before he found her, knew he could take it again. He smiled. If she didn't leave tonight, he would throw her out: let her hitch-hike to Charleston for all he cared.

In the kitchen he scrambled two eggs, the last two, and ate them from the pan while yesterday's coffee reboiled. He thermosed the coffee, and built two baloney and onion sandwiches for his lunch pail. He found some cold corn-bread and a raw turnip in the refrigerator, packed them. He drank off the rest of the coffee, picked grounds from his teeth with a fingernail. Curt would have to pay them next week or they would flat starve.

Putting on his miner's cap, he stepped outside. The sun struggled to sift into the hollow, and greenish fog held back the light. He crossed the foot bridge over the creek, walked past dead stalks of sunflowers Sally had planted, and slipped through the fog to the secondary. All the way to the dog-hole mine, he thought how it had started.

Over a hundred years ago Thacker's had owned the ridges around Echerton, farmed and fought on it, looked down on the people in hollows. An acre at a time, his family had sold themselves to hope and addresses Buddy had lost long ago. Only Curtis stayed, tried to dog-hole coal on his own ridge, to scrape the last life he knew into bread and beans. Buddy knew the time had come for Curtis to quit, too.

He walked through all that was left of Echerton: boarded storefronts and rows of company houses. Weed stalks stuck between rusty spur tracks, and windows of storage areas above the storefronts were splintered from rocks. Ahead, in half-light, he made out the rotting tipple. His father had been crushed there just ten days before the big mines shut down, and the miners were left to do scab-work and D.P.A. The tipple crackled in the cold as the sun touched it, and on a pole beside it, an unused transformer still hummed. The big coal was gone, and he did not know why he had stayed.

Sally was right to go, but somehow he wanted to stay. This place was his, had been his too long to leave, and he would stay until the last shack rotted, filled with snakes and weeds.

One light burned in the grocery store—a one room affair for the families too poor to give up, move to the cities. Buddy checked his pockets, found a quarter, and went inside. The store was warm, and he smelled fresh coffee on the hot plate.

SURVIVORS[4]

•••••••••••••••••••

AMANDA SAT by the window, looked beyond her face in dark glass and down through the foggy valley where streetlights hid under haze, down at lights too far to touch. There she had cleaned the power company offices all night, still smelled of piney suds; there she had called the state home again, asking what time the ambulance would come for her mother. Higher on the slope, the last cedars stood, and higher still, the oaks with early blue light on patches of solstice snow between them. She rested one cheek against cold glass, waited for day, for the falling of cedars, and long before the first crows passed over, she heard their calls drift into the fog.

The wheeze of her mother's breathing came from the bedroom, and Amanda got up, put more coal in the burner, let the tarry smell come strong into the room. The house was small, too hot, but she kept it hot even these last hours for the old woman. Since her stroke, the old woman slept in the daylight, lay waiting for night to fold over day in the shadows of her yellowed eyes. Amanda closed the burner door, looked at her mother's two bone-china ballerinas on the mantle. Years ago her mother had carried them from the house in town, kept these memories of quality long after Amanda's grandfather had driven them from his door. She touched the broken one, cracks yellow with glue, and wondered if the waiting time would smother her or leave her like the old woman—alone, all but dead.

Turning to the table, she straightened the stacks of legal papers—copies of Medicare forms, the commitment of her mother to the state home; on every line Amanda's answers were printed, then in bold script at the bottoms, Amanda Crepps. She had not liked the state home with its green tile hallways and knocking pipes; she had not liked the dog that slept on the lobby couch or the old man smoking butts left in the ashtray, and she looked long at her name on the papers. She took up the bank ledger, wrote "Cedars $500.00," in the black-lined column; now she waited for the real estate office to find her title so that she could add the price of the hillside, move to town.

She closed the ledger, slipped on her coat, and went out to the porch. Day came to the ridge with a red sky, and a small wind shook the broom hedge. Down the hillside she could see the first terrace of the switchback road, lined with stumps and piles of limbs, the road had carried away the cedar logs—centuries old—and the smell of sweet pitch rose with the fog. Under limbs now piled for burning she once played alone, picked violets and ferns for her mother or lay looking into the clouds for her father's face. Now through the swarth the sand had made, she saw only the secondary road where, her mother once said, her father had been run down, the road Amanda had walked to work and back for fifteen years. Tonight she would walk it again, a last time, into town.

She turned uphill on the path from the porch, and in the brighter light where the cedars gave way to oaks at the ridge-top, she saw the grave marker of concrete, and knew her mother had lied.

She heard Samp's truck straining up the grade, and she pulled on her coat, went out to meet him. Day had come to the ridge with a red sky, and a small wind waved the broom sedge[5] around the house. Deep in the cedars, rain-crows howled, and she wondered where they would winter once the cedars were gone, but the squawking radio in Samp's truck drowned them. He was crowded into the cab with his two boys, and when he got out, she saw them stare. Samp pushed back his cap, walked to her.

UNTITLED FRAGMENT[6]

•••••••••••••••••••

THE WHOLE thing came to him that Friday night as he lay there under five blankets with a bottle of whiskey: To do anything but make love, you needed a hell of a lot of equipment. Sweat a bug? Blankets, whiskey, T.V., hot room. Cope a mope? A cigarette without a filter so it would dangle properly from the lip. Do a dutch act? A warm bath with cold steel, a lead bead placed neatly in the brain, a tall building to jump from.

He thought of his mother. Even a good mackerel snapper had equipment—beads, a bible, all those ribbons, etc., and he thought of all the money made in the world on equipment, and he agreed with himself that there was a goodly amount of equipment involved in making love, but he hadn't gotten low enough to buy any yet.

Then he started thinking about going to confession tomorrow. He could see it now: a big hole burning in the curtain while he talked, and the holy water the priest threw on the fire gushing up like gasoline. And he thought: So this is what it's like to have some green. The lowest goddamn thing in the valley of the shadow of death, lower than whale shit in the Marianas Trench,[7] but you can afford to have the flu.

He watched Johnny Carson tell jokes, but they still weren't funny. He remembered being poor, hitch hiking all over the southwest like a good hippie. And that was where he met

Martin, a wetback with a little scratch and an idea about getting more.

It was so hot in Phoenix, that at night it got down to a snappy
109. While trying to catch some cool under a bridge on the south-
side, he saw Martin chasing a body as it rolled into the gulch. He
took out his baggy and rolled a humpish joint, watching as the
Mexican leafed the wallet for green. The little man started back
up the gulch, leaving the cold-cocked body, and spotted him,
toking away in the shade.

"Hav-a-hit?" he said, offering the cigarette.

"You think you pretty cool, huh?" but he took a puff.

"Beats the street, man."

"The street is O.K. A few rats, not too many."

"No rats here, man."

"Where you going?" he eyed the backpack.

"Maybe Mexico."

"Very nice in Mexico. You go deep in the jungle. Is cool there,"
and he handed over the hot roach,[8] disappeared to the bridge
above.

In an hour the Mexican came back, but the body in the gulch
still had not moved.

"I think I go with you, man," Martin said. "Big money in pot-
tery—you know—the national art?"

They caught a ride all the way to Nogales with a bunch of
freaks in a VW bus. The train was $18—sounded good, so just
outside of Nogales they beat up and rolled the hippies.

Johnny Carson tried to catch a bottle of beer to hold up for an
ad, missed, and Joe laughed. It was then he decided to cap the
whiskey and cop a snooze until Linda came back from the hot
shit political dinner for her father. He dreamed he ran up and

down the sewers, looking for Linda. He carried the rusty old Mauser Martin bought for him in Mexico from an oyster sales-man. A couple of kids stopped him in the sewer, asking about Martin. Blue bottle flies sucked the edges of their eyes, but they didn't wave them away, they stood there, asking about Martin. Joe wanted to wave the flies away, but they wouldn't let him, so he leveled off his Mauser. They sniggered at him, pointed, talked in Spanish, and they were still snickering when he drilled them both.

He heard Linda come in, but it was a long time before he could open his eyes, and when he did, she was naked, pulling at the covers. He grabbed her.

"You'll get my bug," he warned.

"So what, I want it with you now," and she climbed in.

"How's the dinner?"

"You know daddy," she said plowing her hands through the covers to find him.

"Um," he said, and let her mount him for a change while he dreamed of the green clouds of parrots over the Mexican jungle.

NOTES

1. Shouting Victory] Also titled "The Tongues of Men and Angels." The text printed here follows Thomas E. Douglass's transcription of Pancake's handwritten draft, published in *A Room Forever: The Life, Work, and Letters of Breece D'J Pancake* (University of Tennessee Press, 1998). Douglass changed the third-person past tense sections of the story to first-person present tense, following Pancake's example. (Pancake had begun to rewrite the story in first-person present tense.) Milton historian Caudwell Dudley had provided information for the story. The two men were planning a research trip together to Frazier's Bottom, West Virginia, where snake-handling is still practiced. With Dudley's death in 1976, the trip never materialized, but this rough draft of the story survives.

2. Conqueror] Also titled "Samaritans." Pancake wrote the following short outline that suggests how the story might have been developed:

> Bailey picks Max up at ------- and a few towns later, stops to buy a fifth, lets Max drive. Bailey talks about his son—a failure, about his wife—a teetotaler old bat, about his war days. He is mild, friendly and thirsty.
>
> Halfway or so, Max stops for lunch and coaxes Bailey to leave the bottle in the car because there's beer inside. In the restaurant, Bailey almost starts a fight, but Max steps in, "He's just a drunk old man. I ain't drunk or old." The challengers back off and Max shuffles Bailey out to the car. He passes out and we get Max's reflections on the situation: Lost Colony [located on Roanoke Island, N.C.] Max tosses the bottle out.
>
> Bailey awakens, claims to be getting sick; Max pulls off on a fire road. Bailey gets the dry heaves and Max feeds him water until it all comes up. Bailey whimpers something about when he was a kid, his mother told him, "Now you gone and put a little pison in your stomach and you'll never get it out." A car load of high school kids pull up, football players types, and razz Bailey's tags: Disabled veteran. Bailey straightens, stops leaning on the hood: "Reach under the seat and hand me my .45. I'm gonna' ventilate their engine." Max reaches, but there is no gun. The bluff works and the car backs out.
>
> Bailey looks for the bottle as Max drives. Max won't own up, but Bailey knows he's tossed it. He orders Max out of his car, cursing: "Goddamn the man that'd pour out another man's drink." Bailey pulls out, weaving and Max looks out across the bay bridge until Bailey's car disappears on the other side. He sees the giant Ferris wheel glistening in the sun, its colors barely discernible in the white sky. He is too late

to set up, too late even to work. Behind him are the stagnant swamps. He looks in his wallet, picks up his suitcase and tools. He could lay up in a motel for a few days: it was still spring, and the college kids wouldn't have the good jobs yet. He started walking across the bridge.

See also Pancake's letter of March 21, 1978, to the Mary Roberts Rinehart Foundation, on page 297.

3. Ridge-Runner] This fragment is part of the first chapter of a planned novel or collection of linked stories to be called *Water in a Sieve*. At the center of the novel would have been Buddy and Sally, characters already familiar to readers of "Hollow." "Hollow" would have been the second chapter. It is possible other chapters were written and lost. Pancake made the following outline for the novel:

CHAPTER I	"Ridge Runners"
CHAPTER II	"Hollow"
CHAPTER III	"Politicians" (smoke filled room)?
CHAPTER IV	"Sally Rand" (bar in Columbus)
CHAPTER V	"Just One Chance" (bargaining with Curtis)
CHAPTER VI	"Pappy's" (visiting an old friend)?
CHAPTER VII	"Good Old Boy" (mining and death of Estep)
CHAPTER VIII	"Sagittarius" (birth of Tommy)
CHAPTER IX	"The Big Top" (TV—way it's supposed to be)
CHAPTER X	"Ashes" (the way it is)
CHAPTER XI	"Deer Hunting" (finale—no deer)

4. Survivors] This fragment is part of the third chapter of a planned novel or collection of linked stories that would have begun with "Trilobites" and "In the Dry." Pancake never settled on the title for the novel and refers to it in his notes as both *Generations* and *Water in a Sieve* (Pancake was fond of the latter and also entertained it as a possible title for another, different novel centered on the lives of Buddy and Sally, characters from "Hollow").

5. broom sedge] The typescript at West Virginia University reads "brood sodge."

6. Untitled Fragment] Pancake's biographer, Thomas Douglass, speculates that this fragment was among the last things that Pancake wrote. He comments that the idea for the story encapsulates Pancake's dreams of escape.

7. Marianas Trench] The typescript at West Virginia University reads "the _____ trench," indicating a word to be filled in later.

8. roach] The tyepscript reads "reach."

PART THREE
Selected Letters

1972–1975
••••••••••••••••••••

To C. R. and Helen Pancake[1] ···

La Vista Grande

Phoenix, AZ

March 21, 1972

Dear Mom and Dad,

You should have seen Mexico.[2] I don't think the place has changed in two hundred years. The people are as poor as you could get and still stay alive or so dirty rich it's ridiculous. There is no middle class and that in itself sounds like the perfect hatching for socialism—but it isn't! From age 5 on up till he dies a Mexican boy is put to selling things: shoeshines, jewelry, food, knives, blankets, seashells—everything under the sun. All of this to stay a hand-to-mouth existence with that one grain of hope that, someday, somewhere, someone is going to drop a million pesos on their heads and they'll be rubbing elbows with the rich.

With the girls it's a similar story—someone gives a poor girl a lucky break and she winds up owning her own restaurant. The ones who aren't so lucky are married off at age 14 or are sold off to a madame to keep the rest of the family going.

The old cabin (now serving as a doghouse) that I had as a child was bigger, better furnished, neater, warmer and by far more comfortable than most Mexican peasant homes. Like much of

W.Va. there are old cars sitting dead in the front yard as a testimony to those inside the abode hut that had tried and failed to achieve that wispy, illusive dream of being rich. But in the shiny reflection of that rusting chrome bumper there still remains that faint glimmer of hope that someday, somewhere, someone's bound to drop that million pesos. As long as that chrome shines, as long as that hope glimmers in the heart of a child, socialism will be just another word that is too big for him to pronounce.

Meanwhile back at the rancho, the wheel of day-to-day life turns over, squashing the weak nieth its spokes and allowing the strongest to run only a few inches free of death.

While all of this revolved around me, I was walking about in my fine American clothes with my wallet fat with bills, smiling with my pearly capped teeth (there's more money invested in my mouth than one of these families see in a lifetime), feeling guilty of my prosperity and yet glad I was a rich American who could take advantage of the fine Mexican craftsmanship. I'm a Cadillac Cowboy. The West was won for me, the Indians were put down so that I could camp without a revolver in my hand. The border was barricaded so I wouldn't have to worry about Comancheros. I am the physical product of two hundred years of murder, bloodshed, thievery, slavery (white and black) and social degeneration. I was born to sit back and relax because my father and his father worked too hard to give me this chance. Or was I? Hell No! Who, in his heart, could relax in a plush chair before a fire as long as people continue to sell their daughters to the local brothel? And it's no phase either, we get richer, fatter, happier, while the rest of the world slides into a cess-pool. ***

Aside from running around the country and learning all sorts of neat things to tell people when I get back I haven't been doing much—writing mostly—but I've run up against some problems with "Stuart." I can't decide now whether to make it a novel or a short story. I've written the story but it has 1,001 marginal additions. Who knows? ***

That's about it, my regards to all. Pop, take care. I'll call again next week to let you know what I'm going to do about coming home.

Peace now,
I love you and miss you,
Breece

To C. R. and Helen Pancake ···

La Vista Grande
Phoenix, AZ
March 1972

Dear Mom and Dad,

I imagine the rainy season has come to pass in Milton. Soon, the bottom will be flooded and when the water recedes there will be all sorts of garbage to clean up. Well save all the planks and boxes—good firewood. I miss my fire. Be it ever so humble. ***

In any event, here are my opinions on your suggested methods of coming home. Airplanes are a total bore. *** What do you see from an airplane? Very little! Buses and trains have common problems. One feels obligated to stick to the schedule and can't stop when one sees a particularly beautiful sight. There's no walking around or stopping by a stream to catch crayfish or pausing to lament some dead dog on the road. He was someone's dog, some mother's pup, but that Big Greyhound keeps rolling.

If I were to say to the driver, "Hey, stop this thing, I want to see what kind of rock that is over there," he'd laugh in my face.

What I'm trying to say is that on my way home I want to *know* my country. I want to touch, taste, smell and hear as well as see this land. If it stinks of manure on the fields I want to know it. If the water on any given mountain is sweet I want to know just how sweet. I want to hear the wind in the grass as well as see it push the trees around. But most of all I want to feel all of those things. I want to know firsthand. I don't want the Greyhound company or any other pumping stale, reconditioned air into my lungs or pre-recorded sound into my ears. If I have to be an American (and I do) I don't want to be sold short on my own country.

Joe Hill[3] wasn't an American—he was a Swedish immigrant but he knew and loved this country firsthand before those who call themselves Americans shot him down in Utah. "It's a beautiful country," he said from his jail cell, "and I've tramped over it all north, south, east and west. I love it." A poor Swede, without a penny or a hot meal but he *loved* our country. I'm a well-fed American, soon to stand before a classroom of bright eyes and when they say, "Mr. Pancake, what's it like out West?" Am I going to shrug my shoulders or am I going to say something like, "It's beautiful. I love it and I think everyone should see it firsthand before they die." It's up to me to do it. It's up to you to understand why. ***

You both say you trust me and I believe it, because I trust you. Worry never does any good but I'd be a fool to tell you not to worry. Parents do it—comes with kids, I guess. Package Deal. "I'll have a bundle of joy and a pound of worry!" At any rate, armed with my camping gear, canned food and your trust and prayers, I'll be on the road to home in a couple of weeks. My stuff will probably arrive before I do—pre-paid, would you mind telling the freight people to hold it till I get there? ***

Don't bother yourselves about such trivia as my diet and sleeping accommodations. I'll have three hot ones a day and I'll camp in the woods, well away from the road. I'll put my fire out before dusk so nobody will even know I'm around. If it rains I'll have enough money for a motel but would you please send my plastic parka (the green poncho). I think I left it under my bed.

I'll stay shy of trouble, keep my mouth shut and I'll stay away from those dirty old roadhouses. Should it come to grips—I've learned to run surprisingly fast in cowboy boots.

As far as I know I'll go north to Denver then cut across the nation through Kansas City, St. Louis and into Louisville; from there I'm home free. It's a good route, lots of pretty country and not too cold this time of year. I really hope you understand why I want to do this and I hope you won't begrudge me this little trip. I'm sure you won't know what it means to me. Above all I want peace among us. God knows there's little peace to be found elsewhere. ***

I love you and I miss you.

But I'll see you soon.

Breece

To John and Barbara Shaffer ···

Huntington, WV

Jan. 11, 1973

Dear John & Barb,

Since last you heard from me (Arizona) I've been the rounds. I came home in time to resume my "education"—12 hrs. last summer and 18 hrs. this past semester—a lot of hard work and long nights but I've earned the right to call myself a "dean's list man"—for what it's worth.

I'm taking 18 hrs. again this semester and it looks as if things get worse instead of better—I honestly have no regrets about leaving WVWC but if I am going to work this hard down here I can find no justification for former actions.

My father is better but has been diagnosed as an unsalvageable case of M.S., so much of my free time is involved with him. M.S. is a drawn-out process producing the antithesis of life but he adjusts like a champ and is always enjoying life to its fullest.

I was in Buckhannon in October and meant to drop by but Gilligan and the bottle got in my way and before I knew it I had to get back to M.U.⁴—hungover and blown out. Thank God for pressure valves!

Belcher is here, well so much for that topic. Cebe was around this summer but I didn't see much of him since we both stay pretty busy with class. He did, however, relate the tale of Jay's reaching "manhood"—still nothing to do in Buckhannon—huh?

Well, enough of me, what of you two? I divine that you'll graduate, John,⁵ around May. Correct? Then what? Ah, the golden question! The answer from your guru says: "Get your wife a job." John, with a blessed beauty like your bride you should beg for a job in the salt mines; I mean, nobody should be lucky twice in the same year. It's Un-American!

Well, write if you can, give my regards to all and keep in touch if you move. I'll do the same in hope of one day *seeing* my old friends again.

Love you both,

The Pancake

P.S. Any great expectations? I mean children?

To C. R. and Helen Pancake ···

La Vista Grande
Phoenix, AZ
June 10, 1973

Dear Folks,

It's been so long since I've written to you I thought I'd better get one off before you give me up for dead. ***

Anyway, I went up to Sedona and then Flag to escape the heat. I camped two nights and came home—getting more like Pop daily. Those mountain beds don't agree with my bones like they used to. Getting old and soft, I guess, but the next trip I take probably won't be a camping trip. Maybe I rough it too much—a sleeping bag just isn't good padding for rock. But the lakes were beautiful with the Sacred Peaks rising above them and making the entire area a warm Montana. There weren't too many people either—it's a good piece off the main highway. Saw some deer, ducks, and rabbit but no snakes—still too cold for them, I guess. It isn't too cold in Phoenix—107 degrees—110 at day with an average of 95-98 at night. Night is when the snakes come out and La Vista has its share because the new owners don't cut the weeds or trim the flowers back. Donnetta[6] killed a baby snake night before last. Personally, I don't bother them unless they bother me the way that monster snake did two weeks ago. He scared the hell out of me so I killed him. It was very unfair—he couldn't help it because he was ugly and big and besides two people helped me so Ole snake didn't have a chance.

The stories are coming along and I'll send Beasley[7] the first rough drafts for possible suggestions as soon as they're finished. I'm really proud of "Rat Boy"[8] and I hope *Atlantic* takes it. They pay $100 a page (mine or theirs I don't know) which could mean $1,000 or $200 depending on how you mean it. Doni did the typing and it was perfect. She's a darn good secretary and she works cheap too. I might send off some poems—I'll have to revise them first. That doesn't pay much but it's print anyway and right now that's all I'm after. I have plenty of time to get rich—baloney. It takes *Atlantic* a while to decide on a story but if they get swift, forward anything from Arlington St., Boston, Mass. If they reject it? Big deal. *Atlantic* is the best but not the only literary magazine. ***

I don't want any "help." If I can't make it on my own I don't want it.

Glad to hear you're getting around so well Pop—don't get too close to that riverbank, Pal, the fish have enough to eat as it is. I hope you're enjoying yourself—have a happy Father's Day. Doni and I went together on something for your sitting room. I hope you like it. Well, I'll get back to work now, my regards to all esp. Aunt Julia. I'll write her soon.

Love,

B.D.P.

To C. R. and Helen Pancake ···

Fork Union, VA

Sept. 7, 1974

Dear Folks,

I guess now that Char[9] has gone back to Seattle, the house is settling back into the usual routine. I hope this finds you well.

My students[10] range from creative to brilliant to leaden slugs, but I'll get by, I'm sure. I sort of like working with the little ones, especially the homesick cases—I know just how they feel. I must be getting old; today I decided my hobo days were gone forever—I have no desire to live in Europe anymore, I don't even want to go back out west for a while. I'm going to come back to W.Va. when this is over. There's something ancient and deeply rooted in my soul. I like to think that I've left my ghost up one of those hollows, and I'll never be able to leave for good until I find it—and I don't want to look for it because I might find it and *have* to leave.

I like my work and tolerate most of my co-workers, but there's no animosity—we just don't share the same interests. I've discovered that not everybody likes to read a book a week. It was quite a shock at first, but I'll get by. ***

Anyway, Mom, get this straight; I want to pay my bills. I appreciate your help, but you and Dad have given me my life up to this point and it's time I earned my own and started acting like a man. If I'd been more responsible, none of this mess would have happened.

For recreation, I walk, write and read. Today, I hiked about five miles, saw a passel of snakes—copperheads mostly—a few garters (which have a darker coloring over here) and one timber rattler that I swear must have been four feet long. I've set up a hiking-forest survival intramural program for the boys who don't want to play ball (I know I never liked to), but I'm going to take them on tamer trails until cold weather sets in.

Paula's[11] getting a new place in November or before: Terrace Park East. I've seen it and it's the kind of place I'd planned on retiring to. But she's happy with it so I guess she'll enjoy it.

This place is O.K. if you just keep cool and when the day's over quit playing soldier. There's good noise about me in the commandant's office. "Pancake's Company," or so I've heard. I don't do anything but keep good relations with cadet officers and men—they run this showboat, I just give them pointers now and then, make recommendations and reward good work. And they said war was hell—ha.

My temper? It's almost gone. I've also discovered that life without beer is not necessarily unbearable. But tell the preacher I still smoke cigarettes and have *no* intentions of becoming a Baptist.

It's not all peaches and cream—the dinner tonight *had* to be dogmeat and rotten eggs disguised as—I've forgotten what Sarge called it. I hope I never see it again. Otherwise, the grub is decent.

I was glad to hear about Grandpa and tell him I said to take good care.

Pop, I guess you're taking a bone out of Mom? Don't work her too hard, now. If she'd up and drop dead on you, it might be Sunday before Jimmy Johnson found you. *Then* who'd take care of you? Sure, you'd go to some V.A. hospital, but they don't give love, just medicine.

Well, better get to what they pay me for. Remember, I love you and I'll fly in T-giving. Paula said she'd pick me up at the airport so don't sweat it.

Love you

Breece

P.S. Regards to any who ask.

To C. R. and Helen Pancake ···

Fork Union, VA

September 15, 1974

Dear Mom and Dad,

Friday night duty nearly killed me. I "stuck" half the corps for direct disobedience. Getting "stuck" is being put on report. It involves penalty tours (one hour march for each tour), a visit to the commandant's office, and takes my voice. Ordinarily, I don't have problems with the corps. They know I'm fair, and I don't shout to get my point across. But last night I had to get them into formation and take them—all of them—to the infirmary for their flu shots. I couldn't believe they cried, but I suppose I did at that age, too.

Then it happened. Some joker flushed an orange down the commode—stopped it up—then shit in it and flushed it. I not only made him clean it up, but threatened to make him eat the orange. Instead I put him on report for 25 demerits. 125 more and he goes home for good. A good many lost their leave weekend last night and a good many will lose it tomorrow. I know that sounds tough, but that's the way they want me to do it, so I do it.

Got my first bill from the Agency.[12] Boy, they don't miss a trick—exactly one week before payday. But they know when payday is, and that's when they'll get their money—and not until.

The bill for my uniforms? Two hundred bucks for stuff the Army didn't want. That's $200.00 over the $100.00 allowance for uniforms under the contract. I'm paying it in monthly installations of $25.00.

Will Blue Cross bill me for the Cabell-Huntington or is it just understood that I'll pay half the bill? If so, please send it back to me.

I'm running two checking accounts—one here and one in Huntington, but both books balance out to perfection.

I called Paula today—I hadn't heard from her for two weeks and I was naturally a little worried. It seems she's received only one or two letters from me. I wrote to her about twice a week—so all that was lost. She said she'd written, but I've gotten nothing. Lousy post offices. I condemn them to sore eyes and addresses without zip codes.

Matt Heard,[13] a fellow instructor (and a bartender before he came here), and I are taking our leave weekend in Charlottesville. Movies, libraries, and other tours of interest. Don't worry. Matt's driving. He went back to D.C. last weekend—Mindy, his girlfriend came down to pick him up. Matt offered me his car to "run home for a weekend if you want." Later, I found out he bought it from a friend for $75.00 and the engine mountings are loose. It's a '66 Chevy—just like the monster we used to have, and seems to have the same mechanical problems—like the accelerator sticks—remember, Pop?

So, how much is the plainest Granada? I know it's a good car, but that doesn't tell my checkbook anything. You won't have to go on my note, even if I do decide to buy one. I've got a job and a decent credit rating. If I finance it through 1st Huntington, I won't need my co-signers. At any rate, I'm not buying anything from anyone but Shorty,[14] and not until '76 at the earliest. Do you know what the insurance would be? Hell, I don't even want to talk about it.

One of the officers offered me a Honda 450 for $200.00 and payments. Great. Then I would get killed. Maybe that's the answer—escape your creditors through death—ought to write a book on it.

Don't worry about Morris or James Ross. Edison said: "Show me a totally satisfied man, and I'll show you an idiot." I'm not satisfied with F.U.M.A. for a life work, so if I go to my other place—it has to be up, or I'm a loser. I'm shooting for something better—not necessarily in money. They can take that away in taxes and funeral bills. No, I want peace, and I'll get it yet. You watch me. But once I get it, I can't let myself be satisfied with it—I have to keep getting better. If I don't, I'm just a loser. Might as well bag groceries if I can't better myself in things that can't be taxed.

Freedom of thought is one of the greatest things our nation has given us, and if we refuse—either through laziness or quiet satisfaction—to make use of that freedom, then we may as well chuck it all and give it to Russia or China, or whoever wants it.

Sarge's cooking was divine tonight—steak, cheese casserole, peas, honey-buns and coffee. I ate twice. Mostly it's dogmeat (that accounts for the Richmond Kennels) and rotten eggs—my personal joke to him. Oh well, war is hell.

I'm glad everybody is better, or at least maintaining. Give my love to all. I miss you and love you. Take care.

Love,

Breece

P.S. The back of p. 5 is the test they flunked—now is that hard? Not if you've drilled for two weeks on the subject.

To C. R. and Helen Pancake ···

Fork Union, VA

Sept. 19, 1974

Dear Folks,

My students are taking one of my surprisingly easy tests, so I'm writing this now in the classroom. Since classes began we have worked seven days out of eight, not counting the two days of helping incoming students. To top it off, I pulled duty Monday night (6:00 pm–10:30) on top of my regular work. Then some idiot gave me the high right arm salute of the Nazi Army, and I had to put him on report (two typed pages) and supervise his punishment—the cleaning of our common restrooms in "A" company.

The work is hard, but the long periods of free time on the weekends don't help me much, so I'd rather work. I found a cave, of a sort, in the end of a hollow about four miles from here. That was my first act of colonization. It is a fox den at the present time, but this winter I plan to camp in it on weekends. It's an off grade of granite, so there's no danger of a cave-in.

As far as textbooks are concerned, the days of the McGuffey Readers[15] are over, although what I'm using is just a modernized version of them. To my opinion McGuffey was as bad as Allen Ginsberg's "Howl" except to the other extreme. Ginsberg thought he had something new when he incorporated perversion into poetry, but Sophocles wrote about a son who killed his father and married his mother. This was written nearly four thousand years ago, and it's much finer poetry than "Howl."

I guess I find fundamentalists—hard-shells, foot-washers—even Methodists a bit hard to take at times. Super-dedicated people bore me. They have no sense of humor, no reception to different ideas, nothing—only their cause, and that makes them singly hard-headed, and generally sickening.

No, private schools aren't the answer either. The answer, Dear Folks, is that there is none.

Well, anyway I'm glad to hear the supersleuth is on the trail of the crook that nabbed my wallet. I honestly hope he doesn't find the guy. I know that sounds crazy, but all I lost was some money and a five-buck piece of plastic. The crook stands to lose his job, or even the chance of ever getting another job. I'd rather not see that, because he'll just become a bigger crook without a job.

Tell Shorty[16] I saw a T-V ad for a Granada, and it looked pretty good. I'd like to get some information on it if I could—tell him that no matter what, I'm buying my next car from him.

Well Pop, the forestry you taught me when I was a kid paid off. I have to escape to the woods in my free time to get away from the noise and the kids. I've seen more snakes than you could shake a stick at—mostly because I look for them. There are entire herds of deer, and watching them graze is a beautiful sight. I set a rabbit snare and baited it with an apple. Caught a coon by the paw, and when I found him, he was trying to chew the line in two. He was so mad, I couldn't get close enough to cut him free, so I stayed with him until he had frayed the nylon cord down (to keep the dogs off), freed himself then went off dragging this green string of nylon behind him.

I try to get letters off to Mammaw and Grandpa[17] and Aunt Julia,[18] too. That's tough to do, but it means a lot to get mail. Sort of means that despite age and loneliness, somebody cares about you.

I hope you don't mind if I pass on Janet and Carolyn—we have nothing in common. Instead I'm going to look up some Pancakes just for the hell of it—to find out if they're nicer than the Huntington Branch. Aunt Julia will fill you in on what I've heard to date.

During my wood-treks, I've picked up several arrow-head ferns, some teaberry, some red-green lichens and some moss. I built a box for the window and I've got them in it—now we'll see if they live.

Pop, I hope you're doing O.K. Want you to know that I think about you and Mom a lot. These kids are in one hell of a shape and if it hadn't been for you two, I'd have been that way too. A long time ago we heard a folk song: "There but for fortune, go you and I."[19]

I was very fortunate to have you two.

Love,

Breece

To C. R. and Helen Pancake ···

Fork Union, VA

Oct. 4, 1974

Dear Folks,

I am pleased to announce I've saved a whopping $322.00 for the month of September. I know it doesn't sound like much, but when it's all you have, it's a pretty big sum. I intend to dump about $20.00 in C'ville with Matt,[20] but I've earned it. Got to get these creatures out of my hair at *least* once a month.

I am also happy to announce my adjustment was successful. I was tested today when my hiking team and I strayed through a farmer's field (which wasn't posted) and he gave me hell for trespassing. Said he was going to report me—oh, just generally made an ass of himself—and I didn't explode back. I hope to God my temper remains in check. I apologized, but he said, "Well, sorry's not enough," and I nearly laughed at him. What did he want me to do? Disappear into thin air? So I very politely informed him of my name and rank, told him exactly who to call to report me, and politely apologized again, took my troop, and left. I hope he does report me. If his land is so important, why doesn't he post it thus: "Shit-Faced-Son-of-a-Bitch—Beware of Bastard."

Mom, thanks for the cookies—there was not too much flour! They were delicious. I made the mistake of getting them during my free period, so I had to share, but they were very good. Damn Matt. He hopes I get more! Glutton. Thanks again.

Jezzuz! I've got duty again tomorrow night. Oh, Leave Weekend, where is thy sting?

It will be nearly a month and a half before I come home, and I miss you, but don't worry, I'll get there if the plane doesn't crash. I'm beginning to think I'm jinxed about traveling for a while. Wonder if I broke a mirror? You know, if the plane crashed, it would be my luck to walk away—wouldn't even get a good week's rest in the hospital. I've thought a lot about my car wreck.[21] I should have got out that minute and checked the tire pressure. Like that guy on the bridge—"Be a good time to grease it."

You may tell the Rev. Mr. Pyles that they *make* you go to church here, but it's so watered down that it's easy to ignore it. The Chaplain's a pretty nice fellow, but that's as far as I care to go. I don't like being made to do things in the way of religion, but this is a private institution and I've signed my rights away—or so it seems. So I sit there mentally reciting logic rules and the few fiery words I remember from the Constitution and Transcendental philosophers.

Well, I hope this finds you well and happy—my regards to all.

Love,

Breece

P.S. Ask Bob Reese if he has any Tax-Shelter plan or special investment plan I could enter. The stock market is horrid, and I'd rather have security at 7% than desperation in a depression.

To C. R. and Helen Pancake ···

Fork Union, VA
Nov. 1, 1974

Dear Folks,

Halloween is over, and all the spooks have gone back into the earth till next year. Hope this finds you well, and unhaunted.

Perhaps I should explain my comments of my last letter. I am leaving F.U.M.A.[22] this spring, and heading for Morgantown.[23] That decision was the direct result of the nervous breakdown I almost had last week. No joke. I thought about the "Ripoffsky" plan, but I'm just not cut out for it. There are a number of things I am qualified to do besides teach at F.U.M.A. and I have figured it up, I can pay off my loan by May, and have a little left over. I've started that wheel already, and I'm going to try for law school. With the first loan paid, I'll have no trouble getting the second one. It will mean work and school at the same time, but that can't be the pressure I've been under the last two weeks.

A lot has happened to me, and I've decided the only dependable thing in my life is my own ambitions. Everything else is here and gone, but a dream is something to make you get up in the mornings. When one has sold one's soul the roof falls in, and one must build the soul again. So I will start now. I will eat the food because I earned it, will teach because they hired me to, and will do the best job I know how because it isn't the kids' fault I have to lie to them.

Nov. 2, 1974

Parents day is over. Boy was that a winner. Most of them were pretty civil about their kids' grades, but one father insinuated I was not doing my job because his son made a B, and last year his son made straight A's in all subjects. Hell, I couldn't help it if the kid blew a test. Then there was a very pretty lady who told me she would appreciate it if I or the commandant told her son that his father (her ex-husband) was in jail in Richmond for murder

. . . said she didn't have the heart. As it turned out, neither did I, and W.C. had to tell him.

Excuse the mistakes in the last paragraph; the machine[24] is going haywire on me. I'm still not sure I've got everything together.

My figures on paying my debts would astound you. I get $440.00 after taxes, pay the agency 120.00, the school 25.00, the bank 200.00. The little left over goes into the Breece Pancake Survival Fund, a non-profit organization which contributes to the delinquency of myself. If I can really claim a loss on my car, I'll get 300.00 bucks back from the government, but I'm not counting on that. Yet despite my poverty, the thought of being a free man again is enough riches. I dislike the restriction here . . . both in thought and action.

I know you both are saying I'm dumb to leave with the cost of living going up all the time, but I want the right to be me, even if I have to fight to get it. Thing is I can't see why we aren't allowed to be ourselves. Everybody here has an education, and should be able to handle his or herself, and still do the job . . . guess not, huh?

Well, I'll quit boring you with my prattle.

I'm glad the yard is in shape again, and that you got a boy to do it. Can't believe the people out back raked leaves as celebration. Takes all kinds I guess.

Hope this finds you well, Pop. Don't work Mom too hard, she isn't that much younger than you. I tried to call you all last week, but there was no answer, so I assumed you were out driving around. That's good, and it really helps to get out now and then.

Just three more weeks till I'm home. So get your arguments

against my leaving ready. I've looked them all over, and I can say there are no *good* reasons to stay.

Love,

Breece

To C. R. and Helen Pancake ···

Fork Union, VA

Nov. 10, 1974

Dear Folks,

Many thanks for your last letter. We all want to be understood, and I think that's why humans began to speak, but if you don't understand my dilemma, don't worry about it. You are removed from the real essence of the problem, and I haven't written the WHOLE truth about FUMA because I'm afraid to put things like that in print, and sign my name after it. That's called paranoia.

Rita went to Paris? I'd love to go there, and just sit in a bistro on the Champs Elysees with a glass of calvados. As it is, I am drinking Bosco, and trying to convince myself that my students are *not* as dumb as I thought. If I stayed here another year, I would have to take courses in Special Education just to teach them how to read. By the way, the boy who threw the fit is gone. ***

I saw *Lucas Tanner* [25] too. Matt and I jointly wrote the producer a nasty letter. Told him that his show assumed too much; like one can reach a student, that students are all human, that students care, that parents care, that anybody cares. Personally,

236 | SELECTED LETTERS

I could never deliver a baby if I had to. Education has nothing to do with the real world, and shows like that one only fill a kid's head with a bunch of illusions, and the kid wonders why his teacher can't be a Lucas Tanner. Maybe if they put cameras in my room and paid me $40,000 a year, I'd be able to do what he does for one hour a week.

When and if I ever get into politics, I'd like to work on the quality of public education and public health. West Va. needs a total social medicine program, and a revamped education program. Why should someone like you, Pop, who worked all his life, and payed state taxes have to rely on your workman's insurance alone without any state aid? What about Aunt Julia? Uncle Mont left her well off . . . unless she gets sick. Then she can't go home, because the bills took everything, and she has to rely on her social security, and the nursing home takes that.

There has been so much sickness in our family, and I've often thought of how bad it could be if we weren't prepared for it, and how easier it could be made through a good medical program. I'm glad to hear Grandpa and Mammaw are at least doing better. Sounds as if you've had your hands full, Mom, but it also sounds as if you had a pretty good time.

Donna Poe invited me to her apartment for dinner this coming weekend, and I'm going to take her up on it. "I ain't had a home-cooked meal/and Lord, I need one now." Besides I get pretty bored sitting around here. She's working as a dental technician in C'ville, and I ran into her at a ballgame last week. She didn't know me without my beard, and was pretty mad because I hadn't tried to contact her. But her anger was mostly bark, and she invited me to dinner and offered to come down and get me in the same breath. That, my friends, is a hustle. Don't worry, I can take care of myself.

To top that off, her father came down yesterday for the hell of it (I don't think he believed I shaved). He has shoulder length hair and a mustache, and dresses like I used to. The man's forty-five, but you couldn't tell it. He's selling the West Va. area, and doesn't get home much, but says he's making money. I guess that's what it's all about.

So it is that I have actually worked three months shy two weeks and I'm tired. I'm looking forward to my stay at home. Mom, could I ask for a diet of seafood and greens? This meat and potatoes is killing me. I feel like I'm 100 years old and one foot in the grave.

Give my regards to all. My plane ticket is on its way, and I'll be in when I get there, so don't look for me until you see me.

Til I knock on the door.

    Love,

    Breece

To C. R. and Helen Pancake ··

Fork Union, VA

Feb. 22, 1975

Dear Folks,

Finally I get a chance to answer your letters. This week hasn't been at all hectic, just the routine insanity. I'm getting ready for the next grading period, and trying not to worry about how I'm going to pass the silent majority this time.

I was glad to hear that you complied with my wishes on the insurance. Dishonesty is too rampant in our land to be excused on an individual basis, rather, like charity, honesty should begin at home. The price doesn't matter. As Steinbeck once said, "Anything that just costs money is cheap."

Weather was so good today, I took a friend's bike out for a five mile trip. I'll feel that tomorrow morning. Walked the last mile as one of the gear guides got mucked in with the chain, and the whole damn thing fell apart. That little venture should cost me about $10.00. I hate those English bikes . . . too much junk to break.

I'm taking a bunch of the boys out to the farm for their Survival Merit Badge sometime in the future. They can't take anything with them except a knife, and have to build camp, make fire, all the neat tricks. Boy, that will be a laugh. Can't get Matt to go. Said he wasn't going to let any damn snake eat him. Said I was crazy. Well, I don't consider getting concussions in the rugby field very sane. ***

The impossible happened. Beas[26] wrote me a letter. He sends his love as he is too broke to send himself. He's in Mississippi, not Texas.

Time to go now. Send my love to all as I am in much the same state as Beas.

Love,

Breece

P.S. Mom, cash that damned check. You're fouling up my bank book. bdp.

P.P.S. Paul Newman has no beard. My first duty upon leaving FUMA is to dispose of my razor. Sorry, girls, Paul will have to do.

To C. R. and Helen Pancake ···

Fork Union, VA

Feb. 28, 1975

Dear Folks,

No news. Just a note to say hello. I have to work this weekend, plus I have duty, so I probably won't have much of a chance to notice any news should it happen.

Mom, I hope the world is still intact. I haven't gotten a clipping in ages. Don't tell me Huntington has no new scandals. Somebody might knock up ——'s daughter . . . that would be real news. Tell them to get busy down there. I don't want just another sleepy town.

Pop, you going to take that ride with me? What if I let Mom drive? Would you trust her? Maybe I'd better, I couldn't find a plastic Jesus, or even one of those scented skunks Pop Amick[27] used to sell. I tell you, America has gone to seed.

Enclosed is the monthly. I've got the monthlies now, oh brother, what next?

I'll be in. Don't look for me till I get there. It'll be after Mar. 8, but I refuse to say when.

Love,

Breece

To C. R. and Helen Pzncake ··

Fork Union, VA

April 13, 1975

Dear Folks,

There isn't a whole lot of news in big Fork Union this week. *** For the most part, the biggest thing was my fight and win of a fried egg. I'll explain when I get home. And, by the way, I was accepted into W.V.U. Graduate School of Writing, but still hear nothing from Law School. Will you please get Mike Sunderland's address for me, as I want to ask him about cost of living, jobs, etc.

The most exciting thing I did this weekend was to watch Matt play rugby, and discuss the problems of the world with a C'ville lawyer who probably wishes I'd let her watch the rugby game. I'll say this, if she was any example of a female lawyer, I want into that Law School as of *now*. I've just been away too long.

Something I'd like to know: if Jr.[28] is plowing so much, why isn't my garden plowed? Now, I don't want to be rash, but if I can't garden this summer, I'll get a job and apartment in Huntington, and you can get that Smith laddie to mow the yard. W.Va. just has too many reminders of something I lost to let me sit around. I'd go nuts in Milton if I didn't have something to work the piss out of me. Hope you understand. ***

You may tell Aunt Julia that there is a typewriter[29] just like this one in the Smithsonian. She'd get a kick out of that.

Glad to know Grandpa got somebody to do the yard. Glad (mostly) that he's feeling better.

Well you all take care, and I'll talk to you next week.

Love,

Breece

To C. R. and Helen Pancake ···

Fork Union, VA

May 5, 1975

Dear Folks,

You can always tell when I am running out of typing paper. I type on the backs of things. Please keep this one as it is my only record of a request to the dean at M.U.

Well, I was right. They offered me a contract, and avoided offering one to the poor bastards who needed their jobs—and sadly, they are all dedicated to their work. $5,522.40 isn't enough to make me endure another year of social isolation, educational sins, and institutional food. I dreamt of one of Mom's pineapple cakes the other night, and nearly cried. But despite that, Matt is hacking his way, and it looks as if he'll be back. His father was really upset with the raise they offered—said the cost of living had gone up 12%, and these people have the male organs to offer us 4%, which isn't even maintenance. By refusing mess I & III, Matt[30] got thirty a month out of the deal, and another ten for living in the barracks, and despite that, he didn't make it close to $6,000. Yeah, it's the old Russian game of Ripoffsky. As Lightfoot said, "If you make a mistake, don't make it twice."[31]

Give us your tired, your poor, your huddled masses . . . It says that at the base of the Statue of Liberty, yet we're raising hell over those poor people trying to get to our country. I'm never amazed by Americans. I hit a possum the other night and didn't stop to pick him up for stew, so I'm sure this party can hold a few more people.

Harry[32] might have loved me, but I found Harry no better than Ford.[33] At least he was better than Nixon—Harry was honest. As for clothes, I could use a half sole on my boots, but if I walk in the grass they should last another season. I still wear stuff I bought three years ago. It's just getting to the point where it's comfortable. Nice to think I made it through this year on $1,200 spending money—I didn't go hungry, and I won't have anything to show for it either, but . . .

Did you ever get a bill from the doctor? Slow fellow.

That's about it for this week—I guess the cockroaches will sure miss me when I'm gone—there won't be any Raid to eat. Sure will be good to see home.

Love,

Breece

P.S. Keep the money! For godsake take it while I've got it to give!

To C. R. and Helen Pancake ···

Fork Union, VA

May 11, 1975

Dear Folks,[34]

Mother's Day was started someplace in W.Va. back in the 1800's. That's all I know about it. You see, when I must celebrate a holiday, I must know all about it, and quite frankly, I hope not to become a Mother. But all that aside, HAPPY MOTHER'S DAY, MOM!

About that camping trip[35] . . . Matt went, but I kidded him about sleeping in the car. At three A.M. that ground got the hardest it had been all night, so I spent the next four hours in the front seat of my Whale.[36] Then I rented a row boat, and all they had were canoe paddles—no oar-locks, no oars, just two canoe paddles. Of course, Matt was still at camp, so I had to paddle the jon back to our campsite (we were right on the lake). After making enough circles and figure-eights to qualify for a ticket for drunken boating, I made it back to camp only to be welcomed with, "Oh, I see you got a boat." We explored the vast reaches of Bear Creek Lake, but never found Bear Creek Lake, let alone the Bear, and still can't figure out where all that damn water came from. Maybe they piped it in.

Pop, the ranger at the park was Mr. J. C. Woody. He said he used to work at South Chas.[37] in the gas-separation, and in plastics. He retired around 1960, although he didn't recall your face, he remembered the name. Do you remember him? He was really a nice old guy. Let me use the boat all day for three bucks, then offered to lend me a pole, but I didn't have a license, so I refused. Besides, I'm sure that with Matt and I splashing around out there all the fish were more concerned with when we were going to leave than with food.

Then Mendy came down from D.C. and laughed at us for about four hours. The wind blew my lean-to to pieces, I burned my hand picking up the coffee water, spilled it, and put out the fire. I decided to take a dip, and since the last bit of pride I had left could only be saved by making a good dive from a running start, I did. The dive was one of the most graceful things I've ever done, but the water must have been thirty-three degrees—just one above freezing. The shock sent me swimming back to shore in a speed that must have put Johnny Weissmuller[38] to shame. Matt and Mendy took off for Richmond, and I took a shower (also cold) and broke camp. Next week is the survival thing, and I hope it goes better.

In the meantime, take care.

Love,

Breece

P.S. The nearest testing center for the LSAT is in Columbus on July 26—so don't make any plans for me that weekend.

To C. R. and Helen Pancake ···

Fork Union, VA

May 19, 1975

Dear Folks,[39]

The survival campout was a total loss. First, the original group cancelled out due to a class trip they'd rather go on. Then it rained the first day we were supposed to be out, so I called it off for a day, and caught hell. Finally, with the knowledge it was going to rain later that day, I took them out Saturday. I have never seen a more inept group in my life—they couldn't even build a fire. As I was the only one who was dry and had a fire, I said I was staying. Of course, they were all for it. Since they couldn't get much wetter without swimming, I told them to get hiking around to find the plants they needed for their meal (we'd gone over this a hundred times before the actual trip). After they were gone over an hour, I got into the car, and took off. They had gone at least two miles up the road to another farm, where they were asking permission to use a tarp the farmer had left out. Thatch roofs (especially the way they made them) didn't seem to be dry enough for them. But because they had knowingly gone off, I took them back to school.

Been packing like a rat on a sinking ship. Funny how I'm not leaving with much more than I brought. Matt is talking quitting. While on duty, one of the finer young men called him a "stupid son of a bitch," to which, Matt grabbed the kid by the arm, shook him, and told him to watch his mouth. The kid called da-da, who called Matt, and more or less threatened him. It was really bothering him until I told him that if I'd been called an etc., I'd have probably beaten the kid within an inch of his life, and called Whitescarver[40] two minutes before so that I couldn't be held responsible to the Academy (in other words, quit then beat the shit out of the little bastard, and if his old man wanted to get froggy on the phone, tell him to hop on over and get me). That's what Johnny Cox[41] would have done to me, plus I'd get it from both of you when I got home.

Mom, you knew about my pool-room background. I was one of the best. Haven't played since I left home. Stupid Va. doesn't have a billiards table that's half white or at all safe. I've tried to get a game to bet Matt on, he doesn't believe I'm any good. ***

This week is finals, so I'll probably not write again unless it's a note.

Take care, and remember, I love you.

Breece

P.S. Will be in the 30th.

To UNC Writers Workshop ··

Milton, WV

June 6, 1975

Writers Workshop
Department of English
University of North Carolina
Greensboro, NC

Dear Sirs:

I am writing to inquire about a position in your Writers Workshop. Enclosed is a story Mr. John Casey, Chairman of Creative Writing, and Assistant Professor at the University of Virginia, suggested I send to you as a sample of my work.[42] It was his hope that you might be able to find a space for me.

I spent the last year at Fork Union Military Academy, where I taught English, and paid for my education. I did not find the position conducive to my writing, and refused a contract for the next year.

My original plans were to attend West Virginia University College of Law in '76, and spend a year starving and writing. If, at this late date, you could arrange a situation which would allow me to eat and write, I would appreciate it. I would be quite willing to teach, research, or perform menial tasks for such an opportunity.

Enclosed is an answer card for your convenience.

Sincerely,

Breece D. Pancake

To C. R. and Helen Pancake ···

Summer 1975

Hi Folks,[43]

"Jarfly" Johnson claimed there was a catfish under the big rock at Zoar Church, and it was so big he had to cut his line for fear of drowning.

Well, Jr. Blake and me, we got this idea as to catch that monster. We took his tractor and winch over there with a logging hook, but we still needed live bait. So we got Dick Bias' wig and put it on Ching Ball along with one of Mom's old Lois Lane dresses (you know—with the shoulder pads like a linebacker?), and roped Ching to the logging hook and threw him in.

Ching, he swum under that rock, and directly there was a great commotion. The sky got all dark, virgin timber shook its roots free and ran, and that big old rock, it quivered till the water was foamy as the cup in Glen Perry's shop.

Pretty soon that big catfish came out of there like a torpedo from hell. He was going so fast they had to close the floodgates at Huntington to keep down the waves, and the explosion sent that big old rock clear up into the yard at Zoar Church—five souls were saved on the spot.

Well, Ching crawled out of that mess all slimy and grinning ear to ear, but his wig was gone.

Jr., he said, "What's you do to that fish?"

"I kissed him," said Ching.

We had to buy Dick another wig. It's been that way all summer.

Love,

Breece

To John Casey ···

Milton, WV

August 1975

Dear Mr. Casey,

The hill-country was grand. The fishing only fair, but I brought a few back, and a piece of the hills (enclosed since I can't mail you the fish). This is yours, and you don't have to read it, comment or anything. Mostly I'm sending it to show you I'm still writing. It has been my experience that CW teachers[44] don't believe CW students write. I'm sure there's precedent for this, and justification.

Your house-sitter said you were vacationing. Enjoy it. Teachers are in season before turkeys, you know.

My hometown paper just called, and they want me to do some feature writing. It's only a tabloid, but for the Catch-22 of the job market, it's experience, anyway.

Did you get all that junk I sent to Rugby Rd.? I took the LSAT, and have little hope of ever joining *that* learned profession. Veni, sedi, excessi.[45]

Let me know if any waves break, etc. In the meantime, I remain, etc.

> Sincerely,
> Breece Pancake

To C. R. and Helen Pancake ··

Staunton, VA

Sept. 4, 1975

Dear Mom and Pop,

S.M.A.[46] was even better than I anticipated. Outside of the great pay, the headmaster is a genuine educator, an artist, and easygoing as hell. He's the opposite of Ronnie Clark.

One of the fringe benefits is Mary Baldwin College—next door—a girls school of great size! Of course the snooker table is in walking distance. The rooms are small, but plentiful. I can use as many as I like . . . all unconnected, except by a hallway.

I feel as if I shouldn't have left you at this time, but I want you to know I'll be home as soon as I can. Promise you'll call if you need me. If anything happens, call.[47]

Everything considered, this year promises to be much better than last. I'm going into C'ville to see Casey about "sitting in" on his writing classes. You may inform all concerned that I'm happy (beardless, but happy) and give them my love.

Mostly, my thanks for summer, and my love to both of you. You put up with me, and that says a lot.

More as it develops,

Love,

Breece

P.S. Save my mail until I can send a decent address.

To Helen Pancake ···

Staunton, VA

Sept. 14, 1975

Dear Mom,

Just a note to tell you I've made it back to Staunton.[48] Everything's O.K.

I guess Doni will be leaving tomorrow, and by the time you read this, you'll be wrapped up in red-tape and paper. If you need me for anything, please call, but I trust your common sense will get you through most decisions. Legal matters, however, should be given to Sam[49] since the law is *not* based on common sense.

Soon, the leaves will be turning on Afton Mountain, and I hope you'll be here to see them. You could bring Helen S. and make a dual trip, or you could come alone.

A truck wreck on 60 made me re-route via turnpike—460-N81. A much better but longer route. Maybe you'll want to come that way rather than battle the mountains. See you soon.

Love,

Breece

To Helen Pancake ···

Staunton, VA

September 17, 1975

Dear Mom,

I've been wanting to call you all week, but that probably isn't the best thing since we both have enough Fred[50] in us to waste the time crying.

I worry about you in the house, alone. I hope you are doing O.K. I know people won't leave you alone during the day, but the nights are hard—even for me. You haven't said you'd be over, so I don't know what to think. I hope you come. ***

I'm getting over a very bad cold, and trying to keep up with my work. Things go on the same—it's almost absurd.

Please tell Mammaw and Grandpa how proud I was to have them with us, and I'll try and write them tomorrow. I've written Aunt Julia, but I'm sure you'll hear about that.

You held out so well Mom, but I'm sure the thing has caught up with you now in the same way it has for me. If it helps any, I can assure you that Pop got exactly what he wanted. Many times we talked, and always he realized it could have been a hell of a lot worse. Despite it all, he had a grand sense of humor, and I'll never forget him laughing. I was lucky to have him for my father and friend.

But we have to let him go, Momma. We can't keep him, we can only make him over in our own minds.

I hope I haven't made things worse for you. I'm kind of clumsy that way. Most of all, remember I love you.

Breece

To Helen Pancake ....

Staunton, VA
Sept. 24, 1975

Dear Mom,

Just got off Barracks Duty and will jot this note as I relax before bed.

Thanks for the letter and clippings. Despite the slantedness of the articles, etc. it was sad that he had to die. I've been tempted to buy a pistol before they legislate them off the market, but I don't know. Guns are good for one thing.

Poor Jerry had better stay clear of California—third time is charmed.[51]

Casey finally got "The Scrapper," and used it in his class last night. It went over well, and most of the complaints were things I'd already noticed—minor stuff, like things Cally says, or the snake-eater image. Casey's offered to write a facing letter for the story to *Atlantic* after I've been baptized by fire from *Playboy*. He seems to think it's worth the postage, but I don't—at any rate I've got to send it to *Playboy* before he will write the letter to *Atlantic*—I know that sounds silly but it's the difference between 1,000 and 2,000 dollars, *Playboy* paying the latter.

Going to see the Frazier-Ali fight[52] with Casey next Tuesday. Keep your fingers crossed for Joe; he's waited a long, long time to beat Ali. The fight-game is almost gone but I remember Pop watching the big names on T.V. It was the only sport he ever enjoyed and in that respect I'm his son. I find myself becoming more like him. I've been doing it for years and I guess it was what I've always wanted. At least I'm comfortable at it. He was a good old boy and to imitate him wouldn't be a mistake.

Please tell Aunt Julia I don't want to put her through the desk thing. That desk is very much a part of her life and while she is living it should be with her as a reminder of the well-organized man she loved.[53] "There is a time for every purpose" and now is not the time. I'd much rather have her come here for T-giving if she could make it (and if you're willing to bring her). Perhaps I could come in the following weekend.

Whale[54] is sick. She's took to screaming at me when I want heat or air of any kind. I can't get her fixed before payday but will drive as little as possible until then.

For the first time in over a year I'm really teaching. Things are working out quite well. If only I weren't playing "Big Army" as Danny used to say, it would be quite satisfactory.

Better stop now. Remember to save some coleus this winter.

All my love,

Breece

To Helen Pancake ···

Staunton, VA

Oct. 5, 1975

Dear Mom,

Received your note upon return Sunday. O.K.—around 2 pm the 25th, and plans O.K. all around. As it were, I didn't get to Uncle Ray's or the Heards'. The Heards were leaving when I called from Union Station—going to Harrisonburg, Va. I then called Melinda,[55] whose parents were in from Fla., and she asked me to join their party, etc., and by departure 26 hours later, I'd had a grand total of three hours to talk to Melinda. She's doing well, and I implored the Heards to continue plans as it is only twelve bucks RT and a very nice ride on the train. Nonetheless, I'll get to Rockville before T-giving—I hope to God.

Cellar[56] is quite warm, home, etc. I'm sure you'll love it. Will probably have the money for instant oats when you arrive, so M & G as well as yourself will eat here. What is their diet? I can't cook it if I don't know it. This is important to me. My sanity was ready for this apt. Too long I've been subject to dictates. Both

Preston (Headmaster) and Chuck (Commandant) were here to congratulate me on the place, and drank a stout to celebrate.

Rumor has it that the Alumni Assoc. is planning to buy SMA from Leoffler.[57] This could be the best thing going, but if Leoffler continues to run the place, it only has inches to go before ground. He's a fish (a Born Again Christian), and tries to force Jesus down all our throats. The families are against it, the faculty, the administration, the cadets are all against it. Last mandatory Chapel, I marched my young ass to Mass, and later to the First Presbyterian, then that night to the Baptists. I spent most of that day in one church or another. This country gave us the freedom of religion, and a right to bear arms, and I'll be a shitass before I let someone rob me of my basic rights. Let it suffice that I'm getting on all right. Yes, I'm looking forward to seeing you, and I hope you feel the same. Let me know how everybody's doing . . .

Love,

Breece

P.S. Note from ——— (M's wife) with copy of "Scrapper" in which she compared herself to Cally in the story. Cally was described as "the perfect woman"—God, I feel sorry for Mitch.[58]

To Helen Pancake ....

Staunton, VA
Oct. 15, 1975

Dear Mom,

Many thanks for the cookies, they were great. Unfortunately, I got them in the presence of the entire office, so about half of them were gone before I could get to the coffee machine. The entire staff and faculty at SMA now knows what a good cook my mother is. They send their compliments. Everyone remarked about the black walnuts. That's a clincher.

Grades, writing, and the typing of "Scrapper" has been keeping me out of trouble. I've yet to find the time to change my lesson plans to the point where I don't get ten comps. a day. I've created a monster.

Speaking of creations, the latest (are you ready?) story[59] I'm doing is the one about that girl who stared at the monkey cage too long, etc. Because the simple truth (that the monkeys marked her baby) is too hard to believe, I'm working in incest as a possible reason for the deformity, but dwelling on the normality of the child's mind. I know you don't like my over-abundance of strange themes, but you must remember people read that kind of stuff because their minds are so normal it bores them.

Mindi isn't coming down, which is a big load off. I was really not in the frame of mind to see her again. She said Mr. & Mrs. Heard are doing O.K. I mailed them Matt's watch. I don't think I told you why I had his watch—we got pretty polluted after the first week here, and I woke up with his watch. Never saw him again.

I have duty all next weekend, plus the fact that it's Parent's Weekend. If you don't hear from me, you'll know I'm going crazy. Planning on going to Ray's the first weekend in Nov. Going either by bus or Amtrak. Whale is bleeding me dry on gas. Won't bring her home Christmas, either.

Speaking of Christmas, I intend to be home if Suzanna (not Suzanne) gets it together. Otherwise, I'd like to split up the holiday, and go to Nag's Head for a week and work on a story.[60] But that's all so far away. I'll tell Beas to drop by. By the way, Suzanna was one of my students at HHS[61] and is now at MU.[62] Dr. Carr gave her my address, and she's been writing ever since. Figure that one out.

I'm sorry but I can't get it together to answer Gloria. It's not that I'm bitter or anything. I can honestly say I have nothing to say to her or Paula. In truth, that isn't all that bad.

It just dawned on me that Mitch never did send that ms. he made such a big deal about not taking stamps for. Could you send me his address? I don't appreciate copies floating all over hell and creation for long periods of time. One guy at Iowa just sent back "Fox"[63] after four months.

This is pretty random, but I feel I haven't written enough to let you know I'm O.K. Somehow, cookies in the mail say mother is worried. You're really a great person, and I've been sort of out of it about writing. Forgive me.

Please give my love to everybody especially Mammaw, Grandpaw and Aunt Julia.

Glad to know you'll be working. It'll be the best thing. God knows Milton isn't enough to excite people through that stretch in Jan. and Feb.

No. Don't haul a bunch of junk over here for the winter. I'll need the tires, but that's about all. Again, this is a one year job. This time I'm working on Civil Service (civil). I've got a rating, etc. All I want is a job in West Virginia. Also, something might come up with Iowa or P-Exeter, I'll sign a contract, and if I have to, break it; if I don't, I still have a job.

Hope this finds you well and getting out. I enjoy your accounts of the various trips you've taken. That must be where I get my writing.

I'm meeting my share of people, too, and getting along.

All my love, and take good care. Again, thanks for the cookies. They'll make me fatter than gallons of beer.

Love,

Breece

To Helen Pancake ···

Staunton, VA

Oct. 28, 1975

Dear Mom,

After Nov. 1, my address should read 324 East Beverly St., Cellar, Staunton, etc. After pulling duty all weekend, I was awakened at 6 A.M. by the screams of cadets. Pardon my French, but I said, "Screw this shit."

On my constitutional, I stopped off at Mrs. (Pancake) Mandeville's house,[64] and she told me of the apt. It is furnished with antiques, has a fireplace, back yard complete with squirrel, two bedrooms, dining room, sitting room, garage, and is within walking distance to the Academy. Of course, it's in the best side of town, in the basement of a really neat old house, and a widow named Mrs. Nutt[65] lives above me. She wanted somebody in the house because she's away a lot, or so I gather. On top of that, I can afford it and still save money as long as I eat at the Academy twice a day. ***

Mom, you don't know what a relief it is to get out of these barracks. I must be asocial, but I can't exist under these conditions. I haven't told anybody about it, and plan to keep this room as a sort of stop-over when I pull duty. I'm moving a little at a time so no one will notice. Don't worry about it jeopardizing my job. Preston[66] won't give a good damn whether I'm here or not, as long as I do my job. ***

You can stay at my place, and if Mammaw and Grandpa[67] can take sleeping in the same bed, they're welcome, too. When you come, I'd like you to meet Mrs. Mandeville—she's really a nice lady. I'm so glad you and Pop taught me to respect and be friendly to elders. It's never been a bad thing.

Work to do—Love,

Breece

To Helen Pancake ··

324 E. Beverly St.
Staunton, VA
Nov. 9, 1975
Sunday 8:30 A.M.

Dear Mom,

Thanks for the letter updating me on all the goings on.

Before I forget, I *don't* need curtains, but I would like my plates, pans, silver, etc. There *is* only some (willow) odd pieces and no flatware. That and the tires I need, and if you can't get the rest of the junk in the car—leave it. I realize you have to have a suitcase, etc., and even have doubts about getting those tires in the trunk. (By the way, let some man get those out—they are *too* heavy.)

Yesterday I picked up the rake Mrs. Nutt had leaned against my stoop and began to rake. I thought it was a hint, so I raked up all the leaves in the back. It hadn't been a hint, and she was rather surprised to find that tools fit my hands (*now*, I've really got a problem). She then took me to her farm in Middlebrook and let me fish in her trout pond for free. Caught a 3 lb. rainbow and a smaller spotted, which we had for lunch. She's really very nice—somewhat difficult to relate to her D.A.R. Republican party attitude, but a nice lady. She really wanted to meet you all, but she's leaving for her kid's house the 17th. ***

Granted, I've got it pretty plush here, but I can't count on SMA being here after June. Leoffler is really a sick puppy. Mom, that school has a dedicated faculty and administration—mostly decent kids—it could be so much, yet it's sad to see Leoffler make public statements like, "I hated it when I went there, now I'll see it close." Revenge? Who knows? The turkey's flipped a gobble. ***

Tuck[68] like Grandpa is too good. The world is very harsh for good people. Harsh and hard to understand. Both men have gone on in smiles and tears while people walk on their hearts. It isn't fair.

Mom, there's no place in Staunton worth eating at. All are starchy spoons, etc. Let me cook. Why do you think I rented this place? Because I like privacy and good food.

I'm glad you're proud of me. Hope I can do more and better in the future. Once in a while, the gypsy comes back, but her song means less—is harder to hear.

Better get ready for the organ prelude at First Pres. Bach today, I think.

All my love,

Breece

P.S. Would like my blue wool boatman's coat and blue coffeepot.

1976–1977

•••••••••••••••••••

To Helen Pancake ···

324 E. Beverly St.

Staunton, VA

Jan. 2, 1976

Dear Mom,

Many thanks for your letter. I'm eating hot tuna, and trying to get this out before tonight. Story work slow and hard, but that's a sign—nearly had a breakdown writing "Scrapper." What I have so far is pretty good—one more draft should do it.

Had New Years with Mrs. Nutt, and sundried Pancakes. She had a dinner party. For me I think. At any rate, I was then invited to a party on Waverley Hill (the home of Mrs. Pancake of UVA, Wilson, board fame—now, of course, dead). That turned out to be cousin Robins P. and Emily and Dorie Smith—also cousins. That is the first time I've ever been served creme de menthe for dessert, and I was afraid to ask what it was. Figured it out later. Waverley Hill is a goddamn mansion. Makes Monticello look cheaply built and small. Boxwoods, too. Think I'll introduce Robins to Mindi. He lives in D.C. and has a UVA law degree, isn't bad looking and has a good personality.

Our combined efforts on the family show that I descended from Abe, they from Phillip, and most likely the Huntington clan from Isaac. E.g., we're as close in kin as the pin oak, the white oak and the red oak—if you want to go back to the first tree, they are the same breed.

Amtrak oversold seats, and that was a real bummer of a trip. You know people can really be shits, and they always seem to take it out on the waiters. Spent most of the trip standing up between cars as I did on the way to Mazatlan, Mx.,[69] and talking to the conductors between stops. Just got bored with the people in the cars bitching their heads off.

Been thinking about that certificate you have in the bank for me, and appreciate the thought. Nonetheless, you and Dad gave me a lot, good breeding, background and education. I can take it from there. I want you to keep that money and use it as you need to. You may not need it now, but it can serve you far better than I. I'm young and can make my own place—I'm Saturday's child, remember? Just thought you'd sleep better knowing you weren't so short on savings.

Got to get a note off to Char, then back to work. Love you and think of you often. Regards to all.

Breece

To Helen Pancake ···

324 E. Beverly St.
Staunton, VA
Jan. 11, 1976

Dear Mom,

The story[70] is coming along really well, and may mean something after all—many thanks for telling me that weird story this summer. Without you, I might be writing like John-Boy Walton[71]—soft soap. If you pick up anything else weird, let me know.

Moving again, but not so far—just upstairs. Mrs. Nutt has found a renter for this apt. who promises to stay awhile, so she's offered me a room in the main house, the Library, and kitchen priv's for a lot less rent. Why not?

Preston[72] is leaving soon, and I guess things must get worse from that point on. Nonetheless, I've made my bed for the next few (maybe very few) months, and I'll lie in it. What the hell, Pop put up with much more than this, and I can wear his clothes.

Mom, I'm afraid my being first on the list as Aunt Jul's exec. is pretty worthless. The only thing that matters is the old gal herself—when she dies, we can only say good-bye. I reckon I'll say it as a mourner, and go on my way. Let them take what they want, and as much thereof as they can carry, we knew her, and that's what counts most. By only asking me to do it, she recognized my adulthood, and that means so much to me, I have no words for it. I hope she sees a hundred.[73]

As for yourself, I hope this finds you well. I wanted to call you this afternoon, but I got my bill this week, so I'm being a good boy. Soon the phone will be out, so if you need to call me, just call Mrs. Nutt after five—I'm usually home at that hour. Don't call on a Wednesday. Class at UVA.

Guess I filled you in on the happenings after New Years, so I won't bore you with that. Mostly I've been writing like an SOB, and doing my physical program. The sweats are very handy, and on cold nights, I sleep in them.

First chance, I'll get a letter off to Shorty and Ray Glenn[74]—two fantastic people. We have a fellow here who was once a pilot—pilot?—yeah—and he used to drink a lot. Well, one day his wife called the maintenance office about her furnace being out, and the man said, "Is your pilot lit?" and his wife said, "Oh, is Austin drunk again?"

Wrote to Char and Doni, but no word as yet.

Again, hope this finds you well. Many thanks for the clipping on the bridge as it fit (Silver Bridge[75]) into my story very well. Don't work too long a week.

Love,

To Helen Pancake ···

324 E. Beverly St.
Staunton, VA
Jan. 14, 1976

Dear Mom,

I guess you got the letter I mailed Mon., so there isn't that much news with me. Just wanted to let you know I'm not in the hospital—it seems everyone else is. Also, I'd like to send my regrets to Glen.[76] I didn't know his wife very well, and mostly I was afraid to talk to her—she always scared me. I guess I subconsciously recalled asking for Dale, and her reply. But that really doesn't matter, and didn't mean I didn't like her. She was a good woman and a hard worker.

Also, I'm going to have my ear[77] done in soon, and want you to promise to get your foot worked on this summer. I'll be home and more than willing to wait on you and keep the house while you're down. All I'm going to do is get something to keep the snakes off my legs, and tramp the rivers with Hinton[78] (if the old buzzard lasts the winter). My next project is the mine wars (and to beat Mary Lee[79] to the punch), so I'll start with him. Also, I'll fish in the mornings, and be back home before nine. Good enough? . . .

We are living one day at a time here at SMA, and as Chairman of English, I can assure you Mr. ——, that your son will leave this school with vertical and horizontal articulation. I don't know what it means either, but I put it on a lot of report cards. Yeah, if the place lasts, I'll be happy for a few more months—I only wish I could deliver a better program, but the Big D won't fork the money we need for materials. I can only get what I make the boys buy, and that's almost always books. We need the aid of posters relating to the themes, things to inspire some imagination, and better prepared lessons. ***

Just about the time I move in with a permanent chaperone, I get a girlfriend in Staunton, Mary Baldwin girl, and quite intelligent, but a little crazy. I always get the weirdos, don't I? The major thing is that she's from only a mile away from Gloria. Fortunately, she doesn't know Gloria exists. Anyway, she's some kind of companion until May—I never need girls after May anyway.

Hope this finds you well, and let me know when you plan to leave for AZ—WA. Give my regards to Mammaw and Grandpa and Aunt Jul.

Love you,
Breece

To Helen Pancake ···

324 E. Beverly St.

Staunton, VA

Feb. 29, 1976

Dear Mom,

It has been something of a trying week, and the worst is yet to come with grades and duty. The coast of Mexico has never looked better in my mind, but I'd feel as if I was letting you and Pop down if I flew the coop.

It looks as if I'll be taking German all summer at MU, so there goes any idea of a vacation. Still, I may get some fishing and roaming in. This is for the grad language requirement, therefore important to get over with. May have to arrange some room with Mammaw and Grandpaw, as I don't want to be shuttling back and forth during the week.

Yesterday I put the top down and drove over to the plant[80] I helped build, visited the Poes and FUMA, then came home. It took the day, and got some of the gypsy out of my system. The Blue Gill[81] is trucking right along, and giving me 35 mpg. If the weather is this nice at break, I'll drive it over the mountains.

Bob Nutt wants me to help him do some write-ups about the farm, and I'm mulling over an article about the Staunton interest in WVa coal to circulate free-lance (and probably for free). To top that, I've promised John a story[82] by the end of March, and I have very little time to write it. May have to put the Staunton article on wraps until I finish the other commitments.

Also, Bob hinted at my living in the cabin[83] on the farm this summer (fish for free in the back pond), but all these good things come when I can't take them. So I hinted back at a rain-check.

By now you have the *Rivanna*, and I hope you enjoyed the story.[84] Getting in print has a strange effect—you feel like writing more because "everybody's read that one."

Hope you are enjoying your job and social life. Mrs. Nutt throws about three parties a week, and it really helps her. I'm convinced she'd die without them.

It looks as if the crops will be bad this year unless we have a wet spring. Guess I won't have my garden—again.

Give my regards to everyone, and I'll be home the last week in March. Dig some worms.

> Love you,
> Breece

To Helen Pancake ···

> 324 E. Beverly St.
> Staunton, VA
> March 28, 1976

Dear Mom,

Been writing all day, finished first section of "Hollow," and just burned out on second. So I quit for today—with any luck I'll get this done in a week or so. It would have been much harder to write without the visit to Ky. truck mines, and talking with Mr. Caudill.[85] He's a great old salt, and was very nice.

There is, however, one thing I hate worse than shaving— that is a dry county! This, I discovered too late, was the case in Letcher County *and* Bloody Harlan. No wonder they're so wild.

Wanted to tell you how much I enjoyed staying home and talking with you. I'm sorry I couldn't get the lid off that mower

—I'm sure the fuel-line is clogged up. At any rate, thanks for the stay, and if you need anything, let me know. I'm looking forward to being there this summer, but hope you can stand the smell of home brew—the beer prices there are too much!

Not looking forward to getting back to work, but I'm sure nothing short of knocking Webb on his butt could dislodge me now. If they give me any hair shit, I'll quit shaving. Let 'em fire me! Only kidding—I'll be cool.

Anyway, if you want to come over sometime, just remember you'll have to entertain yourself during the day. Would love to have you.

> Keep truckin!
> Love you,
> Breece
> P.S. *Save* mail from Educational Testing Service in Princeton, N.J. It contains a ticket I'll need at M.U.

To Helen Pancake ....

> 324 E. Beverly St.
> Staunton, VA
> April 12, 1976

Dear Mom,

Obviously some time has lapsed—I've finished "Hollow," sent it to Casey, gotten a letter (finally!) from U.Va. to confirm my appointment,[86] and sent (again—Mr. Taylor's letter[87] didn't get to Robie Macauley before they sent my stories back—this is getting expensive—$3.00 every trip to Chicago!) my mss. to *Playboy*'s Robie Macauley.

Buddy's nuptial[88] came as more of a shock than you might have imagined. The main character of "Hollow" was named Buddy, so whatever chemistry took place launched a spaceship—"Hollow" was giving me royal pains until your call. I guess the great respect I've had for Buddy sticking out a hard life made him sort of a demi-God—he had the guts to do something I could never do, at least as long as I knew there was an easier way to get from A to B. But Buddy getting married? That's like saying Hitler found Christ—it just don't mesh. Nonetheless, I'm glad to know he isn't sleeping under a bridge or with a whore. He was always good to me, and I liked him—he'll be a good father—hell, he knows enough tails to wag that boy's ear off. If you get his address, send it. I'd like to congratulate him and wish them well.

When you come over, I'll "get sick"—take a few days off, and we'll buzz around a little—there isn't much to see, but it takes some driving to do it. Plan the middle of May—that's pretty slack and U.Va. is over with on the 1st. Of course, that's always a holiday—May 1st.

Also, I think I'll zoom to the beach the day school is out (June 6) and remain there thru and including the 10th. My test is on the 12th, and registration at M.U. the 14th or something. Anyway, I'd like to get some sun and fun before school starts—this time back on the "other" side of the desk.

Hope this goes well with your plans. No word from my "silent sisters." What gives?

Pulled my left leg playing rugby, and can hardly walk—Mrs. Nutt thinks I should put in for Medicare, and I mean it. But I've cut down and lost about five pounds. Gave up meat—not sure for how long, but it seems to be working—and limit myself to six beers—never before nine p.m.—and eat mostly wheat, fruit, cheese, vegetables and fish. No reason for doing this—except to avoid the mess hall, and feel better. There's an interconnection, you know.

Well, I hope you are doing a lot—having some fun along with work. Look forward to seeing you soon.

Love,

Breece

To Helen Pancake ··

One Blue Ridge Lane
Charlottesville, VA
Sept. 2, 1976

Dear Mom,

My assumption that the rush of life would cease once settled in Farmington was false. My pins feel like two long-running sores. Registration, orientation, et al. was insanity inspired and put to action. I have not been this busy in years.

I talked with Perdue[89] yesterday, and my fears were realized. He preferred the "scholarly" paper on narrative style—hard work from here out. Peter Taylor is going to dissolve class after the first few meetings, and that means that most of my work—both for Taylor and Perdue—will be done on my own. That leaves only Chaucer class twice a week, and happily, only one final exam this term.

I bought health insurance, the car is being inspected, and I still have a million errands to run. My room is ready and moved into—for the most part—I left my guns at David's, and haven't been back since. ***

The people here are friendly and as exhausted as I am. You know, it's funny to watch new students—they're scared, but they make up for it with dramatic scenes of emotion. I must have seen twenty scenes like Doni makes at registration. ***

SMA is like a tomb. Nonetheless, Leoffler[90] is still living there—selling bits and pieces of junk—guns, tables, chairs, but as yet, no real estate. Kegley[91] seems to think Leoffler might try to re-open the place, but I doubt that.

I can say this much for sure—I wish someone would buy the place and do something with it. It looks so lovely up there.

Looking ahead, I'll be glad to have a job again and not have to study. So many of these turkey-students are staying in for Ph.D.'s, but the whole orientation theme was telling them they couldn't get work with twelve Ph.D.'s from Harvard.

I guess there comes a time when you decide the sky isn't the limit and the road doesn't go on forever, and that's where you stop. And I guess I prefer the real world to these ivory towers of learning. ***

Already the sycamores are turning yellow-green, and I know you must be thinking of Pop. I think that's O.K. to do, but remember, he didn't live very long, but he lived his life very well. That's what counts. Better get to the library.

Love you,

Breece

To Helen Pancake ···

One Blue Ridge Lane
Charlottesville, VA
Sept. 14, 1976

Dear Mom,

*** Went to Staunton this weekend, stayed with Mrs. Nutt, fished, and had a great time. I really felt at home, and really didn't want to leave. She told me I could have "Far-Away" (the cabin on the farm) for Thanksgiving, and any other time. That would be a great place to hunt and write. I really sort of miss being there, at least in any capacity of living other than at SMA— and even seeing it closed hurts a little.

Got to know the Meades[92] a little better, and Mrs. Meade has a piece of needlework reputedly made by Mary Queen of Scots which she invites you to come see. Also, they are going to put us in touch with the guy who can finally tell the truth about the Pancake's beginnings. He's married to, get this, Anastasia, the chick who claimed to be the lost daughter of the Czar of Russia, and rightfully heiress to the Throne.

Of late my Sunday has been spent with Nancy Ramsey at the old swimming hole, and I roughly resemble a sailor lost at sea. Nonetheless, I ran into Lynn, my throb from a year ago, and the big date that flopped. She was repentive, talkative, and asked me to escort her this weekend, at no personal cost, to a party. Why not. Besides Nancy is sane, and it probably wouldn't work out. But I'll keep swimming with her.

Paid my bills. I'm considering substitute teaching this winter.

I want you to write out the stories you told the tape—I'll explain later, but please do it as soon as you can. They were: the monkey story, the token jelly jars, and your dad's token. This is very important. Also, if you can, I'd like the newspaper film prints on the girl and boy who murdered their parents because the parents wouldn't let them marry. As it turned out, they were cousins. I have no idea how to start, but if you start around '67 and move up, you've got it. I realize this is a lot of work, but maybe you can ask around for a better date. Let me know if you can do this, or who I should write to. All this before Nov. Also, this lib. here can't find Oliver Makin. Who should I write to find this stuff? I'm writing John Stuart, but hope for nothing.

Love you,

Breece

P.S. Tell Aunt Julia hi from me, and tell Grandpa I almost got a deer, but figured the car was worth more. Tell Jr. I let the gas out of his beans, but it didn't do any good. He'll say I didn't do it right.

To Helen Pancake ....

One Blue Ridge Lane
Charlottesville, VA
October 20, 1976

Dear Mom,

Thanks for your call last night. I've been up since 3 am, writing longhand on this teaching paper, and I'm done for. It is now 5 p.m. You see, I go to bed before the news goes off, and I'm up in the wee hours. This because I can get nothing on the radio, have to leave the stereo off, not tempted to a beer since I just got up, can't look out the window since it's dark—nothing else to do, may as well study. That's discipline for a chicken fried rat—which is what I am.

I did get some therapy today. It was pouring rain, so I soaped the can, and let the rain rinse it. Saved fifty cents. Roof leaks so I'll have to waterproof it soon. Did I tell you I fixed the electrical problem with 13 cents? A fuse. Wish it was all like that.

Enclosed are copies of the *Declaration*.[93] At this time I can't say how "Cowboys and Girls"[94] will look, but Chris told me a picture went with the story, which is O.K. There are also some back issues with "Hollow," but it's an old version, still the girls haven't read either one, and if you want to send them a copy, that's O.K. too. I just can't afford the postage.

Peter Taylor is driving me nuts with "Will-o-the-Wisp."[95] He wants a D.H. Lawrence story, and that ain't what she's about. I don't know what the hell to do . . .

I wish the hell I'd taken John's advice and just taken the money to write. As is, I'm so busy reading and writing papers for class I haven't got time to write stories. I was so burned out Monday, that I took rod in hand, and kept everything I caught. Ate it too. And the fact that it was under limit size did not give me heartburn. ***

Well, better go. Miss you much, and reckon I'll see you before long. Love you.

    Breece

To Helen Pancake ···

One Blue Ridge Lane
Charlottesville, VA.
October 24, 1976

Dear Mom,

***Talked to Doni night before last, and all sounds well. We got maudlin about the Old West, and she reports she is headed to these parts in Jan. I will be home for about a week (5 days?) in early Dec., but try to bring her across the mountains as I plan to have the cabin on the farm the remaining time. You can sleep together, and shit in the same outhouse. Sounds inviting doesn't it?

Many thanks for the goodies. On All Saints' Day, I'll fast and pray, but before Hallow Evening, I'll eat what I like. Have a dinner date with the Livingstons in Staunton for that night, and wish I had a pumpkin to carve, but will be satisfied to write my name in the frost.

Tomorrow the Underwood types up another paper. Been working pretty hard this week, and owe Peter Taylor a chapter from the novel Mike is anxious about. Must get to that.***

Mrs. Meade is throwing a party for the Eng. Dept., and had the gall to ask me to tend bar. Said if I didn't she'd *have* to hire a colored, and they don't mix a good drink. That tells me where I stand as a Hillbilly—one notch above the colored—only because I can mix a good drink. If Mrs. Meade later forgets herself and invites me, I'll decline on the basis of not having any shoes, and having to tend to my still and welfare check.

Every time I hear a hard luck story from a millionaire's son or daughter, I think of you and Dad on 18 bucks a week, a war, etc.

You lived *hard but well*, and that makes *character*—not money. Seems to me I read about a fellow who was born in a barn one night. He got pretty pissed off at rich folks, and even wrecked their meeting place more than once. But it just wasn't in him to hate rich folks or folks period. Anyway, I think he was like that because he had *good parents* and *loved them*. I have to thank you and Pop for that, too.

Love you,
Breece

To Helen Pancake ··

One Blue Ridge Lane
Charlottesville, VA
November 8, 1976

Dear Mom,

I don't know when you'll get this, but I may as well write now, as time is coming I'll be going nuts again.

Today, the first day of small game season, I listened as the rats with bushy tails laughed at me from just out of range. And with deer season only one week away, a four point buck walked within ten yards of me, stopped, stared, walked off. Tell Glenn and Jr.,[97] because I won't see another one, I'm sure. There I sat with the shotgun, no slugs, and the season a week away. I could cry rivers. I have been tracking this fellow for a week, but never saw him in that part of the woods, so I'm not as smart as I thought. But it was a nice sight, and I thought of Dad, sitting there in his hunting clothes.

Peter Taylor is starting another magazine,[98] and has invited me to help edit it, but that remains in the shadows, as P. T. is often other-worldly about plans. He wants it to be a mag. for regional stories like my own and others. I think he is rebelling against the so-called new story, and trying to get a clique of southern writers together again—much like it was when he was young. I asked him how much he was going to pay me. There will be money, says he. Sure. In the words of Sally in "Hollow," they's always *gonna*, but they ain't never any.

Richard Jones[99] asked me if he could buy some of the game I get this fall, but in England, they do that. I told them they throw the key away if you do that here, and he said that it was "barbaric" to do such a thing to a man.

Many thanks for the check. It's in the tobacco can if I need it. The thing is, you don't have any money if this keeps up. Granted, I left two C-notes with you, but as I recall, it was because you were short. I don't want this becoming a habit because I don't want to get used to the extra income, and two, I don't want you counting your pennies. Right, you do have bread in the bank, but that's a cow of a different color. You are working for what you live on, and you had better keep it. When Carter[100] gets through, they may close the country down.

Well, I've been up since four, and I'm going tomorrow. Somewhere there is a critter with my name on him, just waiting to become pot-meat.

Love you, and have a nice trip,
Breece

To Helen Pancake ··

One Blue Ridge Lane

Charlottesville, VA

Nov. 19, 1976

Dear Mom,

*** I don't think there's going to be any money in Peter's mag. I sometimes wonder if it isn't just a pipe dream.

I've seen so dog-gone many doe it's sickening, and not one buck since the last report. George and some of his friends hunted the farm second day of season, but I had to leave early for class, so I don't know if they got anything, but it sounded like a war, so they saw something. Tell the men back there that I sit on my stump and count shots—three or more, and I know that sucker couldn't hit the side of a barn. Tell grandpaw I go out with my rifle, and before I ready to leave, I potted two or three squirrels. Only I do it with a shotgun. Actually, I found out nobody over here ever heard of hunting small game with a shotgun just a .22 rifle. They must be more concerned with sport than eating.

I've been getting along on three hours sleep since the season opened two weeks ago, and now I'm hitting the sack for the entire weekend. Just get up long enough to eat a sandwich and drink a milk. Really, I'm zonked. Running through the wood with two guns has taken a lot out of me, but I'll be better after some sleep. By the way, send me a recipe for cooking game, I'm not too good at it, and it tastes raunchy, but I eat it.

O.K. write me a letter about your trip.

Love you,

Breece

To Helen Pancake ···

One Blue Ridge Lane

Charlottesville, VA

Jan. 31, 1977

Dear Mom,

Your consideration toward my wardrobe is touching but unmerited. I'm quite warm, although redundant in fashion, i.e. the same four outfits all the time. But it's O.K. since I'm never seen by the same group for more than an hour. If you'd read my mind, you'd know what I really wanted was my harmonica. I got along by borrowing a "C" (I play a "G" with limitation) and investing in a bottle of Listerine. I'm stealing an idea from a story from W.Va. History 1700's by McWhorter[101] (from Buckhannon, 1915). Because I want it printed in *Shenandoah* mag., I'm stealing a line from "Oh, Shenandoah" for the title. Ergo the need for the harmonica.

Saw Sarah[102] yesterday. Bob talked most of the time (2–6 pm), so there isn't much news. Mary Moore's car rolled down the hill and took out a nice piece of Wilson's Birthplace Wall.

Tell Grandpa not to worry about my car. It runs. I drive slowly and pray a lot, and I promise to buy a new one as soon as I get a steady job. ***

You could do me a big favor—take my old newspaper (the Indian Fighter) out of the frame in Pop's room, put it between two pieces of cardboard and mail it to me here. Give it the Library Rate because it's research material.

I've got to get a haircut pretty soon—I look like a worn out mop. And the other day my cigarette lighter was too full, and on lighting a butt in the wind, I singed one side of my chin down to a day's growth. I don't go out in public much since then. Got the brownies, but will ration them—one a day, so I won't get fat. They sure are good, and many thanks. When the weather (or if) gets better I'll start walking to school. 10 miles a day should put me in decent shape for a good long walk in May (up to Rhode Island or over to Milton). I'm eating well, but can't believe the prices. Can't wait for my tax refund! I can eat steak for a week, at least.

Give my regards to all.

Love,

Breece

To Helen Pancake ···

> One Blue Ridge Lane
> Charlottesville, VA
> Feb. 7, 1977

Dear Mom,

Enclosed please find some stuff Charlotte[103] sent here for reading—as if I don't have enough to read. She and Bob went on this winter trip, but as she tore a muscle, they were sent back before they could camp in the snow. When I was in the mountains in Calif. and nearly froze with my army blanket and a trench-fire, I would have been pretty comfy with all that downy crap on their backs. But the point is, I'd never have that story to tell, or the pride of having stayed alive when it was easier to go to sleep. ***

Mostly I worked this weekend, but I did get away Sunday night for a Bogart movie. It's so funny to watch him work with

Bacall—you can tell they neither one give a hoot about the acting. I saw him in *Casablanca* last week when he worked with Grace Kelly,[104] and the quality of acting was much higher.

Mary Lee Settle[105] had me over Fri. She's working like crazy on the mine-wars, and Mother Jones. Matter of fact, she's starting to talk like her . . . losing that Brit. accent from all those years in Eng. Anyway, if you can send me the correct title and—strike that from the record. The old guy who wrote the Pipestem book[106]—the one you sent last year—if you could xerox the segment called "Death in the Bonepile," I'd appreciate it. I spent twenty minutes in Alderman[107] Friday and brought out scads of stuff Mary Lee couldn't find or hadn't read. Maybe I'll get a free copy, huh?

We haven't had it much better, although our weather has been sunny, and we avoided the snow. Actually, it's getting close to fishing time, and I can't get through the ice. The car is still running, and ask Grandpaw if he got that animal tail on his truck.

No news is good for the story at VQR,[108] but now that the first shock is over, I'm resigned that they probably won't take it. I'm in competition with seasoned vets like Ward Just from *Atlantic*, etc. Although I'm putting in to St. Joe[109] for work, I'm going to try magazines around to see if I can't get a readership or man Friday job—what the heck, it's worth a try.

Hope you are feeling O.K. How do you like that dog?[110] I crack up thinking that Charlotte said in her letter: ". . . wish she could have stayed longer (without that weirdo dog, of course) . . ." Weirdo is right, and I'm convinced they are all that way. In D.C., I thought Jewell's dog was different, but by the time I left she decided to attack. Give me a bluetick.

One other thing, Mary Lee wants to meet you—she wants to

meet anybody who thinks she's famous or talented. She's really funny, and doesn't drink much at all—a beer or two, but that's surprising for a writer who's in their 60's. ***

More later,

Love

Breece

Again thanks for the check.

To Helen Pancake ···

One Blue Ridge Lane

Charlottesville, VA

Feb. 25, 1977

Dear Mom,

Now Feb. 25, so at least I mean well. I got busy as usual and had to put more pleasant matters aside in order to get some writing done. This story[111] just started out to be homework, but I think with the proper time and effort, could be a really fine story. The only thing about writing first drafts is that it's just as much a drain as Basic Training. I've been at it since seven this morning, and at two-thirty, I feel whipped. Wrote seven pages—I know that doesn't sound like much, but I assure you I bleed with every word. ***

Poor Richard Jones went to ask next year off so that he and his wife could go back to Wales and mourn the loss of their daughter.[112] They told him to go ahead as they didn't have any more openings for him—ever. People here are pretty heartless.

Between being sick and all, I haven't got much of a social life together, and this will be the fourth weekend I've played the wallflower, but it sure gets the work done. Besides, I still haven't met a girl worth her salt in this place yet. I go to movies alone and when (matinee) I want, so it costs less all around. See *Rocky*[113] if you can—a funny, good movie, which really should be rated "G."

Met a nice (but flighty) girl from Trinity College in one of my classes, so I asked her if she knew Matt.[114] She did, but didn't know he was dead. "What's Matt doing now?" "Pushing up daisies." "Oh."

Thanks for finding that thing for Mary Lee.[115] Haven't gotten it of this date, but that sort of thing always takes longer—the photocopy of that trial of the two cousins took three weeks. ***

I'll write to Mary Lou first chance I get. Don't worry about my getting a job—The Navy Needs You, that's what the billboard said. Only kidding.

No other news, just putting pen to paper. Give my happiest to all and tell Betty Fr. is making me read more than my classes do,[116] so I'm giving up church for Lent. Again, only kidding. (Why do I have to tell you when I'm kidding?)

    Love,

    Breece

To Donnetta Pancake ··

> One Blue Ridge Lane
> Charlottesville, VA
> June 6, 1977

Dear Doni,   D-Day

    Many thanks for your saga, and sorry this can't prove to be

the same, but I'm off today, and need a haircut. My golf course is city owned, open to the public, and I don't have to charm the golfers. We get some ragged customers. Got a long talk with a guy who tried to tear his wife's jaw off—the whole time the cop who threw him in the clink is sitting there laughing along. Just grist for the mill . . .

If the "girls" there want to meet me, you might warn them that I'm so horny the crack of dawn has to be careful around me. Or, as was said of old, I'd take a naked leap at a rolling doughnut. I'm dating, but these children don't do much for me—takes a thirty-year-old woman to even get a good conversation going. Gloria and Libby[117] are both getting married . . . and the other night I dreamed of Lib. She was standing on a stairway, trying to impress me with the importance of her body and mind. Oddly, I was in a Navy uniform and cowboy boots. I turned, walked away from her yakking, and one of those cold winds that takes your breath away was beating me head on. What would Freud say about that one? Pussy-whipped? Too many Tuborgs?

Have you heard of Diane Fossey and her study of the great apes in Indonesia? I'd take you up on that rt ticket if I could spend the entire time talking to that woman. I saw her on a Nat. Geo. special, and she is flipping brilliant, brave as a snake, and is dedicated as a nun. I ought to say that A. Earhart has always been a secret love of mine, and D. Fossey is alive, and therefore seems less perverse. But you should look her up—seriously—as you'd both get along. ***

As for the news—you assisted me more than you know. Those two trips to AZ blossomed the seeds of experience, made me know myself and others more deeply, and gave me a basis to view from. Somehow, you can't look back without having been away. I think Wolfe[118] was right—you can't go back expecting the same, but it's the re-evaluation that makes going home a truth. Not like love is a truth—that takes two of one state of mind. Going home is only something that one person can understand, making it presentable to others—trying—is the hardest part of writing. Over the past three years I've looked so far into myself and found very little I could make others understand. It wasn't until recently I found out everybody is alike on that score, too. Pontificate, pontificate. See, you even taught me that word. ***

But a guy named Tom Waits is a new discovery of mine. His version of "Phantom 309"[119] is a prime example that the story is in the telling. ***

Love and miss you,

Breece

Dear Doni,

Made it! *Atlantic* bought "Trilobites" for $750. Don't know when they'll print it, but Manning[120] wrote personal congrats and said they'd have some editorial comments at a later date (?). This has really set fire to Wilson Hall and the (Cross yourself) English Department. Poor second rate citizen Pancake who can't speak the King's English, who lost the Balsch prize by one, who just never was good enough for Peter Taylor to take seriously, who (God forbid) went to *work* when the money ran out—that turkey made it. I went to Mass that night, work the next day, and I still put my pants on one leg at a time. I stay out of Wilson Hall, too. Since I have a letter from Little-Brown to look at a collection, I'm thinking of writing the National Endowment for the Arts. If Erica Jong can get bucks for that *Fear of Flying* nonsense, why not me? Hell, an *Atlantic* First and forty cents will buy you a cup of coffee anyplace short of New York.

I owe Jim McPherson[121] a lot for this—he got me beyond the mail-room, and that makes all the difference in the world—otherwise it's sort of postal ping-pong. Jim's a funny sort. He's never invited me to his house or asked me to meet his wife, but I'm the only person here he'll hang around with. Everyone in the Dept. calls him "The Spook Who Sits by The Door" because he locks his office during office hours, and never sits with other teachers. He's an intense thinker—throws out heavy-duty ideas on every subject brought up, and is the only person I know who questioned the purpose of McDonald's in human existence. *That* is something to boggle the mind. We share a common distaste for the preppy-class and a common bond for pool halls and beer.

The funniest thing is that I'm experimenting with tenses (time in language) and images (ideal space) as making the greatest impact in telling a story, and know little about the technical aspects of either. If I've learned anything this year, it's the fact that a teller switches voices in midstream for effect, and that the words "He was walking down a darkened street" and "I am walking down this dark street" and "I walk the dark street" all mean something different in terms of time and space. I may be making TNT without knowing it. BOOM. Otherwise, all's well. Hope you get back in time to have a small party over some roast trout or bluegill (summer) and not rabbit. Jim bought his first gun so we could hunt this fall, and I'm hoping he's quieter in the woods than in the pool halls, or we'll never see anything. He brandished the damn thing in the parking lot and said—"I want

all you white-people to be in Cleveland by midnight." Told him
I'd rather be in Milton. "O.K. all you white-people go to Ohio,
and Pancake can stay here and be my slave." Got to go to work.
Take care and come home soon.

Love,

Breece

P.S. I'm going with the name B. D'J. Pancake. J from John,
my Confirmation name, and I dropped Dexter, but kept the D.[122]

To Helen Pancake ⋯⋯⋯⋯⋯⋯⋯⋯⋯⋯⋯⋯⋯⋯⋯⋯⋯⋯⋯⋯⋯⋯⋯⋯⋯⋯⋯⋯⋯⋯⋯⋯

One Blue Ridge Lane
Charlottesville, VA
August 12, 1977

Dear Mom,

While I have thought of you all week, this is the first time I've
had to sit down and peck out something. I know you must have
thought the railroad[123] put me in jail, but I never had a bit of
trouble, and the conductor was the nicest I've ever met.

All week I have been looking for loopholes to avoid paying
tuition this fall, thereby collecting more of my salary. This is
a "company store"—you never see what you earn, just work,
starve, and don't make waves. Since that part of the system can't
be beaten, I may as well make use of it and finish the degree. I
found a way around two classes I don't want, and actually will
learn more my way. I'm creating two courses before 1800 for
myself, will be my own boss, do my own research, etc. It's much
harder this way, as there is nobody to tell you how to think, but
in the long run, much more interesting. So it looks as if I'm after

just one more useless degree. You can be proud of me the rest of my life while I stay home looking for work.

Dr. Kellogg[124] is trying to get another course for me to teach—two pays more than one—but I'm not sure he'll come through. Meanwhile, I'll pump John for the same deal next year.

Next comes insurance. If you can put me on your Blue Cross for a year for less than 85 bucks, do so NOW and I'll pay you back. If not, tell me, and I'll buy the crap they have here. It's required, so there's no way around it. I tell you, they bleed you dry then wonder why you don't have any money. It would be O.K. if we were all rich.

I want to thank you for the good food and company while I was home—even if I got none of my favorite pie (kick that dog for me, will you?). My thumbnail is scarred from the little witch. Thank heaven that the next time I come home, I won't be bayed in my own front yard. If you get a dog, get something nice, O.K.? I've seen copperheads on the hill with better personality.

Now I'm planning classes, and should be one step ahead of them by Sept. Writing drags and drags, but that's a darn good sign it will pan out to something. Nothing good was done soon. *** Otherwise I want you to rest your worry gland for me on the day of my oral exams, as Kromer[125] will probably turn in his grave. WVU has given me permission to see his papers, but I have to go there. I'm now trying to arrange a ride. All is well, and I hope you are fine and the dog has the squirts from my pie.

Love,
Breece

To Helen Pancake ···

One Blue Ridge Lane

Charlottesville, VA

August 19, 1977

Dear Mom,

Got another class appointment—means twice as much money this term, 3 times the work, but if I eat, who cares? So, I will do quite well all considered. Writing going *very* well.

John and Jane[126] arrive today, but will give them time to unpack—like a week—and get over the shock of being in high prices again.

Many thanks for the *History of Milton*.[127] Needed that. But wanted *you* to read *Everything in Its Path*.[128] I have a copy I got from a reviewer (free).

Yours,

Breece

To Helen Pancake ···

One Blue Ridge Lane

Charlottesville, VA

October 18, 1977

Dear Mom,

Just a note to thank you for my socks—they are truly warm, and very comfortable. I should imagine they'd be good to hunt in—should I ever get time to hunt.

I'm happy to report a woodpecker busily at work on the wooden part of One Blue Ridge Lane. He's got a hole about the size of a baseball and improving on it daily. While I have no objection to either him making merry with Meade property, or his noise, I find myself getting rudely called from bed just before dawn every day. The problem is that with all this work, I'm not getting to bed soon enough to co-habit with this redhead.

But all that aside. I'm doing well enough considering—and although I have gotten no word on the new job, I feel sure they hired another. No job teaching is ideal, but this would have been better than most and I'm sorry I lost out. Don't mention it to Homer, please, as that would only embarrass me.

After shivering through Mass, I attended Em's church.[129] The heat was on high, and they were begging for money. Just like the good old days at Milton Methodist. Em's church is undergoing too quick a change in attitude and threatens to fall apart. If I could find a nice old-fashioned Catholic Church, I might convert her, but she doesn't go for new outlooks. I believe I told you, she's Episcopalian. (I'll strangle the first one who says they are "just like Catholics.")

Peter Taylor is ill, and not of much help. He's got diabetes and still fighting over the recent death of his closest friend, Robert Lowell.[130] While I try to be patient with him, I wish he would be the same with me and think about my story[131] before judging it.

Unfortunately, Casey is the same way. His father is dying of cancer (82?), but I think he's got some hatchets yet to bury, some peace he finds hard to make with his old man. Of course, he is taking the crazy attitude—thinking of quitting U.Va. and moving to New England. I don't think he has any money or work, but if there's a free lunch handy, John would screw it up.

Only McPherson is his usual hidden self.

Em and I will be in Milton someday. T-giving is out since her major papers are due thereafter. Christmas is out because she has to hold two jobs to make ends meet. I would imagine I'd be home Christmas—but I can't see much sense in a $40.00 train ride for three days. That leaves us somewhere between Jan. and Easter—I might even get brave and drive her over. Anyway, barring flood and the A-Bomb, I'll be home in a few days and remain approx. 10 days—so bake a *ham*. I might seek rides and therefore arrive earlier—around Dec. 20.?

Sorry this is just a scribble-note—can't get much else out these days.

> Love to all,
> Breece

To Helen Pancake ···

> One Blue Ridge Lane
> Charlottesville, VA
> October 30, 1977

Dear Mom,

Many thanks for your long letter. The letterhead[132] was really great, only I was unclear on who gave it to you, Grandpa or Uncle Tucker—and for whom you were writing. Send me an address & I'll answer.

I don't think there is much danger in Em becoming a Catholic, so don't let it bother you—it doesn't bother me. Thanks for the sermon—I'll skip it.

Got the Alumnus & read the article on H.B. Lee.[133] Actually, I figured he was dead, but he gets around as well as Aunt Julia. Maybe we ought to get them together. Also, if you could get any of his books you might have handy, I could use them. I don't need *Bloodletting in Appalachia*, as I've studied it, but the others might be nice.

I'm not sure the St. Andrews Society sounds too cool. It does sound racist (pro-Celt) in some sense. I'm sure there were Scots on welfare, but they just couldn't find them (or didn't look). I'd wager they are as prejudiced against the Irish Catholics as Fr. Terrance is against converts. I don't like to align myself with people like that & ignore Terry along with the KKK. Basically he's a good fellow, but he's old school—that's what your buddies at St. A's are. We've got too many good things to work with to waste time with bitterness.

Glad to hear you got to go to Bob Evans' Farm.[134] That must have been a great break for both of you. About all I can recall is that the food is good, and they had a ground hog in a cage. Also, it is my first memory of a really big Ohio farm, the kind that made Sherwood Anderson's stories so vivid in my mind. Without Anderson, I'd never have written a word.

Letter from Doni & she is happy enough in the City.[135] She said I was going home T-giving, which I hope, you have straight by now.

Staunton Military Academy re-opened this fall—in Newport News, Virginia. They kept the same name, added girls to the student body, and now have all twelve grades. Other than that, it is a complete mystery to me. I haven't been up there since July & that awful time I spent in Sarah's house.

I'm shanny to say anything about the Dept. Suffice it to say I'd rather be working where I have some future.

It seems something slipped from your wallet and had been folded into my last letter. Please find it enclosed. If you must, I'd like a pair of high (knee type) lace-up boots for Christmas. Put this toward them. 10 1/2 D.

Got to get to work. Don't take any wooden nickels—Fred Ball[136] can't figure out how to get them into the slot machine at the VFW.

1978–1979

....

To Helen Pancake ....

One Blue Ridge Lane
Charlottesville, VA
March 3, 1978

Dear Mom,   3 AM

Guilt has the better of me, so I'd better write while I have time. It's snowing here—already 3″ with more on the way. Can't say I enjoy this Vermont weather in Virginia. Interesting you should mention Plimpton's coming to Jay's party: Jay, Plimpton, and John Casey[137] all went to Harvard at the same time. Harvard shit big that year.

Will relay message re Grubb/Settle,[138] but can't promise a return. MLS never remembers what she's doing from day to day, as she is currently preoccupied with the Paint Creek novel.

Charlotte[139] wants me to prove Indian so she can work for the white-middle-class social group trying to turn Indians into 2nd class whites. Actually, I'm looking, but not because I care whether Grandma Pancake was or wasn't part Indian: what I want to know is did they make you legally claim it at marriage? Everything else is secondary.

Sara had Em and I to a really fine dinner with Mary Moore,

Frank and GG,[140] Mrs. Frank, and assorted Nutts . . . all in all a fine dinner: two salads, two stews, two desserts—really good.

Doni blessed me up one side and down the other for buying a used car. I agree it is stupid, but assured her I didn't deserve the raving I was getting. At this stage in the game, used cars are the best I can do. As I recall, the Porsche is a "used car" with a VW engine, isn't it?

Did you see *Awakening Land*?[141] I watched one episode with Em and when that guy grabbed Elizabeth Montgomery's tit on national T.V., I swore off the Tube for life. I guess I'm thinking of children growing up with that in their living room. Somehow learning the facts of life from Steve Spence behind a backstreet church seems right and fair now.

I'm writing to find out if I have a teaching position next fall. John is slower than steam off of shit in making position assignments and if I finish in December, I may not have work for the spring. Back to frying hamburgers and looking for schools.

Enclosed please find another will. Tear up the old one—the only thing I changed was literary executorship for your protection.

Back to work.

Love,

Breece

P.S. Regards to all.

P.P.S.: The last paragraph of the will is to insure my burial according to my beliefs. I know you'd comply with my beliefs without question, but it's hard to tell what the girls would do. Love you. B.

To Helen Pancake ··

One Blue Ridge Lane

Charlottesville, VA

March 20, 1978

Dear Mom,

Sorry I haven't written, but I'm sure you know what I've been through with this paper—yesterday I took it to my typist (don't tell Doni, O.K.?), and await the finished product. There really wasn't time to wait for D. to do it, and Jenny makes good all mistakes on the spot. Now I don't know what to do with a free Sat., and as you can tell from the type—I'm at Eisenhard's.[142] Em is working on getting an idea for her paper (she's smarter than I, so the work is finished sooner), and I've been told to come to dinner at suppertime—whatever that means, and I have no idea as to what will be served, except that it will probably be good.

Easter was wet but good. I never stop being surprised at how hard Fr. Pat[143] works and how hard Fr. Terrance works to avoid work. Together with many others, Pat and the parish put on the whole of Holy Week while Terry watched TV. I don't begrudge the old boy for being tired, but 55 is too early to retire. Terry drafted me last night to sponsor a new member Sat. Night, and got so flustered with the service that he forgot to include about one third of the Mass. It wasn't as nice as Regis's service but then Regis[144] worked all day for one Mass. My "godson" seemed rather at odds as to how to handle himself, but I assured him later that he was in for better or worse. He's a nice kid, and I hope to do more for him than John has done for me. I didn't see or hear from John[145] the whole season, and I've grown tired of asking him to come to church. Lastly, tell Betty Holly I'm not

ignoring her nice note, but will answer as soon as time allows.
***

Again, thanks for the check, but you haven't seen the last of your money, I assure you.

Not much else is news here. Now I have to study for orals and the final in the Bible course, then find out what's going on next year (can you believe the writers have no idea what's happening until the term is over, but all others know mid-March?). Now that Peter Taylor is back from the Keys, things should move a little faster. I'm applying to a New York Foundation[146] for a grant to write this summer, but hold little hope of getting it— grants are funny creatures, and harder to catch than a talking crow. Even if I get the grant, I should lose weight this summer.

I did get a laugh out of the clippings you sent—Milton will do its damnedest to keep from settling in one place. Are they going to move it all to 64 in hopes of getting people to stop? We could put June Blake and Bliss[147] on one of those revolving poles with red and green lights—or better yet both yellow, as one should always enter Milton with some degree of caution.

Speaking of caution: if you talk to Charlotte before I do, tell her for me that the records of Tazewell County, Va. show no record of a Virginia Woodell or Waddell or Wadell marrying any William Pancake or anything close to it. It may have been any western Virginian county, in which case one might hire a genealogist at the rate of ten bucks an hour, and even then you may not get what you want. Woodell/Wadell is like Smith in London, and the chances of getting solid records in backwoods counties are slim. Just between you and me, they could have been married in a brush-arbor by a circuit preacher who probably couldn't read or write.

Well, hope this finds you in good spirits and working but not too hard. If I get, by some accident, the grant, I'll be over for a while this summer. If not, for a week in July (near the end of the month). If you want to come over, try to plan your trip for just after finals—May 1.

Love you much,

Breece

To Mary Roberts Rinehart Foundation ···

One Blue Ridge Lane
Charlottesville, VA
March 21, 1978

Mary Roberts Rinehart Foundation
516 Fifth Ave. Room 504
New York, NY 10036

Dear Sirs:

I wish to be considered as an applicant for the Foundation's Award in order to complete five stories and thereby begin their collection and my first novel. My first story, "Trilobites," appeared in the Dec. '77 *Atlantic Monthly*, and the same magazine recently purchased a second story, "In the Dry," to appear some future time. A third story, "Time and Again," was accepted and soon will appear in *Nightwork* (Richmond's local magazine). I propose to complete the following stories:[148]

In "Joe Holly and Buck," two hill-countrymen, one black and one white, begin their friendship on a bus migration from the hills and coal camps of West Virginia to Detroit's auto plants in search of something better than mining. While there, the black man readily adapts to city life, but the white man is sucked into a hill-countryman ghetto, and his only contact with the brightness of the city is in meeting his black friend in pool halls. The story is about Joe's attempt to break out of his ghetto, but the ghetto eventually breaks him, and he returns to the hills a beaten man.

"Conqueror" is a story of alcoholism and war. A fifty-nine-year-old disabled Vet takes his son on one last camping trip before the boy goes off to college, and for the first time in the boy's history the man goes off on a bender of vodka and Pepsi. In his stupor he relates to the boy why he once drank (due to the things he saw men do to one another in Germany), why he now drinks (because of atrocities he has never related to anyone), and why he expects the boy to do his duty in Vietnam. A tussle ensues while the boy pours out the hooch, then the old man retires to the tent, leaving the boy by the fire all night. The boy is not afraid, except perhaps for his father.

"Of Time and Virgins" is a stream of consciousness narrative as a young man tries to make a decision whether he should propose to a virgin he just met. He reviews the four great loves of his life, sees how each falls prey to sexual promiscuity in a different way, and eventually decides he is tainted, but not beyond help. Since he has been with this girl more than a year without bedding her, he decides she is more to him than the others and decides to "propose" tomorrow.

"A Room Forever" is roughly what becomes of Huck Finn when the raft is no longer a possibility. An unnamed orphan narrator temporarily works on an Ohio River tug as refuge from a recent Naval discharge. On the last night of shore leave, he encounters a young prostitute who derides everything he wants: home, family, love. After their argument in a wharf bar on New Year's Eve, she goes to an alleyway where he later finds her, both her wrists slashed. The cold rain has clotted her blood, so she will live. Until now he has soaked himself in pity and whiskey, but now feels his lot is not so bad. He leaves the girl to be helped in the bar. He goes to meet his boat.

"Southern Crescent" is a tribute to the death of good passenger service and the death of a kind man. Claude, retired from the Air Force and wasted with stomach cancer, takes a last ride on a train he ran in steam days. In the club car he talks with a young college student coming up from Virginia to Washington for a job interview. En route the student is not willing to concede that Claude's life is any richer than his own. Not until the two are held at knife-point in Union Station's men's room and Claude backs the thief away with an imaginary gun does the student realize his own gutlessness.

I believe I can complete these stories in as many months. My rent is $55 a month for this complete 12x12 cell (even the fox has a hole), and I spend about $125 a month to eat. I'm 25, single, and have an appointment to teach as a grad ass. next fall at the University of Virginia. I have a B.A. ('74) from Marshall University, hope to have my M.A. from Virginia next year. Before that I spent two years teaching in military secondary schools.

Many thanks for your consideration.

Sincerely,

Breece D'Jon Pancake

To Helen Pancake ···

One Blue Ridge Lane
Charlottesville, VA
March 27, 1978

Dear Mom,

Many thanks for the Easter Gift. Consider Christmas and June 29th taken care of as well. This week finds me finishing up on the Lit. use of Bible paper after which I must spend almost all my time on Ch. 2 of the novel.[149] I've applied for a Grant this summer, but hold little hope of getting it unless the foundation is crazier than I think. Emily and I had a fine Easter dinner and drew up a truce long enough to go to one another's church. Fights start again tonight! (Some of that Holy Water hit her, so she's the same as Catholic now.) Let me know your plans.

Love,

Breece

To Helen Pancake ···

One Blue Ridge Lane
Charlottesville, VA
April 3, 1978

Dear Mom,

Many thanks for your letter on April Fool's. Even mail of that sort is welcome. Sounds as if you're getting along well enough, but I think you're dreading upcoming vacations where you work. I guess you won't be here for the spring—at least that's the way it sounded, but I understand. For the time involved, you could fly to Miami quicker than drive here.

I was surprised at all the ghosts you dragged out in this letter—Midget Morgan, Jim Ross, etc. Somehow it can't be real that they're married and have kids—it's like I'm frozen in time writing. I guess I'll settle down sooner or later, but it's a matter of jobs and years. Fr. Terrance told me not to worry about it so much, so I won't.

Em and I finally have enough time to run to Staunton this weekend, and I have to call Sarah[150] today. It's good to get out of Charlottesville, and see the rest of the world for a change. I think I'll take Em fishing—haven't wet a line since last summer (I'm really in bad shape), and I don't want to forget what a fish looks like.

As for the Grant:[151] I've got enough to get through the summer, and will take a job before long as well as write. As you know, I'm going west in July to make some money and take a vacation (first in three years). I want to revisit some old Spanish missions after traveling with Doni's summer camp on wheels—that is if I survive the summer camp. My back isn't used to dirt beds. If the grant comes through, fine: I quit the job, and go west just the same. If not, fine. In any event, you needn't worry about me.

The paper's finished and turned in.[152] I told him I had some terms used in a strange fashion, but he was very receptive, and said I was safe in my argument. Em and I have a bet: if I get an A, she has to cook any dinner I want (turtle), and if not, I cook what she wants (steak). Loser pays all. I'm really hoping to place the paper at *Catholic Biblical Quarterly*, although that may be above my head. I can't lose by trying. Did you ever look up that passage? Luke 23: 27-31. Nobody has written much about it, so I'm that far ahead.

Also, Chuck Perdue wants me to read my Oral Narrative paper[153] at the fall meeting of the Virginia Folklore Society, and play the tapes. I'm trying to place that paper at *Kentucky Folklore Quarterly*, and Doni[154] will get that to type very soon.

The Jefferson Society[155] gave me a Jefferson Cup for second place in their fiction contest—nice of them. I didn't read my best story, but tried to keep within the page limit. As it turned out, I was the only one who did. But the first prize story was really very good, and I've got much more going with the *Atlantic* than an eight-dollar cup.

I was glad to hear the family is doing O.K. and that Milton is still on the map. As I said in my last letter, I'll be home for my usual August visit if all works well. Give them my love. ***

Better get this in the mail.

Love you,

Breece

To Helen Pancake ···

One Blue Ridge Lane
Charlottesville, VA
April 15, 1978

Dear Mom,

Many thanks for your letter. I'm happy to hear you might be coming by next month, and will save my Mother's Day gift for then. Em and I have a couple of places we'd like to take you, and one German restaurant where they actually put more on the plate than I could eat (Fred[156] hadn't had anything all day and still couldn't eat it all).

Please don't get the impression we're loafing in Staunton every weekend . . . having finished my painting and spring cleaning, I'm trying to study for exams and put my dossier together for job hunting next year. Also trying to revamp old papers and stories by way of getting something else into print. On top of that, I'm teaching the last ditch of this battle for two more weeks.

By now you know that in addition to Mary Lee, James Alan McPherson won the Pulitzer Prize for *Elbow Room*. I think Mary Lee's writing is good, but I'm not ready to say Pearl Buck is a West Virginian by any fashion. Far as I'm concerned, she's Chinese.[157] Jim lost the Nat. Book Award to Mary Lee, but stole her thunder not four days later.[158] I haven't talked to her since January, but I'm sure if there's something to be put out about with all that, she'll be down in the mouth. Somehow, Jim doesn't seem too happy—I guess because he's the type not to like reporters and the public eye. I was in the office when he got the news, and the hallway was full of NBC/CBS/ABC and every other reporter. He made statements to them about how grateful he was then disappeared. We were supposed to go fishing today, but then we've been supposed to go fishing many a weekend. ***

Not much else in the news, I hope all are well and send them my love. Don't brag on me so much.

> Love you,
> Breece

To Mrs. Sullivan ···

> One Blue Ridge Lane
> Charlottesville, VA
> May 17, 1978

Dear Mrs. Sullivan,[159]

Many thanks for your note—I hope I can keep up the pace I've set for myself. Like Wolfe, I walk a great deal (actually Richard Jones can take credit for that—Wolfe can take credit for the wasps in "In the Dry") & I just walked from my pond ten miles back. I had noticed the Canadian Goslings were disappearing and strayed until I saw a whopping snapping turtle! So much for this year's migration.

Etymologically, you're correct: "will-o-the-wisps" was the original title of "Trilobites" & Colly's mother is assimilating the syllabication—something not uncommon to daily speech (not just in Milton—something similar in Virginia is, "goddamnedyankee").

Certainly the last line is the whole point of that story, but don't you think it odd that only you and I have noticed it?

Finally, I think congratulations are in order more for you than me—after all, you put up with me in home room *and* Civics.

Sincerely,

Breece

To Helen Pancake ···

One Blue Ridge Lane
Charlottesville, VA
May 27, 1978

Dear Mom,

Just a note to say hello. I guess Decoration Day[160] back home is still the VFW's biggest affair—if they didn't use those old army rifles today and Nov. 11th, they wouldn't be happy. Here it's nothing much—people leave town and go to the beach.

Yesterday Emily and I took time to go out to a local lake. They rent rowboats for 50¢ an hour, so we did some exploring and had a fair time watching people. Like fools, we neither brought swim suits or a lunch, so the visit was short. She can't take too much sun at once and I don't care for going without lunch after Mass (can't eat before Mass). Spent the week studying for orals and putzing with this story—which I have to get back to very soon. Emily is still struggling with the great thinkers of 15th-century England in an attempt to net some butterfly or other. She claims I'm a bad influence since my logic is so ass backwards: when she tries to argue her point, I get her so tangled up nothing makes sense.

I've arranged to read "Trilobites" at Randolph-Macon Women's College June 20th. They offered to pay me $100, so I couldn't very well turn it down. I'll take the bus and spend the night—all at their expense—and will talk to three classes the next day. Of course I'd like to get more "readings" around the state (away from Charlottesville—one should never shit where one eats), but I'm not important enough to drag in the big money. Actually,

Davis Grubb[161] has it cinched at WVU and something similar is my life's goal (as with everyone who writes I'm sure).

Glad you're reading *Elbow Room*—the title story is the most difficult to understand, yet in a way, they're all difficult since Jim isn't a simple man. Peter's stories are much more suited to your way of thinking than Jim's are. Peter has some degree of fame—a reputation is more like it—but the Pulitzer Prize should make people listen when McPherson talks, and in the end a writer couldn't ask for more.

The Meades are back from England and I got a verbal "thanks for taking care of the house all month." No mention of forgetting the rent or what they could do for me. Since I have to pay July rent, I "forgot" to pay May rent, and in all the rush to England, I hope *they* forgot too. I don't intend to mention the subject. ***

With this wonderful postal system, it should cost me as much to write letters as it does to call home. Still, I know what it means not to get mail and I'd rather write anyway. Hope everyone is fine. Give them all my best and love to the family.

Yours,

Breece

To Emily Miller ···

Phoenix, AZ
July 1, 1978

Dear Pal,[162]

So far the weather has been more than fair—one might say the sky is "peaches and cream." The smoking compartment on the plane gave a very-distant fine view of such skies, but upon

landing, personally—I found the sun very hot and the surround-
ing stars not nearly so bright as imagination might paint them. I
am, dear Pal, scorching with a wry smile—or a bourbon one—as
you like it.

To backtrack and thereby come to the portent of this, I arrived
D.C. AM. 6/29 only to be rained upon while finishing—soberly—
The 42nd Parallel.[163] Soaked by 9 PM., I tramped in search of a
train—found nothing but a page at Union Station—"Will B. Pancake come to the desk"—trapped like the mouse in your house I
hope is smarter.

But about the rain—at first I managed to seek a hole in the
awning of tenement and okay, I tried to read, but kept thinking
of you—said to you—"My God, Emily I miss you." In the words I
heard the wisdom an unknown man uttered to Pop in his hobo
days—"Boy, you got a home; you better go to it." And I said as
I've always said—"I ain't got no . . . My God, Emmer, I love you."
I knew I had makings for home.

Then, tonight, one of our younger tikes (alone, I tried to
keep the stars from fearing the lack of sun) complained: "I'm
bored with all this." All this consisted of a $16.00 dinner in a
"real" western town with "real" cowboys coming in and out—a
mockup to be sure—nevertheless an effort to show them a good
time. The young'un is twelve with tits agreed, so I laughingly
said to Ruth—"Someday my little girl will say that—and take
a five mile walk looking for her head." The last part was direct,
deliberate, and hells fire. I'm sure my little Burnadette would
be pissed when Pop knocked her one for such a comment—I
hope he wouldn't have to—and it made me mad and it made
me wonder:

Would I? Am I such a ghoul at heart? Is your papa right to ask

308 | SELECTED LETTERS

you to re-consider?[164] He wants his boat-dream for you—what
chance can a pen-pusher provide for? I want Colly in Mexico
there to meet the anger of the "masses" (Marx). I want Ottie
to wander the country, free from the whole great space an inch
of his own, I want Colly in Vietnam's last days, a leg torn off
by our own fire, to see again masses in Mexico, to say "the hell
with it" and go to see his Pop. I want Ottie tired, alone, to give
up the garage in Chicago, to return and finding Sheila gone—
meet with the strong, good woman (a kind of you) and begin
his small settling—and I believe that would be a book[165]—and
a good one to read for any man of any class. The woman will be
written up when I return—she must have four stories to her like
the two men—and they must never be too innocent or loving or
"decadent."

To Helen Pancake ···

One Blue Ridge Lane
Charlottesville, VA
August 14, 1978

Dear Mom,

Many thanks for your letters and the xeroxed stuff I still
haven't had time to read. The letter with the check was stuck
with some other misplaced mail on my windshield—the neighbors had picked it up—so the check is safe . . . My summer classes
are over with only one student good enough to make the grade—
the rest took advantage of my being away as an excuse to goof
off, and I encouraged them to drop rather than fail them. I later
learned I should have failed them—I get paid if I fail them, but

not if they drop. It's all the same to me, I could use the money, but not at another person's discomfort.

I assume I got the readership at *Virginia Quarterly*[166] because I found a stack of mss. with my name on them at the office today—I hope the funds are up to date, too—should get $50 a month to defray the cost of rent. Em and I joined our efforts in an equal battle on the cost of eating. Since I almost always eat supper at her house, I offered to go 50/50 on one meal a day, allowing us both to eat better than we would if we cooked—or tried—our own supper. We've found the real bargains at the Farmer's Market just before dark, and today bought a huge round and had it cut into two small eye roasts, fourteen swiss steaks, four pounds of stew meat, and four pounds of ground round—all at 1.29 lb. We figure around twenty-five meals at that, and plus a few whole chickens (how do you cut those damn things?) at .39 a lb., we have meat every day for a month at .60 a serving, each meal not costing more than 1.00. I can't eat chili in a hash house for that today. Heinermann??

All things considered, God's will and low creeks, I'll be in for the gathering on the 17th.[167] I haven't priced the train, and at that point (we don't get paid til Oct.), I might just drive in. I have emergency towing on my insurance, so don't worry. I have a credit card if anything big happens.

I was sorry to hear Lora Danford[168] died. I still think of the cold mornings, walking to school in the late fall, and speaking to her as she walked that poor old dog of hers out by the funeral home. And I remember going in her shop with you when I was little, and the funny tricks the sun would play on the sheets and towels, and thinking how Uncle Abe's store[169] had been.

I've finished all but three books for my orals, and am working up the proposal. I may postpone them, as I have a tough course to take and will teach two while working at V.Q. I really can't bluff them off, as orals are tricky, and I'm on shaky ground with two of the novels.

I have to give a reading in Staunton at the prison Sept. 8th[170]—I guess I don't *have* to—Sara's oldest daughter asked me to, and I thought I'd like to hear me if I was in prison. It pays a little, but I asked that the money go for books—not enough for two these days. I know I should keep the 25, but hell, put yourself in prison for a minute. Besides, Dad always said he and the guy who lived above the Maryland were the only two of his class to stay out of jail—said I was bound to make it, so he turned out right. He always had a heart for the underdog, like he understood why a fellow would do something wrong to get by—like the war—I'm not sure if he killed anybody, but he was the kind who felt like he'd killed a man just by looking at the body, and God knows he saw the bodies. Anyway, this is for him; he taught me to give a bum a dime because it might give the bum the last chance he needs to sober up. So maybe a book, a hillbilly reading a story or just something to break the stay will shake one fellow into thinking it might not be so bad to get by honestly.

I ain't looking forward to seeing Aunt Julia in such a sad shape. That's pretty selfish of me, I know. That's where your wisdom makes a big difference against my age—I get so tired of thinking that the ones I love draw up like old iris in summer. It seems like it started with Grandad and never has quit—even with Kat and Granny, and how mean they could be, I still hated to see them go. When I think of how you choke up or Grandpaw cries when you all talk about Grandma and Grandpa Frazier, I know you never stop loving them even when they've been gone a half-a-hundred years. I try to understand, Mom, I really try, but if I learned anything from my past, it wasn't intellectual understanding of something as deep as love and death, it was the living of love and the living of death, and now that Aunt Jul is in between, I don't know what to do, and I don't think anyone on the face of this earth can tell me.

Damn me, I'm awful depressing. I guess I'm just homesick and tired. I miss you and love you and hope you aren't working too much. Maybe for the Reunion we could have chicken and beans and potato salad for me to step in. Tell Jr.[171] I've tied my cat to the top of the fence-post.

Love you.

Breece

To Helen Pancake ···

One Blue Ridge Lane
Charlottesville, VA
September 3, 1978

Dear Mom,

Thanks for the check and the letter—I promise to get my teeth taken care of as soon as possible. I'm not in need of glasses (I don't know where you got that idea!), so sorry about that.

This next is pretty touchy, so I'd advise you to sit down. I'd rather you didn't call Emily anymore unless it's an emergency; we haven't broken up or anything like that, and I certainly don't love her any less. Her parents have decided I'm not good enough for her and they've been after her to give me the boot and look for more promising material among her own kind. What "her own kind" means is a good Southern Virginian family. People around here really are snobs, especially if you get seriously involved with their only daughter. While Emily *is* above the age of consent, she also has strong ties to that sort of life—you can't (nor can I) blame her for being reared a Virginian. I think that sort of prejudice is pretty funny until it becomes real. I'm convinced Emily loves me, but much of her heart is with her family as well. Anyway, it would be better to avoid the embarrassment of calling her should we decide to split up. I know I sound pretty cold about it, but it's nothing to be upset about (I know I'm as good as they are), and if I got angry it wouldn't hurt anyone but Emily. Also, this is *not* any of the girls' business and I'd just as soon they didn't know about the reason—only that Em and I (if it comes) aren't dating.[172] ***

Now about your car: You should be able to get a good trade-in on $5,700, and I think it would be worth it to try. I *don't* want you to buy me a car *nor* do I think you should give me your old one. *** So trade in the Galaxy. *** I think Shorty[173] will treat you fairly.

Well, Mom, that's about it. Obviously, I'm not too talkative. Thanks again for the loan—first payment will come in October.

Love,

Breece

To Helen Pancake ···

One Blue Ridge Lane

Charlottesville, VA

Sept. 22, 1978

Dear Mom,

This is the first chance I've had to get off my bread and butter letter. It really was nice to be home, and I hope the next time I'll have some more time to hang around and visit. The return was uneventfully fun—I picked up a stranded trucker and gave him a ride to the Sewell Mt. Gulf Station. He was my age—nothing like Ottie,[174] but a nice fellow. He told me I could get a Kenworth truck for 31 thousand and pay it off in two years. It was an interesting idea to think about, but I'm too set in my ways now to go back on the road. Also, I decided to be cute and take the back roads from Covington to Staunton (further back than my usual trail). Got to meet and talk with a lot of people along the way (one-lane roads with no signs), but didn't get here till 12:30. Still made the class the next day though.

Been enjoying the cheese and sausage and pickles—you have seemed to have given me the whole of the batch—and thanks, but wish you'd saved some for yourself. Emily, who won't eat anything but a strange selection of bland foods, gobbled down the two paw-paws and wants a paw-paw tree. I'd get her one if I could remember the leaf pattern and the texture of their bark—can you find a picture of them in the plant books??

My students are worse this year than last. They're so afraid of grades and credit, and a few of them are down-right asses. Last year things went smoothly, and there was no mention from them or me on grades. I guess the world is moving back to common materialism in favor of learning—sadly these kids have been tricked into believing there's a job waiting for them if they get four years of college. One of my seniors (a really pretty red-headed girl—I don't usually think redheads are pretty) nearly cried when I told them not to worry about hurrying through college to join the ranks of the unemployed. Turns out she did her entire degree in two and a half years and will graduate with honors in Dec. She hasn't found a job—or a hint of one, but I ask you, what can you do with a degree in government? Or for that matter, English?

Rest assured your money will be returned to you post haste. John Casey has been really good about understanding dental bills, and I will make enough next semester and this semester to insure the return of your five hundred. I know it must seem stubbornly independent of me to refuse gifts, but your funds are so slight by today's standards, that any buffer you have between yourself and poverty should not be dwindled by your children. Besides, my profession bears the nasty condition of perpetual poverty in this life and riches for my heirs; I chose it, and I should live with it. And, I further insist, any profit you take in interest on loans, rent, or otherwise be yours and yours alone— even as cash in the box.

I don't know if you and Jack Pancake[175] have settled on any conclusion to Aunt Julia's estate, but in the event you do, remember that I said anything the two of you decide on is with my approval. I assume the distribution of personal property is in accordance with both your powers and will be done with every intention to fulfill the last will.

Better get back to business at hand. Again many thanks for the weekend, and hope to get home again soon.

Love,

Breece

To Helen Pancake ⋯⋯⋯⋯⋯⋯⋯⋯⋯⋯⋯⋯⋯⋯⋯⋯⋯⋯⋯⋯⋯⋯⋯⋯⋯⋯⋯⋯⋯⋯

One Blue Ridge Lane
Charlottesville, VA
Nov. 1, 1978

Dear Mom,

Many thanks for the check—I added $120 to it and return it now—I think only owing you $100.00. Actually—although your gift is well taken, it's taken more in terms of credit to a debit. I thank you for it—and very much.

I bought two pair of pants and now try to mostly show up in class in a shirt, tie and jacket—I know it isn't much of a concession to your wishes, but I'm trying. Also—while it seems I make a good deal of money (600 compared to 200 when I first came here), it doesn't seem to go anywhere—I really do know what you're up against with your income.

As for the work—it goes on. I really can't say this instructor plays either a fair game or with a full deck. I make no promises: try as I will, he's just as apt to fail me as confer a degree on my head. What's worse is that he's my examiner on the oral exam, and his method testing isn't unpleasant if one managed to survive my Church's Spanish Inquisition (torture, burning at the stake, etc.).

I really am too busy for words, and with nothing pleasant to show for it—I can't write and teach and take what seems to be one of the hardest courses here. I guess I'm stupid—but I hope someday you might have my degrees on the wall to justify the grey hair I gave you.

That—morbidly—leads me to Glenn and Katy.[176] I've so much and so often felt fond pain with them over Robert, and I had hoped some good might come of all their troubles. They are the kind of people—real people—one never finds beyond a given valley because, once out of the valley, we never have the time to know that *special* kind of person. Robert's death must have been a shock without mercy—their love in and pride of him was without excess. I still remember the pictures of his sons in Glenn's shop, and I first learned to mouth the word "lawyer" with respect—how could Glenn be any less my teacher than Katy in that respect? But Thomas Wolfe—the "great" writer—died in a cab in New York,[177] and Hemingway blew his brains out. Maybe I'd been better off a lawyer.

Well—have to get up early tomorrow—hope this finds you well.

Love you and miss you—
Breece

To Helen Pancake ···

One Blue Ridge Lane
Charlottesville, VA
December 1978

Dear Mom,

Many thanks for the candy and brownies—they came a little worse for wear, but fresh, and they're both delicious (a little too much so, I've rationed myself). It was good talking to you the other night—although I must say I forgot to ask why you sent me two blank calendar pages of November in December??

The news here isn't all that great—I'm still waiting for word on an interview and imagine that most schools call two days before the convention—it's really a buyer's market. They'll invite five people for interviews & four of them always go home empty-handed. Really not very considerate of our future bosses to spend our money for nothing.

On the cover you see Papa Hemingway.[178] Since nobody will be around to tune his guitar or feed him, I told Em I'd ask you if Papa might spend Christmas with us—Actually, it all depends on how well Papa makes a trial trip in the car.

Everything else is the same old 6 & 7. I'm booking for my last exam, trying to read students' work, read for VQR, make out grades, etc. Emily is in the same boat, only she's finished her course work and is doing French for her upcoming exam (you never seem to finish "exams" and graduate).

I'll leave here early the 19th & will probably take my old route through Buffalo Gap & etc. Will call you if I get snowed in at Rainelle.[179]

Love you—and thanks again—

Breece

Job Inquiry Template ··

One Blue Ridge Lane

Charlottesville, VA 22901

[January? 1979]

I am writing to inquire after any possible opening you may have for a writer with a strong interest in teaching.

I am currently completing my language and oral examinations and expect to have the M.A. in hand by May. As noted in the enclosed vita, my thesis was published in *The Atlantic Monthly* before I made the decision to complete degree requirements, having come here solely to study under Peter Taylor and James Alan McPherson. On the strength of these two stories Edward Weeks at Little-Brown has expressed his interest in publishing a collection of my stories, and Wendy Jacobson at Doubleday has requested a portion of my novel.

In addition to my studies, I have been deeply involved in teaching Fiction Writing, both in the traditional workshop setting as well as in tutorials. While teaching writing workshops at this university, I developed a structural approach which I believe fosters the effective reading so important to fiction writing. I am also interested in teaching Classical Literature, the British and American Novel, and the American Short Story as a national genre.

My dossier is available on request. I would be pleased to meet with you at your convenience, and I thank you for your consideration.

Sincerely,

B. D'J. Pancake

To Helen Pancake ···

One Blue Ridge Lane

Charlottesville, VA

Jan. 11, 1979

Dear Mom,

We are all getting ready for the snow that I suppose hit you today. So far this winter has proven milder than the first three here, but I'm sure we're in for something yet. And I owe you a vote of thanks for the staples (canned goods) you put in the bottom of my stuff when I left—it never ceases to amaze me how kind and thoughtful you are.

I went through a pretty bad experience yesterday in Richmond. I had called to answer an ad in the paper for a Public Relations job which demanded "a flair for writing," stayed up all night writing a new resume that would make me look good for that sort of job, drive down the next morning only to be told I was "over-qualified." I don't believe that. What I think happened is that Snelling and Snelling was trying to spice up the looks of a standard sales position, and didn't know what to say when somebody walked in qualified for the position they'd advertised. On the way down I had even decided that if they offered me the job, I'd take it on the spot and finish school at night. It's depressing enough to be turned down for a job, but it's downright lousy to be turned down for a job that probably didn't exist, and to be made a fool of.

But I'm still trying. Haven't heard a word from Alderson-Broaddus or St. Joe,[180] and have about given up on them. If they were all that interested, I'd have heard by now. Actually, A-B may be so slow as to turn out something at the last minute or even two years from now—but I can't be growing moss on my feet waiting for them.

Emily is hard at work on her French, and I'm still trying to unravel and interpret a novel that seems not to want me to do either one. Apparently what was bugging me when I called was a minor case of the flu—one now over—and I just hope you didn't catch it. Also my foot is much better, and I plan to start walking two miles a day very soon, then get back to running.

I'm still disturbed by the report that Aunt Julia is being mistreated, and I hope by now the whole thing has blown over. Personally, I hope that by the time you need such care I will be in the position to give it to you. I don't think it would be fair to trust other people with your own mother.

I'm sending you a check the first of Feb., and I want you to cash it—I have enough to get me through summer, and it would really bother me to owe you money if I got down on my luck and had to bum my room and board from you to boot. So please don't argue, just cash the check. Besides, it looks as if Uncle Sam won't get my money this year either.

Better get back to work. Give my love to everybody.

Love you,

Breece

To Helen Pancake ···

One Blue Ridge Lane

Charlottesville, VA

Jan. 20, 1979

Dear Mom,

Just a note to say I'm alive and working. Finally finished one paper for Tony Winner—one more to go, then orals and language. Believe me, it isn't worth the trouble.

I've had no contact with Mary Lee since I asked her to return *Snakehunter*[181] last year. I must say she thinks a good deal of herself, and I really didn't think the Nat'l Book Award would go to her head, but I guess it did. John Casey—who stays on her good side somehow—says she's really on cloud nine with the enclosed award . . .

I'm now getting ready to attack the Jr. College job market. I have often thought of creating an opening for myself—I'll find a place I like, simply murder the current job-holder, then apply. All things considered, it makes more sense than robbing a bank (my second calling). But don't worry until you get a sudden postcard from Mexico. I'm also into some part-time offers—will let you know if I get anything.

Was over to see Sarah—she's fine, and was very nice to let us go out to the farm[182] in the pick-up. Em had never been in a truck. I went out to grab a quick fish for John's birthday[183]—Other than that, nothing new.

Got to get to work—

Love you,

Breece

To Phoebe-Lou Adams ···

One Blue Ridge Lane

Charlottesville, VA

Jan. 21, 1979

Phoebe-Lou Adams[184]

Atlantic Monthly

8 Arlington Street

Boston, MA

Dear Miss Adams:

I'm working on some fiction, the likes of which you'll be the first to see when it's finished, your eye being the truest test of a story about two women.

In the meantime, I ask you to examine the enclosed. This came to me by mail through one of two sources: either DATE-LINE (an ad in *The Atlantic* which I confess to answering in a fit of loneliness) or GLOBETROTTER (an ad answered in a fit of feeling seaworthy). In any event, I'm afraid such yellow slavery might be doing better than anyone thinks, and I'd like to do a journalistic story on it—either for "Reports or Comments" or "Life and Letters," depending upon the length desired.

I know this is a big favor to ask, so I'm willing to turn the story over to anyone you might have in mind already on the staff. I think there's something here to write about, and I don't really care who writes it so long as it gets written. You'll see my cf. of two opposing points of view on the Nov. '78 issue of "Cherry Blossoms."[185] I like dogs and cats too, but I'm not sure everybody likes a sixteen-year-old looking for a pen pal in what is obviously a sickly different sort of game.

I hope this year finds both yourself and Mr. Weeks[186] in good shape. I missed hearing from you last time, but Jim[187] assured me you were among the busy—those whose gudgeons are in a constant state of grease. In the meantime, I promise to survive (by the way, I have a very nice girlfriend and promise not to answer anymore to the ads for DATELINE).

Sincerely,

Breece Pancake

To Helen Pancake ···

One Blue Ridge Lane
Charlottesville, VA
Feb. 13, 1979

Dear Mom,

Just a note to thank you for your letters and say all is fine. Many thanks for the underwear—getting such things in one's mail has a touch of strangeness to it. I will wear them in good health and promise to model them for the Women's League next week. ***

Yes, we've had quite a bit of snow—roughly 10"—and more keeps coming. I walked in and back a couple of times, but now everything but the driveway is clear, so I'm O.K. At the coldest it's only been around 8 degrees with the highs in the 20's, so a good walk can't hurt me . . . With gas promising to go $1.00 a gallon, I'm glad I got my foot fixed.

Don't worry about me and jobs: I occasionally get nibbles—the most recent from Kentucky Arts Commission (I've specifically asked for the eastern counties) where I'd lecture three days a week in high schools, North Carolina Arts Commission (same deal), and Western (North) Carolina University. West Virginia has no "Writers-in-the-Schools program" (they buy Davis Grubb a pound of Marijuana—it's cheaper).

The library dinner sounded like a joke. Do you reckon they *planned* for Gene McCarthy and Jay[188] to be stranded in that awful old Washington, D.C.? After all, they still get paid. (I'd get paid for a reading that got snowed out.) And what can a three-man band cost? $100.00 at best, with Gene and Jay sitting by the fire in the Georgetown Club talking the possibilities of Jay's 1980 nomination over Kennedy? (I wouldn't vote for either one.) Boy, I can see that one as clear as day. But your note on Carbide Parties hit home—I remember those. It's hard to keep it from eating at you sometimes, I know, and I'm not going to tell you to stop remembering—just don't stop living and being a terrific mother. ***

I've been busy enough. My class seems bright and I think I've got good control (which probably means they hate my guts). They are writing, although only one could begin to imagine beyond the early stages (I teach writing, not imagination). I'm finishing my last paper of my life—from here, it's pure fiction. I'm also writing my orals proposal, but haven't given German much thought. Figure I can finish in a summer if I get a job. If I don't I have plenty of time. Bill Smart at Virginia Center for Creative Arts has promised me room and meals in return for my services as a painter and fix-it man (can you imagine that?). VCCA will peel, leak, and burn to the ground after I've been there a month. The point is, I won't starve and I'll have some time to write.

Saddest is this: an old, retired professor at VPI wrote me that he has written a novel and asked me if I'd read it and tell him whether or not it's publishable. He offered me $50 to read it and $450 to "fix" it. I doubt I'll get beyond the $50, but I took the job. Because of that, you'll find the enclosed. You told me you wouldn't cash a check for $100, but you can cash one for $50. Anyway, how do you tell an old man he should be writing memories for his grandchildren and great-grandchildren, not bad novels? Speaking of which, is it too much to ask that you send *Saga of a Country Doctor*?[189] I've never really read it and pretty soon I'll have a few hours to spend.

Em is fine. She's still reading a lot of French and plans to take the exam over in case she didn't score 700 (out of 800?). She's also reading for her orals and worrying about the job market next year. She's really worked hard all her life (not like me) to get to the upper levels of education, and I just hope she finds something.

Well, that's about it. Hope you survived the snow and hope all is well with everyone.

Love you,

Breece

To Helen Pancake ···

One Blue Ridge Lane
Charlottesville, VA
Feb. 28, 1979

Dear Mom,

Even if Grandpa got fish to-go at Capt. D's, I'm sure he payed for it dearly. Emily and I innocently went to lunch at McDonald's yesterday, and for two Mac's, one order of fries and two cokes the bill was $3.25. It's getting so green baloney butts[190] are the only bargain.

We got 17″ of snow, and I walked quite a bit. Now it's raining, and the snow has melted down to about four inches. While I didn't move my car for three days, I got in yesterday only to discover that I'd left the lights on during the blizzard. Hiked in, got Carl[191] to come out and jump start it, and now all is well again. Were it not for Em, I'd skip the car altogether, but she can't drive in snow and has no way to the store. When gas goes to $1.00 a gallon, I'm walking in except to get groceries. Pretty soon we're going to be singing "Buddy, Can You Spare a Dime"[192] again.

Alderson-Broaddus[193] finally wrote me. The job includes an ability to teach Journalism, Composition, Literature, etc. If you could get the features (Aunt Julia, Troy Hatfield, Hinton Richmond, and any I've forgotten) I wrote for the *Cabell Record*[194] and xerox them for me, I'll have that to back me up. Boy, they intend to get their money's worth out of anyone they hire. There's also a Va. Arts Commission, and I know the poet who works for them is quitting (they don't know that yet), so I'll apply to them as well. You're right: I'll get a job—it may be in a Pizza Hut, but I'll get a job—I'm too hard-headed to let it get me down for long.

Funny you should mention Glazer's[195] salary: Staige Blackford (editor of *Virginia Quarterly*) does little or nothing (not that much to do when you put out four mags a year), and gets $36,000. That's the job I want someday.

Speaking of the Southern Crescent[196]—the wreck last fall that killed six, remember? Well, one of the six was a black cook. Carter had asked him to come to the White House as a cook, but he turned it down. He said he'd spent 40 years on trains, and once a train man always a train man. He was due to retire this month.

Read the first two chapters of the old guy's novel: boy, is it bad. I know he wants to fulfill his dream, but it would be cruel to tell him it's good. Now, I have to finish it, but there's no hope of it getting published. Hard way to earn $50.

Hope this finds you feeling better. We're fine. Let me know how everyone is doing, and tell Shorty and Mary Jane[197] I'm glad their granddaughter got out of Iran (I may find myself in China if this mess keeps up—gee-whiz, I thought I was too old to fight).

Got to run. Give my best to all. Love you.

B

To John Casey ···

One Blue Ridge Lane
Charlottesville, VA
March 25, 1979

John D. Casey
c/o Jane Casey
Department of English
Wilson Hall
University of Virginia

Dear John,

When you read this it really won't matter anymore, but I offer these thoughts the way a fossil comes back to haunt a geologist—but haunt isn't the right word, and I'm too stupid to think of another. But anyway . . .

Remember May, 1975? "God, why didn't you tell me . . . if I'd known you were this good, I'd have offered you a fellowship." I hadn't told you because I knew I wasn't. Then the summer of bad times when I pounded on doors, got fed-up, went fishing, and bingo they offered me a job sight unseen from Staunton, and bingo my father and my best friend croaked within a week of each other, and bingo I held on for dear life. I held on because of me, but I held on with the help of you. The night we went to see Ali murder Frazier in Manila,[198] that night I nearly knocked your brains out with my driving into the parking-lot abutment. I was trying to think of some way to thank you for going with me to the fights, and I forgot to hit the brakes.

Remember L——? "I know you want me to tell you I've had a great time, but well, I've had a good time." And there were breakfasts with wheat cakes and lemon curd and spring mornings when I'd drive the VW from Staunton. I hit a "tree-rat," as Jane called it, but nobody was up to that for breakfast with lemon curd. And I drove home thinking what a wonderful day it had been, and how my father would want me to stop for coffee at least twice on the way home. I stopped three times for coffee, but when I got home my mother called to tell me Cousin —— had dispatched his brains by a NY lake that morning. I wasn't all that sorry for Cousin ——

Remember May, 1976? Jane said: "We go to the house of my father—it has many bathrooms." I came overloaded in the VW for home, left you the things one needs for long stays away—salt, coffee, whiskey and a blanket. I spent the summer writing what would become "Trilobites," you wrote of hopes of "Liberty." Later I came to Charlottesville, worked up the story, read a good novel in galley, met one Rod Kilpatrick. L—— died and went to heaven on somebody else's cross. I died over a girl who was dry as beans in bed but full of lush on the phone. She moved. I stayed.

Remember May, 1977? I wrote to say a story was sold. I got no answer. I worked frying hamburgers, selling golf balls. Richard had dinner with me before late Mass. I remembered you coming all the way here to welcome me to the Catholic faith. I missed you. I went home and started a story, then I found I would teach next year, so I started my lesson-plans. I finished the story and the lessons when you returned. The story wasn't good enough, and you helped me—soon it was good enough.

Remember Emily Miller? "Then Kerrigan said there weren't any virgins left in this day and time—but—I'm afraid he—well he was wrong." So I decided she was right. I wanted to marry her, but later, when it became clear I would have no work, I wanted to become a padre.[199] Me a padre? I loved this girl. I loved this girl. Still, I had work, and you told me I'd get none. Still, I love this girl, and time flew its course. I sold another story: I called you on a winter's night and you were happy. Still, I love the girl.

Alright—maybe not.

Remember July, 1978? I went to the Southwest, and you went to Jane's Father's house. I loved the girl. I wrote several cards to you but the Post Office was on strike. I loved the girl. I went to a woman I knew in South Phoenix (blacks and Mexicans), but she told me I loved the girl. I went to a woman I knew in North Phoenix (lily white), but she told me I loved the girl. I wrote you from a Big Boy counter on Central Ave., and I had no money, had no place to sleep, had no nothing. And "John, this is the last I'll ask." And it was. You were good enough to give me a clean bill of health with my dentist and then some.

So remember May, 1979? I can't. But as I see it, you'll go on as you have before I came. You're an honest man John Casey— honest at your heart—but what will you do for those who come after? Will you take a clean and simple writer like ———, and by giving him funds turn him into the slop ——— is made of? I could stay, I know, John, were I to beg—I might even have a job were I to stay one more year. Johnny, and you'll have to take a drink now, would you love me if I did? I love you. I love you because when my father and friend were dead you helped me hang on for dear life, told me I could write (and be damned if I haven't done a passing job). Alright then, the bargain is settled. I can write, now, and nothing else matters. You've fought hard for me John—fought hard for five years, and please don't think that by my gruff manner and early temper I am any less the man for you. And by your fight, I hope something comes of me worthy of calling your own name to. I'm not good enough to work or marry, but I'm good enough to write.

Can you find a tear or two in these lines they are mine, and I will hope you shed them in Ireland this summer. Maybe we'll neither of us see Heaven, but if you can bring yourself to it, say a prayer for me (not in any church) under an Irish sky.

May God Bless and Go with You and Yours Always, John Casey.

Breece

To John Casey ··

March 25, 1979

Dear John:

In this country those who have have all, and the have-nots have the bones. When I came to you in 1975 the two met, and I am grateful for your sense of *noblesse oblige*. In this country all a have-not can ask for is a chance to be a have; you gave me that chance, and I thank you; now I'll blame myself if I fail.

I could never (even when I tried) tell you how much you, Jane, and the girls have meant to me. I only regret that I never made a larger effort to become a part of your lives, but my own sense of privacy tells me not to do such things—even when I'm far away, it would be hurtful for us to miss one another.

Short time gone, long time coming. Come hook in the gills, come bullet between doe's shoulders, come long cold and the Cross, come time to lay down, come time to get awake, I'll remember you with love.

Yrs,

Breece

Spring 1979
Introductory remarks, at the reading of "The Honored Dead,"
Methodist Student Center, Charlottesville, VA

Tonight I must read "The Honored Dead," an unpleasing story; unpleasing because memories of war, of love, of lust, of misunderstanding can never be pleasing. In 1968 L.B.J. launched an offensive which later became known as Tet: history records the disaster in two ways; a paragraph in books and thousands of stoney inscriptions. In that brief battle one Eddie Grass of Milton, West Virginia, served as a naval attachment to the U.S.M.C. and was charged to the duty of radio operator on field patrol. He lasted thirty minutes on the job, several grenades having dispatched him homeward. I wanted to say that this reading was for Eddie, but ghosts cannot be put down. I ask instead that you consider this reading thanks to the living, specifically to the one who chanced I could write: This one is for John.

To Helen Pancake ···

One Blue Ridge Lane
Charlottesville, VA
March 1979

Dear Mom,[200]

Many thanks for the card, the papers, and all, and I assure you I enjoy them. I was a little distressed by the dial-a-doll ads in the first paper. Not because it's wicked or anything, it just bothers me that so many people get so lonely as to have to resort to the services of dial-a-doll. For so long, our people accepted their fate without a word, but being alone is something they find hard to accept if the option is a phone call, a hundred-dollar bill.

Last night I dreamed of the "happy hunting ground." I passed through a place of bones that looked human, but weren't—the skulls were wrong. Then I came to a place where the days were the best of every season, the sweetest air and water in spring, then the dry heat where deer make dust in the road, the fog of fall with good leaves. And you could shoot without gun, never kill, but the rabbits would do a little dance, all as if it were a game, and they were playing it too. Then Winter came with heavy powder-snow, and big deer, horses, goats and buffaloes— all white—snorted, tossed their heads, and I lay down with my Army blanket, made my bed in the snow, then dreamed within the dream. I dreamed I was at Fleety's, and she told me the bones were poor people killed by bandits, and she took me back to the place, and under a huge rock where no light should have shown, a cave almost, was a dogwood tree. It glowed the kind of red those trees get at sundown, the buds were purple in that weird light, and a madman came out with an axe and chopped at the skulls, trying to make them human-lookin'. Then I went back to the other side of both dreams.

NOTES

1. C.R. and Helen Pancake] Clarence Robert "Bud" Pancake (1917-1975) and Helen Jean Frazier Pancake (1922-2014), Pancake's parents.

2. You should have seen Mexico.] While staying with his sister Donnetta in Phoenix from January to April 1972, Pancake made a short excursion to Mexico in March. Pancake had two sisters, Donnetta "Doni" (b. 1941) and Charlotte "Char" (1943-2017). Born in 1952, Pancake was the youngest of the three siblings.

3. Joe Hill] Born Joel Emmanuel Hägglund (1879-1915), Swedish-American songwriter and member of the Industrial Workers of the World, an international labor union known commonly as the Wobblies.

4. M.U.] Marshall University, in Huntington, West Virginia. Pancake enrolled in Marshall in September 1972 and graduated in June 1974. He attended West Virginia Wesleyan College (WVWC), in Buckhannon, in 1970-71 as a freshman, before transferring to Marshall.

5. John] David Belcher, Cebe Marpe, Jay Boyd, John Shaffer, and Pancake were members of the student theater company at West Virginia Wesleyan College. James Calligan (Gilligan) was his roommate at West Virginia Wesleyan.

6. Donnetta] One of Pancake's sisters, also identified as Doni in the letters.

7. Beasley] Robert M. "Mike" Beasley, instructor at Marshall University and a friend of Pancake.

8. "Rat Boy"] Apprentice work, first written in Pancake's senior year of high school and later reworked at Marshall University. Pancake had submitted the story to *The Atlantic*.

9. Char] Charlotte Pancake, one of Pancake's two sisters.

10. My students] Pancake taught English at Fork Union Military Academy, in Fork Union, Virginia, during the 1974-75 school year.

11. Paula's] Paula, one of Pancake's college girlfriends.

12. the Agency] Southern Teachers Agency, which placed Pancake at Fork Union Military Academy.

13. Matt Heard] Matthew Heard (1949-1975), a colleague at Fork Union Military Academy and one of Pancake's closest friends. Heard would be killed a year later in an automobile accident near Charlottesville, Virginia, on September 29, 1975.

14. Shorty] Roy "Shorty" Hollandsworth, family friend and car salesman in Huntington, West Virginia.

15. McGuffey Readers] Elementary school primers developed by William Holmes McGuffey (1800-1873), common in the classroom in the nine-

teenth and twentieth centuries, and still used today in some private schools.

16. Shorty] See note 14.

17. Mammaw and Grandpa] Elsie Frazier (1897-1983) and Fred Frazier (1899-1981), Pancake's maternal grandparents.

18. Aunt Julia] Julia Pancake Ward (1881-1981), Pancake's beloved great-aunt.

19. "There but for fortune, go you and I."] Refrain from "There but for Fortune" by American folk musician Phil Ochs (1940-1976), which Pancake slightly misquotes. The song appears on the 1964 album *New Folks Volume 2*, released by Vanguard.

20. C'ville] Charlottesville, Virginia, about forty minutes by car from Fork Union, a trip made often with his friend Matt Heard.

21. my car wreck] Pancake was involved in two car accidents while he lived in Huntington, West Virginia. He totaled the family car in one of the accidents.

22. F.U.M.A.] Fork Union Military Academy.

23. Morgantown] Morgantown, West Virginia, home of West Virginia University. Pancake entertained the idea of enrolling in the Graduate School of Writing or the Law School at WVU.

24. the machine] Pancake's typewriter, a 1920 Underwood No. 5, given to him by Aunt Julia.

25. *Lucas Tanner*] NBC television drama that aired in the 1974-75 season. The title character, played by David Hartman, is a high school English teacher who endears himself to his students with his unconventional teaching methods and empathy.

26. Beas] See note 7.

27. Pop Amick] Owner of the American Oil station in Milton, West Virginia. Later that year Pancake would write a profile of Pop Amick for the local Milton paper: "Pop Amick Is Still Going Strong," *Cabell Record*, August 27, 1975.

28. Jr.] Jr. Blake, a glassblower and part-time farmer in Milton.

29. typewriter] See note 24.

30. Matt] Matt Heard. See note 13.

31. "If you make a mistake, don't make it twice."] Paraphrase of a line from Gordon Lightfoot's "Cold on the Shoulder," the third track on the album of the same title, released in 1975 by Reprise Records.

32. Harry] Harry Truman (1884-1972), thirty-third president of the United States, 1945-53.

33. Ford] Gerald Ford (1913-2006), thirty-eighth president of the United

States, who took office on August 9, 1974, following President Richard Nixon's resignation.

34. Dear Folks] Pancake's letter of May 11, 1975, to his parents is typed on life insurance company letterhead. The letterhead asks *Where will you be at 65?*, below which Pancake typed "On food stamps, you turkey." He wrote a few letters to his parents on the same company stationery.

35. camping trip] Trip to the Cumberland State Forest in central Virginia, made with his friend Matt Heard.

36. my Whale] Pancake's 1964 Cadillac, which Pancake nicknamed "the Great Blue Whale."

37. South Chas.] South Charleston, West Virginia, home to Union Carbide Chemical Company, Pancake's father's employer for thirty-five years.

38. Johnny Weissmuller] The American freestyle swimmer Johnny Weissmuller (1904-1984) won five Olympic gold medals for swimming in the 1920s; after his retirement from competitive sports, he became famous for portraying the title character in the Tarzan movies of the 1930s and 1940s.

39. Dear Folks] See note 34. In response to the question *Where will you be at 65?* on the life insurance company letterhead, Pancake this time wrote "In a hell of a shape."

40. Whitescarver] Colonel Kenneth Tyree Whitescarver, Fork Union Military Academy president.

41. Johnny Cox] Track coach at Milton High School.

42. a sample of my work.] Probably the story Casey suggested is "Fox Hunters." Pancake first met his teacher and friend John Casey in spring 1975, while Pancake was teaching in his final semester at Fork Union Military Academy. This meeting in Casey's office at the University of Virginia is described by Casey in the Afterword to *The Stories of Breece D'J Pancake*. See page 181 in this volume. Pancake sat in on Casey's classes at the University of Virginia before he was accepted into the writing program.

43. Hi Folks] With this tall tale of "Jarfly" Johnson, Pancake was responding to a request made by his mother. In a handwritten note at the bottom of this typed letter, Helen Pancake explains: "Breece's father was very ill and a childhood friend of his also in bad shape. I asked Breece over the phone *to write something humorous*. He did an excellent job mentioning their old friends and locations. This was copied and sent to all concerned. They loved it."

44. CW teachers] Creative writing teachers.

45. Veni, sedi, excessi.] Latin for "I came, I sat, I withdrew"; a play on "Veni,

vidi, vici" [I came, I saw, I conquered], attributed to Julius Caesar after he defeated Pharnaces II.

46. S.M.A.] Staunton Military Academy, where Pancake had accepted another teaching position for the 1975-76 school year. The move brought Pancake closer to home and to Charlottesville; however, he was unaware the school was facing bankruptcy. At the end of the school year the distinguished 116-year-old academy was closed.

47. If anything happens, call.] Pancake's father, who had been battling multiple sclerosis for several years, was now gravely ill. This is the last time Pancake addressed both of his parents in a letter. C. R. Pancake died four days later, on September 8, 1975.

48. back to Staunton.] After attending his father's funeral in Milton.

49. Sam] Sam Harshbarger (1928-1992), attorney and family friend. Harshbarger was a West Virginia Supreme Court justice from 1976 to 1984.

50. Fred] Fred Frazier (1899-1981), Pancake's maternal grandfather.

51. Poor Jerry . . . third time is charmed.] There were two attempts on President Gerald Ford's life in California, first by Lynette "Squeaky" Fromme on September 5, 1975, in Sacramento, and again three weeks later in San Francisco, on September 22, 1975, by Sara Jane Moore. Ford was not injured in either assassination attempt.

52. the Frazier-Ali fight] The Thrilla in Manila, the third and final fight between Joe Frazier and Muhammad Ali, fought on October 1, 1975. Ali won by a technical knockout.

53. man she loved.] Mont Ward (1881-1964), former mayor of Milton, was Aunt Julia's beloved husband.

54. Whale] See note 36.

55. Melinda] Matt Heard's girlfriend. Pancake's close friend and former colleague at Fork Union Military Academy was killed in an automobile accident near Charlottesville, Virginia, on September 29, 1975, only two weeks after the death of Pancake's father.

56. Cellar] Pancake had rented a cellar apartment in Sarah Nutt's Staunton home. See note 65.

57. Leoffler] Layne Leoffler, who had purchased Staunton Military Academy in 1973 and changed its charter to nonprofit in an effort to save the failing school. See note 46.

58. Mitch] One of Pancake's cousins.

59. story] "The Mark." See p. 97.

60. work on a story] Perhaps "Conqueror." See page 196.

61. HHS] Huntington High School, in Huntington, West Virginia, where Pancake was a student teacher.

62. MU] Marshall University, in Huntington.

63. "Fox"] "Fox Hunters." See page 67.

64. Mrs. (Pancake) Mandeville's house] Mary Moore Mandeville was a distant relative, one of the Staunton Pancakes.

65. Mrs. Nutt] Sarah Nutt, a widow, who owned the property at 324 East Beverly Avenue in Staunton. Mrs. Nutt lived in the main house, above Pancake's cellar apartment. Later, Pancake rented a room in the main house when Mrs. Nutt found another tenant for the cellar apartment. Thomas E. Douglass in *A Room Forever* quotes Mrs. Nutt as saying that Pancake "was most generous in bringing . . . gifts, many from the glass factory in his home town. He was proud and did not want to be 'beholden' to anyone."

66. Preston] Preston Doyle, headmaster of Staunton Military Academy.

67. Mammaw and Grandpa] Pancake's maternal grandparents. See note 17.

68. Tuck] Breece's uncle, Clifton "Tucker" Frazier.

69. Mazatlan, Mx.] Pancake visited Mexico in 1972. See note 2.

70. the story] "The Mark." See page 97.

71. John-Boy Walton] Central character in the popular 1970s CBS television drama *The Waltons*, set in rural Virginia during the Great Depression and World War II. Played by Richard Thomas, John-Boy was the eldest child in the Walton family and an aspiring writer.

72. Preston] See note 66.

73. a hundred.] Julia Pancake Ward (1881–1981) would die three months shy of her hundredth birthday.

74. Shorty and Ray Glenn] Two Milton friends. See also note 14.

75. Silver Bridge] The Silver Bridge, which connected Point Pleasant, West Virginia, and Kanauga, Ohio, collapsed without warning on December 15, 1967. Numerous vehicles were submerged and forty-six people were killed. See "The Mark," page 97.

76. Glen] Glen Crookshanks, family friend. Glen's wife, Elizabeth, had passed away recently.

77. my ear] Pancake suffered from recurring earaches and headaches. Pancake's biographer Thomas Douglass speculates the cause was a head injury sustained when Pancake totaled the family car.

78. Hinton] Hinton Richmond (1897–1988) of Milton, West Virginia, an inveterate outdoorsman and walking repository of old-time lore. Pancake wrote an article about Richmond, "Hinton Richmond: Man of the Woods," for the August 13, 1975, *Cabell Record*.

79. Mary Lee] Mary Lee Settle (1918–2005), novelist born in Charleston, West Virginia. Settle was then at work on her novel *The Scapegoat* (1980), set in 1912 at the outset of the West Virginia mine wars (1912–

21), fought between miners and coal companies. Pancake would soon begin work on "Hollow," which depicts the difficult and dangerous labor undertaken by coal miners. Later, after he enrolled in the University of Virginia, he would help Settle with research for her novel-in-progress.

80. the plant] North Anna Nuclear Generating Station, in Louisa, Virginia.

81. The Blue Gill] Pancake's blue Volkswagen convertible.

82. promised John a story] Likely "Cowboys and Girls," later published as "The Way It Has to Be." See page 136.

83. the cabin] A hunting cabin on the Nutt farm in Middlebrook, Virginia, south of Staunton. Bob Nutt, Sarah Nutt's son.

84. the story] "The Mark," which appeared in the University of Virginia literary magazine *Rivanna*, February 25, 1976.

85. Mr. Caudill] Harry M. Caudill (1922-1990), author, legislator, opponent of strip mining in the Appalachian coalfields, and professor of Appalachian Studies at the University of Kentucky. In preparation for writing "Hollow," Pancake had travelled to a coal camp in Harlan, Kentucky. It was on this same trip he met with Caudill.

86. my appointment] In February 1976 the University of Virginia awarded Pancake the Emily Clark Balch and Henry Hoyns Fellowships as a graduate teaching assistant in creative writing for the coming fall term. Pancake enrolled in the UVA graduate writing program in September 1976. There, he would study with writers Peter Taylor, John Casey, James Alan McPherson, and Richard Jones.

87. Mr. Taylor's letter] Novelist, short story writer, and faculty member at the University of Virginia, Peter Taylor (1917-1994) had agreed to write a letter of introduction to Robie Macauley, fiction editor at *Playboy*. Pancake sent "Fox Hunters," "The Scrapper," and "The Mark" to *Playboy*.

88. Buddy's nuptial] Buddy Everett, Pancake's cousin's, wedding.

89. Perdue] Charles L. "Chuck" Perdue (1930-2010), folklorist and one of Pancake's instructors at the University of Virginia.

90. Leoffler] See note 57.

91. Kegley] Probably Fulton B. Kegley, Staunton Military Academy faculty member.

92. the Meades] Everett and Virginia Meade, the owners of the property at One Blue Ridge Lane in Charlottesville, where Pancake had rented a room in the former servant's quarters.

93. copies of the *Declaration*] *The Declaration*, a weekly student publication at the University of Virginia. The September 30, 1976, issue contained "Hollow."

94. Mike] Robert M. "Mike" Beasley. See note 7.

95. "Cowboys and Girls"] Title of early version of "The Way It Has to Be."
    The story was forthcoming in *The Declaration*, October 21, 1976. See
    page 136.
96. "Will-o-the-Wisp"] Extensively workshopped with Peter Taylor, the
    story was published under the title "The Honored Dead." See page 124.
97. Glenn and Jr.] Glenn Perry and Jr. Blake, Milton friends.
98. Peter Taylor . . . another magazine] Taylor's plans for a regional literary
    magazine did not come to fruition.
99. Richard Jones] Welsh novelist (1926-2011), one of Pancake's teachers at
    the University of Virginia.
100. Carter] The 1976 presidential election was held on Tuesday, November
    2, 1976. Jimmy Carter defeated incumbent Gerald Ford.
101. W.Va. History 1700's by McWhorter] *The Border Settlers of Northwestern
    Virginia from 1768 to 1795: Embracing the Life of Jesse Hughes and Other
    Noted Scouts of the Great Woods of the Trans-Allegheny* (1915), by Lucullus
    Virgil McWhorter.
102. Sarah] Sarah Nutt. Pancake remained friendly with his former Staunton
    landlady and continued to see her after he moved to Charlottesville. See
    note 65.
103. Charlotte] One of Pancake's sisters.
104. Grace Kelly] Pancake confuses Grace Kelly with Ingrid Bergman, who
    played opposite Humphrey Bogart in *Casablanca* (1942).
105. Mary Lee Settle] Novelist Mary Lee Settle was a visiting lecturer in fic-
    tion at the University of Virginia. Her book on the West Virginia mine
    wars and labor activist Mother Jones would be published as *The Scape-
    goat* (1980). Pancake assisted Settle with research on her book.
106. Pipestem book] Pancake refers to *My Appalachia: Pipestem State Park
    Today and Yesterday* (1971), by Howard B. Lee, in which the former
    attorney general of West Virginia discusses the history of the Pipestem
    area, including West Virginia's mine wars. Pipestem Resort State Park
    is located in southeastern West Virginia.
107. Alderman] The University of Virginia's Alderman Library.
108. VQR] Pancake had submitted "Trilobites" to a fiction contest sponsored
    by the *Virginia Quarterly Review*. The American novelist and short story
    writer Ward Just (1935-2019), the author of *The Congressman Who Loved
    Flaubert* (1973), *Stringer* (1974), and *Nicholson at Large* (1975), would win
    the VQR contest.
109. St. Joe] St. Joseph Central High School, in Huntington, West Virginia.
110. that dog?] Pancake's sister Donnetta owned a Schipperke.
111. This story] Possibly an early draft of "In the Dry." See page 156.

112. Poor Richard Jones . . . their daughter.] Jones's twelve-year-old daughter, Natalie, was killed in a road accident in 1976. Jones abandoned fiction writing after the death of his daughter. See note 99.

113. *Rocky*] The first of the *Rocky* movies, released in November 1976.

114. Matt] Pancake's friend Matt Heard, killed in an automobile accident on September 29, 1975. See note 13.

115. Mary Lee] See notes 79 and 105.

116. Fr. is . . . my classes do] Pancake, who had been raised as a Methodist, was a novitiate in the Catholic Church, preparing for his Confirmation.

117. Gloria and Libby] Former girlfriends.

118. Wolfe] American writer Thomas Wolfe (1900-1938), the author of numerous books, including the posthumously published novel *You Can't Go Home Again* (1940).

119. "Phantom 309"] Tom Waits's adaptation of Red Sovine's "Big Joe and Phantom 309" appears on the album *Nighthawks at the Diner* (1975). The ballad tells the story of a hitchhiker who is picked up by the ghost of a dead truck driver.

120. Manning] Robert Manning (1919–2012), editor of *The Atlantic*.

121. Jim McPherson] James Alan McPherson (1943-2016), American writer, faculty member at the University of Virginia, and one of Pancake's instructors. The two men, who enjoyed each other's company, were outsiders together on the University of Virginia campus. McPherson was the first African American to win the Pulitzer Prize for Fiction, for his second collection of stories, *Elbow Room* (1978).

122. B. D'J. Pancake] In a 1984 interview Helen Pancake explained her son's unusual pen name: "You see, his middle name was Dexter, even though he told some people it was David, and John is the name he took when he entered the Catholic church. The way I got it was that when his first galleys [for 'Trilobites'] came back from *The Atlantic*, a typesetter had put it down as D'J. And Breece said, 'Fine, let it stand.' God love his heart."

123. the railroad] Pancake had recently visited Milton, taking the Amtrak train from Charlottesville.

124. Dr. Kellogg] Robert Kellogg (1928-2004), chairman of the University of Virginia English Department.

125. Kromer] Tom Kromer (1906-1969), Depression-era writer and drifter born in Huntington, West Virginia, whose single book, *Waiting for Nothing* (1935), is a first-person account of life on the bum in the 1930s. The book made an impression on Pancake when he read it in 1976. In a letter of October 29, 1976, he wrote to his mother: "Please read *Waiting for*

Nothing by Tom Kromer. Every word a warning like Pop used to give me." Pancake had planned to visit Morgantown, West Virginia, where Kromer's papers are held at West Virginia University.

126. John and Jane] John and Jane Casey.

127. the *History of Milton.*] *History of Milton* (1976), by Caldwell Dudley, printed privately. Dudley had provided Pancake with information for a story he had been planning about snake handlers, set in southern West Virginia. A draft of "Shouting Victory" is printed in this volume. See page 191.

128. *Everything in Its Path*] *Everything in Its Path: Destruction of Community in the Buffalo Creek Flood* (1976), by sociologist Kai T. Erikson, which chronicles the collapse of the dam at Buffalo Creek and the catastrophic devastation it caused to the coal-mining community there.

129. Em's church] Pancake had begun dating Emily Miller, a graduate student at the University of Virginia.

130. death of . . . Robert Lowell.] The American poet Robert Lowell (1917-1977) had died the previous month, on September 12, 1977.

131. my story] Possibly "In the Dry" or "The Honored Dead."

132. The letterhead] The letterhead had an image of a mule and plow.

133. H.B. Lee] The alumni bulletin from Marshall University featured an article on Howard B. Lee (1879-1985), attorney general of West Virginia and author of several books on West Virginia history, including *Bloodletting in Appalachia*. See also note 106.

134. Bob Evans' Farm] The restaurateur's homestead is in Rio Grande, Ohio, about an hour away from Milton by car. The Bob Evans Farm operates as a company museum and historical center.

135. the City.] Breece's sister Donnetta was living in Washington, D.C.

136. Fred Ball] Family friend.

137. Jay, Plimpton, and Casey] Jay Rockefeller (b. 1937), then governor of West Virginia, graduated from Harvard College in 1961; George Plimpton (1927-2003), journalist, writer, and actor, earned his degree from Harvard in 1950; and John Casey took his BA from Harvard in 1962.

138. Grubb/Settle] West Virginia writers Davis Grubb (1919-1980) and Mary Lee Settle (1918-2005) both wrote about the West Virginia mine wars, Grubb in *The Barefoot Man* (1971) and Mary Lee Settle in her "Paint Creek novel," *The Scapegoat* (1980).

139. Charlotte] Breece's sister.

140. Frank and GG] Frank and Gigi Pancake, of the Staunton Pancakes.

141. *Awakening Land*] *The Awakening Land*, a three-part NBC television miniseries staring Elizabeth Montgomery and Hal Holbrook that aired

February 19-21, 1978. Based on a trilogy of novels by Conrad Richter, the story depicts the lives of a family of white settlers in the Ohio Valley.

142. at Eisenhard's.] Pancake was house-sitting.

143. Fr. Pat] Father Pat O'Connor of St. Thomas Aquinas Church, who would later deliver the eulogy at Pancake's funeral. St. Thomas Aquinas serves the University of Virginia.

144. Regis] Father Regis O'Connell of St. Thomas Aquinas, who signed Pancake's Certificate of Baptism, April 11, 1977.

145. John] John Casey, Pancake's godfather. See note 42.

146. a New York Foundation] Mary Roberts Rinehart Foundation.

147. June Blake and Bliss] Jr. "June" Blake and Bliss Wallace, Milton friends.

148. the following stories] Only "A Room Forever" and a partial draft of "Conqueror" exist.

149. novel.] Pancake had plans for two different novels. One of the plans used "Trilobites" and "In the Dry" as the beginning chapters; this novel would have followed the lives of Colly ("Trilobites") and Ottie ("In the Dry") while introducing a major female protagonist. The other would haved centered on Buddy and Sally from "Hollow."

150. Sarah] Sarah Nutt. See notes 65 and 102.

151. As for the Grant] The Mary Roberts Rinehart Foundation grant, which Pancake would not get. See pages 270-72.

152. The paper's finished and turned in.] On Luke 23:27-31, written for his Bible as Literature class at the University of Virginia.

153. Oral Narrative paper] Pancake was writing a paper based on oral tales told to him by some of the older men in Milton.

154. Doni] Pancake's sister Donnetta.

155. The Jefferson Society] A student organization at the University of Virginia.

156. Fred] Fred Frazier, Pancake's maternal grandfather. See note 17.

157. Pearl Buck . . . she's Chinese.] Pearl S. Buck (1892-1973), the daughter of missionaries, was born in Hillsboro, West Virginia, but lived much of the first half of her life in China. In her 1938 Nobel acceptance speech, she chose as her subject the Chinese novel.

158. Jim lost . . . four days later.] Mary Lee Settle won the 1978 National Book Award for her novel *Blood Tie*. James Alan McPherson's story collection *Elbow Room* was awarded the 1978 Pulitzer Prize for Fiction.

159. Mrs. Sullivan] One of Pancake's junior high school teachers.

160. Decoration Day] Memorial Day.

161. Davis Grubb] Davis Grubb (1919-1980) was a writer-in-residence at West Virginia University.

162. Never mailed, this letter to his girlfriend, Emily Miller, was found among Pancake's notebooks. Pancake was in Arizona at the time, chaperoning a youth group from Washington, D.C., on a trip to the West.

163. *The 42nd Parallel*] The first novel (1930) in John Dos Passos's U.S.A. Trilogy.

164. to re-consider] Pancake had proposed marriage to Emily Miller. Emily's parents were opposed to the prospect of their daughter's marriage to an aspiring fiction writer.

165. a book] One of two different plans Pancake had for a novel or collection of linked stories. Colly and Ottie are characters in "Trilobites" and "In the Dry," respectively; the novel would have continued their stories. "Trilobites" would have been the first chapter in the novel, and "In the Dry" the second. The third chapter would have been "Survivors," which introduces a major female character named either Alena or Amanda. According to a brief sketch Pancake wrote, the novel would have ended with Colly's death in Vietnam and Ottie's return to Rock Camp: "Ottie returns to Rock Camp—everything is different. Valley full of houses to shelter families working for Chemcorp—an indirect link to Dupont's napalm co. Ottie sitting at roadhouse bar debating on whether to join union so he can get a job. Meets Alena—they talk—she tries to convince him to give up & join union, talk turns to how valley has changed—he asks if she knows 'Punky' Collier—comes out Colly is buried in Akron. Ottie pushes his drink away slowly. 'Had enough of this swill to float a fucking battleship.' Alena, 'Have another.' 'No thanks. Have to get to work in the morning.' He goes outside. She follows—'Need a place to stay?' They go to her place—talk—he decides to go union. They make love & lying after she asks him what he's thinking. He's been thinking of 'Punky'—[but] he says, 'Nothing.'"

166. *Virginia Quarterly*] *Virginia Quarterly Review*, where Pancake was working part-time as a reader.

167. the gathering on the 17th.] Pancake family reunion.

168. Lora Danford] Mortician and partner at the Heck Funeral Home in Milton. Danford had passed away on August 6, 1978.

169. Uncle Abe's store] Abraham Pancake's store.

170. a reading in Staunton at the prison Sept. 8th] On September 8, 1978, the third anniversary of his father's death, Pancake read "Trilobites" at the Staunton Correctional Center, a medium-security prison for men. Sarah Nutt's daughter Janet Lembke (1933-2013), an essayist, naturalist, and translator, had arranged the reading.

171. Jr.] Jr. Blake, family friend.

172. aren't dating.] Emily and Breece continued to see each other, despite Emily's parents' reservations about Pancake as a prospective husband.

173. Shorty] Roy "Shorty" Hollandsworth. See note 14.

174. Ottie] Character from "In the Dry."

175. Jack Pancake] A second cousin.

176. Glenn and Katy.] Glenn and Kathryn Perry, family friends. Their son Robert died in a car accident on October 28, 1978. Glenn was Milton's town barber.

177. a cab in New York] Thomas Wolfe died in Johns Hopkins Hospital in Baltimore. Probably Pancake conflates the biographies of Wolfe and James Agee (the latter had a fatal heart attack in a New York cab).

178. On the cover . . . Papa Hemingway.] The greeting card shows a cat playing a guitar. Biographer Thomas Douglass explains that in Fall 1979 Pancake and Emily Miller adopted a stray tom cat, which they named "Papa" for its gray, tufted whiskers.

179. Rainelle] Rainelle, West Virginia, with an elevation of over 2,400 feet.

180. Alderson-Broaddus or St. Joe] Alderson-Broaddus College, in Philippi, West Virginia; St. Joseph Central High School, in Huntington, West Virginia.

181. *Snakehunter*] *Snakehunter* (1973), a novel by Chuck Kinder.

182. the farm] Sarah Nutt's farm in Middlebrook, Virginia, where there was also a cabin that she permitted Pancake to use.

183. John's birthday] John Casey's birthday, January 18.

184. Phoebe-Lou Adams] Pancake's editor at *The Atlantic*.

185. "Cherry Blossoms."] Published in Stehekin, Washington, *Cherry Blossoms* advertised "Oriental ladies" interested in finding male companionship in the U.S. Thomas E. Douglass, writes in *A Room Forever* that "Breece understood this to be a thin veil covering the yellow slave trade, and apparently he had plans for writing a fictional story and a 'journalistic' piece."

186. Mr. Weeks] Edward Weeks (1898-1989), then editor emeritus of *The Atlantic* and husband to Phoebe-Lou Adams.

187. Jim] James Alan McPherson, who sat on the editorial board for *The Atlantic*.

188. Jay] Jay Rockefeller (b. 1937), then governor of West Virginia

189. *Saga of a Country Doctor*] *The Saga of a Country Doctor among the West Virginia Hills* (1940), a memoir by Dr. Floyd Farnsworth of Milton.

190. green baloney butts] In a memorable episode in Tom Kromer's *Waiting for Nothing* (1935), a butcher offers to sell the vagrant Tom Kromer "green baloney butts" for three cents. See also note 125.

191. Carl] Carl Beckman, a friend from Charlottesville.
192. "Buddy, Can You Spare a Dime"] Depression-era song composed by Jay Gorney, with lyrics by E.Y. "Yip" Harburg.
193. Alderson-Broaddus] Alderson-Broaddus College, in Philippi, West Virginia.
194. the *Cabell Record*] Pancake wrote five pieces for the local Milton paper: "Country Music—More Down to Earth," *Cabell Record*, August 6, 1975; "'I'm Thankful I Can Still Get Around': Julia Ward Is 94," *Cabell Record*, August 6, 1975; "Hinton Richmond: A Man of the Woods," *Cabell Record*, August 13, 1975; "Opus One: Records, Plants, and a Thriving Business," *Cabell Record*, August 13, 1975; and "Pop Amick Is Still Going Strong," *Cabell Record*, August 27, 1975.
195. Glazer's] Fred Glazer (1937–1997), director of the West Virginia Library Commission.
196. Southern Crescent] Amtrak line, running from Washington, D.C., to New Orleans.
197. Shorty and Mary Jane] Roy "Shorty" Hollandsworth and his wife Mary Jane, family friends. See also note 14.
198. Ali murder Frazier in Manila] The Thrilla in Manila, October 1, 1975.
199. wanted to become a padre] Pancake had contemplated becoming a priest.
200. Dear Mom] In a handwritten comment on the original typed letter, Helen Pancake explains: "This is the note Breece wrote me just before his death and John Casey mentions it in the Afterword." Pancake died on April 8, 1979.

NOTE ON THE TEXTS

This volume contains the posthumous collection *The Stories of Breece D'J Pancake* (1983), five story drafts and fragments, and a selection of Pancake's letters.

Assembled and published through the efforts of Pancake's mother, Helen, with the assistance of James Alan McPherson and John Casey, Pancake's literary executor, *The Stories of Breece D'J Pancake* contains the completed stories found among Pancake's papers after his death. Left out of the collection were a few pieces of obvious apprentice work (also not included in this volume). Only six of the twelve stories in that landmark volume had appeared in print in the author's lifetime: "The Mark" in *Rivanna*, February 25, 1976; "Hollow" in *The Declaration*, September 30, 1976; "The Way It Has to Be" (under the working title "Cowboys and Girls") in *The Declaration*, October 21, 1976; "Trilobites" in *The Atlantic*, December 1977; "In the Dry" in *The Atlantic*, August 1978; and "Time and Again" in *Nightwork*, September 1978. After Pancake's death, two additional stories saw magazine publication prior to their appearance in *The Stories of Breece D'J Pancake*: "The Honored Dead" in *The Atlantic*, January 1981, and "A Room Forever" in *Antaeus*, December 1981. "Hollow" was reprinted in *The Atlantic*, October 1982, and "The Way It Has to Be" was reprinted in *Rolling Stone*, April 14, 1983. This volume prints the text of the 1983 Atlantic–Little Brown Books edition, including the Foreword by James Alan McPherson and Afterword by John Casey.

Pancake was a firm believer in the process of revision and preferred to put his stories through multiple—ten or more—drafts. On a draft copy of "The Honored Dead," he wrote to his teacher Peter Taylor: "Mr. Taylor: Yes, you have seen this before. Yes, I've changed it quite a bit. Yes, this is the 8th draft. Breece." Pancake biographer Thomas Douglass posits that only three or four stories in *The Stories of Breece D'J Pancake* were able to receive the kind of revision Pancake desired: "Trilobites," "The Honored Dead," " In the Dry," and perhaps "Hollow."

The five fragments and drafts published here all date from 1975 to 1979, the same five-year period in which Pancake wrote the twelve stories that became *The Stories of Breece D'J Pancake*. They share the preoccupations of—and sometimes characters in—the finished stories. Of the story fragments and drafts printed here, only "Shouting Victory" exists in a complete but rough first draft. The text printed here follows Thomas E. Douglass's transcription of Pancake's handwritten draft, published in *A Room Forever: The Life, Work, and Letters of Breece D'J Pancake* (University of Tennessee Press, 1998). Douglass changed the third-person past tense sections of "Shouting Victory" to first-person present tense, since Pancake had begun to rewrite the story in first-person present tense. All the other fragments follow the typescripts held at West Virginia University's West Virginia & Regional History Center. "Shouting Victory," about a "Glory" meeting that involves the consumption of strychnine, comes from the time of Pancake's close association with Milton, West Virginia's Caldwell Dudley, author of *History of Milton*. The two men had been planning a trip together to Frazier's Bottom in West Virginia to attend a serpent-handling service before Dudley's death in September of 1976.

"Conqueror," concerning an alcoholic war veteran and a carney worker, draws on memories of Pancake's father. The fragment entitled "Ridge-Runner" is closely related to the completed story "Hollow," both part of a planned novel or collection of linked stories to be called *Water in a Sieve.* "Survivors" was intended as part of another planned novel—sometimes also called *Water in a Sieve* or alternatively *Generations.* It would have followed "Trilobites" and "In the Dry" as the third story or chapter in the novel; in this novel, the lives of Colly ("Trilobites"), Ottie ("In the Dry"), and a "strong, good woman" named either Alena or Amanda ("Survivors") would have intersected. Thomas Douglass speculates that the untitled fragment, set in Mexico, may have been among the last things written by Pancake.

This volume prints the text of Pancake's unmailed letter of July 1, 1978, to Emily Miller as it appears in Thomas E. Douglass's book. Otherwise, it presents the handwritten and typescript texts of letters held at West Virginia University's West Virginia & Regional History Center and the University of Virginia's Albert and Shirley Small Special Collections Library. Sometimes excisions have proven necessary, but the texts of the letters are otherwise presented without change, except for the correction of spelling and typographical errors. Excisions are indicated by a series of three asterisks. The Pancake archive at the University of Virginia's Albert and Shirley Small Special Collections Library contains typescripts, setting copy, and galley proofs of *The Stories of Breece D'J Pancake* as well as a considerable amount of other material related to John Casey's activities as literary executor of the Estate of Breece D'J Pancake. The Albert and

Shirley Small Collections also houses a small number of letters or notes from Breece Pancake. West Virginia University's West Virginia & Regional History Center holds about 250 letters by Breece Pancake written primarily to his parents, handwritten and typescript drafts of stories and fragments, and much other material of interest to scholars.

ACKNOWLEDGMENTS

This volume would not be possible without the groundwork undertaken by Thomas E. Douglass in *A Room Forever: The Life, Work, and Letters of Breece D'J Pancake*. Library of America would also like to thank Jayne Anne Phillips for her dedication to this project; John Casey, Literary Executor of the Estate of Breece D'J Pancake, for granting permissions and taking the time to answer numerous questions; Michael Carlisle at Inkwell Management for his guidance; the staff at the University of Virginia's Albert and Shirley Small Special Collections Library for their help and for granting access to materials; and the staff at West Virginia University's West Virginia & Regional History Center for their assistance and for granting access to materials.

INDEX

•••••••••••••••••••